JEROME

MW01048493

# REDBUD
# RECKONING

## A CODY HOUSTON SERIES NOVEL

outskirts
press

# CHAPTER 1

Maxine's restaurant was already buzzing with patrons as the man let the door close behind him. It was early evening, but the place had a combination of happy hour and dinner business under way. He made his way over to the last two available spots at the bar and threw his phone and sunglasses on the bar top next to himself to hold the empty stool for his anticipated guest. The proprietor, Kirt, was reviewing the bar stock with the bartender, and nodded at the tall man as he settled onto the stool.

The man slowly surveyed the small bar and momentarily made eye contact with a well-dressed lady as she was placing her wallet back into her purse. She seemed slightly embarrassed and irritated that she had been caught checking him out and clumped off toward the front door rather hastily. Cody watched out of natural male curiosity as her ample backside fluttered in vertical upheaval in the tight dress as she passed his view window.

Kirt smiled approvingly as he sauntered up with a double Jack Daniel's over ice and a glass of ice water. He softly placed the whiskey in front of the man and the ice water in front of the empty stool to further lock down its committed status.

"Better not study that too hard, Cody. You are being kind of obvious, which isn't like you."

"That ass looked like two cats fighting to get out of a bag," Cody responded. "Couldn't help myself."

"I was just waiting for your date to show up and catch you eyeballing another lady and make a scene. Bad for business." Kirt mockingly disapproved.

1

"No date tonight. Dillon is coming to meet me. Ever since I brought him here, he cannot stop going on about your skillet lasagna. You would think he never got anything to eat at home. You know me, I am fifty/fifty lasagna or cioppino. I believe when you find something you like, you stick with it, but I like to have more than one thing."

"Well, you definitely cover that shift well. It took you years to order anything other than the lasagna, but now that you did, I never know which way it is going to break, lasagna or cioppino. Either way, it's been nice having you around more lately."

"Do me a favor, Kirt."

"What would that be?"

"When Dillon gets here and orders lasagna, tell him it's off the menu now. I just want to see his face."

The two men laughed at the inside joke. Cody took a sip of the brown pour and savored the familiar flavor. He enjoyed the scent and the strong burn as the liquid made its way down the hatch. Kirt broke away to attend to other business as Cody pulled up the Internet on his phone and began perusing the news of the day as he awaited the arrival of his friend.

Cody had just transferred over to his brokerage account app to monitor his stocks when Dillon burst through the door and made a beeline for Cody. Cody stood up and the two men gave each other a bro hug and some affectionate back slapping.

As the two men sat down on their bar stools, Kirt came over and offered a friendly handshake and welcome.

"Good to see you back, Dillon. You came over to keep Cody out of trouble tonight?"

"Yeah, that is me. Parole Officer Dillon keeping wild man here from getting off the reservation."

Kirt laughed at the pitiful joke and asked, "What are you drinking tonight?"

"Give me one of those good beers that I was drinking last time I was here. Forget the name."

"No worries, I remember. They are my favorite too." Kirt stepped over and pulled out a green bottle and dispensed with the cap by flicking it into the wastebasket before he slid the cold brew up to Dillon's big paw.

Dillon took a greedy pull on the beer and held it up in front of himself, staring at it admiringly. "That is a good drink," he said as if it was the first time he had ever had a taste of beer.

"You either need to change your jokes or change your audiences, Cupcake." Cody looked at his friend in mock seriousness.

"You know, a guy invites his best amigo out to his favorite restaurant and offers to buy him dinner and drinks in the spirit of friendship, and all he does is make fun of your jokes. I think you need some help, Kemosabe. You have serious issues." Dillon used his fingers to make imaginary quotation marks for emphasis when he said the word *issues*.

Cody smiled and settled against the chair back on the sturdy stool. "Well, as a matter of fact, I was kind of surprised to get this sudden invitation to dinner completely out of the blue. And it is good to see you, by the way." Cody offered up the customary fist-bump that the two friends had developed over the years as their standard confirmation.

Dillon casually bumped the offered fist and broke into a broad smile and leaned in close to his friend. "I have some big news."

"No shit. Do not tell me that Laura is pregnant again? I thought you guys decided two was enough."

"No, no, not that." Dillon shook his head for emphasis and took another big pull on his beer. "The two we have is all I can handle. It is putting me in the poor house just keeping those boys in groceries. You know how much those two eat? Holy crow! Get me another one of these beers while I go to the bathroom, and I will tell you when I get back."

Dillon made his way around the bar in a determined line toward the small restroom in the back of the restaurant. As he passed the vacant stool that the woman abandoned earlier, he did a slight back-and-forth shuffle with a tall, slender young man of swarthy complexion who was trying to take ownership of the vacant stool. Cody saw Dillon break out his trademark toothy grin and clap the man on the back in a friendly greeting as he passed. The man looked intently at Cody and locked eyes with him across the bar for what seemed like an unusually long interval after Dillon passed. Cody made note of it and filed it away in a mental contingency file. He was glad to see Dillon and he looked forward to a nice meal and a few laughs with him tonight. Cody waved the empty bottle at the bartender, who immediately nodded and brought out a new, cold beer to Dillon's spot.

Dillon made his way back to his stool and slid his rear end into the seat while grabbing the new beer with his wide hand. He leaned against the bar top and grinned at Cody with a mischievous, crooked smile. "You aren't ever going to guess what I am going to tell you."

"Can't you just be normal? What the heck is wrong with you? Just tell me."

"Buzzkill." Dillon took a long pull on his beer and air belched quietly while scanning the room. "So, this is what it's like to be single."

At that moment, Kirt walked up to the two friends at the bar and interrupted. "Dinner orders, gentlemen?"

"Lasagna for me, Kirt," blurted Dillon.

"Oh, sorry, Dillon. We are out of that tonight. I thought Cody told you. What else can we get for you?"

Dillon looked stunned. "You have to be shitting me! I drove

halfway across the state in this stupid Orlando traffic for that lasagna."

Cody looked at his friend with mock concern. "Why don't you try out their excellent vegetarian charcuterie board?"

"What the hell is that?" Dillon pouted indignantly.

"Don't get your panties all wadded up, Princess. We are just messing with you. They are already making your lasagna in the kitchen. I ordered it earlier for you." Cody and Kirt high-fived and laughed at Dillon's screwed-up face.

Dillon rallied. "Yeah? Had to punk me out on the lasagna, huh? I thought we were friends. You are so funnnnyyyyyyy."

"I was worried you were going to start crying in public there for a moment. Better get Dillon another beer there, Kirt." Kirt nodded and made his way over to the cooler and smoothly pulled a chilled bottle out and removed the cap in a single motion.

"What are you getting, then? Vegetables?" Dillon looked at Cody like he was an unknown quantity.

"Getting the cioppino soup like I did last time we ate here. It's delicious. You should try it next time." Cody turned and looked directly at his friend. "So, tell me what the big secret is."

"Last weekend I took the rider course at the dealership and got my motorcycle license." Dillon looked like a little boy grinning widely as he looked for the reaction from his friend.

"You are kidding me! Laura finally relented and let you get your license, huh?"

"Well, actually, no. She didn't." Dillon took another swig of beer while he looked directly ahead.

"So, she doesn't know you got it?"

"Something like that." Dillon turned to look at his friend and smiled. "She doesn't know that I bought a bike either."

"Oh shit." Cody was surprised. This did not seem like something Dillon would do. "When are you planning to break the big news, stud muffin? What kind of bike did you get, by the way?"

"Got a Street Glide like yours, but it's blue. Used, with low miles."

"Nice!" Cody smiled at his friend. "Can't wait to see it. Now I have a riding buddy!"

Cody offered his drink glass for a clink with Dillon's beer bottle. The two old friends grinned at each other for a moment and then toasted again.

"To many good rides together!" The two clinked drinks again. "Let me see a picture of this bad machine."

Dillon fished out his phone and immediately produced a picture of himself sitting on a gleaming blue Street Glide on the dealership floor.

"When are you taking delivery?" Cody asked.

"Tomorrow."

"So, you are planning on telling her about this tonight when you get home, right? I know you can't hide this thing in the garage from her."

Cody looked over at his friend, who was not reacting to the question. He nodded at the bartender and pushed his glass over to the edge of the bar for a refill. He leaned back in his chair and relaxed while he waited on a response from Dillon. Suddenly, it occurred to him what the dinner invitation was about. He decided to make it a little easier on his friend.

"Well, you know, if you need a little time to soften her up, you could keep it over at my house. I have plenty of room. Might go down a little easier if you let her know about all this in stages. She will come around if you give her the chance. A month from now she will be riding on the back with you."

"Really? Man, that would be cool. I thought it would be easier to tell her, but suddenly, I am not so sure right now is the best time. I do not want you to think I am pussing out here, but you know she really hates motorcycles. I told her I had to work all weekend while I was taking the class. She is going to get pissed off about that too."

The two old friends clinked drinks again as the server set down their food. Cody laid his napkin in his lap while he watched Dillon attack the lasagna with gusto.

"So, I am off tomorrow afternoon, and my appointment to pick the bike up is at two o'clock. That means I can be at your house around three thirty. You going to be around? I will need a ride back to the dealership to pick up my car. Can you handle that, Kemosabe?"

"Sounds like you might have had all this already all worked out in your head."

"You aren't the only one that can make a plan, Chief."

The two friends enjoyed a good laugh.

# CHAPTER II

The sweat was streaming down his brow and into his eyes as Cody dug deep to increase his pace over the last half mile of the run. He had slept in late and spent a good part of the late morning cleaning house and doing domestic chores. He was very self-sufficient and chose not to hire a housecleaner for the inside of his house, nor a landscaping service for his yard. He was leery about strangers coming into his personal space and simply preferred to take care of his own chores to avoid that intrusion. He reminded himself that his bird feeder and bird bath needed refilling, as well as the hummingbird feeder that his ex-girlfriend had installed for him. He smiled as he thought of himself becoming quite the gardener and bird and butterfly watcher since his ex-girlfriend Jennifer had planted all the butterfly attracting plants around his yard and sweetly convinced him to install the bird feeder and hummingbird feeder.

He was breathing heavily and sweating profusely as he lengthened his stride and focused intently on his form and keeping his arms and shoulders loose while rounding the last corner into the homestretch to his house. His breathing was ragged as he ran down the middle of the lonely street that ended in the round asphalt cul-de-sac that his property surrounded, and he felt a deep burn in his lungs. There were other lots that fronted the circular dead-end, but Cody had purchased the vacant lots on both sides of his as they came up for sale over the years, to control what happened around his home and to maintain peak privacy. An annoying pain on the backside of his thigh began to throb as his leg muscles got stressed from a relatively recent wound that was still healing.

He was battling to keep his stride from breaking down into an irregular lope when he noticed the blue truck with the pair of cowboy boots sticking out of the driver's side window, midway down the block toward his house. He noted the Oklahoma plates on the back of the truck, and he loped past and stole a glance at the boots sticking out the driver's side window of the cab. The truck was out of place and parked on the side of the road within one hundred feet of the entrance to his driveway. He went huffing past the truck without stopping to question the occupant. There was no way that he could do a full investigation of the occupant while running, but he did not want to succumb to the impulse to stop and question the driver as to why he was so close to his driveway. He made a mental note to immediately enter his garage and retrieve the nine-millimeter Walther pistol he kept concealed inside. This was a highly unusual situation for Cody since he almost never had unplanned visitors.

Breaking from his usual practice of slowing from a run to a walk at the start of his driveway, he ran down the length of his driveway without decreasing pace. His friend Dillon sat atop his gleaming blue and chrome motorcycle, grinning like a mule eating cockleburs. He dismounted as he saw Cody hustling down the drive and stopping at the keypad to open the overhead door. Cody ducked in as the door cleared his waist and reappeared almost immediately tucking the black pistol into the back of his shorts.

"Give me a minute before you start shooting people, Code." Dillon walked up carrying his helmet. Cody punched the button to reclose the door as he turned to focus on Dillon.

"You obviously saw the guy in the truck parked out on the road, right?" Dillon held his arms out to slow Cody's advance down the driveway.

"Saw the truck and some boots sticking out the window," said Cody.

"He came and talked to me while you were out running. I told him to go back to his truck and wait until I could talk to you."

"What does he want?" Cody asked.

"Well, you need to talk to him about that." Dillon smiled broadly. "You ain't going to believe it."

Both men looked as the blue pickup truck slowly made its way down the driveway.

"Give him a chance to talk to you before you shoot him." Dillon's eyes twinkled brightly as he enjoyed his private joke.

Cody scowled at Dillon. Clearly, his friend didn't live in his world and couldn't understand the potential number of people who might be wanting to exact some kind of revenge on him.

The driver of the blue pickup truck stopped approximately one hundred feet away from Cody and Dillon and slowly extracted himself from the cab. He left the door open to the truck and moved toward the side of the front hood and placed both hands palms up on the hood of the truck in obvious sight of the two men.

"My name is Wiley Harris," he said. "I am a police officer from Oklahoma, and I want to talk to you. I am not armed. I came here to share some good news."

Cody looked at the man carefully. "I saw you at the restaurant last night across the bar."

"That was me." The man paused briefly. "I have been here for about four days."

"How do you know where to find me, and why are you looking for me?" Cody was unrelenting and cool to the man's approach.

"My maternal grandmother was a lady by the name of Alice Taylor from Tishomingo, Oklahoma. I believe she was married to your dad after my mother was born and given away for adoption when Alice was a teenager. If it's true, then you are my uncle, and you and I are co-inheritors of 160 acres of land near Tishomingo, Oklahoma, that was an original undivided Indian allotment parcel that still has the restrictive covenants recorded against it. The owner who passed away is a direct descendant of the original allottee and was fifty percent Chickasaw. So, the Bureau of Indian Affairs restrictive covenants still apply. In order to get the covenants removed, we will have to jointly file a petition with the District Court to enable us to take joint title or sell the property."

Cody silently held up his hand to motion the man to stop talking.

"You didn't answer the most important question to me yet. I can't process anything you are telling me until I know how you found me and why you think we are related."

"It's a long story, and I have some records to show you. I knew that you might not be aware that my mother was your half-sister. Alice Taylor died from complications of your birth. Based on a review of your birth record and her death certificate, I know that you never knew your mother."

"Still waiting." Cody stated curtly.

Dillon spoke up. "You need to tell Cody how you found him."

"I told you, I am a cop." The man was slightly exasperated. "I used the skip tracing resources we have at our station to search for utility connections in your name and got hundreds of records from all over the country. I got the IRS to confirm addresses of tax returns for your name and cross referenced the two databases and corroborated the active utility information and tax records for target addresses. It took a while, but I filtered out the top prospects from my list and then did some more digging on several of you. I got Mom's birth certificate, located her birth mother's name, and then looked for marriage licenses in Oklahoma and Texas. I got to your dad's name from that, and then found and

11

read his obituary, which had you living here in Florida. From there, I ran down the Florida addresses for your name from the two matches for this area, and this is the only one that appeared to work based on your age. I know quite a bit about you from all of this research, including a summary of your military record and your college transcripts. I think we are related, and I think we are the rightful heirs to this estate that has been tied up at the BIA for some time as restricted land held intestate from your maternal grandfather after he passed away many years ago."

Cody looked at the young man. "So last night, you were staking us out? How did you know we were going to that restaurant?"

"I didn't. I followed you there and came in after you did. I was waiting on a stool to free up at the bar in a location where I could watch you when Dillon nearly ran me over."

Cody was slightly relieved that it had been so problematic for the cop to trace him. He did not appreciate being followed or traced. "So, you have been following me around for four days?"

"Yes," he answered truthfully.

"I have never heard any of what you are telling me regarding your mother and my mother." The truth was, it had been so long that he had heard his mother's name that he almost did not associate it when he heard the man say it. He hadn't heard her maiden name spoken in so long he couldn't remember when he heard it last.

Cody could not process everything he was being told. He looked over at Dillon, who was still grinning. "I need to help my friend Dillon here through some domestic crisis. I can't deal with this at the same time. What are you doing for dinner tonight, Wiley?"

"Hoping to break bread with my uncle," he said, smiling for the first time. He was sensing a breakthrough.

"Let's take things a step at a time. Meet me at the same restaurant as last night and bring your records with you. Meet me at 7:30 so we can get a table; happy hour crowd will be gone by then."

"I know this is a lot to deal with, and no notice. I will bring my paperwork and we can talk about it tonight." He wanted to approach and shake Cody's hand, but sensed that it wasn't a good idea to push that yet. "I will see you tonight."

Cody stared intently at the young man. He slowly lifted a hand with one finger extended.

"Before you go…"

"Yes?" The man stared intently back at Cody.

"You never said what police force you are part of."

"Chickasaw Light Horse Police Department, Ada Precinct. It's the tribal police department for the Chickasaw Nation. I know it sounds podunk to you, but we have fifty-five officers and run a very well-regarded police force covering a good part of Southeastern Oklahoma. I live in Tishomingo, but my office is out of Ada. And don't forget, I found you, didn't I?" He grinned proudly about the last statement.

"So, you are Chickasaw?"

"Yep. So are you. You just don't know it yet."

"You don't object if I call to check on you, do you?"

"Nope, feel free. My boss and precinct offices are in Ada, Oklahoma. Anybody you talk to there will know me. You can find the contact information on the Internet. If you look at the website you will see a picture of me on it. Group photo, I am in the middle row left side. I am a patrol officer and part of the SWAT team for the department. I am also an Army veteran. I was a Ranger and served in First Battalion in Iraq doing counterter-rorism raids."

Cody did not immediately respond to the information pro-vided by the young man. He took a moment to look him over briefly, and squinted slightly as he studied his face. He noted that as he spoke about his involvement in the SWAT team and his service in Iraq, the young man stood more erect and shifted to a more military bearing. Cody could tell that he was proud of his service and wanted Cody to recognize it and appreciate it for what it said about him.

"I will see you tonight at 7:30. Don't be late, and bring your papers."

Wiley did not respond to Cody. He stared at him for a brief moment and got into his truck and backed down the driveway without saying a word.

Dillon looked critically at Cody. "Well, you didn't need to be so friendly, dude. I will be surprised if he shows up now."

"He is the one who came looking for me. He will be there."

"You think he is right about what he is saying? You think he might be your nephew?"

"Hard to say. He didn't seem like a dumbass or kook."

"Well, he seems like a fairly good guy to me. I talked to him for quite a while before you came back. I told him to back out of the driveway and wait in the street. I was hoping to talk to you before you went all Special Forces on him."

"Dillon, you have to appreciate that there are people from my past who won't ever forget what I did to them. I know you can't live in that world with me, but you have to appreciate that I worry about you as much as I worry about myself. If anything ever happened to you because you were with me, I would not be able to forgive myself. Besides that, you believe everything anybody says." Cody looked up at his friend and saw the surprise on his face from the jab after the heartfelt comment.

"I understand and I appreciate that. Just listen to the kid and give his story a chance. I cannot come up with a reason that he would just show up with that story for no reason. Like you said, he did not seem like a dumbass. And just for the record, I do not

14

believe everything everybody says either. I just like people, that is all. I tend to give them the benefit of the doubt until I have a reason not to. Doesn't make me a bad person because I don't run around being all hard-ass like you all the time."

"Got it." Cody removed the pistol from the waistband of his shorts and strode over to reopen the garage door. "Bring that bike in here," he said as the door slowly opened. Cody walked over to the door and entered the code to open the door again and walked over to the far side bay of the triple-car garage, as all three of the overhead doors began opening, revealing a new three-quarter-ton diesel truck on one side, a 1969 Shelby GT 500 in immaculate condition in the middle bay, and two Harley-Davidson motorcycles in the end bay.

"Damn. A guy doesn't show up for a few weeks and things really change fast around here. New truck, another motorcycle. It must be good to be Cody Houston. We just had dinner last night; you didn't even tell me you have been buying all this new shit." Dillon made his usual pitiful face as if he was wounded by the oversight.

"Well, don't be so butt hurt, Princess. The motorcycle was supposed to be a surprise for you when you eventually got your license. Our friend Gordy Hill had it in his garage and had it shipped down here to me. He isn't doing well; the leukemia is catching up with him and it looks like he is on his last leg. It's a nice bike; I like those customized handlebars and that tricked-out LED lighting system on the underside of the bike. It's only got thirty-five hundred miles on it. His son Nate didn't want it and he thought I might like it. It's a nice Fat Boy custom. It's been a while since I rode a soft tail, but I like the balanced motor and the custom pipes he has on it. I was planning on giving it to you if you ever got your license, but you jumped the gun and got your own first. That is the reason I didn't tell you about the new bike."

"Sorry to hear about Gordy. Good guy." Dillon gravely nodded his head while he spoke and looked downward. He knew Cody and Gordy were extremely tight even though they hadn't known each other long and didn't even talk that often at Cody's request. There is something about working and being dependent on each other on a dangerous mission that will make an unbreakable connection between men.

"Yeah. I got a call from Nate, and he told me that his dad is in hospice at home. He won't go to the hospital, and he won't take treatment. It's getting bad, but he is one tough guy. Old chopper pilots don't go down easy."

"How long do you think he has?" Dillon asked in a low tone.

Cody paused and sighed heavily. "Not long. Couple of days, maybe. They have him on a heavy dose of morphine. He is resting fairly comfortably, but he is out of it."

"Sorry, man. I know you guys were tight."

Cody's tightly pursed lips and gentle nod said it all. Not one for showing emotion, he had trouble finding words for what he felt.

"I am glad I helped him. He was incredibly grateful for what I did for Nate. Best thing I have ever done. Doing it for him made it the best thing."

"You are a good dude, Cody. There might not be anybody else in the whole world who would have taken that on."

"Well, I don't know about that. I just did what I thought was right. Glad I could help. Nate is a good kid, and he was worth saving, that is for sure. Proud of him. He is going to finish his doctoral thesis this summer and will graduate in the fall. He is teaching quite a few classes too. He told me there is a chance that Stanford might hire him to teach astrophysics at their university. He had a conversation with the dean about it already."

"That's awesome! Teaching at Stanford would be a real plum

position. I am sure Gordy is proud."

"Well, there is one thing. I volunteered you and your boat without asking you first, but I know you, and I am sure you will be happy to help."

"I trust you, Code. What did you volunteer me for?"

"When I was planning that rescue of Nate down in Mexico, I told Gordy how people take cremation ashes of people they love out to the Gulf Stream in the Atlantic and put them on an eternal journey around the world by scattering them in the Gulf Stream. He really took to that idea apparently. He told Nate to ask me to take his ashes out to the Gulf Stream once he passes. Nate asked me if we would do it for him. He wants to be able to assure his dad that he has it all arranged. I told him we would be honored to do it. Hope you don't mind."

"You know I will help. Just give me a few days' notice to get the old barge ready and fueled. It would be an honor."

Cody looked at his friend and nodded slowly. "I knew I could count on you."

"I appreciate you letting me keep my bike over here in your garage. I just need a couple of weeks to get Momma to warm up to it."

Cody could not help but smile to himself. He knew the motorcycle would probably be a permanent fixture in the garage. Dillon wanted to be his own independent man, but he needed his wife on board with his decisions. He adored her and respected her; his desire to have a bike put him in a weird position. Cody knew that he had acted on impulse to buy the bike and now didn't have a way to fix it since he did not want to face the reality of his choice.

"Why don't you talk to the dealership about taking the bike back and just ride this second bike when you want to go riding? You know you don't have to ride with me if you want to use it. I will give you a key and you come and get it when you want it and bring it back when you want just like it was yours. You don't need to own your own bike now that I have this one as a spare."

Cody could tell that this remark insulted his friend. He could see the irritation in his flushed face.

"I don't want to ride your orphan bike! I am my own man, and I will get Laura on board with it. You just let me handle that. I want us to go to Bike Week, ride up to St. Augustine, ride the Loop, ride over for Biketoberfest, hit Leesburg Bike Fest and all the other things I have been hearing you talk about for years. I am tired of being Mr. Minivan. I need this, man. I am so ready for this. I want to ride down to the Keys and get drunk in Key West."

Cody held out his hand to calm down his friend. He had never seen him act or talk this way before about his life at home. "Calm down, Dil. You keep this thing here as long as you want or need to. I got your back. You know that."

"Good. Thanks."

"It is a good-looking bike, dude. That blue sparkles; it must have metal flake in the paint."

"Yeah, it does look good, doesn't it? I had them put some extra chrome on this thing, a cell phone holder, and I am looking at some of those slip-on mufflers." Dillon lit up like a child at Christmas talking about the bike. He was grinning and shifting his weight back and forth between his feet and waving his hands for emphasis about everything he said. He looked proud to own the beautiful machine, and Cody understood that feeling.

"Well, good then. Leave me a key so I can move this thing around if I need to. We will make plans to hit Bike Week next year. Maybe we can catch the coleslaw wrestling at Cabbage Patch."

"Hell yes! Farm girls in bathing suits wrestling in slaw. Now that is what I am talking about! What I really want to do is go on one of those trips with you to ride the Grand Canyon. Ever since you told me about that trip, I haven't been able to stop thinking about getting my license and getting my own bike. My wife is just going to have to accept this as something I need to do."

"I know you will get her there. I would love to go on a ride with you to the Grand Canyon, dude. Just you and me. We would have a good time."

"Right on. I am down for that. You just wait. I think you should give that bike to your nephew." Dillon shot Cody a lopsided grin challenging him to embrace his nephew even though he knew Cody would need time and evidence to support the claim.

"What makes you think he would want it?"

"He couldn't stop looking or talking about my bike. He told me he wants one but can't afford it on a cop's salary."

"Speaking of that, I need to drop you off at the dealership and start some research on this guy who calls himself my nephew. It's been a long time since I did any research on my mother, I hate to say. If what he says is true, I may be learning a lot more about her than I know now. My dad talked to me about her when I was a child, but to be honest, we didn't talk about her much after that. He was always involved with other women in one way or another, and they became the subject of our conversations."

"I think you should just hear him out, my friend. It looks like he came loaded with a full file."

"Strange way to meet your relatives." The two men shared a hearty laugh. "Come on, Dil, let me get you back to the dealership. Give you a ride in my new truck."

"Cool. This thing is a beast, man. You have to get a special license to drive this thing? Oh, and by the way, what is with all the bird feeders, flowers, and hummingbird feeders in your yard? Jesus Christ, I thought I was at the hummingbird sanctuary, waiting on you. They were everywhere!"

"Jennifer planted a bunch of red bee balm plants around the

yard, and the things are taking over. I have hummingbirds hanging around all over the place now because they love that plant. On top of that, she put some sugar water dispensers around close to the plants. She also planted some butterfly-attracting flowers, and now I am getting mobbed by butterflies. I guess that is what you get when you date a park ranger. She is crazy about her wildlife." Cody three-point turned the truck out of the garage and slowly made his way down the long driveway.

"That girl could do anything she wanted in my yard, man. She is a smoking hottie; total smoke show! I suppose she wants to throw a cub with you, too? Every woman you know wants to have your children within two months."

"Well, I was going to tell you the story about her last night, but to be honest, I am still digesting it and don't know what to do."

"You want relationship advice from ole Dil, huh? I knew it would come to this someday."

"Not that desperate yet. Nice offer, but no thanks."

Both men chuckled as Cody accelerated on the paved road.

"Right. I wouldn't take relationship advice from me either. Have to hide my motorcycle like a little bitch from my ole lady."

"You just need a little time to get the right opening. You love the woman, and you don't want to upset her. I get it. Nothing wrong with that. You want me to tell her for you?"

Again, the two men snickered like grade schoolers.

"So, tell me what is up with you and Jennifer? Last I heard, I thought you liked the girl. Hard to keep up with your romantic life, dude."

"Well, turns out that Jennifer is engaged."

"What? Engaged to who?"

"High school sweetheart. She has been dating him for fifteen years. She is getting a lot of pressure from her family to marry him like they have been planning since they were in high school. She is moving back to Ohio."

"You are kidding me? That girl has a bad case of you, man. There is no way she is going to be happy if she goes back to him."

"She never left him. I was just the side piece. She has known all along that she was going to do this. You know me. I keep things casual. That was always fine with her. She would go up there once a month and give the dude his conjugal visit and then come back. Occasionally, she would disappear and not call me for a few days when he came down to see her. I don't ask a lot of questions and made no promises. She didn't make any to me. That is how it is. The monkey died and the show is over. Moving on."

"Dude. Sorry to hear that. I know you liked her."

"Yep. Don't worry about me. She and I had a nice time together, but it's over; I thought it was strange that she never asked anything about me and never told me much about herself. It was kind of too good to be true. If it's not one thing with my relationships, it's the exact opposite. She told me I was exactly what she needed before she got married. Now that she had her fling with me, she can settle down."

"So how did she tell you this?"

"She came over. I gave her the hairy puppet show, and she broke the news."

"Well, at least you closed it out right."

"It isn't easy being me, Dil. Not as good as it looks."

"Sorry, man. I know you. You will be hooked up with someone else soon."

"We'll see. Good to see you two days in a row. Haven't done that in a while." Cody changed the subject.

"Yeah, man. Appreciate you warehousing my bike for me. Sorry I got so amped up on you earlier. Just get tired of being dumped on at work and pushed around by the old lady and not saying anything about it because she works so hard taking good care of the kids. I need something for myself. The bike is it and I am keeping it."

"Good. Just keep it at my house until you are ready to roll it out at home. It's not hurting anything around here."

"Ten-four." Dillon nodded solemnly. "Still can't believe that girl is going to be able to get over you. I think she will be back." After that prophecy, the conversation turned to the weather, fishing, and lobstering. Dillon thanked Cody again at the dealership, and Cody hustled back home to learn more about his potential nephew.

# CHAPTER III

**C**ody eased into a chair across the table from Wiley, who had several rather thick manila folders stacked up next to the small plate in front of him with papers bulging and paper clips on the edges holding specific sheets of paper to the covers.

"You are kind of young to be a sergeant, aren't you?" Cody asked as he pulled his chair up to the table. Wiley had nodded as Cody pulled up, but had not stood or offered a handshake.

"So you called to check on me, eh?"

"Yes. They said nice things about you and confirmed that you were in Florida looking for me. I saw your picture on the website too."

"So does that mean you believe me?"

"It means I believe you are a cop."

"Well, I guess that is a start. What do you want me to show you first?"

At that moment, a large, well-endowed blonde woman ambled up to the table and cheerfully nodded at Cody. "Two nights in a row. Do you come here every night?" She stared directly into Cody's eyes with no sign of embarrassment or discomfort over being so forward. "I noticed you checking me out when I left last night. Lucky for you, I like tall guys. I am six foot one in heels and I need a big man to make me feel feminine."

"I come here when it suits me." Cody looked at the woman. Something about her seemed familiar. Suddenly it occurred to him where he recognized her. "Aren't you a reporter on the local news channel?"

"Wanda Collis at your service. Got anything you want to tell me?" She winked heavily as she offered her standard line. She was heavily made up and had false nails, false eyelashes, and appeared to have hair extensions in place to make her hair fuller.

"Not tonight." Cody smiled as friendly as he could. The woman was gorgeous from the shoulders up but had hips and legs that looked like tree trunks to support the enormous backside he had watched heave as she walked out of the restaurant last night. He didn't see himself being attracted to someone who wore that much makeup. "Maybe we can get acquainted another time." Cody nodded toward Wiley as if in explanation.

"Okay. You going to tell me your name at least?"

"Of course." Cody stood up and offered his hand. "Name is Cody. I will check in with you next time I see you here."

"Okay, then. Look forward to that." She gently shook Cody's hand and turned to leave. Cody made a point of not getting drawn in to watching the earthquake beneath the tight dress as she made her way back to the bar.

Wiley looked critically across the table as Cody sat back down. "That woman has some serious cankles. You made the good call there, Uncle Cody. Does this happen to you a lot? I mean, women just coming up to you wanting to meet you? Does not run in the family, because it never happens to me. Not even the ones with cankles." Wiley smiled coyly as if he now had something to needle with.

Cody placed his elbows on the table and put his chin on top of his thumbs extended out from his clasped hands. He stared intently at the young man across from him. "So show me what you have that makes you think your mom was my sister that I never heard of."

Cody had to give the young man credit. He came prepared and had done his homework. More than that, he had his information down cold and knew his facts without needing to refer to his files. He took every opportunity, however, to support everything he told Cody with copies of birth certificates, marriage licenses, death certificates, adoption papers, and obituaries.

Cody listened intently without interrupting or asking any questions. They sent the waitress away twice during the fifteen-minute download of his information and support for his claim. When Wiley finished and put his last file away and leaned back in his chair, Cody made a comment that he hoped would not offend the young man.

"Compelling evidence, and I tip my hat to you for doing such a good job investigating all this. I just have one request."

"What is that?"

"Let's take DNA tests to confirm."

"I was hoping you would say that. I happen to have a couple of collection vials. All we have to do is spit in them and send them off. We will both get the results in about ten days. We can do it after dinner. I got those courtesy of the Light Horse Police Department."

Cody was initially slightly suspicious of using the DNA tests that the young man provided and did not immediately respond. He wondered why he was so suspicious about everything after thinking that.

"Don't worry, Uncle. I set this up so we both get the results for both samples separately delivered to us by the testing company. We both seal up our samples and then we drop them in a mailbox together and wait for the results to come back via mail and email. We should know in about ten days. I don't have any doubt, but I did all the research and have the benefit of knowing for sure that it matches; I know this is a lot to digest so quickly for you."

"What if it says we aren't related and what if it says we are?" Cody was curious where this young man saw this going. As for himself, he had no idea what to do if it did show them to be relatives.

"Well, if it says we aren't related, that is an easy one. We won't be seeing each other anymore."

Cody nodded slowly. He was warming up to this young man. He found himself secretly hoping that the DNA matched.

"And if it says that we are related?" Cody asked.

"Then I think you need to come out to Oklahoma and learn about your sister, visit her grave, get signed up with the Chickasaw tribe, and meet a few people. We will need to hire an attorney to file a petition with the court to present to the Bureau of Indian Affairs to get that property covenant removed so we can take the case through probate and take title to the land."

The waitress timidly approached again for the third time, and both men ordered drinks and dinner. After ordering, Kirt immediately personally brought their drink order over.

"Everything good, gentlemen? Looked like an intense conversation."

"All good, Kirt. Meet Wiley. Wiley, this is Kirt. He owns the place."

Wiley stood up and offered his hand. "Nice to meet you, Kirt. Great food here."

Cody watched approvingly as the two men shook hands and exchanged pleasantries. The kid was tall, slender, and muscular just like he was, and Cody had noticed that they both shared the same green eyes that his mother had. He suddenly felt confident that the kid was likely correct in his belief. He fought off the impulse to tell Kirt that he was Wiley's uncle. That would have to wait until the DNA confirmed, he thought. It wasn't like him to get swept away in something like this until he knew for sure. Time would work things out and there would be opportunities to brag about this kid later.

Kirt returned to the bar as food got delivered to the table, and Cody watched as Wiley swallowed a healthy bite of his dinner. "So, tell me about this piece of property. The 160 acres that you said we might inherit. Is it improved at all or is it just an overgrown mess?"

Wiley nodded his head and took a sip of his beer. "Well, it's been sitting there unattended for a long time while it's been tied up, and the Bureau of Indian Affairs hasn't done anything to try and keep it up. It is getting overgrown and the old frame house that sits on it needs a lot of work now. It had a roof leak, and it needs a lot of repairs to make it right again. There is a metal building on it that makes a nice shop. It has power and a nice concrete slab and a couple of overhead doors. There are about twenty acres of native pecans on it around the creek bed. They aren't planted in a grove or anything, but they look like they are productive and produce a pretty nice crop every couple of years or so, according to the neighbors. There are about ten acres of cleared pasture, and the rest is just overgrown blackjack scrub. It's fairly rocky soil with a lot of sandstone outcroppings and natural arroyos and small hills. There were some deer stands and deer feeders on it, but nobody has been putting out salt licks or stocking the feeders. I know a lot of locals hunt the property because nobody protects it. If we get control of it, we will have to shut that down. I have seen people out collecting the pecans when they come into season too."

"So, the property has a creek running through it?" Cody asked.

"Yeah, small creek that runs most of the year. The place needs some fencing work, some clearing, and the house needs a lot of work to make it livable again. There is a water well on it, and Great-Granddad never did strip off the mineral rights to the property, so nobody ever put any oil wells on it, thank God. He was a stubborn old dude according to the neighbors. Everybody was always after him to lease out the oil rights, but I heard he just refused to do it even though everybody else around him did. After a while, they just quit asking."

"Sounds like this might be one of those *be careful about what you wish for* cases, Wiley. This is starting to sound like a real project." Cody smiled warmly at the young man. He liked the energy and enthusiasm he saw in him.

"Don't underestimate me, Uncle. I got buddies on the force that will help me. You would be amazed at what you can get a cop to do if you offer him a beer. My dad says he will help too. You will have to meet him if you come out. He is one in a row. My dad owns a place and keeps some horses. I have always wanted a place like he has. On a cop's salary, this might be my only chance to get a place like this with some land."

"Well, let's take those tests and get this underway. No matter how it turns out, I appreciate you going to all the trouble to track me down, showing me all of what you found out, and if it turns out that this is our land, looking out for both of our interests."

Wiley was trying hard to suppress his smile. This was the first time he had heard Cody warm up to the idea that they might be related. He looked intensely at Cody and shook his head slowly.

Cody continued, "Your dad must be immensely proud of you, Wiley. He has every right to be. Veteran, cop, and future landowner. What more could he ask for out of a son?"

"Well, I don't know about that." Wiley leaned back in his chair and locked his hands behind his head in contemplation. "My dad and I fought a lot when I was growing up. We are both hard-headed guys and I thought I knew everything. He got pretty sick of me; I am sure. We get along all right now, though. Once I went into the service and out of the house, things got a lot better between us." Wiley grinned lopsidedly and took a swig of beer. "When I got out of the service, he really started treating me like

I was my own man and not just a kid anymore. That improved things between us too.

"My life has been a little uncertain with respect to my family. Mom never knew who her biological mom and dad were, so I never knew anything about her family growing up. She did not know she was adopted until she was an adult. She had a falling out with the family that adopted her, and she married my dad pretty early in life and had me. I was an only child, and she and my dad got divorced when I was about nine or so and I lived with her until I was about fourteen, and then went to live with my dad. My dad was on the professional rodeo circuit for about ten years, and he is all busted up physically from bronc and bull riding. He raises and trains a few horses, and he is a fishing guide at Lake Texoma. His family is not real close, and I almost never see them."

"You got a lady in your life?" Cody asked.

"I squire a couple of gals around every so often. Nothing serious at the moment. How about you? Dillon told me you are single."

"Yeah, it sounds like we have that in common. A couple of bachelors."

"Yeah, well, I don't have women chasing me down in restaurants. You got to show me how to get that mojo, Uncle."

"Ninety percent of what I know how to do isn't worth doing, Wiley. Don't use me as an example."

"We'll see. Let's get the check and take that DNA test. We can do it right in the parking lot, and we both send our vials in separate packages." Wiley offered his fist out for a bump like he had seen Cody do with Dillon.

"Sounds good." Cody gave him a solid fist bump and waved for the check. Least he could do was pick up dinner after the kid had done so much work to find him and research their possible connection, he thought.

# CHAPTER IV

**D**oris Loughlin sat in her well-used SUV, idling with her phone in her hand in the vacant parking lot adjacent to a stoplight. She was running late to meet an incoming flight at the airport. Her stomach fluttered with a mixture of fear and anticipation at seeing her boyfriend after he'd been gone for a week. She had pulled over to contemplate whether she even wanted to pick him up. Half of her wanted to flee like a gazelle away from the dangerous and abusive relationship that had developed in such a short time with him, and the other half wanted to fling herself into his arms. In her indecisive spasm of half panic and half anticipation, she had made herself late for his flight without resolving the perpetual internal struggle she faced every day.

She knew she tended to be a submissive woman. She was attracted to take-charge, domineering men. She had never been involved with a dangerous bad boy, however, and the last six months since she met him had started out nice but were rapidly becoming a nightmare as his real personality began to reveal itself. He was threatening her more and more and becoming critical of her, causing her to question herself about everything in her life. He had convinced her to leave her two children with her mom and dad temporarily to give their relationship time to grow, as he put it. He was steadily isolating her more and more from her friends and coworkers and insisting that she become involved with his social circle exclusively. She found his friends odd and distant toward her though. It was as if they did not trust her, and there seemed to be so many secrets about their work, the meetings they had together, and how they made their money. There seemed to be plenty of money, which was always a nice thing to experience, but there never was any discussion about business deals, the economy, or normal things that coworkers would discuss in front of their spouses or significant others.

Sex with him was becoming odd, also. Recently, sex between them was becoming rougher and rougher, and he seemed to enjoy belittling her and becoming physical to the point of pain with her. What had started as playful spanking or hair pulling was becoming domineering and abusive. He seemed to enjoy making her submit to humiliation and domination and using pain as punishment for her bad behavior. At a certain level she enjoyed releasing herself to her submissive, wicked carnal pleasure, but on another level it seemed dangerous, and what initially seemed like harmless bad boy sexual play was rapidly eroding normal boundaries of respect and consideration throughout their entire relationship. When coupled with the isolation she felt from her friends and family, and the unsettling signs of abnormal secret activities, and his refusal to completely reveal to her exactly what he did for the "company" he worked for, there were dangerous red lights blinking all over her involvement with this man.

He was a large and physical man, which she liked. However, what initially appeared to be a calm and easygoing disposition was rapidly giving way to an emerging quick temper and downright vicious attitude of retribution toward people who crossed him. She was sick with worry that she would make him upset and he would turn violent with her. She hated that she felt a visceral attraction to him while fearing him at the same time. She hated that she willingly gave up temporary custody of the children she loved so much at his request. She loathed that she felt too weak to leave him and felt fear that he might abuse her if she tried to and he caught her. He had implied to her, but never directly said, that if she tried to leave him, he would have to hunt her down. She hated that she weakly laughed at his threat and assured him that she would never leave, even though she thought about it any time she wasn't trying her hardest to please him.

All of his friends feared him, and he had shown a vile and explosive temper with some of his circle of friends. They always seemed to forgive him, however, and he seemed to hold an exalted place of high esteem among the ragtag group of sycophant misfits. He referred to himself as a Fixer. Unbeknown to him, she had begun double checking flight schedules of the return flights he claimed he took on the airlines he flew on. His arrival times did not seem to coincide with flights from the destinations he claimed to be flying from. He revealed almost nothing about his trips, and she became convinced that he was not going to the locations that he told her he was traveling to. Initially, she ignored the discrepancies, but the incongruity of his secretive travel life triggered more questions, and she quietly observed and made note of other questionable things he said. Meekly, she said nothing about the things she observed, and after provoking sharp rebukes from him when she asked any probing general questions, she stopped asking. She felt she had allowed herself to be maneuvered into a controlling, dependent relationship with a man she clearly did not know, who seemed violent, abusive, and dishonest, not to mention likely to be involved in illegal activities with moronic cult followers who would do anything to keep him happy with them.

Worse than that, she felt a flutter of sick anticipation in her stomach at the prospect of seeing him again and the vigorous sexual rendezvous that would occur once they got home. This doubleminded, unhealthy attraction was making her ill. She was worried all the time, not eating right, and only felt at peace and right in her world when he was kind and nurturing to her.

Kindness toward her seemed to be ever rarer, which made her crave approval even more and work harder to make him happy with her when he did not grant it. People at her work were concerned for her; they noticed her spiral downward emotionally and physically as she lost weight and her normal happy demeanor.

When the light turned green, she left the parking lot and accelerated hard away from the stoplight and felt her phone vibrate with his call. She answered sweetly, "Hi honey. Did you get your luggage already?"

He answered abruptly. "Where are you?"

"I'll be pulling up in five minutes. Traffic was terrible," she lied. "I brought you some cold beers, though. Just like you asked."

"I will be needing one of those. Hurry up." He hung up brusquely.

She nervously replaced the phone in her purse and accelerated her vehicle hard toward the airport, noting carefully which terminal the airline he was flying on was located. As she approached the arrival gates, she spotted his hulking silhouette leaning casually against a column supporting the roof over the drive lanes. She stopped in front of him and he flung his bags into the back seat and sat down heavily in the passenger seat.

"Where is that beer?" he asked without greeting or thanking her for picking him up.

"Back seat." She pointed backward timidly.

He reached back and lifted the lid to the cooler and liberated one of the cans and roughly opened it. He quickly searched to make sure no police were in the area and took a long pull on the beer as she re-entered traffic and sped away from the airport.

He slowly wiped his mouth and closed his eyes momentarily, leaning back heavily in the seat of the car.

"How was your trip, honey? Were the flights good? Tell me about what you been doing while you were away so long." She sounded ridiculous and sickly sweet, she thought to herself, and she suddenly wondered how she could even think about being with a man who didn't even greet her when he saw her after a week.

"It was all good, babe. Nothing to report. Don't worry about my business."

"Okay then. Just glad you are home." She managed a weak smile.

"So, you been thinking about what we talked about?"

"You mean, quitting my job? I am not ready to do that, Randal. Sorry, I think we need to give this a little bit more time." She surprised herself with the direct response to his suggestion.

He looked away from her out the window and made a tense facial expression. She waited anxiously for his response as she noticed his fists were clenching and unclenching repeatedly on his lap.

"So, this means you don't trust me yet, do you? I've told you I will take care of everything you need. You just need to let go and let me take care of things. It will be so much better for both of us. You will see." He reached over and stroked the back of her head with his big palm and brushed the back of his hand against her cheek. Doris smiled meekly, clasped his hand with hers, and pulled it to her lips to kiss. She felt a fluttering in her stomach at the thought of him being nice to her. She was anticipating a steamy reunion with him shortly, which would make everything right between them.

"Stop by the abandoned property where we get the pecans on the way in. I need to get something I left there."

"It will be dark when we get there, Randal. What is it you left there? That place is spooky, and that old, dilapidated house gives me the heebie-jeebies."

"Just do what I tell you. It's on the way and it won't take long."

The Oklahoma sunset showed its intense full complement of colors as they sped down the highway. She broke the strained silence by making idle conversation about some of his friends, her work, her children, and anything else she could come up with to keep the conversation off of their relationship.

Darkness had set in, and the narrow road offered no street-lights to assist in the rural blackness of southeast Oklahoma. She slowed down slightly, looking for the culvert that provided a crossing over the bar ditch to the long driveway into the property. Randal got out of the car and unscrewed the quick link he had put into the chain to allow him to access the property at will without unlocking the lock. He pushed open the gate and waved for Doris to pull the car forward onto the property, and then closed the gate again after she passed the gate. He reentered the car and leaned forward to try to help her drive in the darkness.

"Turn your bright lights on," he barked. The car creeped slowly down the two gravel ribbons that constituted the remainder of what was once a driveway leading up to the frame house hidden from the road by the overgrown trees and hedges. "Go straight at the curve."

Doris kept the vehicle creeping forward on the grass with the bright lights illuminating the way. After arriving at a hammock of oaks, she slowly brought the vehicle to a stop at the edge of the tree line.

"Get out of the car. I want to show you something." Randal opened his door and glared at the woman. Without comment, she exited the car and walked around back to stand next to him.

He abruptly grabbed her by the hair and leaned her over at the waist. He kicked her legs apart and forced her head down to her waist and moved around behind her while lifting her skirt up and shoved a big hand between her legs, rubbing her softly.

She protested mildly and grunted from the exertion of pressing against his downward pressure on her head. He swatted her backside several times and yanked her panties down her thighs with a savage pull that tore the fabric.

"You know why I brought you here?" he asked roughly while leaning his face close to hers.

"No," she cried softly.

"I wanted to show you where I am going to bury you if you try and leave me or disobey me again."

She sobbed quietly. "I don't think you would do that, Randal. I have told you that I am not going to leave you."

"I am going to kill you and those two brats along with you. I will kill your parents and bring them here and bury them with you. There won't be anything left of your family when I am done."

"You aren't going to do that, Randal. Please tell me you won't do that."

"Do you know what I do? Do you know what I did when I went out of town? I eliminate people. I kill them dead. That is what pays the bills around here. Where do you think my money comes from, bitch? And I will have no problem killing you if you cross me."

Doris wailed at the threat against her family. She wondered how this relationship had evolved into this so quickly. Her sense of survival took over and she recovered her faculties. "Randal, please, you know I am not going to leave you. I love you. I am so happy being here with you."

"You need to quit your job, and I don't want to hear any more about you going to church…fucking hypocrites anyway." He savagely pulled her head up close to his mouth and growled in her ear. "Don't try me on this, Doris. I will end you if you cross me. You understand?"

The tears were streaming down her face, and the pain of his

grip on her hair was overwhelming. "I understand, Randal. I won't cross you; I promise you."

With that he forced her head back down and unzipped his pants. He planned on showing her who had control of this relationship.

# CHAPTER V

**C**ody adjusted his necktie and did a last check of himself in the mirror. The suit hung fashionably on his lean frame. Unlike many modern suits that fit men too tight for his taste, the jacket had ample room for his wide shoulders and covered his long arms appropriately, leaving just the hint of the shirt cuff exposed. The brightly colored silk tie tied in a double Windsor knot was perfectly centered in the white shirt collar. The tie was extra-long, which allowed for the knot and left plenty of length to trail down to the top of his belt buckle. His shoes and belt were buffed out and shined, and he was wearing his beloved keepsake Rolex watch given to him by his father before he passed away.

After the last-minute check of his attire, he opened the door and walked down the hotel hallway with lengthy strides to the elevator landing. The door opened immediately when he touched the down button to descend to the lobby, and he slid easily into the back of the elevator cab after punching the lobby button several times. He laughed to himself as he wondered why he always pushed the button multiple times as if to alert the elevator that he was not messing around. One of his many idiosyncrasies, he thought.

The hotel was in the heart of the governmental district of Washington, D.C. It had been booked for him by his friend Congressman Musselwhite of Texas, who had been a friend of Cody's father. Musselwhite had been encouraging him to visit his office and spend a day with him in Washington, D.C. Cody sensed that the congressman felt lonely in D.C. without his wife at his side. Loretta Musselwhite had stopped coming to the capital with him several years ago because she detested the highly charged political environment and resented the number of people who were always attempting to win the attention and time of her husband. She elected to remain in their hometown of Lubbock, Texas, and focused on her charitable work there, keeping their homestead in order as well as overseeing the staff in his home office. They had settled into the routine, and it seemed to work fine for both of them, but it left the congressman with a certain amount of surplus time on his hands while Congress was in session. Musselwhite had his aide purchase a first-class round-trip ticket for Cody and booked him into the five-star hotel he found himself in as he walked across the beautiful lobby to the side door exit to the adjacent restaurant where he was meeting the congressman after his long day of meetings and hearings.

Musselwhite had utilized his office budget to purchase the flights and the hotel for Cody under the guise that Cody would be offering some consulting for the naval weapons systems being considered by the Armed Services Committee on which he served. Cody had a hearty laugh about the ruse. He knew little about any weapons systems other than small arms and knives. Musselwhite smiled and told him not to worry about it; in the grand scheme of waste in Washington, D.C. this was small potatoes and below anybody's radar.

Adjacent to the Willard Intercontinental Hotel, the Occidental Grill had been serving governmental dignitaries for over a hundred years. It was known for excellent food and service and many interesting photos of high-profile foreign and domestic politicians who had dined there over the decades. As he walked confidently into the entry of the restaurant, he was glad that he listened to the congressman and wore his only good suit to the dinner engagement. The waiters were in tuxes and bow ties and everybody in the restaurant was dressed formally. When the front desk attendant asked for a name for the reservation, it quickly got a nod of approval from the young man, and he immediately assigned a waiter to escort Cody into a private dining room that the congressman had reserved for the occasion.

Cody made himself comfortable in the wide chair facing the door. He would always choose the gunslinger seat, he mused. Force of habit that would never change. The table was oversized for the two chairs and place settings neatly arranged on its surface. The waiter made a huge production of snapping and unfolding the black napkin before expertly laying it on Cody's lap. Before leaving, the man bowed slightly and addressed him in a respectful, low voice.

"Congressman Musselwhite sends his respects, Mr. Houston. He notified us that he would be a few moments delayed, but instructed us to make sure you were completely taken care of. Could we offer you a cigar, drink, or an hors d'oeuvres?"

"Thanks for the nice offer. A little ice water and a Jack Daniel's on the rocks would be fine for now." Cody was surprised at how easy it was to warm up to the elegant service offered.

"My name is Bernard, sir, and I will be taking care of you tonight. While waiting, you might want to acquaint yourself with the offerings of the night in the menu. There are several excellent specials that I will explain to you when the congressman gets here. I'll return right away with your cocktail."

Cody mused about the different ways he had traveled on behalf of the government. Everything from the back of a cargo airplane with a carbine and parachute strapped on, to the front of a jetliner in first class. *Definitely go with first class,* he chuckled to himself. The hotel itself was impressive also. He picked up the menu and started a thorough review. Just as he laid the menu down, Ernie Musselwhite burst through the door with the waiter,

Bernard, in tow and beamed at Cody.

"Sorry I am late, Cody! I meant to get here before you but got held up. Always something cropping up to delay a guy around here. I did catch Bernard though, before he made it back here with your drink and got him to hustle up a martini for me." He took the martini glass off the tray the man held and smiled graciously while toasting him. "Thanks, Bernard. I can always count on you."

"You are most welcome, Congressman. Always a pleasure. Here is your cocktail, Mr. Houston. I will leave you gentlemen to get settled and check back shortly." He set the drink down along with a cup of nuts in front of Cody and quietly disappeared from the room.

Cody got to his feet and held the drink up to clink glasses with his friend.

"It's really nice to see you here, Cody. I don't get much friendly company here in D.C., and I come to this restaurant frequently for business dinner meetings. I always ask for Bernard, and he has become like family to me. They really take care of me here, and that is why I wanted to have you meet me here. I assume everything is okay with your hotel room. Did you make it to any of the museums today?"

"Thanks for the invitation to come here and visit with you. I don't get taken care of like this very often. It is a real pleasure to see how the other half lives life." Cody chuckled and clinked glasses again with the congressman, and then they both settled into their seats.

"Well, I hope you will come back up here again soon, Cody. Loretta is dying for you to come back and visit us in Lubbock again, too. She sends her best and she wants me to get a picture of us together before the night is over, so don't let me forget."

"That's nice of her. Tell her I said hello when you talk to her again. As for getting back to see you guys, that may happen sooner than you think. I have two pieces of news that I couldn't tell you yesterday while we were in the meetings you dragged me to."

"Oh? Tell me the news, son."

Cody looked at the man solemnly. "I have a nephew I never knew about until just recently when he located me and introduced himself. He lives in Oklahoma, and he did quite a bit of research about his mother and my mother. It turns out, Mom gave birth to a baby that she gave up for adoption before she met Dad, and that girl had a baby, who is him. She is no longer with us now, but it turns out that Mom was Chickasaw, and that makes me Chickasaw Indian also. The kid's name is Wiley, and he lives in Tishomingo, Oklahoma, and he is a police officer on the Chickasaw Nation Police Force."

"You are sure about all of this, Cody?"

"Yes, sir. We both took DNA tests, and I got my results back confirming it, right before I left to come up here."

Musselwhite beamed and worked to suppress his smile. "Well, I'll be damned. You never know what life is going to bring you, do you?"

"No sir, you sure don't. He is a good young man too. I want to bring him down to Lubbock to see Mom's grave and introduce him to you guys."

"Well, you know Loretta was good friends with your mother, and she introduced her to your dad. She might have a little insight into the other part of this story too. I will let her tell you what she knows." His eyes twinkled as he looked at Cody. "So, tell me the other piece of news."

"Well, you remember my friend Gordy Hill from Arizona, right?"

"Of course. How could I forget?"

"Gordy passed away a few days ago from his leukemia."

"Sorry to hear that, Cody." Musselwhite lifted his glass and Cody lifted his up again to clink the rims. "Gordy was a good man and a tough hombre. I still can't believe what you two guys pulled off together. How is his son doing?"

"He is good. He is finishing his PhD at Stanford in astrophysics just like Gordy wanted him to. He told me that Stanford was talking to him about staying on for a teaching position, and he is considering it. Evidently he doesn't have any desire to get back into the meteorite hunting business again."

"Is there going to be a funeral service? Are you going?"

"Dillon and I are going to take his ashes out to the Gulf Stream in his boat, along with his son Nate, and put them in the Gulf Stream current that runs about thirty-five miles offshore from Canaveral. He told me that he wanted me to do that for him when we were planning that mission, and he confirmed it with Nate shortly before he passed. Once Nate gets the ashes back and we can work it out schedule wise, Nate is going to fly out to see us, and we will put him in the stream for his eternal journey."

"That is a nice thing for you and Dillon to do, Cody. That Dillon is quite a sidekick, isn't he? I think he would do anything for you."

"He is my best friend. I would do anything for him."

"You guys are lucky to have each other. I lost my best friend when your dad died. It's hard to make good friends when you get to be my age. Then you throw in the fact that I am in politics, and it makes it even harder because you never know if someone is worthy of being a friend or if they are just trying to get something out of you."

At that moment, the door opened to the private dining room, and Bernard entered to check on them. "Everything okay here, gentlemen?"

"Just in time, Bernard. I think they gave me one of those

glasses with the hole in it again. Look, it's empty already! His drink too."

The waiter chuckled at the well-worn joke and smiled at the congressman. "I already ordered you guys two more drinks. I will have them in here in a minute. Can I get your dinner orders?"

The congressman looked at Cody and motioned in an exaggerated fashion. "Cody, trust me on this. Let me order for you. You have to try this Chilean sea bass they serve here. Will you allow me?"

"Of course, sir. That is exactly what I was thinking about ordering," he politely lied.

After a lengthy discussion about how the congressman wanted the meals and salads prepared, the waiter left them to their private conversation.

"What time is your flight out tomorrow morning, Cody?"

"Flight is out of Reagan Airport at 9:00."

"I'll come and get you at 6:30. Pick you up at the front of the hotel. That will give you plenty of time to get there and checked in. There is a lot of early morning traffic at that airport on Fridays. You need to get there a little earlier than you think."

"You don't have to do that, sir. I am fine riding the shuttle."

"You aren't riding the damn shuttle if I have anything to say about it, son. I will be there to pick you up at 6:30 and I will drop you off. They have good coffee at the hotel there, so make sure you bring me a cup when you come out. And quit calling me sir. You are about the only family I have left that I can stand to be around."

The two men shared a good laugh. "Okay then," Cody said. "I will count on you for tomorrow. Thanks for taking such good care of me."

"My pleasure. Least I can do for you since I couldn't get away to spend time with you today."

# CHAPTER VI

Appaloosa horses originated as a breed in the Pacific Northwest by Nez Perce Indians. The name is a derivative of the Palouse River, where the Nez Perce were located. White settlers originally referred to the beautiful animals as "Palouse Horses" in recognition of their origin on the Nez Perce homeland, which was split by the Palouse River in what is now known as eastern Washington, Oregon, and north and central Idaho. Over time, the name morphed to "Appaloosa," which remains the official name of the breed today.

The Nez Perce first acquired horses of many different breeds and appearances from the Shoshone Indians around 1730. The tribe proved to be excellent horsemen and breeders since they found themselves in an isolated territory free from intermingling influences of stock other than their own. They soon developed the practice of gelding inferior stallions and selectively breeding their best mares to the stallions that matched the desired characteristics. Once their herd of horses developed the desired tall, rangy, narrow-bodied traits desired, the Nez Perce began breeding for the notable spotted coloration patterns that define the beautiful breed. In the early 1800s, the Lewis and Clark expedition made explicit reference to the quality of the horses bred by the Nez Perce people in their writings about their encounters. The original Appaloosas were striking, tall, lean mounts with convex facial characteristics inherited from their original Andalusian thoroughbred influences favored in Spain at the time horses were exported to the New World by the conquistadors. As opposed to the unremarkable quality of much of the horse stock in the New World, Lewis noted that the beautiful Appaloosas were the equal of the fine chargers seen in royal courts of England.

The Nez Perce emphasized spotted, blanket snowcap, and snowflake coloration schemes on the horse hindquarters and frequently featured overall body freckled dark or white spots on contrasting undercoat, which led to the notable appearance of their breed. The Nez Perce became successful livestock traders, and their horses were sought by discriminating horsemen of the era willing to pay a large premium for the fine horses produced by the tribe.

The beautiful breed was almost lost when the Nez Perce tribe was scattered, and their herd decimated in the Nez Perce War in 1877. Determined breeders salvaged the remaining breed stock and formed the Appaloosa breed registry in the 1930s. Over time, other physical characteristics were introduced into the breed from quarter horse stock to make the horses better mounts for tending cattle and other equestrian pursuits. Today, the breed features a wide range of body types and emphasizes the traditional coloration patterns for which it's known as the defining characteristic. The breed thrives in the United States as one of the most popular equestrian types because of their willing, durable, and versatile nature.

In the late afternoon furnace in southeastern Oklahoma, the shirtless man labored in the stall as the beautiful sorrel Appaloosa mare watched him use the flat shovel to clean her premises and carefully toss the manure mixed with straw into the wheelbarrow parked in the center of the spacious wooden stall. The man paused to lean on the shovel handle to wave away the nuisance flies swarming his exposed face and upper body. The mare gently neighed and purposefully approached her owner, draping her head over his shoulder in their customary embrace. The man wrapped his long arms around the mare's neck and gently stroked her as he spoke softly to his old companion.

"You are a beautiful old girl. Let your daddy finish this stall and we will brush you down and saddle up. Wiley is coming over and we are all going out for a ride just like old times." The slender horse had athletic, fine lines and a beautiful sorrel base color with mottled snowflake blanket on the hindquarters. He had purchased the horse as a foal and had been the only owner she had ever known since being weaned from her mother. He had bred her with other Appaloosa stallions that featured the traditional narrow body build and athletic lines of the Andalusian ancestors favored by the Nez Perce breeders who established the breed.

The mare had given him a dozen beautiful offspring that had helped him establish a small but high-quality bloodline of beautiful Appaloosa foals that had grown up to be even-tempered, high-quality, healthy specimens of the traditional Nez Perce Appaloosa as he believed they were conceived by the original breeders. At her age, she was no longer breeding, but over her life she had given her owner eight beautiful mares that he still owned and was actively breeding with a selected group of carefully chosen stallions that he evaluated and mated with his herd. His foals were highly prized and brought premium prices in advance by a small but devoted group of equestrian followers. Over time, he had steadily raised the prices on his colts to the top shelf price of $10,000 each, which normally covered the expenses on his small ranch when he sold the annual colt harvest, with some left over as a contribution to his living expenses.

The horse breeding was a good side hustle, but didn't provide enough income to allow him to live independently, so he still worked part time as a striped bass fishing guide on Lake Texoma during the spring, summer, and early autumn months to earn additional money to make ends meet. He also worked as needed for some of the other ranchers and landowners when he wasn't fishing. He was respected by the other area ranchers as a good horseman and a hardworking, no-nonsense ranch hand who could repair fence, shoe horses, run equipment to clear pasture and create terraces for erosion management, cut and bale hay, and perform generally any other kind of ranch work needed without supervision. Between the different endeavors he pursued to make a life for himself, he rarely took time off, but he enjoyed his life and made enough money to be comfortable and keep his small ranch paid for and his beloved herd of horses well taken of. He was fiercely independent and proud of the life he had built for himself. He was closing in on paying off the mortgage on his place, which would then take a lot of the financial pressure off his lifestyle.

The old mare loved being gently brushed and taken care of by her owner. She was in the final stages of her life at twenty-five years old, but she was still a willing mount for a trail ride and had surprising spirit for an animal of her age. She was strong and still had a beautiful coat and full mane and tail that complemented her graceful, athletic lines. She was an easygoing, well-mannered horse and eager to please. Like the traditional Appaloosas favored by the Nez Perce, she was gaited and had a smooth shuffle evenly spread over four beats that made her a pleasure to ride over long distances. She had the gait known in the time of the Nez Perce breed development as the *Indian Shuffle*, which was prized by the breeders. This trait was one of the principal features the man sought in his selection of stallions to breed with his mares, along with the basic athletic, narrow body lines and convex facial features that favored the historical lineage of the Andalusian influence. These characteristics differentiated the Appaloosa from the normal quarter horse, Morgan, and thoroughbred influences that normally featured more stocky, muscular hindquarters and thicker bodies in other breeds and in some Appaloosas.

The man was of native heritage and felt a calling to be a steward of and faithful to the original characteristics of the breed the Nez Perce established. He felt a kinship with the native vision for the beautiful, easygoing Appaloosas and wanted to maintain the integrity of the original breed concept, including the gait, the coloration patterns, the body shape, and facial characteristics. His efforts included a detailed knowledge of the dominant sires featured in the Appaloosa bloodlines and an understanding of the expression of different features that would manifest in the breeding process. His knowledge came from direct personal experience and careful observation and detailed note taking. He frequently consulted with a friendly group of other like-minded breeders and took advantage of their knowledge and opinions as they did with him. He also carefully followed the progression of his colts to adulthood and called the owners who had purchased colts from him for photos and details on temperament and training and any potential genetically impacted diseases and conditions. He carefully documented each of the bloodlines of his colts to keep from inbreeding and overpopulating with certain sires.

He called his mare Mercedes, after the high-quality German cars he admired. He hoped his breeding would achieve the excellence of that brand. He felt that the beautiful old beast had been the equal of the brand and produced magnificent, sound offspring of beauty and temperament. He was proud of his work in the field and maintained a connection to each of the colts he sold and a lifelong relationship with each of their owners from whom he eagerly sought feedback and information. This obsession kept him in touch with his clients and helped solidify a devoted following. Despite her advanced age, the old mare was as beautiful as ever and he still loved riding her whenever possible. She was always eager for an outing too. As the man placed a saddle blanket on her back, her ears went up and a sense of excitement became evident as she snorted and began pawing the floor in anticipation of the ride.

The sound of the truck pulling up close to the barn caused the man to look up from his inspection of the tack resting on a sawhorse in the tack room outside the stall area. He hoisted the saddle from the sawhorse and carried it to the stable where Mercedes was waiting with her head protruding over the gate to the stall to allow her to observe who had arrived. A uniformed young man rounded the turn on foot carrying an old pair of boots in his hand and a pair of jeans and a shirt draped over his shoulder.

"Hey, Pop!" the young man exclaimed as he made a beeline for the mare, who was carefully watching him approach. "How's the old girl today?" He set down the boots at her stall to offer a gentle rub and laughed when the horse began sniffing in search of the customary apple that he always brought her. "Okay, okay, girl. Here it is." He fished the apple out of his back pocket and held it for her as she took eager bites of the juicy fruit. He turned it for her ease in removing meat from the core and stroked her neck as she made quick work of the apple. When she approached the end of the treat, she turned and looked at the young man as if expecting more.

"She's been waiting for you, Wiley. Anytime I come in here to clean up and brush her, she thinks we are going riding and she begins expecting you to show up with her treat. She loves her apples. I appreciate you stopping by to help me keep these horses exercised and ridden. Some of them are getting downright ornery. I rode Dynamite the other day and he tried bucking me when I first got on him."

"Well, Dynamite didn't know who he was messing with, did he?" Wiley laughed. "I hope you didn't get all rodeo cowboy on him."

"No, we worked it out. He just forgot who the horse was

and who was the cowboy." The man smiled. He enjoyed spending time with his son and appreciated that he made time to help him ride the various horses he owned and maintain them as well-behaved mounts. Not riding a horse tends to make them sloppy and unresponsive. With the number of horses he kept, regular riding of them took an effort.

The older man quietly studied his son as he spoke. Their relationship had been rocky, and at times explosive, even physical at times. The two butted heads while Wiley was growing up, and the confrontations had sometimes led to fights. There had been periods of estrangement and resentment between the two after his divorce from the boy's mother and then, later, her death from a car accident. Early in the boy's life, he had been on the professional rodeo circuit and missed important bonding time with his son. The man's hardheaded devotion to buying and keeping this ranch had also impacted his ability to bond and spend time with his son. Too many times, he had chosen work over family. His son had come to live with him a few years after his divorce with his mother, and their relationship had been difficult. His time in the Army had changed his son, however. He became serious about his life and focused on what he wanted. It was good for the man to see how much his son enjoyed being part of the police department. Given all the rebellion of his youth, being a police officer was the last thing he ever anticipated his son would become. He felt proud as he watched his son strip off his uniform shirt and pull on a faded Army brown T-shirt.

"Saddle up on Lily when you get your boots on, son. Been a while since I have had her out."

"Sure, Dad. Before we go, I want to talk to you about something, though."

Shane Harris squinted and carefully peered at his son. He couldn't remember ever hearing his son say he wanted to talk about anything. He put one leg up on the saddle horse and sat down. "What's up?" he asked.

"Remember I told you about that guy I went to look up in Florida about the property I thought Mom was in line to inherit?"

"Yeah."

"Turns out, everything I thought was likely is true. He is Mom's half-brother. We both took DNA tests, and they came back positive. He is my uncle."

"No shit. Damn, that is some good work, son. I know how hard you worked on all that research. What did he say?"

"He was completely surprised. He seems like a good dude, though. He is a bachelor, doesn't talk much. I talked to him on the phone, and he wants to come out here and get to know us. He is driving out here, leaving next week. He is going to take me to Texas to show me where my grandma is buried and introduce me to some family friends from down there. He wants to meet you and learn about his sister."

"Is he going to sign the papers and go to the judge with you to get the land?"

"Yes. He didn't know he is Chickasaw. We are going to get him registered. I told him to bring his papers so we can get him signed up. You know my friend Jennifer down at the tribal registrar office? I have been telling her about him and I broke down the whole relationship for her and got her prepped for his application. She did some research and confirmed everything I told her."

"You still dating her?"

"No. She is not for me, Dad. Too damn dramatic. She gets upset about every stupid little thing and then acts like it was nothing once she is done being mad. Can't take it. How about you? Ever hear from Doris?"

"No, Doris is still with that crazy asshole, Randal. I haven't heard a peep from her, but everybody in church is telling me that she is miserable and looking for a way to get away from him. She is afraid of him and what I hear is that he won't let her come to church anymore, so I don't ever see her. She has her kids at her mom and dad's house, and she is living with him part time at that crazy compound out there. I do not trust those people and I don't think everything out there is legal. I don't understand what she sees in him."

"Pop, I don't want to scare you, but I can tell you that I know it's not a good situation out there. Doris does not know what she is getting herself into. That Randal is no good, and not just because he is a bully, either. He is a bully and a thief, and they are hooked up with some bad people. Doris needs to get herself out of there. I hear bad things at the station about what is happening out there at that compound."

"Yeah, I know. There isn't anything I can do, though." Shane dejectedly looked downward, feeling an ache in his stomach from the anxiety of knowing someone he cared about was in trouble. Even though they had never really had a romantic relationship, he had carried a torch for Doris for years from their involvement at their church. She was quite a few years younger than he was, though, and had gotten involved with Randal recently, which had concerned and frustrated him. "You want to bring your uncle over for dinner when he gets here?"

"Once he gets here, we will check in with you and work something out. I am going to need to take him out to Mom's grave. You want to come with us?"

"I will probably let you guys do that on your own."

"I understand. Let's get riding. I'll grab a saddle and get Lily saddled up. Where do you have her, anyway?"

"She is outside waiting on you in the side corral. I brought her in earlier this afternoon."

Wiley smiled. *Just like Pop to have everything organized.*

# CHAPTER VII

The ankle holster strap snapped solidly, and the man pulled his trousers back down over the compact nine millimeter semi-automatic pistol. He leaned back in the driver's seat of the large SUV and used a knuckle to punch the button turning on the dome light. He looked into the rearview mirror and carefully adjusted the necktie knot in his collar. Lightly slapping the area under his eyes, he cursed as he made note of the bags that seemed to grow more noticeable every time he studied his own face. It was evening and the end of a long day of driving. His face looked tired, and he felt the fatigue throughout his body. He hated meetings like the one he had just arrived to attend. These redneck goons seemed unpredictable and unstable, and he wished he didn't have to meet them without some muscle backing him up.

*Tonight should go smoothly*, he thought. He was bringing a payoff and the potential for three more lucrative assignments to this ridiculous gang of clown show misfits. He opened the briefcase on the passenger seat next to him and pulled out the three folders with material on the cases he had been instructed to review with them. They had performed on six assignments to date, and his bosses were giving them a chance on multiple assignments simultaneously now that they had a track record established.

He opened the heavy door of the truck and slid down to the ground with the files in his hand. He opened the rear door and pulled out the cash box he had brought with him from Kansas

City. He had carefully counted and recounted the money in the box to verify that it contained the full twenty-thousand-dollar payment due to the gang for carrying out their last assignment. They got half up front and half after they killed their mark. All the executions were staged to appear like accidents.

He worked for a shadowy financial company that purchased assignments of beneficial interests in life insurance policies from unsuspecting policy holders who needed cash for various reasons. To generate money, the victims would sell their future life insurance benefits to his employer at a substantial discount to the face value. The victims did not realize that they were signing their own death warrant when they signed the papers. Once his company had the assignment, they were not going to wait for a natural death to collect the face value of the policy. The company waited a few months and then put one of their gangs on the case to create an execution that appeared to be an accident, to hasten the collection of the death benefit. It had proven to be a highly lucrative proposition for the company, and they had developed a network of assassins who performed the *wet work* of killing the insured parties. The groups ranged from skilled paramilitary professionals to hillbilly numb-nuts like this Oklahoma crew. The leader of this crew seemed withdrawn and intense, but he and his misfit band of acolytes had performed on the previous assignments, leading his bosses to reward them with some new opportunities against his recommendation. They needed people from varied parts of the country because they only used assassins brought in from outside the area to keep the chatter down after the job was done.

The man debated locking the doors to his vehicle once he closed the SUV up. He was a creature of habit and he sighed to himself as he set down the cash box on the vehicle bumper to fish out his keys from his jacket pocket and used the key fob to lock the doors. He didn't want anybody rifling his car during his meeting. Long, hard experience in life had brought him to the realization that he could not trust anybody. The lights flashed and the horn did a short double honk as the security system activated. He looked up to the upstairs window of the room overlooking the front yard of the old home and saw the curtain pulled back and the silhouette of a large man framed in the window.

The front door of the ramshackle old farmhouse opened as he was coming up the steps.

"Good to see you, Lucas."

"Hey, Randal. Sorry I am running a little late. Long drive from KC."

"No problem, dude. Come on in. I have everybody upstairs waiting on you. Get you a beer or a drink?"

"I will have a beer with you guys."

Lucas followed Randal up the stairs and into a room with well-used chairs in a large semicircle and an old table pushed to the side of the room.

"Ricky, get this man a beer. Sit here, Lucas. Guys, this is Lucas from Kansas City. He is the guy I have been telling you about."

"Thanks, Randal." Lucas looked around the room at four bearded, scraggly men in jeans and T-shirts who were sitting in chairs, staring back at him and nodding in acknowledgment of his presence.

A large, shuffling man came up with a bottle of beer and opened the top before he handed it to him. "My name is Ricky," he said in a goofy way that made Lucas realize he was not completely right mentally.

"Ricky, sit your ass down. Nobody gives a shit who you are." Randal leaned forward and glared. Ricky quietly put his head down and shuffled over to a chair across the room.

"Thank you, Ricky."

Ricky turned around and smiled at Lucas and took a seat.

"Idiot." Randal shook his head. "Sorry about that, Lucas. He is not right in the head."

"No problem."

"Your show. These guys are waiting to hear what you got to say." Randal leaned back and crossed his arms as he watched Lucas take a long pull on the beer.

"Thanks, Randal." He set the beer down and picked up the cash box. "Just wanted to personally hand off this payment on the last contract and thank you guys for a good job. Looks like it went exactly like you planned it, and that is what we like. On behalf of everybody in Kansas City, we want to say thanks." He handed the box off to Randal to applause and whistles from the small group.

Lucas waved his hand and thanked them for the acknowledgment. "Doing what we said we would do just like you guys did what you said you would do. Good partners follow up and take care of each other. This makes six assignments that you guys have pulled off, and they all went well." More applause and laughter and foot stomping from Ricky.

"Ricky, shut the fuck up. All you do around here is get beers and wash dishes. Quit acting like you had anything to do with it." Randal brutally admonished the young man, who shamefully looked down and went silent. "Get me another beer."

Watching this unnecessary humiliation of the young man caused a visceral upwelling in Lucas. He shot a lingering look at Randal and silently made note of the upbraiding. He was too professional to intervene or comment about the way Randal managed his crew, but at a human level, he saw no reason to be so harsh about an innocent celebration. Lucas found himself hoping for a future opening to humiliate Randal in front of his guys in retaliation. Ricky shuffled back to his seat after handing off a chilled beer to Randal.

"We have three more cases we want to put in front of you guys to see if you want to consider them," Lucas continued. "Two of them are in California and one is in Ohio. We need all three of these taken care of within the month, which means you will have to scout these people out and develop an approved plan in short order. One of the California insured is a fisherman, and as you guys know, we like boating accidents in remote locations. This guy goes offshore frequently, and we want a plan that takes this guy out offshore.

"Second California insured is a hiker, climber, and camper. Based on our preliminary surveillance, we are thinking that a climbing accident might be the ticket if we can find him when he is by himself. The lady in Ohio is a homebody. We think a house fire might be the only recourse on her, but we are willing to listen once you guys scout it out. Details on her are still kind of sketchy based on our limited surveillance. You guys need to come up with a good plan. Arson is hard to pull off without leaving evidence. Think this one out carefully."

Lucas scanned the group slowly and looked over each one of the men. Each one earnestly stared back at him and looked over at Randal. "Any questions or comments?" he asked.

"Thanks for coming out to meet the guys, Lucas. We appreciate the vote of confidence. Let me review the information in these folders with the guys and we will work up a plan to review with you. We can handle this. Don't worry. We will call you in a day or two."

Lucas nodded and stood up slowly. He waved at the men and made his way carefully down the noisy stairs that creaked with each step and walked back out to his car. Once there he opened the car door, sat down, and started the car and leaned back in his seat. He needed to call Kansas City and let them know that the meeting went well, and it looked like this gang wanted to cover all three of the assignments. He turned the SUV around in the front yard of the house and pulled out the driveway feeling glad to get out of the weird environment these people lived in and away from this strange clique of hillbilly misfits.

# CHAPTER VIII

The oral history of the Chickasaw Tribe indicates that the tribe migrated east to eventually settle in northeastern Mississippi from the west. It's not known when this occurred, but the Muskogean native language they have in common with the Choctaws supports the numerous theories that they were at one time part of a tribe that included the Choctaws. Some archeologists theorize that the tribe migrated from west of the Mississippi River in prehistoric times and split from the Choctaw and settled into what the European explorers knew as their homeland prior to European contact. It's believed that Hernando de Soto first encountered the Chickasaw near Tupelo, Mississippi, in 1540. Although initially well received by the tribe, records indicate that differences arose between the Spaniards and Chickasaws that led to a nighttime raid by the Chickasaws and hasty departure by De Soto after nearly being destroyed in the attack.

As with many other eastern woodland native tribes, the Chickasaw were in the way of European settlers who were making a westward push for settlement of the immense frontier. Chickasaws were commercial hunters, traders, farmers, and ranchers and traded freely with other tribes and English and French settlers of the day. As growth in the new, vibrant, young United States took hold, pressure and conflict mounted on the tribe as settlers encroached on the desirable land controlled by the tribe. The Chickasaws eventually relented to pressure and signed the Treaty of Pontotoc Creek in 1832, after the State of Mississippi outlawed tribal self-governance and contracted to sell their historical Mississippi homelands to the U.S. government for three million dollars. Five years later, they negotiated to purchase the western portion of the previously resettled Choctaw Nation reservation in Oklahoma for half a million dollars in what was known as the Treaty of Doaksville. Notably, it eventually took thirty years for the government to pay the Chickasaws for their historical Mississippi homelands. Adding to the historical tortured legacy of the Chickasaw displacement, the forced relocation to Indian Territory on such a dangerous and deadly march, and the bad faith tactics employed by the federal government in dealing with them, the federal government took away from the Chickasaws half of the land they had legally purchased from the Choctaws after the Civil War as punishment for the tribal support of the Confederacy.

On July 4th, 1837, 3,001 Chickasaws assembled in Memphis, Tennessee, for the relocation march to Oklahoma. Over the course of the pilgrimage, 500 members of the tribe would die from dysentery and smallpox. Stubbornly, the survivors dug in and began their new life. Initially, the federal government administratively treated the Chickasaws as part of the Choctaw Nation and did not separately recognize them. After disagreements arose between the two nations, Chickasaws created and declared for themselves a new constitution and reformed their own government in 1856 to separately govern themselves independent of the Choctaws. When Oklahoma became a state in 1907, the federal government assumed the responsibility of appointing the officers of all the tribes, and their independence and sovereignty were eliminated. Ultimately, in 1970, the U.S. Supreme Court ruled in favor of tribal sovereign control for the five civilized tribes over their own affairs, and elections were held, which led to the Chickasaw enacting their own current constitution in 1983.

Today, the Chickasaw Nation is flourishing with over 60,000 citizens and a portfolio of over sixty gaming, medical, contracting, banking, manufacturing, and other commercial interests that fund a generous offering of benefits to their citizens for educational scholarships, medical and social support services, and a judicial system including a police force that serves the thirteen counties forming the historical Chickasaw territory. They are the fourth largest employer in Oklahoma and have benefitted from stable, disciplined business management and long-term planning and investment.

Within the modern governing principles of the Chickasaws as a society rests an ongoing commitment to the historical native cultural values of respect and care for their elders. The native way also includes matrilineal descent in which clan and inheritance are descended from the maternal line, and affords elevated status and influence of women in their society. Native cultural values also include appreciation for the environment with kinship and respect for all living creatures in harmony with the earth. Native religious tradition focused on a spiritual relationship with the creator, humility in one's earthly existence, and maximizing one's journey in preparation for the next life. Native people tend to be generous, kind, and respectful of government and authority in communal life. They value integrity and honor in interpersonal and governmental dealings. As one traverses the paths of the Chickasaw Nation, helpful, kind, respectful people emerge at every stop.

Cody Houston studied the rough-hewn blocks of red granite that formed the exterior walls of the handsome three-story building constructed by the Chickasaws in 1898 to serve as their tribal headquarters. The building is topped with a metal roof featuring twin dormers over an arched entry door and a domed steeple with a widow's walk centered over the complex. Cody contemplated the paradox of a people constructing a building of such elegance to serve as their governmental complex two years after signing the Treaty of Atoka, which declared that the Chickasaw and Choctaw governments would cease to exist after March 6th, 1906, in preparation for the upcoming evolution of Indian Territory into the State of Oklahoma. The building was to serve as a monument to a people who refused to die, refused to go away, and through sheer force of will and persistence now enjoyed prosperity and independence as they reclaimed their sovereignty, and who now elegantly emerged as descendants and caretakers of the heritage of their ancestors. Cody paused at the thought of the Chickasaws being evicted from the building by the formation of the State of Oklahoma in November of 1907. The building remained vacant until purchased in 1910 by Johnston County for use as a courthouse. After the resurrection of the Chickasaw Nation in 1983, the Chickasaws repurchased the building in 1992 and converted it to a museum. Cody noticed the care with which the grounds were kept and the quality of the landscape and hardscape. *My people are proud of this place*, he thought. He smiled as he contemplated the righteousness of the Chickasaws repurchasing this property originally constructed as a testimonial monument of their presence; a building taken away from them by a cruel and unaccommodating society anxious to disenfranchise them and force them to assimilate into an unwelcoming civilization that mocked them and ridiculed their practices and sought to break up their community bonds and culture.

"What you thinking about, Uncle?" Wiley asked. "You look deep in thought."

"I am glad you brought me here, Wiley. As I sit here and look at this building after having studied the history of the Chickasaw people and what I learned today after touring this place, a couple of important things come to mind. This place represents revival and rebirth of the Chickasaw spirit. A downtrodden people overcame oppression and emerged victorious with the repurchase of this beautiful building. This place is victory. Chickasaws reclaimed what was theirs and reestablished their independence and cultural identity and reconnected to the brave ancestors who walked so far to come here in hope of a better life when they bought this building back. The Chickasaws are warriors. You and I are descendants of the survivors. I feel at home here."

"Damn, Uncle. I never thought about it in that way. I think you are already more Chickasaw than I am." Wiley smiled broadly. His uncle was a tough nut. Cody was hard to read and didn't talk much, but his reaction and intuitive understanding and connection to the struggle of his people made him feel proud. Somehow Wiley knew that his uncle had fought his own battles, and through those understood the fight of the Chickasaw for redemption and independence.

"Let's get on those bikes and ride home, Wiley. Been a long day. The cemetery, Turner Falls, Lake Texoma, Chickasaw National Recreation Area, and now back here in Tishomingo. I am ready for one of those cold beers at your house." Cody grinned at Wiley as he spoke. It had been a long day of riding and taking in important sights around the area, as well as visiting the grave of his sister at the family cemetery. His nephew had proven to be a very capable rider and immediately jumped on the bike that Cody brought down for him like he had been riding it for years.

"I love that bike you gave me. Never had anybody just give me something like that before. I have always dreamed about getting a Harley, but it was never in the budget."

"That bike was given to me. Like I told you, the owner was a hell of a guy who is no longer with us, and I think he would be proud to know that another Army vet is now riding it for him. It would just be sitting around not being used if I didn't give it to you. I look forward to telling you the whole story about it someday. I was impressed by what a good rider you are."

"Sounds good, Uncle. I look forward to hearing about this guy soon. A couple of my buddies have bikes, and I have spent some time learning from them and riding theirs. I got close to getting one but just did not want to take on the payment. By the way, remember that my dad is expecting us for dinner at his house tonight at six. He isn't the best cook but whatever he makes won't kill you. Sometimes I stop and get a burger on the way over to his house to keep from starving to death just in case. He always makes way too much food and then he tries to give me some to take home. Please don't bring any home with you. And don't drink his coffee, either. He always makes coffee after dinner, and you never had anything that strong, I promise you."

"Okay." Cody chuckled. "Dinner sounds real promising. We can't talk him into going out to eat?"

"No, he is stubborn. He thinks family eats together at home. You can't talk to the guy once he has his mind made up. We better get on our way, though. After dinner tonight we are going to meet up with some of my friends at Blake Shelton's bar, Ole Red. You ever hear of it?"

"Heard of Blake Shelton, but not his bar." Both men swung legs over their saddles, and the two motorcycles sprang to life with the press of a button.

"It's a cool place. They have live music on the weekends. Should be a few women there in case you want to show me some of your moves on the dance floor. Might even have some with cankles. I know that is what you like." Wiley spoke over the lilting chorus of both idling motorcycles with a mischievous grin.

"I don't know how you would know if they had cankles or

not, nephew. I haven't seen a woman around here yet that wasn't wearing cowboy boots."

Wiley smiled broadly and checked traffic both ways. "Jeans and boots, Uncle. Get used to it." He smoothy accelerated into the traffic lane and Cody followed.

# CHAPTER IX

"**H**er name was Rachel Wilson before I married her. Since she was so young when she was adopted, they changed her last name to Wilson at the adoption, and then when she married me, she took my last name and became Rachel Harris, which is what is on the headstone. She never changed her name after she divorced me."

Shane Harris used a strange-looking metal hook to scrape out the mud from the center of the horse's hoof. Wiley looked intently at his dad as he studied the inside of hoof. "Lily got something in her hoof, Pop?"

"No, doesn't look like it. I saw her favoring this leg earlier today and just wanted to check. If she had something, it came out."

Wiley smiled. His dad knew everything about his small herd and noticed everything about them. They had enjoyed a better-than-expected chicken fried steak dinner in the house with some limited conversation. They decided to move around a bit after dinner and show Cody the horses he raised.

"I am sure Wiley told you, but Rachel had a bad automobile accident caused by a drunk driver when Wiley was about sixteen years old. She left me when he was ten years old because I was too stubborn to quit the rodeo circuit. When Wiley was fourteen, she sent him here to live with me because she couldn't handle him. He wasn't a bad kid, but he just wouldn't do what she told him to and wouldn't focus on his schoolwork. I always hoped that she and I would get back together, but she got killed in that accident. She was a good woman and she deserved better than what I gave her. By the time I realized how wrong I was and tried to make amends and get her back in my life, she was killed a couple of months later. She and I were talking about reconciling and making another go of it. It was really hard on me; I felt like I lost her twice."

Cody asked, "Did she ever know anything about her birth family or her biological mother?"

"No. Wiley was the one who tracked that down. He has been investigating the hell out of all this for over a year now."

"After Mom died, I went back and did research on her original birth certificate and traced her birth mom down. As I researched it, your mother, Alice Taylor, was flagged in the Chickasaw system as an inheritor of BIA land that was tied up intestate pending resolution of heirs." The three men leaned on the split rail fencing surrounding the corral. There were six horses milling around, and suddenly, a beautiful sorrel gently ambled up and began sniffing Wiley's pockets and neighing softly.

"Mercedes wants her apple. I wondered how long it would take for her to come over here looking for it." Wiley laughed and pulled the apple out of his pocket and let the horse munch on it as he held it in position for her. Gingerly, the other horses slowly surrounded the three men hoping for a similar offering.

"This is why I told you to bring that apple, Cody. Let Lily and that gray horse, Blizzard, share yours and I will split mine with Dynamite here. Here is your apple, Pop." Shane caught the tossed apple and shared his with the remaining horses. The three men enjoyed a nice moment surrounded by the beautiful horses as they greedily fed on the apples. They slowly made their way back into the house and sat down for a moment after the horses demolished every morsel of the juicy apples.

"Cody, I am going to make some coffee. Would you like some?"

"I already warned him off on your coffee, Pop."

Shane looked at Cody. "He doesn't know shit. I would not listen to him. I make good, strong coffee. You sure you don't want any, Cody?"

"No, I don't sleep that well as it is, Shane. I try to avoid caffeine at night."

Shane carried on in the kitchen as he started up the coffeepot. "I am what they call Chick-Chock. Part Chickasaw and part Choctaw, which is not that unusual around here. Wiley was already registered as a member of the tribe through my family, but his mom did not know that her biological mother was also a member and that she was eligible to be a member, also. What can you tell us about Wiley's grandmother?"

"My mom is deceased. She died shortly after my birth from complications. I never really knew her. I have some photos that I gave Wiley, and we are going down to Texas this weekend to visit her grave and some family friends. Might be some additional information from that visit." Cody felt embarrassed that he did not have more to offer his nephew. A lifetime of managing his emotions and distancing himself from connections left him limited on family information. He was pleased to learn about his sister Rachel and glad to know that she had been loved by Shane and Wiley.

"You guys are planning to be back for the hearing on the property, right?" Shane seemed concerned about the trip.

"Hearing isn't until 10:30 Tuesday, Pop. We will be back Monday night, for sure. We are heading out to Ole Red tonight to meet some people. You want to come with us?"

"No thanks. Just make sure and be safe, guys. Cops watch that place and arrest people when they leave if they think they have been drinking too much. You are the last person that should be out drinking and driving after you have been in a bar, Wiley."

"That's why I have my designated driver, Uncle Cody, along with me, Pop. He has my back, right, Uncle?"

"I will get you home, nephew."

Wiley hugged his father and Cody offered a handshake to Shane. "Nice meeting you, Shane. Thanks for dinner. It was better than advertised."

Shane looked at his son and said, "You been talking shit about my cooking too? Starting to hurt my feelings." He smiled and looked at Cody. "No respect for elders. Just remember I told you. Talking shit about my coffee is one thing, but my cooking?"

All three of the men walked to the front door and Shane waved goodbye as they drove away. "You didn't have to tell him that I warned you about his cooking, Uncle. Damn."

"You didn't tell me not to. I thought the food was rather good, actually."

"Better than usual. He must have been trying to impress you. Good thing you passed on the coffee, though. Lethal brew." The two enjoyed a chuckle about the exchange.

The blue pickup truck rolled smoothly through town as Wiley began looking for street parking. Surprisingly, there was little available parking, and Wiley turned down a side street to find a spot, and they disembarked from the truck. Cody followed Wiley as he began striding toward their destination. After being waved in by the bouncer sitting outside the small club, they quickly made a beeline for the crowded bar. Wiley nodded and waved at several people as they covered the short distance to the bar. They slid into a vacant space, and Wiley was greeted by a short, plump bartender with a pierced nose and numerous colorful tattoos on her fleshy body.

"Hey, Wiley! What you boys having tonight?" The question came out in a thick, slow drawl.

"Hey, Virginia. This is my uncle Cody visiting from Florida.

Two Jack Daniel's on the rocks."

"You quit drinking beer?" quizzed the bartender.

"Drinking with my uncle tonight, Virginia. Sticking with Number 7 tonight."

The drinks and good conversation flowed over the next few hours. Wiley introduced Cody to several friends and coworkers as they held down a spot at the bar. Wiley was engaged in an animated conversation as Cody excused himself to go to the restroom and strode past a table with a striking brunette and a man with a military haircut who appeared to be her date. The woman locked eyes with Cody as he worked his way through the crowd, passing the table where she was seated. Although it seemed awkward to lock eyes with a woman obviously on a date in public, Cody shamelessly stared her down as he walked past. The woman did not look away and casually held her beer to her lips as he walked by, as if in mock salute. Cody entered the bathroom and filed the encounter away for future thought as he waited his turn.

Returning to the bar, Cody was surprised to find Wiley in conversation with the woman. Wiley and the woman both stopped speaking and watched him as he returned to his half-finished drink.

"So, your nephew here tells me that I am not your type because I am too slender and don't have cankles. He said you like women with a fuller figure and you would not be interested in me. I told him that it seemed like you were pretty interested in me when you walked by the restroom." The woman coyly tilted her head when speaking.

Cody looked at Wiley with surprise. From behind her, Wiley was making a ridiculous face and could barely keep himself from laughing. Cody turned to the woman and made a quick close-up appraisal of her. She was tall and athletically built, with fine skin, a beautiful, friendly smile, and sparkling blue eyes. She would be any man's dream come true and she knew it.

"Well, I do like a muffin top on a woman. I guess we could still be friends, though. Thanks for trying out."

Wiley could not contain himself any longer and slapped the bar top and snorted. The woman scowled at Cody in disbelief and shook her head. "Thanks for trying out? What kind of B.S. is that? Who do you think you are? You aren't so much."

"Just a guy who knows what he likes. Doesn't make me a bad person. By the way, does your date know you are over here talking us up?"

"That isn't my date. Just a friend from work. He is over there talking to those girls, trying to see if he can get a dance. He is tired of dancing with me. See how they all seem to be enjoying themselves? My guess is he is being nice to them and not insulting them. He is a gentleman, not like other guys in this place who won't even buy a girl a drink when she crosses the bar to introduce herself."

Cody turned and looked at Wiley. "You been insulting this woman, nephew? And then you didn't offer to buy her a drink?"

Wiley shrugged and leaned back against the bar. "We just met right before you walked up, Uncle. I didn't have a chance to offer."

Cody looked over at the woman and smiled charmingly. "My name is Cody Houston. Would you like a drink?" Cody looked over the bar and motioned to the bartender. "Virginia, need some help over here when you get a minute."

Cody looked at the woman, who was still standing with her arms crossed and scowling as if uncertain. Cody stared down her angry look and said, "I am not buying anybody a drink who isn't going to tell me what their name is. Against my policy."

Wiley took his cue and slid out of the conversation to go talk with some coworkers near the dance floor. The bartender arrived and expectantly awaited the upcoming order. The woman silently held up her empty beer bottle and showed the label to the bartender.

Cody turned around and said, "Longneck for the lady and another Number 7 on the rocks for me." The lady slid into the now open spot vacated by Wiley and sat down on the stool next to Cody.

"So why do you like large women so much? I never heard of any man that liked cankles."

"Well, I would like to explain the whole thing to you, but we still have this pesky policy violation that we need to resolve. You haven't told me your name yet."

"I haven't decided that I want to tell you yet, Mr. Chubby Chaser. Maybe you need to answer the question first."

"All right, then. We are just going to call you 'Tiny Dancer' and go with that in the meantime. Flagrant policy infraction and serious breach of protocol, but we will move forward."

"Where is this policy manual you keep talking about. I know a little bit about *policies,* you know. I am in the military. I would like to review this policy for myself."

"No kidding. Wouldn't have guessed that."

"Yep. I am in the Air Force and I am a pilot. I have read a few policy manuals. My name is Lisa. Captain Lisa Combs, to be specific."

"Pleasure to meet you, Captain." Cody reached behind him and retrieved their drinks and offered a clink with his glass on her beer bottle. Lisa smiled and softly touched her bottle to his glass.

"Nice meeting you, Cody. Thanks for the beer."

"My pleasure. Am I free to call you Lisa, or do you prefer Captain?"

Embarrassed, she waved her hand and smiled. "Please call me Lisa. I am not going to be in the Air Force much longer anyway. I need to get used to it. I didn't mean to get all big shot on you."

"No problem. I did a little time in the Navy myself. Now, getting back to your original question about liking big women. That is just a joke between me and the nephew there." Cody nodded at Wiley, who was apparently having a good time in an animated conversation with several women. "He likes to bust on me about that because of something that happened recently and was just using you to do it. All harmless and not true. Sorry you got dragged into it."

"Oh, I see. You are not a cankles-loving Chubby Chaser then? So, tell me, what brings you to Oklahomastan, Cody? Long way from Florida, isn't it? What is it you do in Florida, anyway?"

Cody chuckled at the reference to the area. "That's a lot of questions." *Here we go again with the "what do you do?" question,* Cody thought.

"I have time." She smiled sweetly and then took a pull on the beer bottle.

"Just visiting my nephew here, getting the lay of the land. Brought him out a motorcycle from Florida. Taking care of a little family business." He smiled kindly at her as Wiley walked back over and rejoined them.

"You guys make up?" he asked with a smirk.

"No thanks to you, nephew."

"Well, you didn't tell me not to tell her." Cody could not help but smile as he recognized Wiley turning the tables on him from earlier regarding Wiley's opinion of his dad's cooking. His nephew was a handful.

"It turns out that Lisa is in the Air Force, nephew. She is a captain and a pilot. She is planning on leaving the Air Force soon, though. Now you are all caught up."

"No kidding. What kind of plane do you fly?" asked Wiley. "You must be stationed over in Altus, then."

"C-17 Globemaster. And, yes, I am at Altus," she answered

without hesitation.

"Really? I have been in the back of a few of them before. I bet you have too, Uncle."

Lisa turned to look at Cody, who did not respond to the comment. She looked back at Wiley and asked, "You hopped a ride in the back of a MAC flight?"

"No, I served in the Rangers. We jumped out of those planes."

"You too, Cody?"

"No, I wasn't in the Rangers," Cody answered. "Been in a few planes including Globemasters, however."

"He won't talk about it, but he was on a SEAL team in the Navy. He talks about as much as a fish," Wiley offered.

"Really?" she asked, nodding her head slightly. "Impressive."

"Proud to serve." Cody wanted to change subjects. "It was a long time ago."

"Why are you leaving the Air Force since you are a pilot and all? Sounds like a good gig to me," Wiley asked.

"Tired of it. Tired of my life and want a change. My ex-boyfriend is a married colonel on the base, and he won't stop hassling me and trying to keep me around as his concubine because he won't leave his wife. Tired of his grief and all the Air Force politics. They want me to re-up and take the test for major, but I told them I wasn't interested. I get out in a couple of months."

Cody looked at his watch and saw that it was past midnight. He knew that they needed to get home and grab some sleep. He could tell from watching Wiley that he was too drunk to drive and he was probably over the legal line himself based on the number of drinks he had consumed. He tapped on his watch behind Lisa's back and made a sign signifying that they needed to move on. Wiley made a face and held both of his palms up in disbelief.

"Lisa, it's been good meeting you. We are heading out early tomorrow for Texas and need to get some rest. Can I look you up when we get back next week?"

The woman looked at Cody with steely eyes. She was obviously interested in him, but she did not want to get blown off. "How you going to *look me up?*"

"You are going to give me your cell number, Captain Combs."

"You seem fairly sure about it. Are you married?"

"I am not married." Cody pulled out his phone and opened the screen. "What is your number?"

The woman looked at Wiley and asked, "Is he married?"

Wiley shook his head slowly and said, "Nope."

She gave him the number and Cody gave it a confirmation call, which she answered and hung up on. "Should I save this under Captain Kickass or Wonder Woman? You should give a guy a break, babe. I am a very likable person if you give me a chance."

She smiled sweetly and said, "Giving you a break probably isn't going to happen, Chubby Chaser. Call me if you want when you get back." With that she waved her fingers and walked off.

"Attitude. I like it," said Wiley.

"Are we paid up? Get your girlfriend Virginia to bring us our check and let's get out of here. You are going to have a hard time getting up in the morning, nephew."

"You don't need to work my shift, Uncle. I will be up before you will." With that, Wiley promptly belched and made a writing motion with his hand. The bartender walked over and picked the slip out of a glass situated in front of him and slid it across the bar to Wiley. She could tell from the way he was acting and talking so loudly that he was very drunk.

"You aren't driving, are you, Wiley?" she asked.

"My uncle has it under control. Don't worry about us. How much we owe you?" Wiley picked up the check and was studying it when Cody slipped the bartender a hundred-dollar bill.

"Keep the change." Cody smiled at the harried woman.

Things had gotten busy and there were numerous people trying to gain her attention.

Wiley stood up slowly and was trying to steady himself for the walk outside. Cody grabbed his arm and draped it around his shoulder. After a couple of steps, a man walked up and took Wiley's other arm and draped it over his shoulder.

"Hey, Wiley. Remember me? Ricky from high school. I will help you." The pronunciation of the words made Cody look at the man closely. It seemed obvious to Cody that there was something off about the person, but he couldn't exactly put his finger on it.

The three men made it outside, and they sat Wiley down on a bench outside the front door of the bar. Cody took the truck keys from Wiley and took off to retrieve the vehicle. He started the truck up and pulled up to the front of the bar as he saw Wiley's friend storing a number in his phone. The man was helpful in assisting Cody get Wiley into the truck cab, and Cody turned to thank him.

"Thanks, Ricky. Appreciate the help. He normally drinks beer, but tonight he got off on the Jack Daniel's and it looks like it snuck up on him."

"Yeah, snuck up on him." Ricky smiled goofily at Cody with a contorted face. "He is my friend," he said, pointing at Wiley slumped over in the seat. "He is a police officer."

"Well, thanks for being a good friend, Ricky. Better get him home now. See you around."

"Yeah, get him home now." Ricky vigorously shook his head and briefly walked in place in a low shuffle by standing up on his tiptoes and leaning to each side. "Jack Daniel's snuck up on him." Ricky made a brisk sideways waving motion at Cody with an open hand. "Bye-bye, mister."

Cody started the engine and reached over and fastened

Wiley's seat belt before pulling out into the road. Wiley was already passed out. *Thank goodness he lives close,* Cody thought. He pulled the truck out into the lane and slowly accelerated. Wiley started snoring during the drive back to his house. When they got there, Cody helped his nephew to his room and Wiley collapsed on the bed.

He took his nephew's boots off and brought him a glass of water. He made him sit up and take a drink before he left his bedside, to help him re-hydrate. It would help reduce the hangover the lad was sure to have tomorrow on their trip to Texas. Cody favored getting an early start on road trips, but he sensed that an early start tomorrow was not too likely. *Wiley had enjoyed himself tonight.* Cody smiled to himself. *It was nice to see him engaged and having fun with so many friends. The kid should probably stick to beer, though.* Cody carefully shut the door to Wiley's room.

Wiley lived in a small, simple home with two bedrooms and a gravel driveway. Cody's truck and the trailer with their motorcycles loaded was already connected and facing toward the road in the front yard ready for the planned early departure in the morning. Cody had parked Wiley's truck in the gravel driveway close to the house, providing an opening for his truck and trailer to exit without having to move Wiley's truck again. The early departure part of the program was increasingly suspect as Cody heard Wiley begin snoring loudly.

Cody was making his way across the house to the bedroom he was occupying when he looked out the front window of the little house and saw bright headlights shining through the windows. The driver of the vehicle gunned the engine and then turned the bright lights on. Cody immediately went into self-protection mode and made a mental note of the location of his ever-present nine-millimeter handgun and did a mental rundown of anybody who might have taken offense during the evening or had some reason to come around so late.

Cody was peering out the window at the commotion when he felt his phone vibrate. He stared at the screen and smiled as he pushed the button to answer the call.

"Missing me already?" he asked.

"No. I just came over to see Wiley," she snorted.

"I see. Well, unfortunately, you are stuck with me because Wiley is already passed out in his bed. I am the only one awake in this house. Sorry to disappoint."

"Sorry to stalk you, but I just wasn't ready for the night to end yet. I followed you from the bar."

"Turn off your car and come in. I can get you a beer if you like." Cody was surprised by the turn of events, but he knew what was called for from here. He had a fairly good idea how this night was going to end.

"I should just go home," she said softly into the phone. She wanted Cody to argue for her to stay. "I definitely don't need any more beer."

"You don't have to stay, but I think it would be a complete waste of fuel for you to have driven over here without at least coming inside for a moment. I have a surprise for you."

"Ha! I just bet you do have a surprise for me, Chubby Chaser. I didn't fall off the turnip truck right before I met you, you know. Besides, it was just a few blocks from the bar. Not that much fuel or effort to come over here."

"Okay, then. I am coming outside and bringing my surprise with me." He opened the front door and walked out into the bright headlights and covered his eyes with his hand to shield them from the direct bright beams. She quickly turned off her car lights and shut down the engine. He walked up to the driver's side, opened the door, and stuck his head in and gave her a deep kiss without saying a word. Initially she protested and tried to withdraw her lips, but then gave in and vigorously responded by putting her hand around the back of Cody's head. After the intense connection, they separated lips and she looked at his face with half-opened eyes.

Cody pulled his head out of the car and took her hand while he backed up out of the car. Without saying a word, she rotated her legs in the seat and followed his cue. She wrapped her arms around his arm and followed him into the house, leaning on him as she walked.

"I knew you would be a good kisser," she said. "I am such a pushover for a good kisser."

They entered the house and made a beeline for Cody's bedroom. Cody shut the door and gave her another sizzling kiss that seemed to last for an eternity. He leaned back and looked at her sweet face and saw that her eyes were closed as he pulled away from her.

"Turn around," he said.

She slowly did as he asked. He reached around with both hands and gently began exploring her breasts and then started unbuttoning her shirt from the top down. He gently bit her neck and then pulled her hair as he nuzzled her face with his own. Her breathing picked up noticeably, and she reached around behind herself to feel his body.

"You are a very naughty boy. A seriously naughty boy. How did you know I needed this?" She leaned forward as Cody pulled her shirt off of her arms.

"Just a lucky guess," he replied in a whisper. He pushed her one step toward the empty bed, and they fell together onto the comforter. *Things are looking up for the home team,* Cody thought. He might be the one struggling to get up early tomorrow. He chuckled.

# CHAPTER X

**"I** am doing okay, Momma. It's just complicated between me and Randal, that's all."

Doris adjusted the phone as she looked down from the second-story bedroom window at Randal, surrounded by his buddies at a picnic table in the backyard of the house they referred to as their compound. He frequently referred to his followers as *The Crew*. They were a motley bunch of bearded, unkempt, redneck tweakers and stoners who worshipped Randal as their leader. A weak overhead light dimly illuminated the area they were occupying, and Doris could see a thick cloud of marijuana smoke surrounding the group. There was a hatchet-throwing contest underway, with Randal competing against one of his sycophants as they took turns launching rotating hatchets into a large tree stump ten feet away.

"Honey, you know I love you and I don't want to get into your personal business, but I found out some things about him that I have to tell you. Please hear me out and don't get mad at me."

"I'm listening to you, Momma. I have found out a few things myself lately." She whispered hoarsely and leaned against the wall, preparing for more bad news as she stared down at the floor with her arms closely against her sides.

"Honey, I asked around at church and I found someone who knows Randal from his childhood. He has been a disturbed person his whole life, according to her. He was a troubled teenager who was violent and abusive even as a child. He was known to torture animals and he used to drive around looking for roadkill deer to take home and cut open and mutilate. He had a weird fascination with mutilating animals as a child. He was known to kill cats and even dogs."

Doris took another look at the group downstairs through the window. The full weight of the disturbed history of Randal was crushing. She felt tears well up in her eyes.

"I hadn't heard that before, Mom. Who told you all these things?"

"Loretta from church was Randal's neighbor and a friend of his mother when he was growing up. And that is not all, either. He was kicked off the sheriff's department for being cruel and abusive to people, you know. After he left the sheriff's department, he started competing in those tough man competitions, and it's the only thing he has ever been good at. Loretta thinks he is into some type of criminal activities. More than that, she said that some people think that he has Sheriff Edwards involved in it some way."

Doris slumped to the floor in despair. She knew Randal was a troubled man, but she thought she recognized some shred of decency and caring inside his gruff outer personality. The way her relationship with him had gone recently, and the way he had treated her and threatened her, made her feel differently about him now. She was trying to plot a way to escape from him without putting her two children and parents at risk for attack in retaliation. She had come to believe that he was capable of anything. More than that, when she had initially observed Randal's ongoing relationship with the sheriff, it had encouraged her to believe that he might be legitimate and supported his explanation that his dismissal as a deputy was a misunderstanding rather than abuse. The revelation that he might have the sheriff involved in his crimes was a sign that his criminal activity could be even worse than she had imagined. And worse yet, she might not be able to rely on the sheriff's officers for protection from Randal. A deep chill flowed through her body as she contemplated that reality.

"Honey, are you there?" The concern in her mother's voice was real.

Doris shivered violently. "I am, Mom. Are my babies okay?"

"They are, honey, but they miss you. Please come back to us. There is one last thing I need to tell you about Randal."

"What is it?" Doris felt an involuntary convulsion take over her shoulders.

"Loretta told me that Randal's last girlfriend just disappeared, and nobody knows where she went. The sheriff did a real quick investigation, but didn't find any evidence of wrongdoing. Loretta thinks Randal had something to do with her disappearance. There is a rumor that she was trying to leave him, and he killed her."

The air gushed from Doris's chest, and she suddenly found it difficult to breathe. She could not respond to her mother's last comment. She rolled over onto her side and went into a fetal position as the tears streamed down her cheeks. She wondered how someone like her could suddenly find themselves in such a dangerous situation.

"Honey, are you still with me? Daddy and I just want you to come home."

Doris sat upright on the floor and wiped away the tears from her cheeks with a trembling hand. "I am coming home, Mom. I just need to pick my timing. I think it might be better to wait until Randal goes out of town again." Doris heard loud footsteps that stopped at the closed bedroom door. She quickly whispered, "Gotta go, Mom. Call you back later" as she disconnected the call and set the phone down.

There was a soft knocking at the door, and Doris slowly crossed the room and partially opened the door.

"Oh, hi Ricky. What's up?" She had always felt sorry for Ricky. He was mercilessly abused and made fun of by Randal. He was mentally slow and had several odd but harmless habits including half hopping and walking in place when he spoke and repeating what other people said to him. She felt he had a good soul, and he had always been kind and gentle with her. She had developed a friendly and affectionate relationship with him, and he was one of the only people she felt she could trust.

"You are crying." He noticed the tear streaks on her face after she opened the door. "Don't cry, Doris." The observation was making him upset.

Doris stepped over to him and gave him a quick hug.

"Ohhh, don't worry, sweetie. I am going to be fine. Just a little sad and missing my kids." She smiled bravely at him and wiped her face.

"Just a little sad. Missing your kids." He walked in place momentarily as he repeated her words and nodded his head knowingly. "I'm hungry," he said.

Doris immediately understood that Randal had sent him to get her to fix him something to eat. They did not allow Ricky to use the stove or prepare any food for himself after several near accidents with food fires. Fortunately for her, he was easy to cook for.

"You go on down then and I will be along in a minute. How about a grilled bologna and cheese sandwich?" she asked, knowing that it was his favorite food and he never seemed to tire of it.

"Hmmmmm…" He squealed excitedly in a high voice while walking in place. "That's my favorite!" he said excitedly as if she had just guessed a well-kept secret.

Doris could not help but feel better watching him get so happy about something so small. She hugged him again tightly. "You are my favorite, Ricky. I will be down in a minute."

"Okay. Down in a minute. You are my favorite, Doris." He vigorously nodded his head up and down and then innocently waved at her before turning to shuffle back toward the stairs.

Doris watched his uneven gait and suddenly blurted out, "Ricky, wait!" She walked briskly down the hall to get close to him. She put her hands on his arm as she questioned him in a forceful whisper. "You remember you told me that Wiley is your friend?"

The mention of Wiley made Ricky smile broadly. "Wiley is my friend," he answered.

"You remember that I told you Wiley is my friend too, right?" Doris made note that she was grasping his arm in a fierce grip and relaxed her hold on it.

"Wiley is your friend too. He is a police officer." Ricky looked up and made a circling motion with his head and gave Doris a toothy grin.

"So, you promise me that if anything bad ever happens to me, you will tell Wiley about it, right? Because he is both of our friends, right? And you and I are friends too, aren't we?"

"Tell Wiley. Tell Wiley because he is our friend. You are my favorite friend, Doris."

Doris hugged him closely again and buried her face in his chest. He was the only decent thing in this hell hole she found herself in. "Thank you, Ricky." She had no idea if he would remember or was capable, but at least she was doing what she could. Somehow she felt that he would come through for her if she needed him, as long as it wasn't too complicated.

"I will see you downstairs in a minute and make you a sandwich just the way you like it." She smiled sweetly at him and rubbed his face lightly with her hand and then spun away from him and ducked back into her bedroom.

Doris quietly shut the door and buried her face in her trembling hands. She was frightened and uncertain about what to do. Survival instincts told her to play her cards carefully and patiently wait for her chance to escape, instead of acquiescing to her impulse to flee immediately. She knew that Randal would be watching for signs that she wanted to make an escape. She needed to keep her wits about her and maintain a façade of commitment to him until her opportunity appeared. She quickly looked at herself in the mirror and wiped away the tear stains on her face and straightened her blouse before opening the door to let herself out of her bedroom.

# CHAPTER XI

**C**ody took a sip of the steaming brew. He enjoyed the taste of the bitter, strong, jet-black coffee as it washed down his throat. The smell of the bacon cooking was making him hungry. His body ached all over from the exertion of the previous night. He smiled at the memory and looked over at the woman as she delicately flipped bacon grease over the top of the eggs she was cooking. She was wearing panties and one of his T-shirts. Despite the previous night's activity, Cody felt a stirring inside as he looked over her lean physique and nicely formed legs and backside.

"This is how my Gramms taught me to make over-easy eggs. You splash the bacon grease over the top of the sunny-side-up eggs, and it cooks the top of the egg without having to flip the egg and break the yoke." She smiled sweetly and tilted her head as she turned to look at Cody.

"She taught you how to make good coffee too."

"Nope." She giggled. "I learned how to make good coffee in the military. You can't hang out with a bunch of pilots and not know how to make strong coffee. You get crucified if you make a pot of coffee that won't peel paint." She removed the bacon from the pan and laid it out on napkins and blotted the top of the strips. "The only bread in this house was so moldy I had to throw it away, so there won't be any toast. Your nephew does not seem to cook much. Half the stuff in this refrigerator is out of date also. Lucky he had this bacon and some eggs. Otherwise, I wouldn't be able to cook you breakfast."

"Don't ever trust the things you find in a bachelor's refrigerator." Cody sagely nodded as if revealing the hidden nugget of knowledge that would define modern culture. His mind was slowly waking up from the night of drinking capped off with the multiple rounds of amorous entanglement with Lisa once he got Wiley in bed. She was a screamer and highly sexually charged. Apparently it had been a good while since she had been with a man, and she was making up for lost time with Cody last night.

Just as she laid out the two plates of food on the table and sat down to join Cody, Wiley appeared and croaked, "A guy goes to sleep at night thinking he can trust his uncle to take care of his place if he has a few drinks and then he wakes up to find a woman in panties in his kitchen cooking breakfast. A guy would think he could trust his own family."

Lisa quickly picked up the response. "Well, I can tell you don't have any women hanging out around here. Any man that uses that prison-grade toilet paper is not going to be able to keep a woman. You can't do any better than that, Officer Wiley?"

Cody chuckled out loud at the insult. Wiley looked at him with a wounded face and blurted, "How did she know I never have any women over here?"

"Nephew, I just met her. We damn sure didn't spend any time talking about you last night. Just take it easy. You look like ass."

"I feel like ass. Last time I go out drinking Jack with you, Uncle. I am going to stick to my beer from now on. And yes, I did get that toilet paper from the office. Nothing wrong with saving a buck or two wherever you can. Didn't know people were so fussy about their wipe."

Lisa slid her plate across the table to him, got up, and poured him a cup of coffee. She set the coffee cup in front of him. "Here you go, tightwad. Next time I go shopping I will pick up a six-pack of normal TP and ship it over to you so you can upgrade your hospitality. If you ever do get lucky and actually get a woman in here, you don't want her to know you steal toilet paper from the local jail to save five dollars. What you have in there is so meager it would not wipe the snot off a gnat." She patted him on the back and then padded off to the bedroom, leaving the two men by themselves. Both men turned to admire the shapely backside as she exited the kitchen.

Wiley stared at the eggs and bacon with an uncertain look on his face. He looked up at his uncle, who was staring at him. "What are you looking at me for? I have lived in this house for over a year now, and I haven't ever had anybody stay over yet. You come here and I wake up to a lady in panties making breakfast after your second night. I should be staring at you. How did she wind up here?"

"Nephew, if you are going to pass out so early in the night, you are going to miss some of the action. Try to keep up." Cody smiled pleasantly.

The two men locked eyes for a moment until Wiley relented and looked down at his plate. He began wolfing down the food and shook his head. As he sipped the coffee, there was a loud disturbance on the front porch and the muffled sound of a deep voice shouting loudly.

"Oh shit." Wiley held up his hand as Cody immediately stood up. "That is just my crazy neighbor. He probably saw me come in drunk last night, and he is out on the front porch praying for me. He is a terrible snoop and watches everything that goes on here night and day." Cody followed Wiley toward the front door.

"What kind of weird bullshit is this?"

"It's just Pastor Tiberius. He isn't right in the head, but he is harmless. He comes over here to pray for me regularly, but he watches my place and I trust him."

"Pastor Tiberius? What the hell kind of cockeyed nonsense is that? Is he your pastor?"

Wiley shook his head as he opened the door and stepped

outside. Cody followed and observed the most unusual-looking man he had ever seen. Pastor Tiberius was almost as wide as he was tall. Standing just over five feet tall, holding a Bible in his left hand and thundering away in a deep voice, the little man was red in the face and sweating from the effort of his forceful prayer.

"I know I don't look like an angel, but I am an angel. You can't see the wings on my back, but they are there. I bring the message of God to this den of sin. All the wicked Philistines in residence at this sinner's hovel need repent! I lay my hands on your foreheads and say, 'Demons be gone!' I say be gone from these people—Satan, retreat from these fornicators and remove the devil's intoxicating drink from their systems! Jesus, protect these nonbelievers from their wicked sins!"

"Pastor Tiberius, isn't it kind of early for you to be over here saving us from our sins?" Wiley looked exasperated as he confronted the round man. "We are leaving for our trip."

"Confronting sin is a twenty-four-hour job, Wiley. Jesus calls me to encourage sinners to repent and follow the Lord's will. I pray for you every day. You are a good man, stranded on a sinner's island. You need to change, son. Embrace the word of the Lord and chart your new course. You have a Jesus-sized hole in your spirit, and you will only find peace through his message. You need to stop the wicked drink and fornication and go to church like your daddy does."

"Thank you, Pastor. My uncle and I were just about to leave for a few days on a trip. We will be back soon, though. Can you watch out for my place while I am gone?"

"As always, Wiley. I am your ever-vigilant servant. I walk in the Lord's grace with a servant's heart. I will pray for you and your uncle and your wicked, fornicating strumpet inside."

"Do you watch this place every minute, Tiberius? How do you know everything all the time about everybody?"

"I am a vigilant guardian for the Lord, my son. You can count on me." The short man bowed magnanimously and beamed at his audience. His eye had a persistent tic that caused a twitching of his face. He carefully made his way down the two steps leading up to Wiley's front porch and waddled back to his house on a well-worn path.

Once he was out of earshot, Wiley remarked to Cody, "The guy is not all there upstairs, Uncle. I always ask him to watch my house when I am gone because I know he will anyway. He has a key to my place, and he comes in and takes all my beer and liquor and drinks it. He tells me he is saving me from myself, but everybody knows he drinks all the time. He takes my groceries too. He is a sad case, but he is harmless. Always preaching the word and acting like he is saving people, while he drinks like crazy. The pastor at Dad's church finally asked him to quit coming to services there. Everybody calls him pastor, but he never has been a preacher anywhere. Just a nutjob that claims to be an angel."

Cody shook his head slowly. "He looks like a refrigerator with a head. Never seen anybody so vertically challenged with that much girth."

"I always leave a few beers for him and some groceries. When I am gone, he comes in and takes them all over to his house. He tells me the groceries were spoiling and that he is saving me from myself by taking my beers and pouring them out. He doesn't know it but I have him recorded on my security camera drinking beer while he is leaving my house."

The two men returned inside and met Lisa as she was exiting the bedroom where she and Cody had spent the night. She latched onto Cody's arm and redirected him outside with her. Wiley stopped and admired the view again as she walked past.

"Not driving in your panties, Captain?" Wiley couldn't help himself.

"You let me know when you get some real toilet paper in here and maybe I will bring my panties back. Who was that outside?"

Cody smiled. "Nosy neighbor. Nothing to worry about. Better get yourself ready, Wiley. Remember we need to get an early start on the trip to make it there for lunch with my friends."

"Ten-four, Uncle." He turned and headed for the shower.

Cody and Lisa walked out to her car, and she leaned against the driver's side door. "I borrowed your toothbrush and toothpaste."

"No problem." Cody admired the red Corvette she drove. "Nice car. What is she, a '94 or '95? That looks like a six-speed with an LT-1 motor. Doesn't look like it has the ZR-1 badging."

"It's a 1995 with LT-1 engine. I have had this old girl since I went to flight school. She has been good to me. Usually, I drive around with the top off, but I put it back on when I get on the highway." She smiled sweetly at him over the compliment about her car.

"Nice. I bet you look good in it with the top off."

"Well, some guys seem to think so." She moved in closer to him and put her arms around his neck. "So, you know, I fly training missions to Patrick Air Force base periodically, and I have one of those trips coming up soon." It wasn't a complete lie. She did need some training flights from time to time, but the destination was usually left up to her discretion. She was confident that she could work out a good reason to make it to Patrick Air Force Base, which she knew to be in the general area where Cody lived. "I usually have a nice layover also, which might give us a chance to spend some time together while I am there."

"That sounds promising." Cody smiled. He liked this lady and the thought of her spending some time with him in his area sounded nice. But he felt it was too soon to bring her to his home. "Maybe we could sneak down to Miami and spend a few days in South Beach or Coconut Grove."

"You afraid to introduce me to the wife?" She enjoyed being pushy about the topic. Too many years of fending off advances from married men had left her depleted on this issue.

"I am sure we can work something nice out. See if you can set it up on your side, and we will work out the rest of the details." He smiled warmly and looked into her eyes. He was remembering the sight of her in panties smiling at him while she cooked the eggs, and it caused a stirring inside his loins. If he had not just pushed Wiley on getting ready, he might have been tempted to lure her back into the house for a repeat performance before she left. He cupped the back of her head and pulled her in for a sweet kiss goodbye. He noticed that she closed her eyes and sighed at the end of the kiss. Cody opened the door to her car and closed it behind her after she slipped into the driver's seat. "You have my number, sailor."

"Yes, I do, ma'am. I will call you later today after we get settled in at our destination. I am glad you came over. You can count on it."

"That would be nice. I would like to say that I don't normally do things like this, but the truth is, I am glad I followed you and threw myself at you. I would do it again."

"Well, it was a surprise, for sure. But I am glad you did it also. You drive safe and I will talk to you later."

She backed out of the driveway and waved at him as she drove off. Cody turned around and headed back to the house. He noticed Pastor Tiberius watching intently from his front porch next door. Cody waved at him to make sure he knew he was being watched too.

# CHAPTER XII

Cody and Wiley worked in silence as they loaded the two bikes up on the small three-rail trailer. The trailer was wide enough for two bikes but also had a middle rail to support a single bike, if desired. After ratcheting the tie-downs to the nylon looped straps on the handlebars of the bikes, the two each checked their respective bike. Cody motioned silently to Wiley to watch while he went through the process of disabling the security system on his bike so that the lights and alarm would not go off while being towed. After finishing, he motioned for Wiley to do the same to his bike.

"Now, you do yours." Cody watched as Wiley expertly turned on and then off the ignition on his bike and then depressed both turn signals until the bike responded with a single flash of both signal lights. "Now when you see that single flash, you are in transport mode. In that mode, your bike alarm won't trigger while you are towing it. Before I figured that little detail out, I showed up with my battery completely discharged the first time I trailered my bike."

"Gotcha." Wiley looked over at his uncle and smiled. "Good ride today. Thanks for showing me Grandma's grave. I guess we both wish we could have known her."

Cody was uncomfortable on this subject. He had dealt with the loss of his mother over the years by not focusing on it, and sharing this issue with someone seemed out of step. "Wish I had more to share with you about her."

"Well, at least you got your dad and her in the same part of the cemetery. They are close together."

Cody laughed. "My dad loved my mom, but he loved a lot of other women too. I am not sure who I would bury next to him. I had quite a few mom-figures at different times in my life growing up. Better to not make a choice, I think. Keeps the peace that way. He never had children with anybody else, though. Can't change it anyway; the plots next to Mom were already taken, so I just got the closest one I could when Dad passed."

"What was your dad like?" Wiley asked. He had a cautious look on his face as if he knew he might be crowding Cody and encroaching on sensitive territory by asking. He found his uncle to be a real enigma when it came to talking about his family.

"This guy might be the best person to ask," Cody deflected as Congressman Ernie Musselwhite walked up holding two dripping wet longneck beers that had been opened already.

"You guys have a good ride?" Musselwhite boomed out as he passed out the ice-cold beers.

"Yes, sir." Wiley was in awe of the congressman and extremely respectful in any engagement. The two seemed to hit it off well, and Cody was pleased that Ernie was warming up to his nephew.

"Ernie, Wiley was just asking me what my dad was like. I told him he should ask you." Cody winked at Ernie and hoisted up the bottle. "Thanks for the beer."

"Well, let's go get comfortable in the backyard. Loretta has put out some snacks, and I have an ice chest loaded up that needs to get emptied. I will tell you all about him. I have known Cody since he was a little cub, you know. His dad was my best friend from childhood and best man in my wedding." Musselwhite and Wiley started walking toward the backyard. Ernie seemed to enjoy telling the story of his friendship, and Wiley was completely engrossed in the conversation.

Cody called out, "I have a couple of phone calls I have to

make, so I will join you guys in a minute."

Cody pulled out his phone and turned his back on the two men. He heard Wiley making a side comment that Cody needed to call one of his *women* as he started to dial Lisa. He hadn't checked in with her yet after promising he would, and knew he needed to follow up to keep his word.

She answered on the second ring. "I was beginning to wonder if your wife might have shown up or something."

"Nice to talk to you too," he replied. "There I was thinking you would be glad to hear from me."

"Don't get all offended, tough guy. I am happy to hear from you."

"Now that is a little better. What is it with you and all the suspicion about me being married? You don't know any men that aren't married? There are a few of us around, you know."

"You will have to give me a pass. Too many years hanging out with these oversexed, alpha-dog pilots who think they have to nail every woman they meet. And they all usually have really nice, attractive wives at home. So, did you and Wiley get there okay and get your ride in?"

"We did. It's supposed to rain here tomorrow, so we loaded them back up on the trailer. Planning on being back to his house on Monday afternoon."

"That sounds nice. You have the court hearing on Tuesday, right?"

"Yep." Cody was impressed that she remembered.

"So, it's three hours between where I am and where you will be Monday night. Don't suppose you could meet me in Duncan, halfway? I will make it worth the drive."

"Small minds think alike." Cody smiled. "Maybe you need to explain to me exactly how you are going to make this worth my while."

She giggled. "Well, you remember last night, don't you? I would say, similar to that, but maybe better now that we know each other a little bit and I will be able to bring over a little sexy nightie. I felt like I didn't really have a chance to do it right for you last night. It would be worth a ninety-minute drive, wouldn't it?"

"I would run barefoot over broken glass to chase down the laundry truck that had your panties in it." He tried not to laugh as he uttered the cheap, worn-out trope.

Her laugh was infectious. Cody found himself laughing with her involuntarily. After she stopped giggling, she said, "That is complete and ridiculous bullshit, sailor. But it's funny bullshit, so I am going to let it slide this time."

Cody responded, "I will make the hotel reservation."

"Okay, that sounds good. You know I have to be back early for muster here on the base next day, though."

"No problem. I should probably be done by early morning."

"You are so cocky. Is that what I like about you?"

"Glad to know I am growing on you. There for a while I wasn't sure you were going to give me your name. I will get back to you on the location for Monday after I nail down a reservation. Look forward to seeing you then."

"Can't wait, Romeo. See you then."

Cody smiled and hung up and then called Dillon as he started walking toward the backyard of the large home. Dillon immediately answered.

"How is it going out there with Wiley? You guys having fun?"

"It's going well, thanks. We are at the Musselwhite's', just sitting down for a beer. Ernie has been smoking a brisket all day, and it smells awesome here in the backyard. Nothing like a little Texas barbeque." Cody smiled at Ernie as he sat down. Cody covered the mouthpiece and said, "It's Dillon and he says hello."

"Dillon! Let me have that phone." Ernie walked over to Cody with a replacement beer and held his hand out for the phone and empty bottle from Cody. Ernie had the politician's knack of making everybody he talked to feel like they were the most important person in the world.

"Hang on, Ernie wants to talk to you."

Ten minutes later Ernie had completely covered exactly how he smoked the meat with green hickory wood and how he seasoned it and kept the temperature "low and slow," then described how he made his own barbeque sauce. Cody knew that Dillon would be completely jealous because he was a fan of barbeque and loved to smoke and grill meat himself. Over the course of the conversation, Loretta came out and set the outdoor table with pots of baked beans and a large bowl of fresh coleslaw and some Texas garlic toast slices on a dish. Once she had her hands free, Cody gave her a nice hug and thanked her for taking such good care of them.

Ernie let out a healthy laugh and looked at Cody. "Dillon said he is on the way over and not to let you eat the whole dad-gummed thing." He laughed and tossed the phone back to Cody. Cody caught it and resumed his conversation with his friend.

"You still there, Dil?"

"Damn, dude, that barbeque sounds delicious. Making my mouth water."

"Yeah, well, maybe I will smoke some brisket for you when I get back. All Texas men know how to smoke meat, you know."

"I didn't get this big eating salads, man. Why did you keep this a secret? Anyway, enough about that. I have been calling you for a reason."

"What is that?"

"Guess who showed up over here wanting to talk to me about you?"

"Well, given that she has been blowing up my phone and leaving messages, it must be Jennifer. What has she got to say for herself?"

"She showed up here at the house, man. Crying and saying she had been trying to call you but you weren't calling her back. She and Laura talked for over an hour and a half, man. I told you that girl has a bad case of you. She is talking about cancelling her wedding and breaking it off with her fiancé of fifteen years. She misses you and wants to talk to you, blah, blah, blah, blah. She is so confused, Kemosabe. How do you do this to these women? That girl is a total smoke show; you should be in there fighting for that. Listen to ole Dil here."

"Well, did you hold her hand and nuzzle her neck, stud muffin? Just tell her I'll call her when I am on my way home. I am busy now. Tell her I will be happy to give her the slap and tickle when I get home, but that I liked what we had, and she shouldn't break up her engagement with this guy over me. I am not ready for anything else with her."

"Hard-ass. Let me tell you, if I had five minutes with her alone without Laura in the picture, I would be climbing her like a spider monkey."

"Yeah, well, I think I may have found somebody I like better out here in Oklahoma. Wait until you meet her."

"For the love of God. How the hell do you do this? You could cop ass in a convent. Can't wait to hear about this new lady."

"Gotta jump here, Dil. We are about to eat. You need to say anything else to Ernie or Wiley?"

"Tell Wiley I said hey, and make sure you send me his phone number. Tell him I will call him in a few days. And say hello to Mrs. Musselwhite for me."

Cody closed out the call and walked over to Loretta and put his arm around her as she finished bringing out the table settings.

"Dillon sends his regards."

She broke into a large smile and buried her head in Cody's chest. "Oh, that Dillon. Ernie liked talking to him so much and really enjoyed meeting him last time we saw you. Those two have talked a couple of times on the phone since then. Don't know if you knew that."

"That is nice to hear." Cody smiled broadly. The idea that he was responsible for bringing good people together pleased him. "Do you have a piece of paper and a pen? I need to write something down for Wiley."

"Of course, sit down here at the table to write. I will bring it to you." She left and quickly returned to find Cody staring into his phone. "Here you go," she said as she handed it to him.

"Thanks, Loretta. Can you make this easy for me and tell me Ernie's cell phone number to save me from looking it up?"

"Easy one. I call that four or five times a day when he is in D.C." She recited the number and left him to return to the kitchen. Cody slowly printed the number and name and then copied Dillon's number on the paper. He stood up and shuffled over to Wiley and Ernie, who were engaged in an intense conversation about the property that he and Cody were petitioning the court on regarding their inheritance claim. Cody casually lifted the cooler lid and pulled out and opened two ice-cold beers and took a hard pull on one of them. He exchanged the empty bottle in Wiley's hand with the full one, and Wiley held it up and nodded at Cody.

"Never been to a party where people gave you full beers and took your empties before. I am used to serving myself. I hang out with too many cops, I guess. Nice to see how the other side does it." He smiled broadly at Cody and Ernie. Cody nodded back and allowed a moment of pause.

"So, nephew, you like that motorcycle I gave you? You think

that was a surprisingly good gift?"

"Hell yes. You don't even know. Never had anybody give me anything so nice before. Thank you very much, Uncle Cody." Wiley suddenly seemed concerned as if maybe he hadn't thanked his uncle sufficiently for the gift.

"I am glad you like it. You already thanked me a million times for it and I am not fishing for more. You deserve it and nothing makes me happier than giving it to you."

Wiley acknowledged what Cody said with a slow nod. He could tell that Cody wasn't finished. Ernie cocked his head and leaned in slightly while Cody took a long pull on his beer.

Cody affectionately looked at Wiley after indifferently scanning the horizon in a slow gaze and draped his arm over him. "I am sorry I wasn't in your life earlier. I wish I had been. I have enjoyed getting to know you and I couldn't be happier about finding you. I thank you for all the trouble you went to in connecting us."

Wiley smiled broadly. "I had no idea how you were going to take it when I told you about us. Glad it's working out. A guy never knows in something like this." The three men chuckled about the last statement.

Cody nodded and then continued. "I have something else I want to give you. It's the best and only other thing I have that is worth anything." Cody paused for effect. "On this paper is Dillon's cell phone number and Ernie's personal cell phone number." Cody folded the paper and passed it to Wiley. "Dillon is going to be calling you in a couple of days. You will like him, and you can always trust him."

"Thanks, Uncle." Wiley tucked the paper into his pants pocket and looked quickly at both men with a smile.

Cody continued slowly. "Dillon Luther is my best friend and my brother. Ernie here is like my father. You can consider Dillon as an uncle and Ernie to be like a grandfather. I don't have anything else that is worth a damn that I can give you, but I assure you that being family with those two is way better than that motorcycle."

Wiley beamed broadly and chuckled. "Don't you need to ask them about this first, Uncle?"

Cody nodded and acknowledged the concern. "There are two kinds of family in life, Wiley. The family you are given and the family you choose for yourself. Dillon is my brother because we choose to be brothers. Ernie and I are related because we choose to be family. You and I are related, first because we are family, but also because we choose each other. Nothing else in my crazy, messed-up life has ever made me happier than finding out I had a sister I never knew about and then learning she had you. Now, meeting and knowing about you, I see good in you. I see what I could have been if I had not made bad decisions and taken wrong turns. The most important thing I can tell you about Dillon and Ernie is that I do not have to ask them if you are family. If you are family to me, you are family to them. You can always have confidence in that."

Ernie wiped away moisture from his eye and cleared his throat. He roughly put his arm over Wiley and patted him on the chest while affectionately shaking him back and forth. "I think it's time to eat, boys. This is a fine day for our family, Loretta." His voice cracked slightly as he spoke.

The three men grinned broadly as they clumsily bumped hips and made their way toward the table, and it made them all break out in laughter.

Loretta was enjoying the sight of the three men while standing by the table with a martini she had poured for her husband in her hand. She pulled out a chair for Wiley and said, "You sit here next to me, Wiley. I want to learn all about you, and I will tell you a few things about your grandmother. She was my best friend in high school, you know."

Wiley smiled at Loretta as he sat down. "Yes, ma'am. Cody told me that you were close friends with her."

"Well, I have some pictures that I pulled out to show you after dinner. You have a lot of catching up to do." She gently rubbed his back and looked at Ernie and winked. "You are as handsome as your uncle. You two favor each other."

Cody looked at the table and held up his beer bottle. "Here is to Loretta. Sets the best table in Texas. You are the Queen of Texas, Loretta, and Ernie is a lucky man."

Ernie Musselwhite beamed as he reached for his wife's hand and more moisture welled up in the corners of his eyes. He held up his martini glass. "Hear, hear," he muttered softly. It was the best response he was capable of at that moment. He felt proud to be seated at the head of this table. He and Loretta exchanged glances and locked eyes for a brief interlude. Cody and Wiley busily helped themselves to the sliced brisket and sides and were already sampling and discussing his sauce. They did not realize the healing their presence in his home provided.

# CHAPTER XIII

Houston slowed down as he neared the large tractor bouncing haphazardly down the road at its top speed. He glanced into the rearview mirror and checked on the stream of cars behind him. Pulling the trailer with the motorcycles, he was uncomfortable traveling at the speed that most travelers seemed to prefer on the two-lane highway in that area, but he remained steadfast in maintaining his cautious pace and trying to cooperate with the indignant drivers determined to pass him on the road. There was a steady stream of oncoming traffic making it difficult for him to pass the tractor and he leaned back in the seat patiently to await his opening.

"You don't use the GPS, don't play the radio, and you drive like an old man, Uncle. What in the world do you need this new truck for, anyway?" Wiley looked at his uncle with disdain. "You don't even have an aux cord so a passenger can charge their phone up or play their music. The only feature I have seen you use is that hands-free calling. Not that you get that many phone calls or anything."

"I don't know what the heck an aux cord is; don't want to know. If you didn't charge your phone last night, then don't blame me if it isn't working. I like to drive in silence, and I don't need a GPS. It is not like there are so many roads in this godforsaken southern Oklahoma road race that a guy can't get around without his GPS. We are out behind the back of beyond, for goodness sake. If a guy can't find his way around here with a map and a compass, then he is in real trouble. As far as my phone calls, I get all the calls I want." Cody looked out the side window and leaned back. He knew the kid was going to keep busting on him if he didn't blow up in response.

Wiley smiled broadly. "Okay, Uncle. Don't get your knickers all twisted up. Just wondering why we can't turn the radio on or something. You talk about as much as a fish. A little conversation wouldn't kill you, would it?"

"All right, then, I have some conversation for you. How about you tell me who that guy was that helped me load you up in the truck that night at the bar? Who was that and what is his story?"

Wiley nodded his head and chuckled. "That was Ricky Hunter. Friend of mine from high school. Ricky is a little bit slow, but he is a good old boy. I used to look out for him all the time and kept people from making fun or taking advantage of him since middle school. We have been friends for a long time."

"When we were driving back to the house, you kept muttering about him being in trouble. What was that all about? You were so drunk you weren't making any sense."

"Yeah. Ricky is hanging around a group of guys that are trouble. I know Ricky isn't doing anything bad, but the guys he is with are real bad news. You remember when we were with my dad, and he was talking about that guy Randal? The one that his ex-girlfriend Doris is hooked up with now?"

Cody nodded affirmatively. The conversation stopped momentarily as Cody made a sudden acceleration to pass the tractor that had slowed them, when he saw an opening. He mashed the accelerator to the floor and the big truck surged forward with a throaty roar of the diesel engine.

"You go, Uncle! That is what I am talking about!"

Cody couldn't help but smile about the grief his nephew gave him. He smoothly passed the tractor and returned to his lane with no drama and gave his nephew a wooden smile. "So happy you approve. Hate seeing you so nervous over there, pumpkin."

"Right. Don't forget I am family, scary man. Don't make me shit my pants with that crazy side-eye. Ernie told me about what you did down in Mexico for the guy that owned my bike. We have a long way to go yet, and you won't like how it smells if I have a mudslide over here because you are giving me that look."

"Quit talking about my driving. If you shit yourself, you will be riding in the back."

"Sensitive! There I was thinking you were so hard."

They both laughed at the ridiculous exchange. Wiley giggled like a child and slapped his knee. Cody was happy to see him enjoying himself so much and getting so comfortable around him.

"So, getting back to Ricky and Randal and Doris and the domestic drama with all that crowd."

"I don't really know what the story is, to be honest, but I am hearing a lot of bad scuttlebutt about those guys, and from what I hear, the sheriff is involved too. That is what is making me so nervous about it. That Randal is a real cowboy; the rumor is he takes on work as a hitman. I don't have any details, but there is something bad enough going on that he feels he needs to pay off the sheriff to keep doing it. There are a couple of guys that work for Randal that have some skills and a couple of ex-cons that are pretty violent. They are all a bunch of gun nuts and weapons freaks. Ricky is locked in with them now, and I am worried about him. He might know too much for them to let him leave."

Wiley paused, resettled himself in his seat, and continued. "My department is not really related to the sheriff or the police departments in the local towns that would have jurisdiction over him. Some of the sheriff's deputies have talked to some of the guys on our force in private though, and they don't like what they see. Something is bad over there. Something is making the sheriff keep his deputies away from Randal and not respond to anything related to them. They aren't even supposed to write his crew any traffic tickets, from what our guys hear."

Cody glanced over at his nephew while he paused and reflected. He gave him a minute to gather his thoughts in silence.

"Dad dated Doris briefly before she started seeing Randal, but she stopped seeing him just when he was getting serious about her. She took up with Randal suddenly, and from what Dad hears at church, she wants to leave him now, but she is afraid of what he would do to her children and her mother and father if she did leave. Nobody knows what to do about it. The children are staying at their grandparents', and Doris either won't or can't leave the compound where Randal stays. The grandparents are sure that Doris wants to leave, but she is afraid to. It drives my dad crazy because he doesn't know what to do. I am scared that he might do something crazy and get himself in a bad situation trying to help her. Randal is a rough cob, and he is known to be a violent and angry guy."

"Do you know Randal or the guys that are in his crew?"

"I don't really know Randal personally, but I know a lot about him. He is about ten years older than me. He used to fight in a local tough man circuit around here and built a name for himself as a rugged guy. He usually either won or came close to winning most of the tournaments. I saw a few of those tournaments. He is not a real technical fighter, but he is a brutal dude that could take a punch. He has never been knocked down in any of his fights, and he brags about that sometimes. He knocks out most of the guys he fights; he has a pretty wicked overhand right, and he is a big dude.

"The sheriff, on the other hand, is a different story." Wiley shook his head slowly and carried on. "He won re-election easily a couple of years ago, and most of the community thinks he is doing a good job. Some of the guys I work with say that they see him at the casino quite a bit and they think he has a gambling problem and a bad drinking problem. The Chickasaws hire Light Horse officers for off-duty security at the casinos sometimes when they have concerts or expect a big crowd, so some of the officers go there pretty frequently. They say he is always hanging out at the card tables playing blackjack and betting heavy. Nothing illegal about that, but we all know that he just bought a pretty big place after he got re-elected, and he has three kids. His soon-to-be ex-wife is driving a new Escalade around town, so it looks like they are living pretty high on the hog for sheriff wages."

"I heard you talking to Ernie about the sheriff yesterday when I was in the kitchen talking with Loretta. I heard him saying he would help you get a meeting with the right people at the FBI. Something going on there?"

"I am not doing anything about it right now. I do not have any hard evidence that I can share with them, but if I find something illegitimate, I might take him up on his offer. I have been poking around a little but don't know anything substantial yet."

"Just be careful. Don't get into anything crazy."

"Yeah. Look who's talking." Wiley cracked a smile. "So, let's talk about your pilot friend there, Ms. Combs. When are you seeing her again? I heard you talking to her a couple of times on this trip. You don't have to be all top secret about stuff, Uncle. You know I saw her panties."

"Seeing her in panties made your highlight reel, did it? Kind of pathetic that a young man like you is feeding off his uncle's action."

"I just don't have the touch like you do. I thought you were going to coach me up on landing some coitus anyway. A good uncle would do that."

"I think you do better than you let on. All this poor mouthing and sandbagging. I saw those girls hanging around you at Ole Red. I already told you anyway, most of what I know how to do isn't worth knowing. You need to find yourself a nice girl, treat her right, and hang on to her. That is all the coaching you need."

"I guess I get my share. Pickings are kind of thin where I live though. I am thinking maybe you could introduce me to some Florida girls and give me a reason to come and visit."

"So, you are saying that coming to visit your uncle isn't enough to justify a trip to Florida? Hell, you drove all the way out to see me before you even met me. Now that you know me, I have to line you up with a booty call to get you to come and visit? And to think I gave you a motorcycle too. I am thinking about trading you in on another nephew."

"You aren't trading me in! Not at least until after we get the court case worked out anyway. You do remember that, don't you, Uncle? I lined that up for us."

"Okay. Maybe I will give it a few days before I make up my mind. And by the way, while we are on the subject, I am meeting Lisa tonight in Duncan around seven. I am spending the night, but will be back to your house early in the morning for the hearing. Just passing that on so you don't get worried when I leave tonight. I got everything covered."

"Got everything covered do you?" Wiley made a slight up and down motion with two fingers on both hands as he said the word "covered," and he slowly nodded as if he was uncovering some deep secret and made an exaggerated wink with one eye. Just as he finished his mock theater, his phone rang.

"Hey, Uncle Dillon! No, he is sitting next to me here in the truck. We are still driving back to my place about half an hour away. No problem though. I don't mind talking shit about him while he is listening."

Cody shook his head slightly and smiled. Just what he needed. Two guys watching over everything he did and talking about it between themselves. Life was indeed changing for him. He smiled to himself as he lumbered on down the road at his own comfortable pace, listening to Dillon and Wiley talk excitedly about their new motorcycles.

# CHAPTER XIV

The small wall-mounted air-conditioning unit rattled and groaned as it struggled to beat back the fall heat in the stuffy motel room. Cody lay on the bed partially dressed, engrossed in the book he had been reading for the past few hours. He had arrived early at the motel room in Duncan to await Lisa's arrival. He had packed a few beers in one of Wiley's battered old ice chests, a bottle of chardonnay, a half-empty fifth of Jack Daniel's, and some deli sandwiches he purchased on his way out of town. Based on his first encounter with the lady, he did not expect that they would be leaving the room once she showed up. He needed to eat at night and felt like he should at least provide something for them to avoid a late-night scramble to find an open restaurant. He wasn't on familiar turf and doubted that he could find anything other than a possible pizza delivery in a pinch. Even his limited, mangled sense of chivalry dictated that he at least make some dinner provision for them.

Cody felt a need to understand the process that led to his and Wiley's claim to the abandoned land they were to inherit. The book he was reading was a historical examination of the Indian Relocation from the growing southern states through the Indian Removal Act, General Allotment Act, and Dawes Act legislation leading to the death of 15,000 tribal members in the Trail of Tears forced resettlements from historical homelands to Oklahoma, starting in 1830. Eventual subsequent taking of over ninety million acres of historical native tribal-owned land occurred as a result of the enactment of these legislative acts.

Indians were in the way in colonial and post-revolutionary America. The booming young nation was struggling with a growing conflict between restless white settlers searching for land to call their own and the native inhabitants, as white population surrounded the tribal territories, causing conflict with the tribes who were fiercely protective of their communal homelands. These tribes were historically commercial deer hunters for meat and hides, subsistence corn farmers, fishermen, gatherers, and eventually, cotton growers and slave owners as the economy grew and demanded production of commercial crops. They did not recognize private ownership of land in the way of Europeans. Their land was a communal tribal range claim for the use of their citizens to hunt, cultivate, and peacefully enjoy in harmony among the citizens of their tribe. Their claim to the homeland had been defended time and again over the centuries against other native tribes and European encroachers with both treaties and wars. The original inhabitants knew well where the boundaries of the different tribal homelands existed, and no legal definition or deed to property was needed.

The tribes controlled vast swaths of desirable lands in undivided parcels throughout the country. The push of settlers westward increasingly made conflict between the natives and settlers inevitable, however, and made it difficult for harmonious co-existence of native people with white settlers, as the settlers increasingly pushed to gain access over and to historical Indian lands. The Chickasaws were ultimately made subject to Mississippi State laws in 1832, which opened them to white legal exploitation and ended their self-governance, ultimately forcing them to cede their claim to their homeland and agree to seek another home west of the Mississippi River in the Treaty of Pontotoc Creek. Eventually, that resettlement was directed to Oklahoma on land owned by the Choctaw Tribe, and, legally, the Chickasaws were folded into the Choctaw umbrella from the perspective of the Bureau of Indian Affairs. The Choctaws and Chickasaws have a historically complex relationship. With a shared ancestry and language, they are related but have lived separate for many centuries. Tribal legend tells of a story where two brothers led a migration of the combined people, and a split of the two brothers in separate directions along the trail led to a splintering of the followers into two groups. One of those groups became the Choctaws and the other, the Chickasaws. They had adjacent homelands in Mississippi and fought numerous wars. The French attempted to mobilize the Choctaws against the Chickasaws twice before giving up. The Chickasaws sided with the British and against the Colonials in the Revolution and then again with the South against the North in the Civil War. Their support of the British and the Confederacy made perfect sense from the perspective of the Chickasaws, based on their interests of the time, but in the end their choices made it easier for the U.S. Government to abuse them and disavow the treaties and protections provided to them under legislation of the day.

Ultimately, the beautiful, rich, and productive original homeland of the Chickasaws was swallowed whole by the U.S. Government and sold and allocated to predominately white settlers there. Again, in the replacement homeland in Oklahoma, the communal tribal territory purchased by the tribe was eventually reclaimed by the government, and Indian heads of households were given allotment land of up to 160 acres in settlement under deeds restricted for twenty-five years by the Bureau of Indian Affairs. Land was awarded to poor Indian people who had no money for seed stock, livestock, nor farm implements and tools and no access to credit to gain the necessary funds for farming. After the initial twenty-five-year exemption period, the tax exemption expired, and numerous allotment lands were seized by local white governments from poor Indian citizens for failure to pay taxes and were dispersed to white settlers in tax deeds. Eventual discovery of oil and gas deposits in the area led to further exploitation of native land holders and fraudulent conveyance of land title to unscrupulous investors for mineral interests. Many of the remaining intact Indian allotment estates wound up subject to bank foreclosures in the Depression era of the 1930s as the dual blows of the collapsed economy and the dust bowl struck landowners.

Cody considered the sordid history of the Chickasaw citizens and the longstanding abuse they suffered from the government that sprung up around them and overtook their sovereignty. In the long march of time, the estate that he and Wiley were inheriting had survived the turbulence surrounding it intact, with the original deed restrictions in place. He also considered himself a survivor. He was a survivor of many fierce, lethal battles and encounters both of his own creation and in service to his country. Like the gunslingers and lawmen of the bygone era, he rarely contemplated his fate or his luck. In the few moments of introspection he allowed himself to consider his past, however, he was struck by the parallels of this property and his own life. His ancestor had stubbornly fought off the invasion of greed, societal pressure, and disregard, to maintain it intact from its original establishment as an independent parcel. As the possessor of similar qualities in his own existence, he recognized and appreciated the qualities in that which he encountered. He was the obvious inheritor of this obstinate sole survivor. He smiled to himself as he recognized the righteous kinship.

Fate had connected Wiley to him to bring him knowledge of his past and a reckoning with their joint future. He felt an obligation of stewardship for the abandoned estate and a strong connection with its past. The stubborn Chickasaws were a story of triumph and victory of hope over oppression and disrespect. If awarded this property by the court, he and Wiley would care for this land in a manner befitting its history and the heritage of their stubborn, independent ancestors. Cody smiled at the reconciliation of history and future in his mind as he closed the book. He took a last swig of the remaining beer in the bottle on the nightstand and glanced at the clock. He was anticipating Lisa's arrival shortly and entered the small bathroom to start the water in the shower.

After the steamy shower and a quick shave and a change of clothes, he was reorganizing his duffle bag on the bed when he heard a soft knock. He quickly peered out the peephole and saw Lisa in her military fatigues standing outside his door with her cap and sunglasses on. He saw her smile as she heard the click of the latch slide open. She smiled widely and he slowly cracked the door and placed his foot sideways against the bottom to prevent further opening.

"What do you want?" he asked suspiciously.

"Open the door, stud muffin. You know what I want," she snorted in reply.

Cody opened the door widely and smiled as she sauntered in and put her hands on her hips while turning her head slightly.

"Sexy enough for you?" she asked as she pulled the bottom of her fatigues top out for inspection.

"Do I need to salute?" he asked.

"What you need to do is quit being a smartass and give me a kiss and a hug and tell me how good it is to see me again."

Cody pulled her in tightly to him and planted a wet kiss on her lips. She had her eyes closed and sighed contentedly when he finished. *It was going to be good to be him tonight, he thought.*

# CHAPTER XV

**D**oris fidgeted nervously in her chair while she watched Randal review his notes and maps and photos. He had several files spread out in front of him on the table centered in the small room. This was his conference room, where he held meetings with his "crew," as he referred to them, and sometimes used it as a place to have confidential phone calls.

Randal had recently started having his guys station vehicles closely in front of and behind Doris' car when she got home from work. Initially, she did not think anything of it since there was always a parking shortage in the front yard of the "Complex," as the house was referred to. Lately, however, she had been trying to avoid parking in places where she could be blocked in, but four-wheel drive trucks would be quickly staged around her car shortly after she arrived back home at night from work. After several days of experiencing the same practice, she knew it was no coincidence.

When she left work, she noticed that she was being followed. Her tail picked up within a block of her office and continued until she was almost home. Within several minutes of her arrival, her car was blocked in by her follower's vehicle. She felt sick to her stomach with worry about her safety. Almost immediately, Randal had asked her to sit down and join him in the room he was occupying with his paperwork.

Randal looked up at her and smiled reassuringly.

"You ever been to California?" He did his best to make it look like a kindly, conversational inquiry.

Doris suspiciously shook her head negatively. "No," she said quietly.

"I want to take you out there with me on my trip next week. You are going to have to take some time off from work. We might be out there a couple of weeks."

"Randal, I can't do that right now. I already told you that I can't get away from work like that without notice and some planning to make sure we have the right coverage. Let's try and set up a trip just for us sometime next summer." She smiled sweetly while thinking to herself that there was no way she was going to be with this animal next summer.

Randal threw down his pen in annoyance. "Goddamn it, Doris, I have never asked you for nothing. Now I need you and you are not helping me. You need to get on board here and help out." He glared at the woman as he spoke and pointed his finger at her for emphasis.

Doris wondered how the man could toggle from trying to be sweet to being so aggressive and angry within the span of fifteen seconds. She was becoming nervous and concerned for her personal safety.

"Why do you need me out there?" She didn't like where this was headed.

"I can't come up with anything about this guy in California that I can use against him. The only thing we know is that he is single, and he is a skirt chaser. I need you to meet him and get him to take you to a remote place on his boat. Once you get there, we will already be on site and take care of our business. I have a call with my guys from Kansas City in fifteen minutes, and I need to tell them what our plan is. I need to know that you are down for helping out. You won't be involved; you're just bait."

Doris was stunned by the suggestion that she might want to help out with his "business." All of the air was sucked out of her chest, and the dull ache increased in her stomach. She was unable to respond at the moment and stared blankly at Randal with no ability to speak.

"I am counting you in on this, and I am committing to Kansas City that you are on board. Don't cross me here, Doris. Now get on out of here and let me prepare some more; this is an important call for me. They expect me to give them our plan on three assignments tonight. I already have to ask for an extension on one of them, and our plan on the other California job is weak as hell and they might not approve it. This is the only plan that makes sense that we can come up with for this guy in San Diego. He is supposed to be a fisherman, but the marina tells us he never fishes. He uses the boat to entertain women. He is a cock hound. I don't have any other way of getting him out in his boat or knowing where he is going or when so we can catch him out on it. I need a plant. Only way I can work it, and the plant has to be you since I know I can trust you."

Randal glared at Doris with his bloodshot eyes. It did not have to be said; the glare said it all. Everything Doris loved was at risk if she did not cooperate. She knew that. At this point, the only thing she couldn't figure out was how she got into this position. She slowly rose and let herself out of the room with one backward glance. He was staring at her as she exited the room.

In the hallway she leaned against the wall and put her face into her hands and silently sobbed. Her worst fears were coming true. Randal was not only proving to be the violent killer she feared he might be, but now he was also trying to involve her in his work and would not allow her to leave. She was trapped.

She wiped the tears from her face and walked purposefully to the stairs leading to her bedroom. Once inside the bedroom she began pacing and walked to the window. The sky was dark, threatening, and the wind was picking up. She involuntarily began pacing again and shivering with fear. She tried to calm her breathing and forced herself to think about survival and what her best next step should be. She suddenly recalled that Randal kept a loaded pistol in the nightstand on his side of the bed, and she quickly scurried over to see if it was in the drawer. She remembered it vividly. It was a pearl-handled chrome revolver. It was both beautiful and sinister looking at the same time; on previous occasions, when she had seen it in the drawer before, she had been mesmerized by it, and it made a lasting impact on her memory. She slowly opened the top drawer. The zippered case that the gun was normally resting on was there, but the pistol was gone. Inadvertently, tears spewed from her eyes again and a jagged breath left her body. She was feeling exposed and vulnerable; the fact that he had removed it from their bedroom indicated that he was suspicious about how much he could trust her, and that was a bad sign.

Doris supported herself against the wall and made her way to the window again as she noted the darkness enveloping the view outside. The tree branches were swaying and showing significant, stormy wind gusts. Suddenly, large hail started falling on the sloped roof outside the window along with some large rain droplets. She felt melancholy and strongly missed her family. Tears were flowing down her face involuntarily, and she was trembling with anxiety and fear. The thought of potential harm coming to her children suddenly iced her emotions, however, as she considered how her two children would feel if she disappeared or were killed. Her maternal, protective instincts morphed her fear for herself into an angry passion to protect her children, and she immediately began considering different ways to escape and remove herself from Randal's control. She swiveled the window lock at the center of the window sash and pushed the top of the frame to see if she could open the old window. Initially, the window resisted, but she felt some movement in the sash and, suddenly, the window slid halfway open. Droplets of rain splashed inside, and she quickly closed the window again and left the lever open. She made a quick glance at the chair in the corner of the bedroom and slid it over under the window to gain some elevation to make an exit out the smallish window easier. She studied the screen on the window and noticed the vibration it made in the window frame with the wind gusts, and she observed that it appeared to be loose in the frame. The large hail continued coming down fiercely on the roof, and she could watch the large ice balls bounce off the roof shingles after they struck the asphalt-coated surface.

Doris stood up on the chair and slowly partially reopened the window and pushed outward on the bottom of the screen in the corner that appeared the loosest. With almost no effort, the screen popped out of the frame and slid down the roof. Just as she was stepping down from the chair after re-closing the window, a loud knock on her door caused her heart to jump in her chest and pound heavily.

After the second knock, she asked, "Who is it?"

"It's me, Ricky. We are in a tornado watch, Doris. Tornado watch. Tornado." He sounded muffled coming through the door because he always looked down when he talked, but Doris could easily identify his voice and manner of speaking. She knew that Ricky was deathly afraid of storms and always followed the television news reporter's advice carefully. She could sense the concern in his voice.

Doris walked over to the door and opened it a slight amount and stood behind the door as if she might not be properly dressed. She peered out modestly and smiled bravely at Ricky. "I see the hail and wind, Ricky. Are you going down to the shelter?" Tornado warnings were somewhat routine in season, and none of the crew would normally go down to the storm shelter unless a tornado was identified in the immediate area. Ricky, on the other hand, was easily excitable during the storms and only felt comfortable if he was in the shelter. She normally went into the below-ground shelter with him to comfort him and keep him calm.

"Yeah. Shelter. Going to the shelter. Come with me, Doris. Shelter."

Doris closed the door quietly and leaned her back up against it and filled her lungs. She closed her eyes and exhaled softly and thought of her children and her parents. She longed to be in their presence and away from the madness she found herself in. She sensed that this was her opportunity to make a break. Somehow she had to summon the courage to make her move and stop being so paralyzed by fear. She softly opened the door again and looked at him. He would never look anybody in the eye when talking to them.

"You go on down there, Ricky, and as soon as I get cleaned up and dressed, I will meet you down there. Go ahead and go."

"Okay. Go now, see you there. Go to the shelter. Shelter." He turned his body without looking at her and shuffled toward the stairs. Doris closed the door and locked it and immediately began searching through her clothes in the closet to come up with some practical shoes and jeans that would help her withstand the weather. Fortunately, her heaviest jacket was hanging on a hook on the back of the door.

Selecting some warm and sturdy jeans and a flannel shirt along with some tennis shoes, she grabbed some gloves and quickly unrolled the jacket hood from its zippered enclosure and let it drape down the back of the jacket for use in the rain. She centered the chair on the small window and stepped up onto the seat and pushed the sash up as high as it would go. Fortunately, the hail had stopped, but the rain continued in the black of night. She could see and hear the droplets bouncing off the sturdy shingles. She hoisted herself up over the sill and wiggled her way out onto the roof while being careful not to bang her shoes on the wall. After turning sideways to finish extracting herself from the tight portal, she rolled over to her hands and knees and reached up to close the window. After pulling up her hood and putting her gloves on, she was ready to make her way down to the edge of the roof. She had eyed the roof so many times over the past few months and mentally had worked out exactly how she would make her escape. Every time she pulled up to the house, in fact, she studied the roofline from the front yard parking spot and re-confirmed in her mind how she would do it if she found herself in need of a hasty escape from the house.

As children, the kids in the neighborhood where she grew up had all spent time on rooftops in the neighborhood and developed and practiced a technique of swinging their legs down first from a corner of a roofline to allow them to suspend themselves by hanging onto the edge of the roof at the corner before dropping to the ground. This diminished the height of the fall and helped avoid potential injury while they were daring each other to demonstrate their roof gymnastics. She was always determined to show the boys in her neighborhood that she could do it as well as they could, and she was a fearless youngster. They had all eventually gotten permanently chased off the roofs of each other's homes by concerned parents, but the technique remained in her memory, and she believed she could pull it off again if she needed to. Without further thought, she scrambled down the roof incline to the corner she had selected and immediately rolled to her stomach and slowly swung one of her legs over while taking a good handhold on the edge of the roof. Her other leg remained on the roof for stabilization until she lowered herself down on her chest to the point she could no longer maintain it. Once it swung down, she knew she would not be able to maintain her hold and would need to push herself away from the roof and prepare to roll upon impact.

She quickly closed her eyes and mentally reviewed the technique and allowed the leg to drop without another delay. She brought her legs together at shoulder width and crouched for the impact with hands extended to help break the fall. The wet roofing and water flowing down the roof provided minimal friction to retain her grip with her gloved hands, however, and she lost grip in one of her arms, which caused an unexpectedly crooked fall. Doris felt the jolt of pain in her ankle and realized that she had landed wrong and rolled it over severely when she landed. More than that, she had bruised her hands and body by landing on the large hail ice stones lying all over the ground. She lay motionless for a moment and did a quick inventory of where she felt pain and tried to determine if anything was hurt badly or broken.

She then moaned and rolled on the ground before forcing herself to stand up and check her ability to walk. The twisted ankle was sore and caused her to limp badly and impacted her mobility but did not appear to be broken. She bravely limped off into the night in the rain, however, and made a slow and halting escape for the tree line. Her long-planned getaway was off to a bad start in horrible conditions, but she knew everything about her life was on the line. *At least the rainstorm will provide some cover and make it harder to track me,* she thought.

# CHAPTER XVI

Technically, the judge told Cody and Wiley that they would have to wait until the Bureau of Indian Affairs filed the paperwork to remove the restrictive covenant and the estate cleared probate in order for the deed transferring ownership to them could be recorded for the place to be legally theirs. He issued the order, however, and signed it at the proceeding, which essentially gave them the rights to the property since it was unchallenged by anyone else. Since the place was unoccupied and dilapidated, Cody, Wiley, and Wiley's father, Shane, spent the afternoon at the 160-acre farm walking the land and doing some light cleanup by knocking down some of the overgrowth that had taken over the grounds. It appeared that Oklahoma was trying to reclaim the place. Wiley had obviously spent quite a bit of time there and talked enthusiastically about all the plans he had running through his head. Cody was not sure about the house. The place was small and in terrible condition; the roof ridge beam sagged, and Cody pointed out the structural deflection in all the beams and floor joists in the old home. It was obviously a hand-built relic from a bygone era that had miraculously survived the tornadoes and windstorms over the decades, along with the rain, ice, and occasional snowstorms that hit the area. Not wanting to throw shade on Wiley's dreams, however, he kept most of his observations to himself for the moment. There would be time enough to talk things through with Wiley regarding improvements. Wiley seemed intent on restoring the old home because it would be all he could afford to do; he did not realize that his uncle Cody had resources that would make other ideas possible.

According to what was known by long-term area residents, the farm had grown cotton originally, but the land played out like so many other places during the dust bowl and, eventually, the family had converted to raising livestock and growing vegetables. From walking the land, Cody could tell where some original pastures had begun to be reclaimed by the land and would require some effort to clear again. Evidently, an area rancher had been cutting hay on some of the pastureland for his own livestock. Wiley had been indignant about this and promised to end the poaching. Cody calmed him down and encouraged him to go easy on the neighbor. Fencing was down on the property, and it would take a while to restore the place. Nobody in the area was sure who the rightful owner was, and it was obvious that the Bureau of Indian Affairs had not spent any time over the years overseeing the property or maintaining it. From where Cody sat, nobody could get too angry over someone else poaching a little grass if there wasn't someone to ask if they could harvest it. The way he saw it, nature provided it and there was no crime in using it if it helped someone, and no one was hurt while it happened.

The main thing the probate court had done was keep the taxes paid to prevent the loss of the property to a tax deed while the estate had been cleared. Now that the primary land asset could be legally conveyed, Wiley's lawyer assured them that he could get things closed out within ninety days or so with deed restriction removed and recorded shortly thereafter. Fortunately, there had been just enough cash and interest earned on the estate cash to keep the taxes paid until Wiley discovered that he might have a beneficial interest in the estate. He had arranged to make a small loan to the estate to pay the taxes while he did his research and hunted Cody down. Cody reflected on that briefly and smiled to himself as he thought about Wiley taking a chance with his limited savings by making a loan to the estate to buy more time to establish his and Cody's claim to the land.

The three men were making their way back from the creek bank in the cab of Shane's four-wheel drive truck as he slowly made his way through the overgrowth along a winding, barely visible pathway to the yard of the house. Shane's truck had a substantial grill guard on the front with an electric winch. The guard knocked down the brush without harm to the grill or headlights as the truck plowed through the unmaintained areas, and the winch would be useful in getting them out of any wet areas if they got stuck.

Cody looked at Wiley grinning in the front passenger seat of the truck while they rocked viciously from side to side as the truck made its way over the rough terrain. "So, tell me about how you made the loans to the estate for the past two years to keep the taxes paid. I hadn't heard this before."

"Yeah. It wasn't a lot of money to most people, but it wiped out my savings account. Taxes on the place are only about $2,500 per year since it is agricultural land, but the estate had run out of cash, and when I first found out about it, I made a loan to redeem the oldest of the tax certificates to prevent it from being moved into tax sale. I did the same thing again a year later. Had to run up a credit card to make the second payment, though." Wiley laughed. "Dad told me not to do that, but it looks like it paid off, didn't it?" Wiley looked at his father across the cab.

"Yes, son, you believed in this idea of yours and went completely in on it. I give you credit for that; it looks like your hard work, research, and grit are paying off. Proud of you." Shane offered up a palm and the two high-fived each other.

"You never mentioned the money you loaned to the estate to me, Wiley. Let me at least go in with you for my share on it so you can pay off your credit card."

"That would be great, Uncle. I didn't want to mention it to you until I knew it would work out. Didn't want you to think I was chasing you down for that. We are going to inherit at least two years of back taxes and an upcoming tax payment on the property too. We will have to work up a plan to pay those things right away. Now you know why I have been using that prison toilet paper! Been running a little tight in Wiley town lately."

Cody chuckled at the toilet paper reference; it made a little more sense in retrospect. "Are we good for the next ninety days?" he asked.

"No problem. We have until May," Wiley responded.

"Good job on saving the farm, nephew. I will get you a check for my portion of the amount you paid for taxes and for the attorney when I get home. I can handle the back taxes when we get the title in order to get the other tax certificates cleared. Don't worry about those. Least I can do to repay you for all the work you did on this."

"Looks like you got yourself a good partner." Shane smiled at Wiley.

"I got lucky." Wiley smiled broadly again.

"Well, you know I am more of a trim carpenter than a framing carpenter, Wiley, but from what I can see, that old shack is in pretty desperate shape. I think we should talk it out before you go crazy trying to rehab it. I think we should start out by having the well tested and the septic tank looked at. While we are doing that, we should have a structural engineer and a framing contractor come out and tell us what they think about the structure. Since it is not a slab on grade, we might be better off starting from scratch and building a whole new home onsite in the same location if the septic system and well are in working condition."

"What do you guys think about the barn?" Wiley sounded a little wounded by Cody's assessment of the house.

"Barn looked like it was salvageable to me." Shane looked in the rearview mirror at Cody as he spoke.

"I agree. I think the barn could be salvaged. Needs a little roof work and some repairs, but I think it is still sound structurally." Cody was glad to be able to agree.

"We would need to replace all the fencing to keep any horses here, though. That will take a while. Fencing that is out here is all barbed wire, and some of that is falling down. I guess that should be our first project."

Shane put the truck in park in front of the old house and looked over at his son. "Well, you know that is one thing you and I can do. We do it all the time at my place. I will help you as much as I can." He began ducking lower to look outside the cab at the sky. "Looks like we have a hell of a rainstorm coming. Could be a tornado and some hail this time of year too. You boys better get out and get into your truck before it starts raining. I will meet you for dinner at seven per plan."

The sun was rapidly setting for the day as Cody and Wiley entered the cab of Cody's truck. Wiley motioned toward the rapidly diminishing fireball in the sky. "Look, Uncle. This time of year we get a real nice sunset right over the pasture from the back porch of the house. Pretty spectacular."

"Yeah. It is. I think it's going to start raining real hard soon, though. That sunset is just about the only clear spot in the sky right now. We are under some wicked-looking thunderstorm clouds."

"That time of year," Wiley lamented. The rustling of the wind was increasing as the darkness of night rapidly enveloped the landscape. Occasional lightning strikes were appearing and causing rumbling thunderclaps. He could feel the electricity in the air and a drop in temperature. "Might be some hail in this storm. We ought to get this nice truck in my garage to protect it and take my old truck out for dinner."

"Appreciate that, nephew. Damn hailstones can cause some damage. We should try and get the bikes protected also."

"We can roll them up on the back patio under cover," Wiley responded.

Cody accelerated hard onto the asphalt road and quickly got to the speed limit. They quickly navigated the light traffic and arrived at Wiley's house. They efficiently teamed up to do the slight rearrangements necessary to squeeze Cody's truck into the garage of his house and roll the two bikes onto the protected part of his back patio.

Once inside, they cleaned up and changed clothes in preparation for meeting Wiley's father at a local restaurant for a celebratory steak dinner. They arrived at the restaurant and found Shane sitting in a back booth nursing a beer and reading the local paper. As Cody and Wiley slid into the booth and settled in, Shane slid their menus toward them across the table.

"The family that runs this restaurant raises beef on a ranch about fifteen miles from here. They butcher and process the beef locally also and take some of the best cuts for this restaurant. The place is not fancy, but you get a good steak and a generous portion of all the sides. Prices are fair too. It is definitely the best meal in this town."

"Dad, did you catch the news before you left for here? We are in a tornado watch."

"I didn't turn the TV on at home while I was there, but I heard the waitresses talking about it when I got here. Probably going to be a thin crowd tonight. Nobody is going to want to get out in this weather. I parked down the street inside one of the car wash bays to keep the hail off of my old truck. You never know when that stuff is going to kick up. That old truck has been through enough of those storms. I got a cracked windshield a few years ago from a hailstorm. Only good thing about those is that they don't usually last long."

"Did you get all the horses fed and locked up in the barn?" Wiley asked, like he didn't know the answer.

"Yeah. They were all congregated around the barn and ready to come inside. I didn't have to go looking for anybody tonight, thank God. They are all smart enough to know where it's safe. They all just walked right into their own stalls after I let them in. Those damn horses are more used to their routine than I am. They all follow Mercedes. She is the queen bee in that hive, for sure. I lead her into her stall first, and the other horses just walk into their own stalls behind her. It's the damnedest thing I have ever seen. I go into the barn first and open all the stall doors and get their hay and grain in place. Then I go out and lead her in, and the other horses don't want to wait on me to come back and get them. They make it easy on me; they just file in and put themselves in their own stall. I just close all the stall doors behind them, and they settle in for the night. Whole process takes about five minutes."

Shane was finishing the story as the waitress walked up. She smiled broadly at Shane and Wiley and poured water into their drink glasses.

"Well, look who we have here. Shane and Wiley eating together tonight. I see you guys separately from time to time but hardly ever see you here together. You still have all those beautiful Appaloosa horses, Shane? Are those the ones you are talking about?"

"The very same." Cody could feel the pride that Shane had for his horses.

"They are all so beautiful. I would love to bring my daughter out sometime to show them to her. She is crazy about horses, and I know she would love seeing them."

"You bring her out anytime, Kelly. Just come on out when you want to."

"That is nice of you. Thanks, I will do that. Now who is this tall gentleman with you in the Mexican wedding boots?"

Wiley and Shane snickered and guffawed. Wiley hooted and the two high-fived each other.

Cody could not help but laugh at the two of them rolling around in the booth, snorting and hooting like two teenagers.

"This is my uncle Cody, Kelly. I wasn't going to say anything about those boots, but now that you mention it, they do look like something you would see at a Mexican wedding."

"How are you doing there, Uncle Cody? Welcome to Tishomingo. Where did you get those dandy boots, anyway?"

"At the gittin' place." Cody was trying hard not to get insulted.

"Oh, okay. I just never seen anything like them before. Just thought I would ask. I know you didn't borrow them from Wiley. He is way too cheap to buy anything that fancy. He is getting better, though. He almost tipped me a whole dollar last time he came in. A couple of more cents and it would have been a whole dollar. I will give you fellows a few minutes to look at the menu and come back. Soup tonight is minestrone."

Wiley looked over at Cody and started snickering again. "I knew she was going to do it. She has to say something. She talks shit about everybody, but she does it so nicely and she does it to your face. Got to respect that about her."

"Well, just for the record. These are Dan Post boots, and they are made out of python skin. Now you two goat ropers might not know much about that type of thing, but these boots set me back a little bit of change, and it would be nice if you would act suitably impressed. I bought them just before I came out here for the sole purpose of trying to fit in during my visit."

Shane smiled easily and leaned back slightly. "Dan Post boots;

you don't say. Well, now, Cody, the truth is Wiley and I know a little bit about cowboy boots, and, well sir, those are some damn fine-looking kicks. I just advise you not to leave them around Wiley's house. He has a reputation for walking off with stuff from time to time. About half of my tools are over at his house."

"Oh, for the love of God. You are not going to start talking about that goddamn crescent wrench again, are you? That was five years ago, and I was going to bring that back to you. I just didn't have one big enough to fit that trailer hitch nut. Sweet Jesus, you never forget anything."

Shane and Cody looked at each other and laughed. Cody was glad that nobody else was talking about his boots anymore. He looked out the window into the street and saw the hail striking the street and sidewalk outside the restaurant and heard the wind blowing canopies and signs and pushing the glass against the frame, causing it to rattle.

Pleasant conversation between the three about the potential future of the ranch followed, and the men shared a few good laughs at Wiley's expense on different subjects. They all ordered steaks and when the salads came, they were consumed in hurried fashion with little comment. Within minutes of clearing the salad plates, Kelly returned with three massive steaks overhanging the plates on which they were served. Appreciative sounds from the three men greeted the woman as she expertly laid down the plates and placed her hands on her hips in an exaggerated fashion.

"Anything else you need, Shane? Wiley? And how about you, Uncle Cody? I think you are going to be getting those fancy boots wet on your way home tonight, you know. It's raining pretty hard out there."

"Nephew will go get the truck and come and get me. How about some steak sauce for this gut buster?"

Wiley winked at the heavyset woman and immediately went

to work cutting a piece of the steak off from the huge beef slab.

The meal carried on with limited conversation until, one by one, the men gave up. Wiley was the last to stop eating, and he leaned back in the booth and looked skyward. "It's a TKO. I can't finish it."

"Not for lack of trying, hombre." Cody looked at the remnants of the steak on the plate and compared it to the amount left on his and Shane's plate. "You did better than your dad and me."

"Yeah, well, you might have to drive home tonight, Uncle. That was an epic battle. I need a nap now."

Shane looked at Cody and shook his head. "So much for going to Ole Red for beers then. I was looking forward to finally going there. Been open for a couple of years now and I haven't ever been."

Wiley looked down at his phone as it started to vibrate next to his plate. He picked it up and showed it to his father. "This is that high school friend of mine, Ricky Hunter, who is working with Randal. I am going to see what he wants."

Cody and Shane watched intently as Wiley answered the call. "Hey, Ricky! What's up?"

Wiley listened silently for several moments. He briefly closed his eyes and put his hand on his forehead. He sighed heavily and said, "Don't worry, Ricky. Doris is going to be all right. Do not tell anybody you talked to me, okay? You understand, right? Don't tell anybody you talked to me." Wiley looked up at his father, who was staring intently at him.

"Doris must have slipped out of the house and ran off. Ricky says that Randal and his crew are out looking for her."

Shane stood up without saying a word and made a beeline for the register at the front of the restaurant. As he walked over, he made a motion with one hand asking for the check.

Wiley looked at Cody. "Dad's going to go look for Doris,

and I have to go with him. You don't have to get involved in this, Uncle. It might be a little dangerous, and he is probably going to want to go over there on horseback."

Cody looked at Wiley carefully. "This sounds like a family issue to me, Wiley. Don't discount your family. We are the only ones you can really count on when you need us. You just tell me what you need me to do. I am not that great on a horse, though. I can sit one if I have to and I have done some riding, but I didn't grow up riding rodeo like you guys."

"I will tell Dad. He will probably put you on Mercedes. You can completely trust that horse. She is very dependable and does not cause trouble. Dad has trained her for twenty-five years. Let's go. I will ride with Dad, and you follow us in my truck." He slid the keys to his truck over the booth top toward Cody.

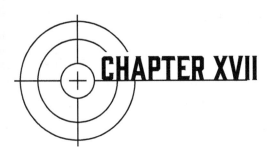

# CHAPTER XVII

Cody carefully pulled out his cell phone from the side pocket of the old trail duster overcoat he was wearing. All three of the men had wrapped their phones in small, clear Ziploc plastic bags to protect them from the steady rain, at Wiley's suggestion. Since they immediately separated to cover more ground once they got mounted, it made sense to make sure they could communicate with each other. The coal-black darkness of the night was interrupted occasionally by another lightning strike that would provide fleeting illumination. All the gear Cody wore had been loaned to him by Wiley and Shane. His cowboy hat was wrapped in a plastic cover with an elastic band at the bottom. The cover kept the dark felt hat from absorbing the rain. The wide brim was essential to keep the rain off his face and out of his eyes. It had been many years since Cody had donned a cowboy hat, and he had never owned or worn a duster overcoat before. The cold rain and wind gave him a quick education on why they were essential items when a person found themselves on horseback in the rain. The overcoat was knee-length and featured a lengthy slit in the back to allow the coat to drape over the back of the horse and protect the rider without bunching up. The hat was invaluable and kept the majority of the rain from striking his face and allowing him to see into the darkness of the night.

Cody wished he had brought the nine-millimeter handgun he kept in his vehicle attached to his belt in a clip-on plastic holster he kept along with the firearm. Since he had ridden with Wiley to the restaurant in Wiley's truck, he hadn't been able to return to

Wiley's house to retrieve it. Wiley had loaned him the gun that he kept at his dad's house, a nickel-plated .357 Magnum caliber Colt Python with a four-inch barrel in a leather holster. The Python was famous for being one of the highest quality revolvers ever made, and the double-action revolver chambered in the brutish .357 Magnum caliber was lethal within its firing range. Cody had noted that both Wiley and his father had brought their Winchester 30/30s in scabbards along with their semi-automatic handguns. They apologized that they did not have another one to offer him.

He was surprised that the boots he was wearing had not bled moisture through yet. He was certain it would only be a matter of time before the lightweight skin got saturated and wicked moisture through to his socks and feet, however. He could not help but snort in laughter at the waitress's reference to his dressy boots. Colt Python, carried by a guy in python skin boots. *You can't make this shit up,* Cody thought. The weapon was holstered onto his belt beneath the duster overcoat. It may not have been what he would have selected for himself given a choice, but it was a potent firearm and would serve the purpose in a close-range gunfight. There had not been time to do his usual thorough planning and gear selection.

After driving from Shane's small ranch to the vacant property Cody and Wiley had just inherited, they made short work of offloading the three horses from the trailer. Shane and Wiley had dug up three pairs of fence cutters to allow them to cut through any wire fencing they needed to cross to conduct their search for Doris. Cody's responsibility was to search around the road rights-of-way in the area. They quickly sketched out a rough map of the area for Cody and gave him some benchmarks to maintain his bearings. The plan was for him to make his way toward Randal's compound, as close to the road as possible on both sides of the compound and on both sides of the road. Cody confirmed the direction to town and decided to work the right-hand side of the road headed toward town first, since that seemed most likely to be the way that someone would naturally take in escaping.

Shane was anxious to get on with the search, and there had not been much of a strategy session beyond assigning the area closest to the road to Cody, and for Shane and Wiley to each pick up one side of the road and work their way toward the compound on their respective side of the road. The weather was dreadful with a full-pitched gale, scattered lightning, and steady rain. The clay soil was saturated, and water was ponding in low spots. The soil was slippery and soft in the higher areas. It was sloppy, uncomfortable, and the wind made exposed flesh cold. In the absence of other gloves, Cody had put on his fingerless motorcycle riding gloves, which helped but were not the perfect choice. On balance, Cody felt grateful for the duster and the hat. It would have been hard to be in the elements without those two garments.

Cody quickly deduced that the horse had better night vision than he did. He allowed the mare to pick her own way in the general direction he steered her, and she slogged through the slippery clay mud and muck fearlessly, walking through any standing water without hesitation. Cody felt comfortable on her and could feel the steely strength in her legs as she powered them up inclines and through ravines. She was fine-limbed and not heavy in the hindquarters the way many quarter horses and Morgans were built. Nonetheless, she was surefooted and powerful and attentive to any command he gave her. She was easy to ride and instinctively anticipated what he wanted her to do without any fuss or hesitation. She seemed to trust him completely, and smoothly executed any command he gave her. As he grew comfortable with her, he gradually just let her find her own way through the underbrush and low-hanging limbs without direction from him.

Cody knew the horse was making a lot of noise crashing through the brush, and that would be heard by anybody in hiding. His hope was that it would be Doris who heard him and not one of Randal's thugs out looking for Doris. He maintained a vigilant scouting posture as he made his way. After about fifteen minutes of working through the overgrowth and pasture, the horse suddenly stopped. Cody peered at the brush line and saw that the brush had overgrown a barbed-wire fence. Fortunately, the horse had seen it and knew to stop. Cody dismounted to take a closer look and pulled out the fence cutters. It was a five-strand barbed-wire fence with metal fence posts. Cody walked down the fence slightly to a clear spot and quickly cut through the first four strands and was bent over snipping the bottom strand when he heard the four-wheeler slowly making its way through the pasture on the other side of the fence line. As the buggy cleared the top of the ridge, Cody saw the headlights beam upward toward the sky and then sharply bounce downward as the front wheels cleared the ridge and entered the depression on the other side. The buggy was bouncing vigorously as it slowly crept through the rugged terrain.

Cody knelt down in the wet soil to avoid making a silhouette. He looked backward to check on Mercedes and saw the mare patiently standing in the same spot where he left her, looking downward to avoid the rain. Cody remained motionless for a moment, looking across the meadow to the tree line where he had observed the four-wheeler. He could still hear the vehicle but could not see it. Suddenly, he saw a figure break through the tree line in his peripheral vision. In the darkness, he could vaguely see the backside of someone moving slowly back into coverage and out of sight. From the way they moved, they appeared to be wounded or hurt.

Cody skirted back to the mare and draped the reins around her neck. He swiftly mounted and walked the horse up to the fence to allow it to inspect and confirm that there was no wire. Gingerly, the mare eased through the opening, and Cody steered her down the fence line to reduce his profile. The rain continued and the occasional lightning strike illuminated the sky. Cody could hear the four-wheeler growling softly through the brush and periodically stopping to idle while the driver scanned the area for signs of Doris. The mare had closed in on the area where he had seen the person duck into the woods. Cody dismounted from the horse and led her into a thicket. As he was tying off the reins of the horse, he heard someone hoarsely whisper.

"Shane! Is that you? Is that you, Shane?"

Cody turned around to see a slight woman leaning on a walking stick, trembling in fear and completely soaked. She abruptly kneeled down when she realized that Cody was not Shane. "You aren't Shane! How did you get his horse?" she uttered through a ragged sob.

Cody knelt down where he stood to get to her level. He was approximately ten feet away from her and sensed that he needed to reassure her that he was there to help her before he advanced closer.

"My name is Cody. I am Wiley's uncle and a friend of Shane's. Wiley and Shane are out here looking for you too," he whispered.

The woman wanted to believe him, but it seemed unlikely to her that they would have had a way to find out she needed help. "How did you know I was out here?" she asked.

"A guy named Ricky is one of Wiley's friends. He called Wiley to tell him that you ran away, and Shane and Wiley wanted to come out and see if they could find you and help get you away from these guys. I came along with them to try and help out. Shane gave me Mercedes to ride since I am not an experienced rider." Cody could see a glimmer of hope in her eye at the mention of Ricky and the mention of the horse's name.

"Doesn't sound like Shane to loan Mercedes to anybody else to ride." She was shivering from the cold, and he could tell that her ankle was causing her pain.

"Well, he and Wiley saw how bad a cowboy I was and took pity on me." He smiled at her when he said it, and she returned a hopeful look but refused to smile. "Looks like you are in pain."

"Twisted my ankle real bad getting off the roof of the house." The shivering was giving way to shuddering and convulsing. He could tell that she was close to going into shock from the cold and pain of the ankle. "It's hard for me to walk."

Cody reached in behind the duster overcoat and pulled the plastic bag out that contained his cell phone. He lit up the screen and dialed Wiley's number while listening for the four-wheeler and peering through the brush for headlights. Wiley's phone flipped over to voicemail, and he redialed the number again. This time Wiley immediately answered.

"Was having trouble getting my phone out of this coat. You there, Uncle?"

"Yeah, Wiley. I am here. I have Doris. We have a four-wheeler out here close by looking for her. We are hidden right now in a thicket waiting for them to move on. Say something to her; she doesn't know me or know for sure if she should trust me." He handed the phone over to Doris. "It's Wiley. He is out here too, on the other side of the road looking for you there."

Doris took the phone and held it up to her other ear. In a very meek voice, she asked "Wiley, is that you?"

Cody watched as she covered her eyes with her free hand and began sobbing. "I am sorry, Wiley. I am so, so sorry. I just don't know what to do. I am just so scared. Thank you so much for coming to get me. I am so glad Ricky called you. He is such a sweet boy. Okay, okay, I know I can trust him completely. I will tell him." Doris looked up at Cody and smiled at him for the first time. "He wants to talk to you."

"Hey, Wiley. Yep. Meet you back at the truck. You call your dad and get him headed back. I can still hear that four-wheeler around here, so we are going to have to stay hidden from them on the way back. I am going to have to put Doris on the horse and walk the horse back because she has a twisted ankle. It's going to take me a bit to get there like this. We need to clear out, though, because these guys are looking for her all over the place. I have heard at least three different four-wheelers out here searching." Cody looked over at Doris, who had moved in closer to him and was now leaning against him. He draped his arm over her to give her a hug of reassurance. "Right. See you there." He disconnected the call and placed the phone back in the bag.

"Looks like the rain is slowing down." He peered outside the thicket and contemplated the implications of that. It made it a little easier to get around, but it improved the visibility and conditions for Randal and his gang. He could no longer hear the four-wheeler engine. That meant that the rider had either left the area or was in a listening mode. "I am going to get you up on that horse and lead you back to where we left the truck and trailer. I think it's about a mile that way on the other side of the section line road. We need to stay hidden on the way back, though."

Cody went over and stood by the mare and gently caressed her neck and said some soothing words to her as he untied her reins from the tree branch he had secured her to. The easy, calm demeanor and willingness of the gentle beast to perform her rider's instructions amazed him. He had never been around a horse this well trained. She followed him over to Doris without complaint and stood motionless while Doris stood up and embraced her neck with a hug. "Hey, sweet girl. You remember me, don't you?" Doris laid her head against the horse's neck and closed her eyes and began crying again.

Cody walked over and put his hand on her shoulder. "Which ankle is hurt, Doris? We have to get going now. I know you are hurting, but I need you to be strong until we can get you back home."

"I know, I know. Sorry. My right ankle is the one that is hurt. I can mount her from the left using my left foot in the stirrup if you will help push me up."

Cody was relieved to note that it sounded like she had some experience riding horses. He helped her stand up and move over in position to grab the saddle horn. He then leaned his shoulder into her outside hip from behind. "Now go ahead and lean your hip over and put your weight on my shoulder, and I will help lift you up so you can swing your leg over the saddle."

Doris did as asked, and Cody easily assisted her to get properly mounted. She leaned forward and soothingly spoke to the mare. "Good girl, Mercedes." She smiled at Cody as she rubbed the horse's neck and reassured the gentle old mare. He took a moment to listen for the four-wheeler and searched through the darkness for any evidence of headlights or a flashlight beam.

Cody gathered the reins and gave them to her. "Follow me," he said.

The rain dropped steadily on Cody as he made his way through the brush. He did not want to use the flashlight to illuminate their path to avoid detection. For the immediate moment, they had the advantage of sound, however. Walking as they did produced limited noise and allowed them to listen; conversely, their pursuers could not listen for them over the noise produced by their mechanical transportation. The advantage was significant. Even though they were outnumbered, Cody felt confident that they could make it back without detection if they were careful.

As always, Cody's mind shifted to the tactical breakdown of the situation. They needed to remove themselves, the horses, and

Doris from the area without detection or confrontation, if possible. The point of highest exposure for them was returning to their truck and loading the horses onto the trailer. Cody assumed that would take a minimum of ten minutes, during which they would be highly exposed to detection. A chill came over him as he contemplated the possibility that Randal and his gang might have detected the truck and horse trailer. Cody recognized that in their haste to get underway with their search, they had failed to stage the truck and trailer on the property in such a way that it could not be detected from the road. For sure, Randal would have had people patrolling the roads and undoubtedly would have seen the truck and trailer.

Cody pulled out the fence cutters from the side pocket of the duster and kneeled down to clip the bottom strand of the barbed wire first. He rapidly clipped the remaining four strands and pulled the wires away from the opening to create a wide area for Doris to pass through. He regretted opening up another section of the fencing, but he did not want to take time to walk back up the fence line to the location he had already cut. Doris smiled at him bravely.

"You came prepared," she remarked as she passed by.

"Short notice, but we did the best we could." He gave her a friendly pat on the leg as he caught up with her. "You doing okay up there?"

"Oh yeah. Mercedes and I go way back. Shane always put me on her too. This is way better than hobbling along on my ankle. Randal's guys have about three of those four wheelers, though. I know they are all out here looking for me; he will not let them stop looking. They kept driving right past me a number of times before I ran into you."

Cody knew time was not his friend at this moment. Restarting the walk back toward the vehicle, he felt himself easing into an operations mindset as he ran through probabilities of outcomes on alternatives. One possibility was not to return to the truck tonight. They could ride all the way back to Shane's house on horseback and come back later for the truck and trailer. Cody knew that plan was messy and complicated since it would involve them riding along roads at night with Doris, leaving the opportunity to be discovered by Randal's crew or being hit by traffic.

After summarily dismissing the possibility of staying hidden all night after watching Doris shudder from the cold, Cody knew that the only real option was returning to the truck and driving out tonight. He gave some thought to the idea of calling the police to defuse any possible confrontation. After a moment of contemplation, he turned around to check on Doris and held his hand up in signal for her to stop at the thicket he ducked into for cover.

"I need to call Wiley again," he explained. He pulled out the cell phone and redialed the number.

"Nephew. Listen, just thinking this through. I think it's likely that Randal will be waiting for us back at the truck. We should have hidden the truck and trailer in the back part of the property by the barn. I am sure that Randal or one of his guys would have been driving and seen your dad's rig parked there and noticed that it was out of place. What do you think about calling the police?"

There was an awkward silence. Cody could hear the sound of the rainfall hitting the brim of Wiley's hat while he waited on his nephew to respond.

"You are right, Uncle. We should have hidden the truck. I didn't think about it."

"None of us did. I think we need to rendezvous before we get to the house and scout out the property before we just barge in there."

"Right. Let me call Dad now before he gets there. Where you at?"

"Making our way in that direction, about 150 feet away from the road. Reason I say I think they would have noticed the truck is because of the amount of traffic I have been seeing on the road. They are out driving around looking. I know they would have noticed your dad's truck at the property and knew it was out of place."

"Ten-four. Standby. Call you back."

Within several minutes Cody felt his phone vibrating with a return call from Wiley.

"Dad says to stay put. He will sweep in toward the road. Look out for him and flash your flashlight at him three times if you think you see him or hear him. If he thinks he sees you, he will use the same signal. I am crossing the road and am almost at the property. I am going to scout things out on foot and see what is happening. Once I get it scouted, I will start making my way back to you guys."

"Got it."

With that Cody looked up at Doris. "We are going to wait here for Shane to catch up to us. You want to get down and give Mercedes a rest? Old girl has been working hard tonight."

Doris grimaced at him. "I am going to need some help to absorb the shock on my right ankle when I swing my leg down. Can you help me?"

"I have you. Swing it down and I will ease you to the ground."

After Cody helped her dismount and moved her over to a comfortable resting position, Doris motioned for him to sit down next to her.

"I need to tell you something, Cody."

"What is on your mind?"

"Randal is very close to Sheriff Edwards. He comes over to Randal's house frequently. Randal pays him off and Edwards stays off his back. Randal used to be a deputy on the force until he got kicked off for abuse. I don't think you are going to get a lot of help from Edwards, and the sheriff's office has the jurisdiction out here. You can't rely on him, and I don't think he will help us. I would have called them to help me get away from Randal if I thought it would have worked." Doris sat with her arms crossed and her injured ankle extended out from her body to minimize the stress on it.

Cody sat quietly and looked at Doris without comment. He knew she had more to reveal and didn't want to interrupt her.

She continued. "When I picked Randal up from the airport a couple of weeks ago, he took me to the property you and Wiley inherited and told me that if I tried to leave him, he would kill me, my parents, and my children and bury us there on that land." She bowed her head and covered her eyes in shame and sobbed deeply in dismay.

"Randal is a terrible man. He is suspicious and he was a tyrant to me; he would not let me leave him and was always threatening my children and my parents. I just didn't know what to do. He has a terrible temper, and he is violent. He acts as a hired killer for this company that buys life insurance policies. I am not supposed to know this, but I do. He started trying to convince me to help him with an assignment out in California. He wanted me to lure the guy into taking me out in his boat so they could kill him. The company that he works for wants the deaths to look like accidents." She began a violent shudder that she could not control. Between her fear of Randal's threats to her family and the cold she felt, she was nearly spasming.

"Don't think about any of that right now, Doris." Cody talked to her in the calmest voice he could produce. "Shane, Wiley, and I are going to get you out of here and take you to a safe place. You are in good hands. You did the right thing by leaving him; just let us take care of the rest of it. You are just emotional, cold, and exhausted right now. Hang on a bit and it's going to get better."

"Okay." She sniffled and wiped her nose with the back of her hand as she spoke in a small voice. She felt paralyzed by fear of the uncertainty. At least she didn't have to make any more decisions. She looked forward to seeing Shane again. It seemed like a hundred years since she had seen him.

Cody went out outside the thicket to listen for signs of Shane in the brush surrounding them. The rain was slowing down considerably. He was just about to pull out his phone to call Shane when he saw three slow flashes. Cody responded with three slow flashes from his flashlight and got another rapid three flashes in exchange. He started to make his way toward the light to intercept Shane and give him a quick download on Doris and her fragile emotional state. They rapidly intercepted each other about 150 feet from the thicket where she was sitting. Shane had dismounted from his horse and was leading the animal toward him with his pistol in hand. He quickly holstered the firearm when he recognized Cody, and the two men exchanged a fist bump.

"Doris is in that thicket right there with Mercedes. She has a badly twisted ankle from jumping down off a roof, and she is in a real fragile emotional state. She is very cold, and she is extremely scared right now and weepy. Be careful with her and reassure her that we are going to get her out of here and keep her children and parents safe too. Randal has really done a number on her and threatened her life and her family's life too."

"Got it. She will be all right. She is a strong girl."

"Other thing, Shane. I got to thinking about it. I am fairly sure Randal is going to be waiting for us at the truck. Based on the traffic I saw and heard going that way, and the fact that there haven't been any four-wheelers around here, I am thinking they found your truck parked on the property. I think you should keep Doris out of there for right now and let me and Wiley recover the truck. We can arrange another meeting site and pick you guys up after we leave the lot. It will make it easier to manage Randal if he doesn't know we have Doris."

Cody could tell that Shane was concerned about splitting the group up. He looked at Cody. "You don't think you are going to need my help with Randal and his group?"

"You let Wiley and me handle it. You take care of Doris. If things do go bad with Randal, I want you to get her out of here and get to safety. It is best if Randal does not see her. I am going to tell him that we didn't find her. He won't know that you were with us."

Shane shook his head in understanding and looked over at the thicket. "In there?" he asked.

"Yep. You go on over there and talk to her. I am going to call Wiley and try to tell him where we are so we can meet up here."

Several minutes later Wiley rode up to Cody's flashlight signal and dismounted to check on Doris. Cody held the reins to his horse as Shane and Wiley came out with Doris.

Shane had his arm around Doris as she limped gamely toward Cody. "Doris and I are going to ride double on Mercedes over to a bridge on the section road that crosses this road in front of us. I know a way to get there along the back fence line of this property. Wiley will drive down that road to pick us up. You take my horse."

Cody walked over to the horse that Shane had been riding and pulled out the carbine from the scabbard. "You leaving me this?" he asked.

"You can take that. It's a 30-30 Winchester lever action. You familiar with it?" Shane asked.

"Model Ninety-four with a twenty-inch barrel. Five in the magazine and one in the chamber?" Cody studied the side of the carbine. He had learned to shoot on a similar carbine. He knew it packed a substantial, high-powered round that had devastating impact on a target within 200 yards.

"Yep. That is it. I don't ride with one in the chamber, though. It only has five in it, and I forgot to bring extra ammunition. Sorry about that."

Cody looked over at Wiley. "You have the same thing?"

"Yes. Identical. No extra ammunition, either."

"What are you packing for a sidearm?"

"My nine-millimeter that I carry for work. A fifteen-round Glock with an extra magazine."

"What are you carrying for a sidearm, Shane?"

"I am packing a .38 revolver."

"Okay, then. Wiley and I ride up to the truck, and you head out to the bridge. When we get there, it will be one of two situations: they will either be there, or they won't. If they aren't, we will call you and you can turn back and ride to the truck and load up with us. You keep riding toward the bridge unless you hear from us. Wait at the bridge for thirty minutes. If you don't hear from us or see us there in thirty minutes, you ride back into town and get with the chief of police in Tishomingo. Don't call us and don't go to the sheriff. Go to the chief of police in town. You got it?"

Shane nodded his head. "Got it. One thing, though. I want to swap horses with you now that you are riding with Wiley. My horse has the scabbard on it for the Winchester, anyway."

"No problem. That Mercedes sure is a nice horse, though."

Shane looked over at Wiley and said, "Bring Mercedes out here, Wiley."

Wiley turned and brought the mare over and handed the reins to Shane. Shane looked over at Doris and said, "Just liked we talked about. I am going to lay her down on her side and I want you to get behind me and sit down on her hindquarters, and we will stand her up with both of us on her."

With almost no hesitation, Shane pulled the mare's head down toward the ground, and she knelt down on her front knees and rolled over to her side. Shane straddled over the saddle and Doris straddled behind him. On Shane's command the mare extended her front legs and then effortlessly rose up on her strong hind quarters with both riders astride.

Cody chuckled out loud and said, "Well, now that is a trick. What a well-trained horse she is."

Shane reached into his front pocket and tossed a set of keys to Wiley. Doris wrapped his torso with her arms. He looked at Wiley and said, "You guys be careful. Don't do anything stupid with that idiot if he is there."

"We will be all right, Dad. We will call you as soon as possible."

With that, Shane tipped his hat, and the horse calmly strode off into the tree line. Wiley looked at Cody and said, "Well, at least the rain stopped. Let's go get our truck and haul ass out of here. You want me to call for some backup? I can have a cruiser or two here in fifteen minutes."

Cody walked over to his horse and pulled the Winchester out of its scabbard and inspected it. He levered a round into the chamber and then continued cycling the carbine until all five rounds spit out into his palm. He checked the chamber and verified that the gun was empty and then replaced the ammunition back into the tube.

Wiley watched him and smiled slightly. "You don't trust anybody, do you, Uncle? I guess that means no on the backup."

"Not with my life, I don't." Cody wasn't in the mood for playful back and forth right now. He was in warrior mode, and he was tired of hiding from a redneck bully. "I am sick and tired of hiding from this dude Randal, and I am ready to get home and get in bed. Let's head over to our property and take care of our business."

The two rode the fence line along the road frontage to a culvert in the ditch at the section line crossroad before their property, cut the wire fencing, and then rode in the road up to their property. They both pulled their carbines from their scabbards as they rode right up the driveway to the vehicle. They dismounted at the back of the trailer and did a quick scan of the property to see if anybody was watching. Cody saw fresh four-wheeler tracks all around the truck and trailer from multiple four-wheel buggies.

Just as Wiley was lowering the ramp to the trailer, three four-wheelers came roaring out of the brush at the tree line and stopped approximately thirty feet from their location. A large man driving the middle four-wheeler stood up and dismounted.

"What brings you fellows out tonight in this weather? You guys looking for someone?" Randal asked in a defiant manner.

"What makes that your business? Why don't you tell me what you are doing trespassing on my property?" Cody responded.

"Trespassing? How do you figure that, tough guy? This property has been abandoned for decades. You just decide it's yours?"

"It's mine as of yesterday because the court said it was mine. It's mine and you are trespassing, and I say you need to get off of it and stay off of it."

Wiley racked the lever in his rifle and loaded a round into the chamber of his carbine. He surveyed the three men in front of him and made a choice as to which one he was going to fire on first if it was required. It looked like his uncle might be close to making a move.

"I say you are going to have to show me some paperwork before I believe that, hoss. Meanwhile I am not going anywhere, and neither are you. I think you guys owe me an explanation on what you are doing out here this time of night in this weather. Like I asked earlier, you looking for somebody?"

"I don't owe you an explanation for anything, big mouth."

Cody purposefully strode over toward Randal. Wiley raised his rifle and aimed it at Randal while watching the other two men carefully. He had mentally selected which of them to shoot first, if required. Once Cody got within two strides of him, Randal took a defensive step to his left to avoid an attack and reached for a gun holstered on his right side. Cody quickly pivoted on his left foot and took a giant stride toward him and thrust the muzzle of his carbine savagely in an upward motion directly into Randal's solar plexus, which doubled him over immediately. Cody raised the butt of the carbine above his head and rapidly smashed him in the back of the head three times, leaving him unconscious. The big man face-planted forward on his knees onto the muddy ground. Cody stepped on the unresponsive man's wrist and pried the .45 caliber pistol from his fingers. He bent down, rolled him over on his back, and looked the man in the face and pulled him up slightly by the shirt.

"I guess you didn't know who the wolf was, did you?" Cody hissed.

Cody levered a round into the Winchester and pointed the carbine in the face of the closest of the two men. The man immediately raised his hands as if in surrender. He had a shocked look on his face after watching Randal get dispatched into unconsciousness so quickly. The eerie scene of these two tall men in their dusters and cowboy hats knocking their leader unconscious and disarming him so easily put them in an unknown position. They had never seen Randal unable to intimidate his adversary. Seeing him so easily dispatched and injured was unsettling to them and scrambled their sense of the world order.

Cody spoke slowly in a low voice to the closest of the two men. "Load that piece of shit up and haul him out of here. You tell him the next time I see him on my land I am going to shoot him on sight. Don't ever come back here or I am going to bury you next to him. You got it?"

The man shook his head in agreement. "Yes, sir."

Cody looked at the other man, who appeared even more frightened than the first. "How about you, princess? You aren't coming back here either, are you?"

"No, sir." The two men quietly picked Randal up as he began to moan and protest and loaded him on the back of one of the four-wheelers. They rode the spare four-wheeler to the road right-of-way and staged it next to the road for recovery later. Cody kept an eye out on the men while Wiley loaded up the mares into the trailer. As he started to close and latch the gate, Cody stopped him and stepped onto the trailer.

"I am riding back here." He positioned himself in the center of the trailer with a good hand hold on the center bar with his carbine in hand. "Call your dad and tell him to meet us at the bridge."

Wiley laid his carbine on his shoulder and took a long look at his uncle. "I guess what Dillon and Mr. Musselwhite said about you is true, isn't it?"

"I don't know what they told you, Wiley. Just remember what I told you. Most of what I know isn't worth knowing. The only important thing you need to get out of this encounter is that nobody is going to come on our land and tell me what to do. Full stop. Nobody. Our ancestors fought too hard to keep this place to allow someone to come over here and punk us out while we are standing on this property. We are Chickasaw. We are descendants of the survivors of a long, hard trail. We respect all, but bow to nobody."

Wiley closed the gate on the trailer and nodded in agreement. "Gotcha, Uncle. Gotcha. Nobody is going to tell us what to do on our land. I am down with that. I have your back and I know you have mine. Ole Randal just didn't know who the wolf was. Guess he found out, didn't he?" He smiled and studied Cody intently, waiting for some confirmation that was not offered. His uncle was still in warrior mode and was intently watching Randal's crew as they loaded him and headed back to their compound.

Wiley made the turn around the corner of the trailer and shuffled stiffly toward the truck cab. He was a little sore from all the riding. He smiled slightly as he reviewed the night. He couldn't wait to tell his dad how easily Cody had taken Randal out. Knocked him out and took his gun. They had gone full Tombstone on Randal and his guys and bitch-slapped them like grade-schoolers. *Just wait until word of that gets out on the street,* Wiley thought. That information was going to damage Randal's tough guy reputation.

# CHAPTER XVIII

The hood on the Corvette opened from back to front and un-covered the entirety of the car from the windshield to the bumper. Cody stared at the front light mechanisms that used a vacuum-powered mechanical lever to flip the headlight buckets mounted in a carriage bracket from facing backward to facing forward when the headlights were illuminated. Several YouTube videos into his research had powered his effort with just enough information to make this headlight replacement task seem pos-sible, but did not seem inclined to make it easy. Wiley looked at the engine compartment of the twenty-five-year-old car as if he were the janitor at the Space Center launching the shuttle. Cody had hoped for more mechanical prowess from his nephew. He rubbed his face and knew that it showed the exhaustion of the all-night hunt for Doris the previous night.

"I thought you Oklahoma boys knew a little more about cars." Cody noticed that Wiley's eyes were larger than usual as he tried to make sense out of how the headlight system worked.

"I don't know where you got that idea, Unk." Since that morn-ing, Wiley's moniker for his uncle had been reduced to Unk.

"You know. Country boys will survive. All that horseshit."

"I got to tell you, I don't see you doing all that much in here, either. Maybe we need to haul this old thing over to the mechan-ic's shop and let them handle it."

"It might come to that. I got to try and be the good boyfriend first, though."

"Is she staying the night?"

Cody looked at his nephew with a quizzical face. "Probably. Is it a problem if she does?"

"Oh, no. No problem. I was just wondering if you could get her to cook us breakfast again in her panties. I like that."

"You need to quit poaching on my action and scare some up yourself." Cody wondered to himself how a guy with the DNA of people who can get a horse to lie down on its side in the mud and stand up with two riders on its back could not know the difference between a flat head screwdriver and a Phillips head. Wiley wasn't going to be much help on this project, he thought.

At that moment Lisa walked out onto the front porch and smiled sweetly. "How is it coming along out here? You think you boys can pull this off?"

Cody looked at her standing on the porch with her hands on her hips in short cutoff shorts and long, shapely legs and immediately came up with something that he would prefer to be doing.

"Still researching it," he replied.

"Ummm… Okay. Let me know what you come up with when the research portion of this activity ends, and the actual installing part of the work happens, and I will be happy to bring the new headlights outside for you. You two top-shelf technicians left the repair parts inside here on the coffee table. You guys look like a couple of monkeys dry humping a football out there."

Cody squinted at her as he pondered the implication that she thought that he and his nephew were incapable of replacing the headlights on her car. "I am sure we will figure it out."

"Well, don't worry about it if you can't. I have several guys on the base who have offered to help keep my little red Corvette running right. I have been driving this thing since I got out of college, you know. You don't want me to have to make a car payment, do you? In fact, my old boyfriend, the colonel, said he would take care of it, if I needed him to. I told him heck no.

I didn't need him to do it since I have a new boyfriend and he would know how. I was just sure you guys could save me from getting a ticket for driving around at night with a headlight out." With that, she smiled sweetly and let herself back into the house with a finger wave and a wink.

"What color panties does she have on, Unk?" Wiley's ball cap was on slightly crooked, and he had a wad of chewing tobacco in his mouth, which made him appear to have a puffy cheek.

"What makes you think she has panties on, nephew?"

"You killing me." He spit a long stream of brown juice outward away from the car and wiped off his chin with the back of his hand.

"I have to get these headlamps changed out. Do you have any ideas for me, or what? Quit talking about my girlfriend's knickers and put some brain power on this subject for a minute."

"Best thing I can come up with is let me go over next door and get Tiberius. He loves doing this kind of shit. I can't help you, Unk. If you need a door busted open or someone arrested, I can help. If you need a horse broke or ridden, I am your man. Helping fix a car? No skills. I can't help you. Besides that, I am worn out from all that riding last night."

"Well, go get Tiberius then. Must run in the family; after watching two videos on it, I am not sure I can do it either. I am exhausted from last night, too, and taking care of her needs this morning on top of it. I can't even concentrate right now."

Wiley nodded, slowly acknowledging the fatigue, and walked slowly across the front yard and almost made it to his property line when the vertically challenged Tiberius rounded the corner with his bag of tools in hand.

"Hi, Wiley!" he exclaimed. "Looked like you guys might need some help. Brother Tiberius, at your service."

"Hey, Tiberius. I was just coming to ask if you would help

out. You know how to change out the headlight bulbs on this Corvette here? One of them is burned out, and the owner wants both the headlight bulbs changed."

"As an angel, I always do the bidding of those in need. Even though that is the vehicle of a fallen woman, I act as Jesus would and wash the feet of the unworthy. I am here to be a servant, including to those who have strayed from the path of righteousness, Brother Wiley. Tiberius, at your service." The short man made a slight bow and looked up at Wiley with his facial tic spasming, causing a slight winking action in one eye and a proud look of acknowledgment that he was needed.

Tiberius immediately swarmed over to the open hood of the car, nodded at Cody, and began talking to himself as he familiarized himself with the apparatus. Almost immediately, he recognized the device that manually cranked the headlights open and then spotted the method to unscrew the bulbs from the bracket by opening them up halfway. Within a couple of minutes, he had the first of the two bulbs unplugged and removed from the carriage bracket and had begun on the second.

Wiley entered the house and returned with the bag containing the new bulbs for the car. He set the bag down next to Tiberius and slapped him on the back. "Doing good here, Ty. Right man for the job. You need something to drink?"

"Well, yes, Wiley. As it turns out, I am rather parched. What do you have to offer a brother to drink?"

"Unfortunately, Ty, the only thing I have in the house to drink is cold beer. Terrible thing, I hate to admit it, but I haven't been to the grocery lately." Wiley looked over at Cody and winked.

"Only beer, eh? Cold?"

Yes, Tiberius. Nice cold ones. The kind that makes a righteous brother want more than one. Sometimes I get weak and drink three of four of them in a row."

"Well, now, Wiley, you know I wouldn't normally, but since I am so thirsty and that is all you can offer me, I don't want to offend your hospitality and I don't want to stay so dehydrated, so maybe I should have one. Yes, yes, I will have one and thanks so much for the kind offer." Tiberius looked at Cody in explanation and said, "I don't normally drink alcohol."

Cody sagely nodded his head in agreement, cleared his throat, and replied, "It's bad for a man. Makes him do things he wouldn't without it." He could not ever remember this much discussion over a beer before.

Tiberius studied Cody as if looking at him for the first time. "What church do you attend, Cody?"

Cody did not want to launch into a discussion of his religious belief or non-belief. He wanted this troubled little man to finish this job, however, and did not want to upset him. He didn't care to lie about his position, either, so he just took the path of avoidance.

"Not currently attending church regularly, Tiberius."

Tiberius looked up at him and surprised Cody with his response. "Me either. I got kicked out of my last church. They thought I was crazy, and they caught me drinking. I lost my driver's license due to DUI after that and they asked me not to come back. I am still an angel, though. I am going to open up my own church soon. I am working on it. I know it's in the Lord's plan for me."

"I am sure it is, Ty." Cody felt exhausted and just needed him to finish this chore so he could get back to sleep.

"Maybe you and Wiley and I should get together sometime and read some scriptures and have a Bible study."

"Yeah, maybe. I will talk to Wiley about it." Cody was happy to change the subject. Wiley came out with three frosty longnecks that he had opened and handed one each to the others. Wiley and

Cody took moderate swigs of their beers and watched in amaze-ment as Tiberius completely guzzled the entire bottle without stopping. After finishing, he wiped his mouth and immediately started working on the remaining lightbulb without comment.

"You want another one, Ty? You must have been really thirsty, man." Wiley looked over at Cody with amusement.

"Yes. I was thirsty. Very thirsty. Doing the Lord's work makes a servant thirsty." He would not look up at either of the two men and was completely focused on his task.

"I will get another one, then." Wiley set his beer down and returned to the house for another beer.

With practiced precision, Tiberius completed the installation of the other bulb and tightened all the screws holding it into the bracket. He was picking up his tools when Wiley returned with the additional beer.

"Here you go, dude. You made that look easy, Ty! Right guy for the job."

"Those headlights should be adjusted. You will need to get the car in front of a wall and turn the lights on and then use these two screws on the top and side of each bulb to adjust them. I am sure you guys can handle that. For right now, just turn the lights on and let's make sure they work."

Cody went over to the low-slung car and looked inside for the light switch. After a few seconds, he located it and turned them on. They rotated and clanked open, and Cody could see the left light shining on Tiberius's wide body.

"Are they both working?" he asked.

"Yep," Wiley confirmed. "Try the bright lights."

Cody pulled the turn signal stalk backward and got the thumbs-up from Wiley, confirming that the bright lights illumi-nated. He turned the light switch off. The headlights properly ro-tated back to their hidden position with a slight clunking sound.

With that, the three men looked at each other as if uncertain the task was completed.

Tiberius held up his beer bottle in mock toast to his companions and promptly guzzled two-thirds of the beer in one greedy swig. He pursed his lips and held the bottle up for inspection as if looking at his first bottle of beer. "That's a good drink," he said.

"Mighty kind of you to help us out on this task, Ty. We were a little stuck until you came along. You really were an angel for us on this project. Thanks a lot, my friend. You need a beer for the road?"

"Tiberius at your service, Wiley. I do the Lord's work whenever I can, as you know. Your uncle and I were discussing holding a Bible study earlier when you were in the house. I think we should start with John 8:24—unless you believe that I am who I claim to be, you will die in your sins." He looked upward at his two tall companions from his low center of gravity. His facial tic was causing a slight quiver of his cheek jowl and a flutter of one of his eyelids.

Cody and Wiley looked at each other with uncertainty over the Bible study proposition. As they were each contemplating a response, a gray four-door sedan slowly began easing into the driveway and parked close to the road.

"Who is this, nephew?" Cody asked tersely.

Wiley ejected another long stream of brown juice from his mouth. "Not sure. Looks like a cop car, though. It's not a normal cruiser, but I can tell by the license plate that it's a government vehicle."

Tiberius immediately began walking briskly toward his house with his tool bag without saying a word. He had dropped the empty beer bottle at the front of the vehicle and was walking away at maximum velocity.

The man emerged from the driver's side of the car without

turning off the car engine. He strolled over to the Corvette in unhurried fashion. "Morning, gentlemen." He surveyed the scene casually and stared at Wiley.

"Morning, Sheriff Edwards. What brings you out here?"

"You are Wiley, aren't you? We met out at the shooting range during the SWAT team's competition, right? You are on the Light Horse force if I remember correctly." Wiley affirmatively nodded and the sheriff continued. "You are Shane Harris's boy, aren't you?"

"Is this a recruiting call, Sheriff?" Cody immediately didn't like the smug attitude the sheriff assumed. "What can we do for you?"

"Who are you?"

"I am Wiley's uncle. Like I asked already, how can we help you?"

"I have a report of an attack on a local citizen last night and a stolen firearm. You two know anything about that?"

Wiley and Cody looked at each other, and Wiley gave a slight indication that he wanted to take the lead on responding to the questions.

"No attack occurred, and no firearm was stolen, Sheriff. My uncle and I just inherited some vacant property through a court action that concluded yesterday. Last night, we were visiting the property to discuss our future plans for the place that we now co-own, and we were accosted by three armed men on four-wheelers. They were questioning us about what we were doing and trying to stop us from peacefully departing our property. My uncle here stopped one of the men from drawing down on us and disarmed him. We took the firearm for our own safety. All legal and well within our right to defend ourselves from armed attackers on our own property. I have the court order inside and the firearm in my truck if you would like to see them."

"Yes. Let me have a look at that court order."

Wiley went inside to retrieve the court order and the sheriff looked at Cody. "You the one driving that white truck with the Florida tag? Why are you parking it in the garage?" He pointed over to the open garage.

"Yep. That is mine. It's a new truck; my nephew offered me the garage to keep the hail off of it last night."

The sheriff silently nodded and seemed to accept that explanation. "I understand you guys were on horseback last night. Is that right?" The sheriff had pulled out a small notebook and was writing down the license plate number on Cody's truck.

Wiley returned with his folder containing the paperwork and pulled out the order that they picked up from their attorney signed by the judge at the end of the hearing.

The sheriff perused the order and confirmed the judge's signature. He jotted down the case number of the document and looked at Cody. "You are Cody Houston of this address in this document? You have identification?"

Cody nodded and fished his pocket wallet out of his front pocket. He pulled out the driver's license and handed it over to the sheriff.

After comparing the name and address on the license to the document, the sheriff wrote down Cody's driver's license number and returned it to him. He turned and looked at Wiley and asked, "Your last name is Harris?"

"Yep."

"Need some phone numbers from you guys then, and I need to pick up that firearm. I will return it to the owner."

Wiley recited his phone number to the sheriff and went to his truck to retrieve the firearm that Cody had taken from Randal.

"So, how about you, Florida? Phone number?"

Cody recited his phone number and bit his tongue to refrain

from further comment. It was all he could do to keep from letting the sheriff know how transparent his actions were. The simple fact that the sheriff himself was investigating the incident rather than assigning it to an officer for follow-up revealed an unusual interest in the case.

"You fellows stay safe. I recommend that you stay away from those guys for a few days to let things die down. They are pretty stirred up right now." He accepted the firearm offered by Wiley and slowly strode back to the sedan that he had left running. Cody noticed that the dash camera of the car was focused right where all the discussion was held, and that the entire interaction had been recorded. He was glad that he let Wiley take the lead answering the sheriff on what they were doing.

"I think maybe you ought to tell those clowns to stay the hell off of our property, Sheriff." Wiley's face turned red as he finally let loose.

"I will pass that on. I will be watching you guys. Keep things between the lines out there, Officer. Be a shame to work as hard as you did to gain title to that place and then wind up kicked off the force and out of work." He slapped the open palm of his hand with the small pocket notebook and slipped it back into his shirt pocket before trudging back to his cruiser.

Cody and Wiley looked at each other and remained silent until the sheriff departed. As Cody secured the Corvette, he removed the keys from the ignition after raising the windows and closed the driver's door. As they walked toward the house, Lisa opened the screen door and looked at them both with obvious alarm on her face.

"What was that all about?" she asked while staring at Cody.

Cody decided to level with her. "While we were out last night at the property, we encountered some guys that live in the neighborhood, and we had a little altercation. We took a firearm from one of the guys to keep things from going to a bad place, and the sheriff came to ask us some questions about it and get the firearm to return to the guy we took it from."

"Jeez, welcome to the neighborhood! Nobody got hurt?"

"Nobody got badly hurt." Cody thought it best to keep things vague at the moment. "Don't worry about it. Everything is under control. Nothing bad happened." He draped his arm over her and walked her back inside the house. That seemed to relax her and put her back in her normal chirpy mood.

Wiley changed the subject. "That Tiberius sure hightailed it when the PoPo came around, didn't he? I never have seen him move that fast." All three of them laughed at the comical way Tiberius slinked out of the picture when the police showed up.

Lisa followed Cody into the bedroom they were sharing and leaned against the door frame while he peeled his shirt off and prepared to shower and shave for the day. She had texted him during the night while he had been out searching for Doris, and he had encouraged her to come over if she could get away since he was leaving tomorrow. She had appeared early in the morning after driving over from the base.

"So, thanks for fixing the headlights for me. I love that old car. I have been through the wringer with that girl. She has never let me down, either."

"You keep it in nice condition, for sure. I don't think I told you, but when my dad died I inherited his 1969 Shelby GT 500. I keep it at home in Florida. When you come out there, I will take you for a ride in it. Since you are such a car person and all, you might enjoy it."

"Well, finally! A little personal information, and confirmation that you want me to come and visit you." Lisa patted him on the back and made a strange face. "This is my shocked face. Look closely. I have my trip all set up to come out there in five days.

You know, when you fly a two-hundred-million-dollar govern-ment plane around for night flight training, they ask a few ques-tions, and they have to make sure that they have support staff, fuel, and parts on hand for it before they let you fly it somewhere. Takes a bit to get all that worked out. Thank goodness you are finally saying something that gives me an indication that I am invited. I went to a lot of work to set that trip up without even having a real invitation."

Cody looked at her with a bewildered look on his face. "Did I miss a turn somewhere? A minute ago, we were talking about our cars and what a good guy I was for getting your headlights replaced."

Lisa looked at him and shook her head slowly. "You are going to be a project, dude. Don't you worry about it, though. Captain Combs will have you flying in formation soon." She patted his chest and gave him a sweet smile.

Wiley walked up to the open door, witnessed the exchange be-tween the two, and stared blankly at Lisa. "You have any friends like you? You know, who like to cook breakfast in their panties?"

Cody shook his head and looked at Lisa. "It's hard to soar like an eagle when you are surrounded by turkeys. The man is ob-sessed with seeing you in your panties the other morning. Sorry about that."

"Hey! Hey! I am not being all weird about it or anything. I just liked it. I would like to get a girlfriend who makes me break-fast in her panties. Like you always say, Unk, doesn't make me a bad person or anything. A guy likes a little egg sandwich served up by a hottie in panties, and suddenly it's a big deal. Last time I checked, there isn't anything illegal about that." Wiley stretched his neck out indignantly as he muttered to himself and slightly shook his head from side to side for emphasis.

Cody reached down and took Lisa by the hand. "We are going

to turn in and get a little nap. Catch up with you when we wake up, nephew."

"Well, before you guys have what you think is quiet sex that I am not supposed to hear while you are taking your *nap*, there is something you might want to hear about first." Wiley used two fingers on each hand to make mock quotation marks when he said *nap*.

"Lay it on me, nephew. What you got?"

"Dad and Doris picked up her kids and her parents, and they all took off this morning for a little getaway down to Dallas to take the kids to Six Flags. They are following your advice and getting out of town for a few days to let things cool down. Doris quit her job and might sell her house too. She is really spooked but happy to be with Dad, and she said to tell you thanks for helping her get out of there. Dad told me to tell you thanks too. He sounds really happy. I am going to be looking after the horses for him while he is out of town. I need to get over there later today and make sure they are all fed and watered, and I need to groom the three we rode last night. They are going to look for a place to stay out of town for the next couple of months. Doris withdrew her kids from school."

"Those are some good horses your dad has. Well trained and beautiful. Lisa and I will come with you when you head over there if you want. I am sure she would like to see them."

"Yeah, that sounds good. Would love to do that, Wiley. Don't leave without us." Lisa seemed genuinely interested in seeing the horses she had heard about.

"Sounds good. You kids get your *nap* now. Chocolate milk when you wake up." Wiley smiled as he pulled the door to the bedroom closed.

# CHAPTER XIX

Wiley sat down at the kitchen table in his blue uniform with a steaming cup of coffee. He blew on the black liquid and then sipped a small dose of the beverage. He nodded his head in approval and set the cup down.

"Good cup of coffee." Wiley looked at his uncle and began examining the leftovers on his breakfast plate.

"Lisa made it. I can't take credit." Cody looked up from his phone at his nephew in anticipation of some remark about what she was wearing when she made breakfast. When no commentary was forthcoming, he added, "She made you a plate and left it in the oven."

Wiley nodded and retrieved the plate from the oven. He snatched the coffeepot and topped off Cody's cup before sitting down again. He began wolfing down the large serving of scrambled eggs and bacon and lifted up the envelope that he found on the table. "This for me?" he asked.

"Has your name on it," Cody responded.

Wiley opened it and read the brief thank-you message Lisa had scribbled before leaving to return to the base earlier that morning.

"That Lisa is a sweet lady. I can't believe I let her get away from me. I was talking to her first, you know. How the hell did she wind up with you?"

Cody looked up again. "I am sure she just felt sorry for me, nephew. Don't take it too personal."

"Well, you know she is more my age than she is your age. Just saying." Wiley smiled smugly as he needled his uncle.

Cody casually leaned back in his chair and stretched his long legs out. He was dreading the long drive back home but was looking forward to returning to his life there. On the other hand, he felt glad to have come to get acquainted with Wiley and his life here. He would enjoy returning when the last of the title paperwork was finished on their inheritance property. He had no idea what to do with it, but he knew Wiley had ideas and he was eager to learn more about those. He looked over at Wiley in his policeman's uniform with his holster, radio, and badge. He wondered what Wiley would think if he knew all the things that Uncle Cody had done in his life. He secretly smiled at the irony.

"I have enjoyed coming out here, Wiley. Thanks for putting me up and showing me around. I look forward to coming back when the paperwork gets finished."

"Me too, Unk. Won't be long now. I will bird dog it and make sure it happens."

"So, what is the update on your dad and Doris? I heard you talking to him last night. Did you tell him what I said?"

"Yes, sir. I told him. For the first time in my life, my father is taking my advice. He is doing exactly what you and I are telling him to do. He and Doris have rented a cabin at Lake Texoma for a couple of months. They will stay out there until things cool down, and they will keep a low profile. I will keep the horses fed for Dad until he gets back and keep his place together the best I can in between working and getting the court paperwork details finalized on our place."

"You told them to make sure they didn't tell anybody where they were staying, right?"

"I did, Unk. Doris' parents have left on an extended RV trip, and they won't be able to be found either."

"Good." Cody nodded slowly and looked directly at Wiley. "That makes you the only loose end here."

"What do you mean, Uncle? You think I can't take care of myself? Those misfits try and mess with me, they will regret it. I learned a few things in the Army, too, you know. I am a peace officer with a badge. I have a full police force and my SWAT team ready to back me up if I need them. I will do a Chickasaw stomp dance on those dimwits if they come after me."

"They would have their hands full if they made the mistake of coming after you. I know that for a fact. I was glad to have you for my wingman when we ran them off our land the other night. The problem is not that you can't handle it. The problem is that these hillbillies aren't smart enough to know when to stop."

Wiley patted the nine-millimeter semi-auto pistol holstered on his side. "I will keep this on me at all times. If they are coming for me, they better bring all they got."

Cody liked his bravado. "You got a security alarm on this place, Wiley?"

"Yes. Never thought I would need one, but being a police officer it's a good idea. It's always seemed pretty safe to me. Plus, I got Tiberius, the human security alarm living next door. That dude watches everything in this neighborhood."

They both chuckled about Tiberius. "Last time I saw Tiberius, he was running so fast I thought he was going to blow his tennis shoe out." Cody slapped his leg in laughter remembering the comical sight of Tiberius dropping his beer bottle and literally running home when the sheriff stopped by.

After the laughter died down, Cody continued. "Seriously, nephew, be careful around here. We kicked over a hornets' nest the other night, and they aren't going to just forget about it. I know a few things about guys like Randal. When they get embarrassed like we embarrassed him in front of his men, they have to do something to reclaim their aura of leadership over their little clan of clowns. His clown show is all he has, and he doesn't want to lose it. This would be a great time for you to upgrade your security system, and I will pay for it. You need to have some more security cameras and a system that you can monitor your place with when you aren't here. A system that notifies you if anyone trips the system when it's armed and allows you to see any one of your cameras at any time through your phone."

"Thanks for the offer, Uncle Cody. Actually, the Light Horse will pick up the cost of a new security system for me. They do that for all their officers for their home security needs. I just never felt like I needed it; I thought the one I had was good enough. Now that I do, I will check it out."

"Well, last thing, then. Make sure you keep that sidearm on you all the time. Don't let them catch you unarmed. I would ask your sergeant for some drive-by patrols too. I wouldn't expect much from the sheriff as you know, but maybe the Chickasaw police chief would be willing to send a patrol occasionally, also."

"Mother Cody! You are smothering me, Unk! I am a grown-ass man here. I got this. You get in your truck and get on back to Florida. Here is Doris's phone number. She and Dad are expecting your call sometime this afternoon. Dad said he would text you the number of the guy that Randal works with from Kansas City, just like you asked for. Doris copied it down from his phone a few weeks ago. Some guy named Lucas. She doesn't think Randal knows that she has it."

"Good. Like I said, I will call them this afternoon from the road. I need to get a little more background on this guy Lucas. I am looking for something that we can use against Randal in case we need something."

"You need any help loading up?"

"Nope, all set. I got it all packed up and loaded before you came into the kitchen. I am ready to roll."

"I am ready too. First day back at work. Kind of looking

forward to getting back into the salt mine. Miss those crazy people." He smiled slightly as he locked the door to his house and walked his uncle to his truck. They turned and looked at each other.

"You drive safe, Unk."

"Will do. You remember everything I told you."

"I do. I will keep you posted."

The two men exchanged an awkward bro hug, and Wiley trudged off toward his truck. He looked back as he opened the car door and waved at Cody when he pulled out onto the street. Cody waved back and smiled. *Kind of nice to have some family to worry about,* he thought.

# CHAPTER XX

The woman knocked on the partially open door before entering. The smell of the hospital was familiar. She had spent six years working there before migrating over to her father's small family practice, where she currently worked. After receiving notification from the hospital that their practice's patient had been admitted for serious injuries, she knew that she had to visit him. He was a high school classmate, after all, and she doubted that he would get many other visitors. She was uncertain about his family situation, and she felt an obligation to look in on him, both as a patient of her father's practice and as a classmate.

His condition was not good. She had gotten the downlow on his admission from a nurse she knew. He had a broken jaw and fractured skull, several broken ribs, and other broken bones. His face was severely beaten and swollen, and he could not talk well. He was sleeping restlessly as she looked at him fondly. The television was playing loudly, and a large standup fan was blowing air over him.

He had been dropped off at the emergency room entrance in a state of semi-consciousness. He had been found at the entrance by an ambulance crew bringing in another patient. It had taken several days for the hospital to get all the information needed to fully check him in. The full story about how his injuries happened had not been revealed yet. The sheriff had been notified about his condition, but no deputy had come and checked on him nor taken a statement from him yet to evaluate for a crime.

She remembered him fondly as a large, friendly, kind soul.

Many of her classmates did not know what to think of him. He was mentally slow, and he had not graduated with his classmates because he had been held back in high school. He took special education classes, and she had lost touch with him as she progressed on in school. She had always treated him nicely, however, and she considered him a friend even if she did not see him often the last few years of high school.

She saw him turning his head and noticed the breathing rhythm begin to change. He was waking up from his nap. She reached over to take the television remote control and turn down the volume.

She leaned over to look closely at him. "Ricky, it's me, Lucy. You remember me from high school? It's your friend Lucy Simpson, Ricky. Are you awake?"

She continued to talk sweetly to him and gently stroked his chest and arm. He seemed startled when he awoke and found her leaning over him. He made some moaning noises that signaled that he recognized her. One eye was not bandaged, and she saw that he was staring at her. He attempted to speak, but she was not able to make out his words. He made a motion at the nightstand and patted the palm of his hand. She noticed his phone on the stand and retrieved it for him. He held up a finger as if to ask her to wait as he turned the phone on. While he waited for the phone to power up, she saw a tear stream from his eye and she wiped it away with a tissue and a kind word.

"I was so worried about you when I heard, Ricky. How are you feeling today? Are they treating you well here? Is there anything I can do for you?"

Ricky clumsily pushed buttons to get to the screen he wanted her to see and then held it up for her to read.

"Wiley Policeman," she read. "Wiley? You mean our classmate, Wiley Harris?"

He nodded in agreement.

"You want me to call Wiley and have him come and visit you? Is that what you want?"

Again, Ricky vigorously nodded his head and attempted to mumble.

"Okay. Let me see that phone so I can get the number. Good Lord, I haven't seen or heard from Wiley since he was in the Army. I heard he was back, but I haven't seen him in forever."

She input the number into her phone and looked kindly down at her friend. "Okay, Ricky. I will call Wiley today and ask him to stop over and see you." She held his big hand and felt a wave of emotion. "You take care, Ricky. I will see you again soon. I am going to have my dad stop by and check in on you, okay? Daddy will make sure you are getting everything you need. I will stop by and see you again soon, too."

She bent over and kissed his bandaged head and gave his hand a pat as she waved goodbye. Ricky nodded his head and then closed his eye. Another tear streamed from his eye, and she carefully wiped it away from his cheek before she left. She could not fathom how anybody could want to injure a sweet soul like Ricky Hunter. Her defensive instincts were aroused, and she wanted to do more to help.

As she approached the nurse's station on his floor, she caught up with her friend and chatted with her about his case. She received assurance that her friend was looking out for him and that she would call right away if his condition changed. When she left the hospital she saw a comfortable-looking bench in some shade and sat down to initiate a call to Wiley. He answered on the second ring.

"Officer Harris."

"Wiley, it's Lucy Simpson from high school. How are you?" She could not help but laugh. It seemed like ages since she had talked with him.

"Lucy! Well, I'll be. I was just asking about you the other day. I heard you were still in the area. I never see you around, though. You doing all right?"

"I am good. I am a nurse now and working for my dad in his practice. I understand that you are a police officer now and working on the Chickasaw force? Katheryn gave me an update on you not long ago."

"Yeah, after I got out of the Army, I tried a couple of different things and then joined the force. It's going pretty well; I like what I do. Keeps me out of trouble. Are you still dating Jack? You guys married yet?"

"No, Jack and I broke up a year ago. He left the area. He decided he wanted to live out in California, and he just took off. I have not talked to him in six months. He wound up moving to Silicone Valley and is out there working. He is engaged already, from what I hear. We were together since high school and all through college. He just didn't want to stay in Oklahoma, and I didn't want to leave. We never were going to be able to work that out. Ten years together and he barely said goodbye when he left me."

"Sorry to hear that, Lucy. I always thought you guys would make it and be together forever. I wasn't that close to him, but he always seemed like a good guy that treated you right."

"He was. I don't have any complaints. We just wanted different things. He did an internship in college out in Silicon Valley, and he could never stop thinking about living out there after that. It was the only place he ever wanted to go for vacations. He worked in Oklahoma City for years and he lived in Norman, so we were able to see each other a lot, but in the end, he went where he needed to go, and I stayed here."

"Well, let's get together and get caught up on everything. I am living outside of Tishomingo now, and I work out of Ada Precinct."

"That would be really nice, Wiley. I would love to catch up with you. I need to tell you something, though."

"Okay. Tell me."

"You remember Ricky Hunter from school?"

Wiley froze in silence. He instantly suspected the worst-case news and was hesitant in his response. "What about him?"

"He was severely injured, and he is in the hospital. Looks like he might have been beaten badly. I just left him at the hospital, and he asked me to reach out to you and ask if you would come and see him."

"Where is he?"

"Mercy Hospital in Tishomingo. I will text you the room number if you want it."

"Please do. I will get over there after my shift and check on him. Anything he needs?"

"I think he is okay for now. Wiley, there is just one thing."

"What is that?"

"He is in really bad shape. He is not able to talk right now. You cannot make out what he is saying. It's almost impossible to understand him. His jaw is broken, and his head is bandaged. Someone really beat him up bad."

After a pause, Wiley replied, "I will make sure I get over there this evening. Thanks for letting me know, Lucy. Appreciate you reaching out to me. I will save your number and reach out to you soon."

They hung up on the call, and Lucy recalled the interactions she had with Wiley over the years. She had always dated her boyfriend, Jack, in high school, and never interacted much with other guys from her high school class. She had left for college shortly after school, and her sole memory of Wiley after was a time when he was on leave from the Army, and she encountered him in town. They had a pleasant exchange and she remembered thinking how tall and buff he was. He had not been so nicely put together in high school. She always liked clean-shaven, conservative men, and he had definitely cleaned up his act since the last time she had seen him. She found herself hoping she would see him again soon.

# CHAPTER XXI

The Cobra Jet 428 motor in the 1969 Shelby GT-500 roared to life with just a few rapid revolutions of the starter motor. The deep rumble of the powerful V-8 engine filled the garage with its lilting energy as the car trembled and vibrated. Obviously, the trickle charger was doing its job maintaining the battery in running order, Cody thought to himself. The crisp baritone of the exhaust barked out the rear of the car. Cody waited a moment for the Holley four-barrel carburetor choke to open and the RPM of the engine to slow before slipping the car into reverse. Once the choke opened, he eased the old street fighter out of the garage backward until he could reverse direction and drive forward down his driveway to the street. The car rolled out smartly as if eager for drive time, and Cody depressed the clutch to slow the approach to the street slightly.

Turning onto the asphalt street, Cody depressed the accelerator harshly to unleash some of the pent-up power from the 400-horsepower drive train and slightly broke the rear tires loose with a smooth shift to second and full-on acceleration after the shift. The old girl felt feisty today, he noted to himself with a smile. The tires rolled out their flat spots within a few blocks, and the exhaust rumble sounded on key. He did a brief check of pressures and temperature of critical fluids reflected in the gauges to confirm everything was sound. The car was mechanically completely original and had its original Gulf Stream Aqua color plan with the gold-colored GT-500 striping accents and white leather interior. It featured an interior roll bar and bucket front seats with safety harness seat belt system. It was a beautiful, classic muscle car that offered head-of-the-class performance for its generation, and the car had many admirers any time he took it out for a drive. Indeed, the car was more than a match for many of the modern performance cars in both handling and acceleration. It was a powerful, high adrenaline drive every time he took it out.

Cody was on his way to meet his best friend, Dillon Luther, for lunch. The long trip back from Oklahoma had required a day off the road for rest, reorganization, and recovery, but he was eager for some seat time in the Shelby and glad to have an opportunity to catch up with Dillon for lunch. He was consciously making more of an effort to spend time with Dillon lately, and his suggestion to meet for lunch on a workday was warmly accepted immediately. He was glad to get the Shelby out for a run and then bring her home for a quick wash down to remove the inevitable dust buildup on the shiny paint. Cody pulled the Shelby into the parking lot of the sports bar that Dillon had suggested close to his office. They had met there numerous times before, and Dillon was well known by the waitstaff since he ate there several times a week. Cody parked next to his friend's minivan and walked into the place.

He scanned the interior and found Dillon perched at the bar watching television with an iced tea in front of him. The television screen was playing a fishing show highlighting fly-fishing technique for saltwater species. Two men on a flats boat were working a mangrove forest, searching for redfish and snook and expertly flipping a fly out to the mangrove branches and slowly retrieving the line repeatedly. They made the casting look elegant and effortless. Dillon looked at Cody with disdain as he approached.

"Now, do you really think this is as easy as they make it look? I would like to learn how to do this, but damn, I see nothing but fouled line and frustration trying to fish in a location like that."

He held out his fist for a bump as Cody took the stool next to him.

"Fly-fishing is probably not for a couple of old meat-eaters like us, Dil. Too much skill involved," Cody replied.

The two men shared a laugh as the bartender approached. Cody glanced over at the beer tap to see what was offered. He looked over at Dillon and asked, "Join me in a beer?"

"Well now, Captain. Normally I would not. But if you are going to insist, I might have one of those beers. I understand it is a good drink."

Cody shook his head and ordered two beers for them and two menus from the bartender. The bartender returned with the beers and menus. Dillon ordered a grouper sandwich without opening the menu. Cody ordered the same thing, and they clinked glasses.

"Good to see you during the week, Dil. We need to do this more often, dude."

"Well, as soon as they smell this beer on my breath at work, I might have a lot more time to hang out with you, Cody. Of course, me and my family will have to move in with you at your house because I will not have a job anymore, but, hey, I know that isn't a problem. Right?"

"You mean you aren't running things at the Space Center? One little beer. You are such a drama queen. Did you get Laura on board yet about the motorcycle?" Cody knew the answer to the question but felt obliged to ask to needle his friend. He turned to look at him with his eyebrows arched as if expecting an answer. "At least if you move in, you will be close to your motorcycle."

"So how was the drive back, amigo? Two days? Took you two days, I guess. Where did you lay over?" Dillon ignored his own question. "How are the butterfly and hummingbird plants doing? Do you need me to send Jennifer over to check things out?"

Cody looked at his watch in mock astonishment. "Gee, Dil, I

can't believe it took two whole minutes for you to bring that up. A world record for restraint."

"So, tell me about this new lady friend, Code. You grieved so long about Jennifer; I was getting worried about you. At least this new woman can be comfortable knowing that you are emotionally completely over your last relationship since you gave it, like, five minutes before you started banging somebody new."

Cody pulled out his phone and pulled up a selfie he took of himself with Lisa and showed it to Dillon. "Captain Lisa Combs, US Air Force. C-17 Globemaster pilot. Getting out of the Air Force soon."

Dillon let out a minor burp and waved at the bartender for a refill on his beer. He looked at Cody in mock seriousness and asked, "Is she moving in with us too? Going to be a full house with me, my two sons, Laura, Lisa, and you. You might need a bigger place. How is my nephew Wiley? You know he keeps calling me Uncle Dillon every time we talk on the phone. You tell him to do that?"

Cody finally broke a smile as the two old friends took turns busting on each other in mock seriousness. "Wiley is good. Once the paperwork gets worked out on the land we inherited, I will head back out there again."

"When are we going to meet this flower?" Dillon asked, while pointing at the picture still displaying on Cody's phone.

"She is coming in for a quick visit in three days. She is scheduled to fly into Patrick Air Force Base, and she will stay with me for a couple of days before she returns to Altus. That is why I called you for lunch. I wanted to see if you and Laura might want to meet up for dinner while she is here."

"Sure. Let me see that picture again. I did not realize this was so serious. I don't usually get to meet these ladies until you are about to break up with them."

Cody showed the photo to Dillon again as their food showed up. He retracted the phone and pulled up a couple of pictures that Lisa had sent him of herself, including one in her dress uniform. He handed the phone to Dillon while he arranged his fries.

"Nice. She has some set of wheels, dude. How do you get all these women interested in your unhappy, moody ass? You are not even nice to them. How does that work? I am happy all the time and nice to people too. Not even my wife likes me, much less a woman that looks like that. Pass the salt." Dillon handed the phone back to Cody.

"I don't really like you either." Both men smiled at Cody's dig.

"So, Wiley told me you had a little altercation with some of the locals in Oklahomastan. I heard the sheriff came and did a little interview. Didn't take long for you to become popular, did it?"

"Wiley's dad's ex-girlfriend got herself involved with some questionable characters. They were essentially holding the woman captive, and Wiley got a call from somebody that she had gotten loose and was trying to get away. We went out and helped her get home. The guy she was seeing, and a couple of his misfits tried to stop Wiley and me from leaving and were trying to hold an interrogation. We had a discussion and got it resolved."

"Ha! Discussion? I heard you and Wiley got dressed up in your cowboy hats and dusters and went all Tombstone on the guy, gutted him in the solar plexus, and then bashed the back of his head three times with the butt of a rifle." Dillon looked in disbelief at Cody. He could not imagine how his friend could try to dismiss a confrontation like that.

"We were being accosted by these guys on our own property, Dil. We weren't looking for trouble." Cody shook his head slowly. "I am worried about Wiley, though. His dad is staying out of town now for a few months with this woman to protect her from those guys, and Wiley is there alone. He could become a target for these idiots. Where he lives and the property that we inherited are all in the jurisdiction of the sheriff who is in the pocket of the guys we had it out with. I think the sheriff is bad news there and can't be relied on. I don't think he would protect Wiley if those guys came after him."

"Well, Wiley is a cop, isn't he? Can't he get some help from his guys if there is a problem?"

"I think he probably can. I hope he asks for some help if he needs it. I am afraid I might have set him up and then left him behind as a target."

"He's a tough guy. I don't think you need to worry about him. He can take care of himself."

Both men went quiet and turned their attention to the fishing show again and worked on their fried grouper sandwiches.

# CHAPTER XXII

Lucy set the steaming Styrofoam cup of coffee in front of Wiley. She noticed how uncomfortable he looked, crammed into the smallish metal chair and table. She could not help but giggle as she sat down next to him.

"What are you laughing about?" Wiley smiled as he looked her in the eyes. It had been a number of years since they had seen each other, but she still had the same sweet smile and demeanor that he remembered from high school, and she had maintained her trim figure.

"I had forgotten how tall you are now. You really grew after high school, both in height and weight. The Army training must have helped with that, didn't it? These little chairs and tables they keep in this cafeteria aren't made for guys like you. Sorry about the Styrofoam cups too. You would think a hospital would make a healthier choice for their employees and visitors. You know, I used to work here before I went to work for my dad in his practice. All those connections I have here is why I can get this wonderful free coffee in Styrofoam."

Wiley smiled about her concern over the Styrofoam cups. "The last time we saw each other, you told me you were working here. I am sure it is a lot better working for your dad."

"Yeah, I enjoy working for Daddy, but I miss my friends from work here and it gets a little isolating. Small town, small practice, you know what I mean. You get tired of knowing everything about everybody all the time!" She lit up with a laugh about the last comment and beamed her friendly smile at him. "So, tell me how long you have been on the police force?"

"I didn't really know what I wanted to do when I got out of the Army. I hung around a bit, not doing much, and then found out that the Chickasaw Police Force was forming a SWAT team. It sounded a whole lot like what I already knew how to do, so I applied, got accepted, and made it onto the SWAT team. I work out of Ada Precinct, but I cover mostly the area around Tishomingo. We all take turns going down to cover the casino and hotel property down in Thackerville at the border as needed. I enjoy it."

"Have you stayed in touch with Ricky? I know you were always his protector in high school. He worships you; you know."

"Yeah, I see him from time to time, but he started hanging with Randal and that group of misfits he attracts, and I lost touch with him. Saw him again recently at 'Ole Red and, unfortunately, I had been drinking a bit that night and wasn't able to catch up with him real well at the end of the night when we saw each other. My uncle had me drinking whiskey that night and I got a little over served. I am usually just a beer guy. Ricky helped me get in the car. That is the last time I saw him. I hate seeing him so busted up like he is now. He is the nicest guy in the world and would never hurt anybody. I don't know why anybody would do that to him."

"I hate seeing him so down. My friend Charlene here at the hospital called me to tell me he was here. She said they called the sheriff to let him know that he has obviously been attacked and a police report should be filed, but the sheriff has not come around to get his statement, from what she told me."

Wiley looked at her fiercely. "You mean to tell me that no deputy has come to take a statement from him even though the hospital called them? Has his mother been alerted?"

"I tried to ask Ricky if he had talked to his mother, and it seemed to me that he did not want me to tell her he was in the hospital. He seemed scared when I mentioned it, but he wasn't able to talk yet, so I didn't know what he was trying to tell me."

"When do you think he is going to be released?"

"I heard they were going to release him tomorrow or the next day. He seems like he is better now, and he is starting to talk again. It is still hard to understand him though."

"He is a strong kid, always was. I know he will heal fine and be just as good as new soon, but he needs to stay away from Randal and those guys. I think I have a little insight on why this might have happened. Let me do some research on things, and when I confirm it, I will share it with you." Wiley looked at Lucy as if he was seeing her for the first time. "Why don't you have dinner with me sometime?"

"You want to get everybody in town talking about us, do you?" Lucy giggled again.

"Well, I could take you out of town to Norman or you could come to my house. Your choice. That way we keep the backchat down in T-town."

"I have a better idea. Why don't you come to my place and I will make you the house specialty."

"Sounds nice. Not that it matters, but what is the house specialty?"

"Best spaghetti and meatballs you have ever had."

"Not that I was going to say no if I did not like what you were going to serve, but I happen to like spaghetti and meatballs. I am down. When is this happening and what can I bring?"

"You can't bring anything. Friday or Saturday night. Your pick: I am open."

"I say Friday, then. You going to text me your address?"

"Yes. I don't live with Mom and Dad anymore. I don't live far away, though. They helped me buy a house in their neighborhood."

"Well, must be a nice home if it's in their neighborhood. Looking forward to Friday. Let's go look in on Ricky and see if he is still sleeping."

They walked down the hallway to Ricky's room and looked inside. The television was blasting as usual, and Ricky was still sleeping soundly. Lucy went up to him and rubbed his arm gently. He responded slightly but did not wake up.

Wiley noted that some of his bandages had been removed and that some of the swelling had gone down in his face. He looked better, and Wiley was encouraged that the hospital was releasing him soon. Wiley could not help being concerned about where his friend was going to stay when he was released, however.

Wiley looked at Lucy cautiously. "I may have to bring him home to stay with me until he gets better. He isn't going to have a place to go to when he gets out. He can't live alone, and I know he won't want to go live with his mom. She is worried enough about him, and she is not in good condition herself."

Lucy shook her head slowly. "You are a good friend to him, Wiley. He is lucky to have you." She had worried about the same thing. There were only a few people in the world who could take Ricky on in their home. Wiley knew that, and he was prepared to step up and make his home available, if needed. She really admired that.

"I might have to bring him over for spaghetti Friday night." Wiley smiled sheepishly. That was not how he drew the evening up when they first planned it.

"You know he is welcome to come. I will make it up to you the next time you come over." She stepped over to him, put her arms around his neck, and pulled his head down for a steamy kiss. "You are a good man, Wiley Harris."

Wiley was surprised by her reaction, but he thoroughly enjoyed it. *Apparently, being a good guy works out sometimes,* he thought.

# CHAPTER XXIII

Sheriff Clay Edwards pulled into the old, dilapidated car wash stall and got out of the car. He occasionally met with Randal at this location to avoid attention from members of the community. Randal was not highly thought of in town by most of the citizens, and the sheriff could not afford to be seen talking with him frequently. He didn't want a record of numerous phone calls to Randal, nor did he want to be observed over at Randal's "compound" frequently either. They had developed a ruse where they both went to the car wash at the same time occasionally to provide cover for a short discussion. It also provided the opportunity for Randal to hand over the cash payments that he made to the sheriff in order to keep the law out of his affairs.

Edwards went over to the change machine and cashed in a couple of bills to provide quarters for a quick rinse of his cruiser. Just as he was switching over from the wash to the rinse, Randal pulled up in his new, tricked-out, four-wheel-drive truck. It was a flashy new addition that drew attention to him and caused people to ask how a man with no visible means of employment and income could afford such an expensive vehicle. Randal casually opened the passenger car door to the cruiser and tossed in a thick envelope with their customary fee enclosed. Randal sauntered over to the sheriff and steeled himself for what he knew would be a tense conversation.

"You are messing up, Randal. I have a lot of people asking me when I am going to start an investigation about the attack on Ricky Hunter. You hurt that kid bad, and I am going to have to look into it. His mother has called me, a couple of the nurses are bugging me about it, and I have this Chickasaw police officer, Wiley Harris, who is up my ass about it. I can't provide cover for you on everything, dude. You lose your temper like that again and I won't be able to help you."

"That Wiley guy is the same one who was with that dude who hit me in the head with the butt of that rifle. You remember that, don't you? Why aren't you arresting him for attacking me?"

"You run up and threaten him on his own land when he isn't doing anything wrong and get your ass beat, I can't protect you from that, either. You better stop being stupid, or your world is going to change fast," the sheriff hissed harshly at close range.

Randal threw his hands up. "All right, all right! Just help me find Doris. I need her back for this job in California. I need your help to find her."

The sheriff pointed the sprayer toward the ground and moved his face to within a few inches of Randal's. "You listen to me. I am not helping you with anything. You want to find that girl, you find her. What makes you think she would do anything to help you even if you did find her? She ran away in a bad thunderstorm with no car. Looks like she wanted to get away from you pretty badly."

"What are you doing to earn this money I keep paying you? Everything I have is on the line with these California jobs. You have to help me find her. I can reason with her if you help me locate her. I can get her back on the team."

"I am not promising anything. Like I told you, if I hear something , I will call you. Haven't seen or heard anything yet. You need to look on your own." The sheriff pulled a chamois out of the trunk of his car and began wiping down the windows of his vehicle.

Randal went over and began rinsing down his vehicle, running down different potential responses in his head. He was rapidly running out of time, and it was making him desperate. He needed a female to help him work out his plan. It couldn't be just anybody. It had to be someone he could manipulate and intimidate into doing what he needed without fear of them turning on him. He had Doris perfectly set up until she got away from him. He roughly twisted the knob on the controller and slammed the spray handle back into its tube. He spun up some gravel from the wash bay as he made his way back onto the road.

He was going to have to switch to harsher methods to cause Doris to come back to him. He could not find her or her new boyfriend that she was hiding out with, couldn't find her parents, couldn't find her kids, so maybe he just had to work with what he could find that she cared about. That had to be Wiley Harris. Since he was out looking for her in the rain, there had to be some connection between them. If he had Wiley hostage, maybe Wiley's father would bring Doris to him to save his son. It was all he had to work with.

He pulled into the liquor store parking lot and turned off the key to his truck. He stretched his arms behind his head as he forcefully struck the steering wheel with both hands. He had to do something, and he had to do it fast. Time was not on his side. He felt the back of his head to see how it was mending. He refused to wear a bandage on the wound, and it had opened up a few times and started bleeding. He saw blood on his hands and swore angrily. Another reason to get even with the bastards who had taken Doris.

Suddenly, his phone started ringing. He stared at the display on his dash and angrily pushed the button on the steering wheel to answer.

"This is Randal."

"Randal, it's Lucas. Checking in on you, cowboy. How you

doing on those assignments?"

"Come on, man. Two calls in three days? You got to give me some time here, Lucas. I have guys in California and a guy in Ohio. We are scouting and working on different ideas based on what we learn about these people. I don't have any new plans to submit to you yet on any of the assignments. I will call you once we have something to present."

"Listen closely. We had an agreed-upon time frame, and you have presented a plan on the first assignment that we approved. Your girlfriend was your accomplice, and she was going to get the guy to take her out on the boat. What happened to that plan?"

"Working on getting it together. My girlfriend is not cooperating now, and I am working on getting her back on board the plan. Just give me a little time, dude."

"We gave you time. You need to be in California overseeing this one, Randal. You need to get your woman under control and make this happen for us. If you don't, the boys in K.C. aren't going to be happy with you. They are going to want me to give those assignments to somebody else. You understand?"

"I hear you, Lucas. Now back the hell up and let me do my job." Randal was spewing saliva in anger when he responded.

"Next phone call on the subject isn't going to be so pleasant. I didn't get this job by being a pushover, Randal. Remember that. You aren't the baddest dude at this barbeque."

"So now you are threatening me?"

"Warning you. Get on it. Make it happen the way you talked about."

The phone clicked and went silent. Randal got out of his truck and went into the store to buy supplies. He wondered how things had gotten off track so quickly. Just a few weeks ago he had everything going the way he planned. He was getting tired of everybody pushing him around.

# CHAPTER XXIV

**C**ody made the turn into the parking lot of the Tiki Hut bar next to Patrick Air Force Base. Lisa had insisted that he meet the two other members of her crew, her co-pilot and her loadmaster. The two airmen had rented a car and were planning on spending their time in the area while Lisa spent her time off with Cody at his home. She had arranged to meet him at the bar so he could meet her "boys" as she referred to them, and they could meet him for their approval. She explained that they were protective of her and were curious about this new man in her life who could cause her to orchestrate this "training" trip so suddenly. She had managed to pick up some cargo in Alabama for transport down to Patrick to give the trip additional validity and avoid command suspicion. The gear pickup had gone well, and the plane landed at Patrick on schedule, based on her text to him. As he parked, he texted her to let her know that he was there.

Cody found himself anticipating her arrival. He had carefully scrubbed his home top to bottom, mowed the yard and trimmed his hedges, washed his car and cleaned the inside carefully, and changed sheets and towels throughout the house to prepare. He had stopped to buy a single red rose to lay in the front seat of the Shelby for her. He was approaching the saturation point of his romantic capabilities. He carefully ironed his jeans and pulled out his favorite heavily starched, dry-cleaned, button-down, long-sleeved shirt. He carefully selected his favorite casual dress shoes and matching belt. He wanted to look nice, but not like he was overworking it. He was satisfied that he had done just enough so she would notice and be happy he made an effort. He had not invited that many people to his place in the past. Women coming over happened from time to time, but usually not with this much planning involved. He laughed to himself.

Entering the premises of the open-air section of the bar, he located an available table that would offer a good view of the entry area and provide nice shade from the late afternoon sun. He settled in and was quickly greeted by a server who took his drink order. Knowing it was likely to be a long night, Cody decided to go with a beer for now. Just as the server was returning with his frosty brew, Lisa and two men rounded the corner in their flight jumpsuits, with Lisa pulling a rolling suitcase. He stood up and waved and Lisa broke into a large grin, walked over, and embraced Cody in a quick hug before turning to address her two companions.

"This is Cody. Cody, this is Elliott and Jacob. Jacob is my co-pilot and Elliott is my loadmaster."

Cody shook hands with both men, and they all sat down. The server had alertly noted their arrival and made short work of their drink orders. Cody inquired about the flight and got a summary from each of them regarding their part of the flight. The summary from each was brief and very military in format with no sensationalism. From what he could tell, everything went according to plan with no drama. Apparently, they were a tight, experienced crew.

Cody recognized the co-pilot, Jacob. "I saw you at Ole Red the night I met Lisa, didn't I?"

"That was me. Elliott was there too, but he was surrounded by ladies, as usual. Lisa tells us that you were in the Navy."

"Yes, I was. A long time ago."

The waitress arrived with their drinks, and Cody swiftly offered a toast in an effort to change the subject.

"Here is to the Air Force and you three guys. Lisa tells me that you are the best C-17 crew in the force." They clinked their glasses, heartily agreed with the assertion, and made an impressive dent in their beers.

"What are you guys planning to do while you are here for the next few days?" Cody asked.

"Well, Elliott wants to go down to the naked beach at Playa Linda and look for women. We are booked on an airboat ride down in Kissimmee, and I need to go to Disney and buy a couple of things for my kids, so they don't disown me when I get back. Two daughters, five and seven years old, and they want to go to Disney so badly. My wife let me know I am going to have to scout some things out for them and bring them for a vacation when we can work it out."

"Well now, this is the first I have heard about the nude beach. How did you guys hear about this?" Lisa made a mock judgmental face to Cody as if in disbelief that Elliott would be interested in a nude beach. "Do you know anything about a naked beach, Cody?"

"Haven't visited this Playa Linda beach myself, but the scouting reports I have gotten on it indicate that there are very few racehorses on the track there, if you know what I mean, Elliott. Hope you aren't disappointed. Just a lot of old people who really should keep their clothes on, from what I hear." Cody couldn't help but laugh at the idea of Elliott's interest in the well-known local nudist beach on Canaveral Sea Shore.

"I don't want to hear any complaining about sunburnt tackle on the return flight, boys. You better make sure you put some sunscreen on the pale areas, if you know what I mean. You have been warned!" Lisa smiled sweetly at the two "boys." It was clear she cared about them, but enjoyed busting on them at the same time. They seemed to have a good rapport.

"Well, I am planning on meeting some of the local talent out tonight at Coconuts to make sure I have someone to apply the sunscreen to the pale areas, if you know what I mean, Boss Lady. I asked Jacob if he would do it for me, and he turned me down. Relying on the compassion of the local civilians to keep my pale areas safe from overexposure." Elliott finished his declaration with a mock smile at Lisa.

"Okay, you two are grown-ass men. Nothing worse than getting sunburned on your first day of vacation, that is all I am saying. Not trying to get into your business while you are here, but I need both of you ready to fly back in a few days, and you know what I always say. Flight comes first. Show up ready and be a professional when it comes time to take off. I expect nothing less than your best and I will always give you my best. That is what has made us the best crew in the force. Remember?"

"Don't worry about us, Boss Lady. We will take good care of our pale areas." Jacob gave a mock salute and then looked directly at Cody. "And what are your plans for tonight and the next few days?"

"Making dinner at home tonight. I figured the Boss Lady might be a little tired after the flight. Might make up a pitcher of sangria to go with it and take it easy. Probably sit around and talk about you guys most of the night." Cody didn't want to share too much information about the expectations both he and Lisa had made clear for each other concerning the plans for the evening. He didn't anticipate much talking and definitely none about her flight crew. "Don't worry, I will take good care of her, and I will make sure we don't go to the naked beach at the same time you guys go."

"Yeah, we don't need Boss Lady checking our pale areas for lotion. Keep her away from the beach tomorrow." Jacob remarked in a dry tone.

"What is on the menu?" Lisa inquired.

"Paella de Marisco, Cody style. Not classical Spanish, but tasty and wildly acclaimed in certain small circles."

"Crowd pleaser! Sounds like the go-to panty dropper to me, Jacob. What do you think?" Elliott stared at Jacob with a weird expression on his face.

"Sounds like Cody is going nuclear. Critical mass, to be exact. You breaking out the Eagles concert DVD also? That always works for me. Nothing but belt buckles hitting the floor. I cook up my renowned go-to recipe of beef, rice, and red wine with the Eagles and that is certified 100 percent lethal. Never been a woman yet that could resist."

"All right, all right. Enough. Enough. I will see you two comedians in a couple of days. Just for the record, Cody doesn't need a 'panty dropper.' We already have all that figured out. Thanks for the concern, though. You guys can just keep your secret recipes to yourself." Lisa stood up and looked at Cody. "This is only going to get worse from here. and it's a good time for us to leave. These two guys get going on something. and they won't leave it alone."

Cody smiled at the two men. "Good meeting you guys. Enjoy your stay here and use plenty of sunscreen. Sun is strong here. SPF fifty or better." He gave them a thumbs-up as he stood up and grabbed Lisa by the hand. She gathered her rolling suitcase and put her arm around his waist and they walked out.

Cody leaned down to give Lisa a proper kiss when they got to the parking lot. "Good to see you, Boss Lady."

"Don't call me Boss Lady! That bullshit started about two years ago when Elliott showed up, and now everybody on the base calls me that. It makes me sound like I am some kind of prison guard or something. I have guys trying to change my call sign to that now."

"Well, what is your call sign? You haven't told me that yet," Cody asked.

"It's stupid. I didn't get a cool name or anything. They named me Fine Tooth. You know, as in fine-tooth comb for my name, Lisa Combs."

"I think I would just go with Boss Lady. Sounds more badass."

"Well, speaking of badass, is this your car? The Shelby GT-500 you inherited from your dad?" They walked up to the beautiful car.

"This is it. I just had some body work done on it, and the whole thing got repainted. It turned out nice. This is a perfect match for the original color, though."

Cody put her bag in the trunk and started the motor. She smiled as she picked up the rose in the front seat and gave Cody a big kiss on the lips after she seated herself. Lisa approved enthusiastically when he revved the mighty engine up. She pulled the seat belt harness down from the roll bar and buckled herself in.

"This car is awesome. Look at that, an eight-track tape player. What are you playing in there?" She pulled the tape out and looked at it. "Creedence Clearwater Revival! What are you, a refugee from the seventies?" She laughed and replaced the tape. "Where did you get that tape?"

"My buddy Dillon found a case of tapes that he bought for five bucks at a garage sale."

"Now that is about a dozen times I have heard you talk about Dillon. Am I going to meet this guy while I am down here?"

"Yep. He is going riding with us in a couple of days, and we are having dinner at his house."

"Good. I look forward to meeting him. Look forward to the ride too. I haven't been on a motorcycle in a long time. Where are we going?"

"DeLeon Springs. They have a little breakfast joint there

where they bring the batter to your table, and you make your own pancakes on a griddle at your booth. It's a fun place. We will head over to Daytona later and do the Loop and head back home along the beach road. The night before, we will be going over to Dillon's house for dinner so you can meet his wife, Laura. Got a few touristy things planned for the next two days, though."

"That sounds really nice. Don't think you have to book us up for every minute, Cody. I am just ready for a little downtime with you. I have been really stressed about leaving the Air Force, and I could just use some normal, everyday time to chill and relax. Thanks for inviting me over and putting me up. This is a big decision for me, and I need to make sure that I do the right thing here. I have sent some resumes out to the airlines, and I am getting a lot of strong responses and interest from them. I don't know if you have heard, but there is a pilot shortage. The Air Force is offering me an incentive to re-up too. For the last six years, the Air Force has been my life. I am just trying to sort things out for myself to see if it will be my future or not."

Cody considered what she said to him before he responded. Out of character, he reflected on his own experience leaving the Navy and decided to share his past.

"I had a harder transition leaving the Navy than I did when I went in. It can seem confusing as you are considering options. I recommend that you try not to overthink it and just go with what your gut tells you. Your instincts will be right most of the time. I think you are fortunate because you have two good options. There probably is not just one right choice in your situation. You listen to your inner voice, decide, and then go make the best of it. The same things that made you a good pilot and good officer in the Air Force will make you a good pilot in the commercial world too. I think you just need to recognize the lifestyle issues associated with either choice and be ready for what comes with each.

I would not let your colonel ex-boyfriend affect your decision. The truth is, when you complete your assignment where you are stationed now, he won't have any real influence over your career any longer. I would not let what he says or does drive your choice either way about staying in the Air Force or leaving if you want to leave. Even though it is a small community in the C-17 flight world within the Air Force, the Air Force is a big organization. It is a lot bigger than one colonel. Either way you choose to go, you are going to be fine."

The car was purring along happily in third gear at low RPM as they made the turn onto the road to Cody's home. Lisa smiled contentedly at Cody and rubbed his shoulder.

"That is the longest you have ever talked to me. Thanks for opening up a little bit and sharing those thoughts. I knew that was in you and I knew that I could trust what you said to me when you decided to talk to me. I have a lot of people giving me advice, but I don't trust them because it always seems like they have their own agenda and just want to get in my business. I appreciate that you did not suggest that I do one thing or the other. Too many people are telling me what to do; I think you hit the nail on the head when you said that I need to listen to my own internal voice. I feel better and more relaxed already. Thank you." She sat up on her knee and kissed him sweetly on his cheek and whispered in his ear. "I am looking forward to my paella dinner tonight, but I don't want to eat until about midnight. I have other things I need first. I hope you don't mind if we flip the schedule."

"Flexibility is one of my strong suits." Cody smiled at her. He turned the car into the driveway and pushed the button to open the garage door. The door opened and revealed his truck and the two motorcycles in his garage.

"So, you have two motorcycles?" she asked.

"No, Dillon doesn't have room in his garage, so he keeps his motorcycle here at my house. His is the blue one."

"Oh, I see. I knew a guy once that left his bike over at his friend's house because his wife did not know that he owned a motorcycle."

Women's intuition always amazed him. Cody looked at Lisa without responding. He closed the trunk to the car and embraced her as they walked together into his house. He was glad to have her here with him tonight.

They crossed the yard to the back door of Cody's well-kept, mission-style, single-story home and immediately swept through the house, illuminating the rooms and placing her luggage in the master bedroom. Cody was an old, solo dog. He struggled sleeping through the night with his lady friends in his bed. He frequently found himself unable to sleep and was either forced to move to another bedroom or lie awake all night while his partner was fast asleep. Years of maintaining emotional distance and connection with people to protect them from retribution directed at him, plus his normal light sleeping habits due to the dangerous, violent lifestyle of conflict and confrontation, combined to make it difficult to sleep with a partner in bed. He found sleeping with a partner the most emotionally intimate act of being involved with another, and it was when he was the most vulnerable.

Normally, he warned his lady friends in advance about his idiosyncrasies in this area to prevent misunderstanding and hard feelings, but he had purposefully not chosen to discuss his issue with Lisa. He wanted to prove to himself that he was capable and did not want to create the issue if he could avoid it. She deserved a man who could connect with her, be there for her emotional needs, and be a guardian and protector for her. He did not want to run from normalcy any longer. He was tired of the violent dreams and fears of his past haunting him. He wanted to wholly connect with a woman and be available and reliable emotionally as well as physically. He had walked a long trail of solitude and emotional isolation with many violent nightmares of past victims haunting his nights and robbing his sleep. His internal self was counseling him to embrace this challenge and trust this soul who seemed to need him at this moment. He was the man of the moment. He needed to rise to the call. He felt he could and wanted to try. Things had gone well so far, and she had no need to know of the past struggles that she would never be able to understand.

He smiled at Lisa as she started the shower and slipped out of her flight suit. The paella dinner was not likely to happen from the way things looked at this moment. Midnight pizza delivery was more probable...

# CHAPTER XXV

Wiley pulled mightily at the jumbled clump of vines and plants with his gloved hands. Armed with a pair of lopping shears, machete, and flat shovel, he was dismantling the overgrowth surrounding the house. He made slight progress with each pull, and the roots finally gave way; he fell back slightly from the effort and then shook the roots sideways to knock off dirt back into the depression created from the removed roots. He tossed the vegetation into the pile he was creating and stood up to wipe the sweat off his brow. It was hard work clearing the overgrowth from the old estate. He studied the poor condition of the farmhouse carefully as the siding became more visible after removal of the vines and vegetation covering it. He was reluctantly beginning to arrive at the conclusion that the old frame house was beyond saving and needed to be demolished rather than renovated.

Wiley turned when the mower ran behind him toward the front of the house. Tiberius was operating his zero-turn mower to cut down overgrowth in the open areas around the trees and brush and to open more walking paths to improve accessibility of the property. He looked up to see Lucy's car pulling into the driveway. Tiberius had evidently seen her driving up from the backyard, and he sped out to meet the vehicle. He had really connected the previous day with Ricky when Lucy brought him out to see the place and the clearing that Wiley was doing. He obviously wanted to come back out again and see them. It surprised Wiley that he was so willing to come back to the farmhouse, which was so close to Randal's compound, where he had been beaten badly after Doris escaped. It was hard to know exactly what Ricky did and did not understand.

Wiley dropped his tools, grabbed his sweat towel for a quick wipe, and then strode out to greet Lucy and Ricky. Tiberius dismounted from his mower to greet Ricky. The difference in height between the two of them was striking, with Tiberius barely breaking five feet in height compared to Ricky's broad, six-foot, five-inch frame. Ricky had always been a happy, gentle giant with impressive strength and size but limited coordination and slow movement. He still had the bandages on a portion of his head, but he no longer had his arm trussed, and the bruises on his face were healing rapidly. He broke into a beaming smile when he saw Wiley and began shuffling toward him to greet him with an impressive hug. Wiley gave him a gentle backslap and affectionate hug and walked him back toward Lucy, standing next to the car with his arm around him. Ricky was one of the few people he knew who was larger than he was.

"My turn, now?" Lucy asked as the two approached her.

Wiley walked up to her and pecked her on the cheek. "Thanks for bringing Ricky out again."

"Is that it? All that driving for a peck on the cheek? You can't do any better than that after the way you were kissing me last night? You nearly sucked the tongue out of my mouth, hot stuff."

"I am just all sweaty, dirty, and I stink, babe. You don't want to get too close to me right now. I will make it up later if you want."

"I do want. I want you to come over and take me for my milkshake at the Sonic you promised me last night. You do remember that, don't you?"

Ricky suddenly lit up and began transferring weight between his feet and swaying back and forth and swinging his arms. "Chocolate milkshake at the Sonic. That is my favorite. My faaavorite."

"You want to come with us, Ricky? Go to Sonic tonight and get milkshakes?" Wiley looked at Lucy to see if she objected, and her pleasant smile gave him all the feedback he needed. She was an easy-to-please, accommodating person and liked taking care of and being with people. She had grown close to Ricky as he healed, and she was going out of her way daily to see him and check on his progress. She had gotten her father to go over and check on him at his mother's house. While he had been in the hospital, she had seen to it that he got the best medical attention that Ricky had ever received. His mother was pleased at the attention he was getting and the friendship that was evolving with Lucy and Wiley and her son. Wiley had also made an effort to check in with Ricky both on the phone and in person as his patrol schedule allowed.

Tiberius approached the group. "Yes, the hamburgers at the Sonic are excellent and the milkshakes are wonderful. I enjoy them also. This angel is hungry. I haven't been able to go to the Sonic since I lost my license."

Wiley laughed out loud at this unlikely group of companions he had. "Well then, it looks like it is settled. I am buying everybody dinner at the Sonic tonight. Burgers and milkshakes for everybody on me."

Lucy excitedly clapped her hands and looked at both Tiberius and Ricky. "You see how easy that was, guys? I knew we could talk him into it." She bent him down to her level and kissed his cheek and whispered in his ear. "You are a good guy, and that is what I like about you. Just make sure you save me some alone time after we eat." She looked him in the eye and winked seductively and touched his nose with her finger.

"Yeah, well, you are going to have to drive because I can't fit this many in my truck. You going to come over and pick me and Tiberius up?"

"Inviting me over to the house, are you? You sure about this?

Big step, you know."

"You already know where I live from what I have told you about it. I will try and behave myself when you are there. I am a gentleman." He winked back at her.

"Come over here and talk to me for a minute before I leave." She grabbed him by the hand and they walked together toward the front porch of the old house. Wiley pointed to a shady spot, and they walked over and she looked up at him.

"Ricky's momma says that she still has not heard from the sheriff on the attack. Nobody ever came to the hospital, and nobody has contacted her from the sheriff's office about filing a report and making an investigation of the attack."

"Did you ask Ricky about it? Did anybody come and visit him while he was in the hospital that we don't know about?"

"I asked him, and he said no, but he doesn't really want to talk about it. I think you need to talk to him and ask him. If he says no, maybe you need to take him down to the sheriff's office and help him file a complaint, don't you think? They can't just ignore an awful attack like that on this sweet boy. Look at him. He is so excited about getting a burger and milkshake tonight. That is all he cares about. He adores you and thinks you are some kind of hero. He was so happy to come out here today." She smiled sweetly at him and paused briefly before saying, "I can't believe I never really thought about you when we were in high school. You are so damn cute. You need to stop teasing me like this; I am thinking about you way too much."

"I will talk to him. And I will stop in and talk to the sheriff again too. This is not right. There needs to be some charges filed on Randal. He can't get away with beating people like that. Give me a couple of days, and I will work up something. You leaving Ricky here with me?"

"Yes. I have to go home and get ready for my big date." She moved in again for a quick kiss, and Wiley willingly obliged her.

"All right. I will take him home with me while I get ready, and we will drop him off at his house after dinner in your car. I didn't mean to have everybody crowd in on our milkshake date. Sorry about that. It just kind of happened."

"Don't worry about it. It will be fun. I will see you at your place in a little bit. You are leaving from here and feeding your dad's horses before you go home?"

"Yes, we will wrap up here now, stop by Dad's place, and take care of things there, and then I need about thirty minutes to get cleaned up. About an hour and a half will do it. That will make it around seven if that works for you. Thanks for bringing Ricky out. I think it does him good to get out some, by the way."

"I think it does help him. He talked the whole way out here. He loves Tiberius. Those two are a pair, aren't they?"

"A good pair, but slightly unusual." Wiley chuckled as he opened the car door for her. "See you in a bit." He turned and looked at the two staring at him.

"Let's get out of here, Tiberius. You leaving your mower here or are we taking it back with us?"

"No, we can leave it here, Wiley. The work I am doing tomorrow I can do with my push mower."

"Okay, then. Put it up and I will pull the truck around. We have to go take care of my dad's horses on the way home. You want to go take care of some horses, Ricky?"

Ricky caught up to him as he headed toward his truck in his flat-footed, halting half run. "Yeah, take care of horses. Horses."

Wiley smiled at his friend as they walked and put his arm around his shoulders. He couldn't imagine how anybody could ever want to hurt somebody as likeable and friendly as Ricky. It was a sorry indictment of an individual to have committed that act, in his opinion. He wasn't exactly sure what to do about it to make it right. But he knew he had to do something.

# CHAPTER XXVI

**S**heriff Clay Edwards pulled the desk drawer open again to check the Wild Turkey bottles for any residual liquid that he could pour into his coffee. It was the second check of the same bottles in hopes that he might have overlooked some during the first search. He grunted in realization that all four of the "handles" of Wild Turkey were dry. Being a sheriff in a small town made it hard to purchase the volume of liquor that he needed to feed his appetite. He normally relied on his administrative assistant to buy his liquor and bring it into the office after hours, but she was away from the office for a week on medical leave. He carefully considered which of his deputies he could call on to purchase a bottle for him. He looked at the duty roster, which had been laid on his desk, to see which of his deputies were working and picked up his phone to call one of his most trusted officers.

"Doug. Clay here."

"Hey, Clay. What's up?"

"Need you to stop by and get me some Fresca and meet me out by the cemetery to hand it off." He used the office code name for Wild Turkey.

The deputy did not make the immediate code word connection and paused before answering. "A little early for Fresca, isn't it, Clay? Liquor store doesn't open until ten. Can't do anything before that."

The sheriff leaned back in his chair and rubbed his temple. "Just handle this for me and let me know when you are headed to the cemetery."

"Gotcha, Clay. Before you hang up, couple of things. First, everything you gave me about that court case involving that Harris kid and the land checks out. He and his uncle did inherit the land. I checked with the judge's assistant, and she told me that the land is theirs subject to a restrictive covenant that the Bureau of Indian Affairs is in the process of removing. The paperwork has been filed with the Bureau and is in the process of signature circulation. As soon as that happens, the covenant will be removed from the title and will have no further effect. As of now, though, the property has already been deeded to them by court order, so the rest of it is just administrative detail. Second, you know that kid Ricky that got beaten so badly by your boy Randal? His mom and my mom go to church together. His mother has got my mom asking me when we are going to file a complaint and do an investigation on what happened there. I got my own mother up my ass on that case; we need to do something there, Clay. Mom tells me that people in the community are talking about it and wondering why we aren't investigating it and pressing charges."

"Quit asking me about that. I will take care of it. Call me when you got my Fresca in hand and do what I told you." The sheriff literally hissed his response at the deputy and breathed heavily into the phone. He was sick of hearing people ask about the attack on Ricky Hunter. *That kid had no sense, anyway, pissing Randal off like he did. What the hell did he expect from a wild ass like Randal? The guy had no control of himself. Wait till he hears that the guys that ran him off the land actually do own it.*

"Ten-four, Clay."

Sheriff Edwards closed his eyes and leaned back in his chair. He hated how dependent he had become on the alcohol to make him feel normal. Drinking had become an obsession for him. He was continually worried about having to go to places and meet with people who might be able to detect that he had been drinking. He almost never felt good any longer, and once he started drinking he had a difficult time stopping. In the mornings he felt so badly that the only thing he could do to make himself feel better was to start drinking again. It was becoming a recurring nightmare on a daily basis. If he wasn't drinking, then he was thinking about drinking and was a terrible grouch, and if he had been drinking, he didn't want anybody to know it, so he stayed to himself.

Combined with his drinking problem, the stress he felt over his relationship with Randal, and trouble at home with his wife, the pressure was getting unmanageable. *The chickenshit bribe money I get from Randal is nowhere near enough to make it worth this headache,* he thought. He found it hard to find a jumping-off point, however, and that just made him grumpier. He needed to find the offramp with this group and he needed to find it soon. Too many people were asking questions and beginning to get suspicious and watching him too closely. He didn't want the scrutiny. Just then he heard a knock on his office door.

"Sheriff, there is somebody here to see you. Light Horse Police Officer Wiley Harris. Want me to put him in the conference room?"

"No. Tell him I am busy, and I will call him this afternoon. I am not seeing anybody right now." He looked at his watch and calculated the time before the liquor store opened.

"You want me to get his phone number?"

Edwards raised his voice in responding. "I got his number from the last dozen times he tried to call me. Just send him away and tell him I will call him when I get a chance this afternoon. Tell him that people are telling me that Ricky is doing just fine and there isn't any problem. Guys get into arguments all the time. I don't have the manpower to investigate every little dispute in this town."

The receptionist returned to the front desk and cheerfully

looked at Wiley. "Sorry, sir. Sheriff is not seeing anybody right now. He said he will call you this afternoon."

Wiley looked at the lady and tried to hide his disgust. "I heard him. Please give him my card so he for sure has the number." He handed her a business card and turned to leave.

"I am sorry, Officer. Sheriff is going through a bad time right now." She leaned over and put her hand up to her cheek and whispered hoarsely. "His wife left him recently."

"Sorry to hear that. He still needs to do his job. Please have him call me. You tell him I am going to keep coming back until he sees me." Wiley nodded his head at the woman and walked out of the station.

The woman walked over to the office door again and knocked softly. "Sheriff?" she asked meekly.

"What now?" he barked in return.

"Just wanted to give you this card from Officer Wiley Harris; he wanted me to tell you that he will be coming back until he hears from you."

"I told you I have his number; I don't need the damn card."

"Okay. I will keep it at my desk just in case."

"You do that. Please close the door." Edwards glared at the woman as she backed out the doorway and gently closed the office door. He picked up his cell phone and dialed a stored number.

"Randal. Clay here. Research on the claim by Wiley Harris and his uncle on that old abandoned 160 acres came back, and his story checks out. They do own it. I can't do anything to them."

"Those fuckers bashed the back of my head in with a rifle butt. You can't do anything about it?"

"Not when you are threatening them and tried to hold them captive on their own land, I can't. Speaking of beating people, I am getting a lot of heat on that Ricky Hunter kid and his case. They want to file charges on you for beating his ass."

"I know you can fix it, Clay. Nobody gives a shit about that kid."

"That isn't what I am hearing, Randal. Next time you beat someone up, you are going to have to double my side of things. You get my drift? Not enough in this for me to keep protecting you for the stupid shit you do. Tired of it. Make sure you lay low for a while. I can't cover you on anything else for a while."

"Well, how about helping me find Doris? You could help me with that. All you have to do is tell me where she is. I don't need you to do anything else."

"Haven't heard anything about the woman. She left town and hasn't been seen. Her parents too."

Randal spat on the ground and growled, "You aren't any damn help."

"Never been my job to do your detective work. You remember what I said. Lay low and don't do anything stupid right now." He punched the button to disconnect the call and looked at his watch. *Might as well head to the cemetery a little early,* he thought.

# CHAPTER XXVII

Dillon flipped the pancakes with surprising agility and skill. The row of pancakes on the tabletop griddle were all sprinkled with a healthy covering of fresh blueberries. Cody and Lisa sat on the other side of the table and smiled as they watched Dillon expertly cook the large pancakes on a mid-table griddle supplied by the Old Spanish Sugar Mill restaurant in De Leon Springs for their "cook your own cakes" breakfast in the scenic State Park. It was a famous local haunt, opened in 1961, inside the park that offered a number of batters for pancakes utilizing different flour mixtures and a variety of different fruits and nut toppings for the pancakes, as well as breakfast meats and eggs cooked in the restaurant kitchen. The trio had ridden out on Cody and Dillon's motorcycles for an enjoyable bike ride and breakfast. Dillon had taken the day off work to accompany them solo.

"Geez, Dil. I did not know you were such a chef, dude. These pancakes are perfect," Cody remarked. Dillon was busily placing a substantial pat of butter on the cooked side of all the pancakes he just turned.

Without looking up from his focus on the pancakes, Dillon responded, "I am Pancake Dude at my house, Code. My boys want pancakes on the weekends, and they expect their Pops to deliver. We make some of the craziest pancakes you have ever seen sometimes! They crack me up with their little ideas. We put food coloring in and make red or green pancakes or pancakes with M&Ms. Pancake Dude delivers on the weekends. Personally, I like mine with chopped pecans and bananas."

Lisa chimed in, "Well, what a way to top off a three-day trip! First, airboat ride and Gatorland, then, fishing on your boat with dinner at your house last night and now, Pancake Dude is making us all pancakes for breakfast on our motorcycle ride. I honestly can't remember when I have had this much fun. I haven't been on a motorcycle in forever. You guys are safe riders; I appreciate that. Too bad your wife Laura couldn't come along, Pancake Dude." Cody winced when she said the last sentence. He knew Lisa was tweaking Dillon about not informing his wife about the motorcycle. He had to tell her about it to keep her from innocently mentioning it while they had dinner with Laura and Dillon at their house the night before.

Dillon surprised Cody with his response. "Yeah, well, the truth is, I haven't told her about it yet. She is not a fan of motorcycles. I got my license and that bike without telling her about it. Cody is kind enough to let me keep it at his house until I get the opening to let her know. She doesn't even know I am taking the day off from work. I just get so boxed in all the time. I am tired of being Minivan Man and Pancake Dude all the time. I need to do this for myself, but I don't want to upset her either. I think she would get upset and I don't want to upset her. Still working it out in my head. I will tell her soon."

"I get it. Some things you just have to do for yourself." She looked over at Cody and smiled. "Right, Cody?"

"Dillon is going to come clean soon enough. He just needs the right opening, that's all. I predict Laura will be coming along the next time we come here."

Dillon jumped at the chance to change the conversation. "So, what time do you fly out tonight? You said it had to be a night flight, correct?"

"It just has to be a night-time landing. My co-pilot needs another night landing to complete his training cycle so he can take over the plane when I leave the Air Force in a couple of months. We are making sure we have all of his training up to date before then so we can submit his application to transition to pilot before I am gone. We are planning on taking off around 18:00 hours, which will get us back to Altus late enough to qualify for a night landing without keeping us out too late. He is going to be flying left seat today and he is going to handle the whole flight as if he were senior pilot. Even though I am not flying left seat, I still have to be at the ready. That is why I can't join you guys in those mimosas, which look absolutely amazing, by the way. Maybe just a sip." She lifted Cody's champagne flute to her lips and took a small sip. "Hmmm…that fresh squeezed orange juice is amazing."

Cody smiled at the woman, and she snuck in a quick kiss on the lips and giggled like a schoolgirl. She had an infectious love of life and seemed to thoroughly enjoy everything they did together. Her stay at his house had gone very smoothly, and she was a pleasure to have around. He was sorry to have her leave so soon this evening, but knew that they would be spending more time together in the near future.

Dillon acted repulsed by the public display of affection between his friends. "You kids try and hold it down a little, will you? They are going to come over and make us leave if you don't. I just want to eat my breakfast before we get kicked out, if you don't mind."

Cody responded, "We will do our best, Dil."

Two servers approached with platters of eggs, biscuits, gravy, sausages, and bacon and left them on the table. Lisa quickly distributed the plates to their proper owners, and they all dug in with intense gusto on the food. The conversation died down rapidly as the food disappeared from their plates. Cody smothered his pancakes with maple syrup and munched on a crispy bacon slice he held in his hand. The sexual temperature had been high during Lisa's short stay at his house, and he had been working up an appetite keeping her satisfied. This breakfast was well-earned, and he felt soreness throughout his body as a reminder of her demanding appetite. All three of them were demolishing the tasty breakfast with enthusiasm and conversation was sparse.

Cody's cell phone rang as he pushed his plate toward the center of the table. He picked up the phone and looked to see who was calling. He looked at Dillon and said, "It's Ernie calling me back. He is going to want to say hello to you."

Cody pushed the button on the phone and spoke. "Hey, Ernie! Just sitting here with Dillon and my friend Lisa, finishing breakfast. We were talking about you earlier. Thanks for calling me back. Dillon wants to say hello first…here he is."

Dillon engaged in an enthusiastic conversation with Ernie over the breakfast menu and promised to come and see him in Texas with his family as soon as he could, before passing the phone back to Cody. Cody covered the mouthpiece with his hand and looked at Lisa. "Excuse me for a few minutes while I talk to Ernie. Be right back."

She smiled at him sweetly and said, "Of course, take your time, babe. I will just sit here and finish these pancakes. I will probably be five pounds heavier when you get back."

Cody picked up his coffee cup and carried it with him to a vacant table out of earshot and sat down with the chair back to his chest. "Ernie. Appreciate you calling me back. This will have to be brief but just have a quick question for you."

Ernie interrupted. "Before you ask, you've got to tell me how things are going with Lisa."

"She came out to spend a few days with me. We are having a real nice time together. She is flying out tonight, but I am pretty sure I will be seeing a lot more of her soon."

"Oh good!" Ernie replied. "Is she still planning on getting out of the Air Force?"

"That seems to be the plan now. You know how it is with the Air Force, though. They need pilots and they are probably going to throw a big bonus at her to keep her. Airlines seem interested in her also, though. She will make her own decision; I am trying to stay out of it as much as I can."

"What is on your mind, son? How can I help?"

"Just need a little advice on how to handle something, Ernie. We have a bad sheriff where Wiley and I inherited that property in Oklahoma. How would a guy report a sheriff that isn't doing his job and is on the take? Who would you talk to about it?"

"I imagine it would be either the attorney general of the state, or you would go to the FBI. Either way, I can probably help out a little. I will have my office contact the FBI and see what they say. I can get back to you tomorrow on that. We will get something set up for you."

"Thanks, Ernie. I will be heading back out to Oklahoma soon. I will make sure I coordinate with you so I can catch you in Texas when I do."

"That is nice, son. Get back to your breakfast and we can talk later."

"One thing, though, before you hang up, Ernie. Regarding the sheriff, I want to send him a strong message that we are breathing down his neck and people are watching him."

"Okay, son. That doesn't seem unreasonable. Let me see what we can do."

Cody returned to the table to find Lisa and Dillon in an intense, quiet conversation about how Lisa recommended that Dillon tell his wife about the motorcycle he had purchased.

Cody looked at his friend and nodded in agreement with Lisa. "You have to remember, Dillon, you are the number one person in her life and in your children's life. She is not just looking out for herself and for your safety, but for your children also."

"Code, getting a lecture about being safe from you is like getting a briefing from a NASCAR driver. Give me a personal break."

All three chuckled at the comment, and Cody stood up. "All right then. If you aren't going to listen to me, then let's get riding. Lisa needs to rest, clean up, and then pack before her flight this afternoon. I have to have her back at Patrick Air Force Base by five for her pre-flight."

Dillon looked at his watch and said, "Better get moving then. I can probably get to the office by one this afternoon and not take a full day of vacation." Cody swung a leg over his motorcycle and steadied the bike on the jiffy stand. He nodded to Lisa, who stepped up on the passenger floorboard and swung her leg over and sat down easily on the bike just as he had instructed her to do. Cody stood the bike up off the stand and started the motor and was quickly ready to ride out.

Dillon had watched how Lisa mounted the bike and nodded. "Okay, now I see it. That is easy. Can't wait to teach Laura how to load up like that." He started his machine and rode out briskly to catch up with Cody.

The two friends took their bikes for a lap around the Loop in Daytona, enjoying the riverside ride, and then split off as they hit the interstate. Cody headed west toward his place, and Dillon carried on south toward his home. He had decided that today was the day that he was going to come clean with Laura and tell her about getting the bike. No more keeping the bike at Cody's house. Lisa had convinced him that he needed to tell Laura, and she convinced him that his wife would be more understanding than he thought. When they split up and Cody went down the interstate ramp, he gave them a salute and a thumbs-up. He evidently planned on recovering his vehicle from Cody's house at a later time.

Cody rested his arm on his passenger's knee while he rode, and relaxed as the big Harley easily cruised the final few miles toward his house. He contemplated stopping to refuel on the way as he normally would, but decided to pass on it to give him more time with Lisa at home. She had a strict scheduled departure time with her crewmembers relying on her for their training completion, so he wanted to be supportive of her commitments. Nonetheless, it was going to be a few weeks before he could see her again, and he wanted to make sure that he sent her off with one last romp. In the rush to get up early that morning to greet Dillon, they hadn't had time for their normal morning wakeup routine. Cody had a plan in his mind to make up the oversight.

When they arrived at the house, it quickly became obvious that they were of like mind. She undressed and followed him into the shower, and they enjoyed a leisurely, mutual sensual wash and rinse with some passionate kissing under the steamy shower. They gently dried each other off, and then Cody embraced her, picking her up and carrying her into the bedroom. She placed her finger on his lips to stop him from engaging another fiery kiss and placed her small hand behind his head.

"Wait, wait. There is something I want to do before I leave. You have to let me do this."

Cody looked at her quizzically "What do you mean?" He was doing exactly what he wanted to do, and it seemed like it was what she wanted also.

"Just let me up and give me a minute. You are going to like it." She gave him a sweet kiss and pushed him off of her. She found her bag and pulled it into the bathroom and closed the door. Cody rolled over on his back and smiled; he was eager to get on with the first plan, but knew he had to let her do things her way.

She came out of the bathroom in a sexy teddy that amplified her naturally sexy figure, holding a candle and a jar of moisturizing cream. She set the candle down next to his side of the big bed and gently bent down to kiss him as he was looking up at her. She lit the candle on the nightstand and blew the match out, then sat down on the edge of the bed, looking at him.

"I have spent the last two years of my life in a relationship with a guy I worked for, and he was married to someone else. Every time we got together for sex, it was rushed or spur of the moment. I never had a chance to take my time and get clean and sexy and enjoy time with my man. I am not complaining in the least when I say this, but you are like a wild man every time we see each other, and I never get a chance to get the full, slow experience the way I want it. Before I leave, I want to take my time and give you a nice, slow massage, with a scented candle and some background music. I want to have a memory that I can relive during those times when I am alone in my lonely, institutional Air Force supplied housing unit."

With that, she stood, retrieved her phone, and began playing music that she had downloaded onto the device. She had recorded a playlist specially for the purpose of this moment. She motioned for Cody to roll over onto his stomach, and she straddled him with her knees bent at his midsection. Slowly and sensuously, she began massaging his back and shoulders in a gentle, soothing way with lotion from the jar. It had been a long time since anybody had touched Cody in that way. He was always like a heat-seeking missile whenever he got his pants off around a woman. He could understand her comment about him. He never took his time for sensuality and connection. Sex to him was an objective to accomplish, not a journey to be enjoyed. He made note that she needed this. He needed to pay attention. This fine lady had needs that only her special man could meet. He was that man; he would have to make an adjustment or two in this area to meet that need. More time, more connection, less fierce, high-intensity physicality. He closed his eyes and sighed heavily. He felt his breathing slow, and his stress level reduce.

The slow, gentle massage was relaxing and soothing. The combination of her gentle touch, the flickering light, the pleasing scent of the candle, and the music played at low volume was sensual and tranquilizing. She was in no hurry. She did not speak. She just lightly rubbed and caressed his back, neck, and shoulders over and over. He felt himself slipping into a relaxed fog of semi-consciousness, somewhere between sleeping and awake. The relaxation he felt was all-consuming, and he allowed himself to completely quiet his mind and take in the full moment. It was an amazing experience.

After an eternity, she bent over and kissed him on the side of his head. He smiled and reached up for her and pulled her downward to him for a passionate kiss. She willingly slipped into his embrace, and he rolled on top of her and gazed into her eyes without saying a word and began kissing her all over her body. He took his time and slowly explored her entire body with his lips. She was soft and sweet.

Their lovemaking session lasted a full hour and ended with him collapsed on top of her feeling completely drained and spent. He rolled to his side and pulled her backside to him for a full body spooning and felt her sigh in complete content. He picked his head up to look at her and saw that her eyes were shut, and a fulfilled smile was on her face. Without opening her eyes, she remarked, "I know I need to get moving, but I don't want to. I was going to make us some salads, because I really need to eat something now to be ready for my flight. It's important that I eat something healthy and easily digestible a couple of hours before I fly."

He thought about it for a minute before responding. "I will get up and make us a couple of salads with tuna while you rinse off and get packed. We have time for that. I will shower off again when I get home from dropping you off. We can make it work."

"That would be nice," she said as she reached around to stop him from getting up. "Just five more minutes, though. This is the most relaxed I have ever felt, and it is so nice. You rock my world, Cody, you rock my world. I don't want to leave."

He smiled to himself and laid his head down on the pillow. This woman was getting to him and working her way into his life. Having her around would suit him fine.

After a couple of minutes, Cody slipped out of the bed and turned the shower on for a quick rinse off. He left it running for her and kissed her gently as he toweled off. "Better get moving, babe. We are going to have to hustle to make it."

She smiled sweetly and stirred. He bent down and gave her another kiss and sauntered off to put together a couple of salads for them. As he was walking toward the kitchen, he picked up his cell phone from the Bombay chest by his front door and confirmed the time and checked for messages. He quickly emptied a tin of tuna each on a couple of bowls of spinach leaves, added some black olives and nuts, and then sprinkled both down with olive oil and red vinegar. He grabbed a couple of forks and made his way back to the bedroom with two salad bowls in hand.

Lisa had gotten up and was in the shower; he placed her salad on a nightstand next to the bed and blew out the candle. He had just filled his mouth with a full bite of salad when his phone rang. Lisa came out of the shower wrapped in a towel and sat down next to him to quickly work on hers.

"Hey, Wiley," Cody answered.

On the other end of the line, Cody heard some distressed breathing. "Cody. It's Tiberius. They got Wiley. They got Wiley."

"What do you mean they got Wiley?"

"We were coming home from working on your place, and some of Randal's guys must have followed us. I unloaded my mower and rode it home. While I was parking it, some guys drove up and pointed guns at Wiley, knocked him unconscious, and kidnapped him. They did not know I was watching. A guy walked up behind him and knocked him out and they put him in their truck bed. They were talking about leaving him in the old house you guys inherited and setting it on fire. I do not know what to do, Cody. What do I do?"

The world froze and stopped cold for Cody in that instant. He felt his insides completely tense up and his breathing got heavier. His hand holding the phone dropped to his leg and he stared at the wall. He could faintly hear Tiberius calling his name.

Lisa looked over at Cody in alarm. "Are you okay?" she asked.

Cody picked up the phone and put it to his ear again. "Tiberius. Keep this phone nearby and keep it turned on. Call you back." With that, he hung up his phone and looked at Lisa. She could tell from the look on his face that his demeanor had completely changed. With the flip of a switch, he had gone into warrior mode.

"Are you okay. Cody?" she asked again.

"Does your plane have a parachute for the loadmaster to wear when he opens the cargo doors in flight like they used to?"

She looked puzzled at the question and did not respond.

"Do they still make loadmasters wear parachutes when they open up cargo doors in flight like they used to?"

"Yes. We don't use it often, but there is a parachute on board for all of us in case we have to bail for some reason. The loadmaster is normally the only one who puts one on and usually only when he will be opening the door in flight."

Cody looked at her closely with steely eyes. "That was Tiberius who called me on Wiley's phone. The guys we had the disagreement with knocked Wiley unconscious and took him hostage. Tiberius overheard them say they are planning on putting him in the home tonight and setting the house on fire. I need you to fly me over Tishomingo and drop me on our house." Cody did not wait for a response. He immediately stood up and walked into his home office to fire up Google Earth to get the GPS coordinates for his house to allow Lisa to plot an approach for his drop.

Lisa was staggered by the suggestion. She could not respond. She got up and followed Cody into his office.

"You can't ask me to do this. This could put me in a lot of trouble."

Cody was sitting in his office chair waiting for the computer to initialize.

"More trouble than Wiley is in?" he asked.

Lisa put her face in her hands and shook her head. "No, not more than he is in."

Cody calmly looked at her. "Look at me and listen. Wiley is all I have. I am not going to let him get taken out without fighting for him. If you can't drop me, then I will start driving right now. It will take me eighteen hours, but if that is the best I can do, then that is the best I can do. I am going to do my best to help him, whatever that is. If you can't help me, then I can't see you anymore. I would never be able to get over it." He stared at her with all the intensity that he had.

"Cody, it's not just that I might get into trouble. I can't throw you out in the dark over some field in Oklahoma and hope you get down okay. It just doesn't work that way. I have to have a vector, knowledge of conditions, a target GPS coordinate, a selected altitude, and other information to make a drop plan for you. I can't take a chance that I am helping to kill the only man that I will ever want to be with. I would never be able to get over that.

I would rather lose you than be part of what hurts or potentially kills you. You can't ask me to do that."

"I'm asking. I'm begging." Cody stood up and put her face in his hands. "Please do this. Wiley doesn't have any other options."

Lisa's lower lip was quivering, and tears began flowing from the sides of her eyes. She embraced Cody with all of her might and looked up at him. "Show me where you want to drop. I will work up a plan. I can't get any lower than three thousand feet. Are you comfortable dropping at night from that altitude?"

"I trust you. Set me up with the best drop you can as low as you can. I recommend this field because it is open and there are no power lines. Come in on this vector, which is the direction we will be flying from. You will be heading 270 degrees here; due west. Fly as slow as you can to minimize the potential error and drift."

"One hundred and fifty knots is the slowest I can fly that bird. So that is the plan? Two seventy approach, 150 knots airspeed, 3,000-foot altitude, and what you just wrote down are the GPS coordinates to the target landing location?"

Cody handed her the paper with his writing. He bent down and kissed her. "Thanks, babe. I need to gear up. Get your luggage ready and get in uniform. Leaving in fifteen minutes."

He walked purposefully toward the side door of his house so he could get to his gear in the garage. Five minutes to go from the most relaxed and comfortable that he had ever felt in his whole life to full-blown savage. *Wasn't easy being him*, he thought.

# CHAPTER XXVIII

**"Y**ou ever done this before?" Senior Airman Elliott Jenkins offered Cody a frosty cold bottle of water dripping with moisture from the ice chest. He held a parachute pack in his other hand and dropped it beside Cody. The big jet had just leveled out of the initial part of the climb to its cruising altitude and was flying smoothly. Cody was strapped into a jump-seat chair against the bulkhead separating the main cabin and the cavernous cargo area.

"Been a while, but yes." Cody's black tactical duffle bag held a vest, a nine-millimeter Glock 19 pistol with three fifteen-round magazines loaded with 115-grain hollow point ammunition, large flashlight, three section collapsible billy stick, sheathed knife, and some basic hand tools. Everything he intended to carry could be inserted into the tactical vest he would don for the jump. He continued, "I have a pistol and three loaded magazines in this bag. I intend to put it on and load the pistol when I get ready. I just do not want to surprise you. Your plane: I am just catching a ride."

Jenkins was all business in his response. "Ten-four. If someone is going to jump out of a plane at night to do something, I would be surprised if they were not up to something that might need a weapon. I don't have mine with me, but when I know people are riding in the bird with weapons, I always carry. Boss Lady didn't tell us what you are up to completely, but I give you props for being willing to go full savage to do it. Not too many people lining up to jump out of a plane at night."

"Thanks for helping me."

"Roger that. I need to go over this plan with you. We are going to put you out this side door over there at 3,000 feet above ground level, going roughly 150 knots when you drop. Boss Lady recalculated the flight plan and has a target waypoint for your exit drop. Your forward velocity during freefall and anticipated wind drift during fall were calculated backward to arrive at the drop waypoint. If everything goes right, it should put you very near the target landing point you gave her. I have already rigged the static line, and we are going to clip this line to your rip cord on the chute so that you will automatically deploy the parachute after you are safely out the door of the plane. I know you have done that before."

"Got it."

"The side door of this aircraft is located behind the wing and engine discharge of the plane. The wing is elevated, and you probably noticed the T-tail tail section is elevated so that there is no way you can strike anything on the plane when you jump out, so don't concern yourself about that risk. The side door is designed for parachuting."

"Got it. Like I said, it has been a while, but I have jumped out of one of these planes before."

"Ten-four. Bear with me. For my own sake, I need to go over everything to make sure I do my best for you, frogman."

Cody extended his fist out to the airman for a fist bump. He appreciated his professionalism.

"Now, here is what to expect. Because the engines are elevated, you aren't going to get too much jet backwash. You will feel some initially, however, and the windspeed will surprise you when you exit even though we will only be going 150. The static line lead rip cord will pull faster than you think, but there will be a slight delay in deploying the canopy. Don't worry if you don't feel it completely deploy right away; this chute will not fill as fast as the wing chutes you probably used when you were with the teams. Give it a full chance to deploy, and I know it will, but if for some reason it gets tangled or doesn't fill right, that bottom pull handle is the emergency chute. Give it every chance for the primary canopy to open, though, before you use the emergency."

"Got it."

"Best to just do the head-down, spread-eagle posture you were taught once you drop. The canopy will pop in a few seconds after you drop even though you will think it takes an eternity, and then you need to steer down the best you can to your target if you can identify where it is. We are going to be on the downside of darkness when we get to the drop zone, according to Boss Lady. Won't be full dark but you ain't going to see much on the ground once you drop. Best to just trust the planning and watch out for trees when you get close to ground. This is not a chute where you try to land standing up. Let the chute lay you over when you hit the ground and then use the disconnects at the top of the harness to release the canopy from the harness. Roger that, frogman?"

"Got it."

"One more thing about the parachute."

"Yeah?"

"I am responsible for everything in the back of the plane including all the equipment. I need this back." The airman was kneeling next to Cody, and he softly backhanded the parachute pack. "I am sure you are going to be busy when you hit the ground, but it would be a big deal to me if we can get this chute back, so I don't have to bullshit somebody to get a replacement. These rigs all have serial numbers, and they keep an inventory of what is on here, so they are going to know on the next audit if this chute is not on board. If you could get it back to me, I would appreciate it. I am probably going to have to get somebody laid just to get it repacked, as it is." The airman grinned at his own joke.

"I will see to that. No problem."

"Boss Lady took over the flight. She is sitting left seat, so she can't come back here to say goodbye. She wanted me to tell you that. I will have communication with her on that headset when we get close to the drop zone. We will get you up and ready well before the drop and get the door opened. She will give me a countdown when we get close to the exit waypoint. You got to move fast when I give you the sign to go. Don't delay getting out the door or you will mess up the calculations. We will get you in the doorway holding onto the handles in advance and just wait for my signal. Once you get out the door, whatever is going to happen is going to happen. The gear deploys itself, so just try and enjoy the ride. You got all that?"

"Got it." Cody felt tense and wished he were more current on his parachuting skills. There wasn't a choice, however, and he had made his decision. Wiley needed him and the adrenaline of the situation made him feel wildly alive. He just hoped he would be on time.

"Good. Last thing. Boss Lady said you better come back to her. Looked like she meant it when she said it. She choked up. She is one tough nut; I wouldn't cross her. It would be best if you just do what she says. That is what Jacob and I have learned. Just do what she says, and everything will be fine." He offered his fist for a fist bump.

"Roger that. Thanks for the good rundown, Airman. Appreciate it." Cody reached out and bumped fists with him. The comprehensive review of the plan made him feel better about the risks of the task. He suddenly felt confident that he was going to get down on the ground just fine. Whatever happened after that was completely unknowable at this point, however.

Elliott slapped Cody on the back. "Go ahead and finish getting your gear together and I will come back in about an hour to check your gear and help you get in your chute. We will adjust the harness and review the rip cord, static line, and exit plan." Cody nodded as the airman left him to finish unpacking his gear and vest. Cody situated the equipment in the tactical vest and made sure that everything was secure enough to withstand the rigor of a jump.

He was dressed in black tactical pants, black long-sleeved T-shirt, and black jump boots. He fought off the cold overtaking him as the plane steadily climbed in altitude. The cavernous back cargo area of the plane was difficult for the systems to keep at a comfortable temperature, and he found himself wishing he had brought a coat. He slipped the vest on to assist with retaining body heat. He decided to suit up into the parachute harness for additional insulation. He adjusted the straps, located and memorized the locations of the different pull cords, canopy release clips, emergency parachute rip cord, and harness connectors. Once he was satisfied that he had full command of all the chute functions, he pulled out the small jar of blackface he had brought along and slowly began applying it to his face. Completing that chore, he put his gloves on to help conserve heat.

He sat quietly in the chill of the cargo locker and contemplated his task. He thought about Wiley and tried to anticipate the various scenarios that could confront him. He believed what Tiberius told him; he had no reason to misrepresent. If it was the plan to burn Wiley up in the house, he would have to act fast. The dilapidated shack would go up like a bonfire the minute flames hit the old wooden structure. The frame house was not stable in its current condition, and any destabilization of the tired old structural beams, girders, or ridge beams on the roofline would cause roof and structural wall collapse and potential overall structural failure and rapidly diminish any opportunity to remove Wiley from inside before he was consumed by the fire. Furthermore, the home was not built on grade; it had a crawlspace as homes of that generation always did, and the flooring system was suspect as is. It would most certainly collapse as the fire progressed and further complicate extraction for anybody attempting to exit.

Cody thought through the competing motivations that would drive the decisions Wiley's captors would make regarding their actions. First, if they wanted to burn Wiley in the house, they would probably want it to look like an accident. Second, they would not want to be seen in the vicinity of the burning house either before or after it was set ablaze. They would want to have deniability. Not wanting to be seen anywhere near the home was more than likely the reason they were waiting until nighttime to start the blaze. Plus, it would delay the fire department response and more than likely delay the time frame for anybody to even report the fire. The more the house burnt, the less evidence there would be to investigate. Third, the best way to make it look like an accidental death and not a crime scene was to place Wiley in the home alive once the fire started so it would look like he got caught in a fire at the house and burned up either trying to stop the blaze or overcome by smoke and flames.

Reflecting on these factors occupied Cody's mind and made the time pass. They were forty-five minutes into the three-hour flight, and Cody felt an inadvertent shudder from the cold conditions overtaking his body just as Lisa rounded the corner. She approached him and kneeled down where he was sitting.

"I am sorry it is so cold back here. There isn't any heating system for the back part of the plane. Let me get you some towels to wrap yourself in." She scurried away and quickly came back with a half-dozen large Air Force issue towels and began draping them over his shoulders and chest. Cody immediately felt some improvement. Their breath was creating a visible vapor. "Elliott uses these towels for cleanup back here; sorry they are stained, but this is the best we have."

"Thanks, I appreciate the wrap," he replied.

"We are at approximately 28,000 feet in elevation right now. At this altitude it is very cold. In about thirty more minutes we will begin a slow descent down to our eventual 3,000 feet above ground level altitude for your jump. It will get slightly warmer as we descend. We need to keep you warm and able to move between now and then, though. I may need to pull rank on Elliott and have him give up his jump seat for a bit to allow you to recover your body heat."

Cody nodded. "I am fine. It isn't that bad; I put the chute on my back to provide insulation on that side, and now with these towels wrapping my front I should be fine. It has been so long since I did this that I forgot why we always wore all that gear when we jumped." He smiled at her. He knew he must look strange in his black gear and black face paint.

"I had to come back here to apologize. I am so sorry that I initially told you we couldn't do this to help Wiley. I just need you to know that it was never about whether I get in trouble with the Air Force or not. I don't care what the Air Force thinks anymore. I am done with them. I am just scared that this is so dangerous, and you might get hurt. Even if you survive the jump unhurt, you don't know what situation you are getting into on the ground with these guys. I am just so afraid that I am going to lose you. I love you already and I am counting on you to come back to me. At the same time, I know you can do this. I am counting on it." Her lip was trembling, and a renegade tear formed in her left eye.

"I notice that your left eye always tears up before your right eye." He put his finger at the corner of her eye, and the tear ran down his finger. "I hope this is the last time I ever see that happen. I promise I am not crazy, Lisa. I am all that Wiley has right now and I have to stand up for him. He is a good man and he needs me. I can't do any less or I wouldn't be worth being around anymore. You can be sure, though, that I will be back. I am coming back to you; I will do everything I know how to come back for us."

She smiled sweetly at him and put her hands on top of his. "I know you will."

"I would kiss you if I didn't have all this face paint on. Your guys would see the evidence."

She laughed softly and sniffled. "I have to get back to my seat. The guys think I am in the bathroom. I am trying to be tough in front of them. Just know I am up there doing my best to give you a good ride and a tight jump."

Cody nodded at her silently and watched as she made the turn toward the front of the plane. *Not only is she a nice person and beautiful woman, but she is also somebody good to have on your side when life requires it. She is disciplined and tough in her own way,* he thought.

Just as she indicated, thirty minutes later the plane made a slight but perceptible deceleration, and the forward orientation of the plane changed from level flight to a very slight downward angle followed by a slow reacceleration to their original cruising speed due to the downward flight path. Elliott returned to check on Cody with a steaming cup of coffee and some beef jerky.

"Everything back here okay, frogman? You found the towels, I see. Good idea. It gets chilly back here and you don't have a coat. Sorry I didn't think about that when we were taking off. You comfortable with the way that parachute harness fits? Put this jerky in your vest, and this coffee will help keep you warm."

"Yeah, I got it adjusted. I just need to confirm what I think about the quick disconnects on the canopy straps and the emergency rip cord. I think we should probably also double check the static line lead to make sure it clips to the static line. I think we have double confirmed everything else." Cody took a sip of the steaming brew and nodded his head. "Surprisingly good coffee, my man. Thank you."

"Boss Lady makes the coffee. She got tired of Jacob trying to make it. I will give your chute a once-over and review everything with you once we get you standing up. I already checked that static line and the clip. I am sure we are good. The only thing I am worried about on this jump is you winding up in a tree. We got you covered on everything else."

Elliott gave him the thumbs-up and made his way back up to his station. Cody placed a piece of the jerky in his mouth and tucked the rest of it into a vest pocket. The salad he had made earlier was long gone, and the jerky would give his stomach something to work on instead of grumbling.

Cody leaned back in against the wall and closed his eyes. He felt some nervous excitement and was impatient for action. Time wore on and his body felt some fatigue from the adrenaline of anticipation. He wandered into and out of a fitful resting that was well short of sleep but did provide a minor amount of calming relaxation. In his head, he ginned up memories of previous jumps to refamiliarize himself with the sensations of leaving the aircraft in flight and falling to earth. He recycled the memories and relived the sensations to prepare himself for the task in front of him. *Elliott is correct about one thing,* Cody thought. *My only real job at the moment is jumping out of the plane. Once that is done, I am no longer in control. The gear will deploy itself, and from that point, there is little I can do until I make ground.* At that moment Elliott returned to the cargo area and made a motion for Cody to clip his lead to the static line affixed to the overhead of the door side of the airplane.

Cody stood up and made his way over to that side of the plane. Elliott went through the procedure to unlock and open the door. The wind volume made a rushing noise that made it difficult to speak. After getting the door open, he came back and did a check on Cody's parachute. He leaned in close to Cody's ear and shouted, "Did you familiarize yourself with how to disconnect the canopy?"

Cody nodded affirmatively. Elliott went on to check the fastening of the harness, the rip cord lead line, and connection to the static line, and then pointed to the emergency red rip cord pull handle at the bottom of the chute harness. "Did you locate and familiarize yourself with the reserve chute?" he asked.

Cody nodded affirmatively again and said, "I did. Everything seems familiar. I think I got it."

"Good. I looked everything over, and it looks like you are good to go. I am going to put the headset on. You see the two handles on either side of the door opening? When we start the countdown, I will wave at you, and you need to move forward smoothly to the door and grab those handles. When we get down to the last five seconds of the countdown, I will use hand signals to give you the count. When I get to one, you jump out the door. You got it?" Elliott demonstrated, and Cody nodded in affirmation.

"Got it," he said in reply.

"Okay, frogman. I am putting the headset on. Wait back here until I give you the wave. Good luck to you and make sure you let us know as soon as you can that you are safe."

Cody nodded in agreement and gave him a thumbs-up. Elliott walked up to the bulkhead and took down the headset and unraveled sufficient cord to allow him to walk back to the door. Cody could see him conversing with the other crew members and knew that communication between them was established. Under some circumstances he could have enjoyed the adventure of this night jump, but the uncertainty of the cause for the exercise prevented that.

Within a few moments, Elliott waved at Cody, and he immediately moved forward to the door and grasped the handles securely. After a seemingly never-ending interval, he started the hand signals counting down from five. When he hit one, Cody immediately jumped out of the aircraft into the night without hesitation.

# CHAPTER XXIX

The breeze slowly dragged Cody over the rough ground in the darkness. The entire jump had taken place in less than three minutes. Without the benefit of being able to see in the darkness, Cody had been surprised when his boots struck the ground. He allowed the canopy to pull him off his feet without opposition and completely relaxed when the ground interrupted his downward drift. He reached up and unfastened both of the carabiner clips that fastened the harness to the canopy and allowed the resistance of the canopy to help right him back to his feet as he began gathering the nylon canopy together for recovery. He quickly pulled the parachute together into an unruly pile and did a quick pat-down to confirm that all his gear had survived the jump. He felt the pistol and the two spare magazines, the compass, flashlight, knife, hatchet, and the various Velcro sealed pockets that contained the simple hand tools he had brought along. He concluded that everything made it down with him. He reached into the side pocket of the vest on his left side and removed the phone he had stashed there. He took a single moment to tap out a quick text to Lisa. "Thanks for ride. Down safely – C"

With that, he removed the harness, opened the pouch, and did his best to stuff the canopy back into the pouch on the back of the harness. Predictably, he could not get it back in without properly folding it, but he did the best he could and eventually got about half the chute inside the pouch with half hanging outside. Nonetheless, it gave him a carriable package that he could sling over a shoulder to transport to a retrievable point. He was doing his best to live up to his word to Elliott for return of the parachute.

Cody looked up to see if he could scan the sky for evidence of the sunset and confirm which way west was. As he departed the plane at 3,000 feet, he had been able to see over the horizon, and the light from the sun in the west had still been visible. Now, down on the ground, however, the light could not be observed, and pitch-black darkness prevailed. He was disoriented from the drop and had no feel for the direction he should travel. From his recollection of the Google Earth satellite photography of the drop zone, he knew that the road bordered the eastern boundary of the property he had selected as his target. Assuming he had dropped close to the target, he would need to move east to reach the road that ran in front of the property he and Wiley inherited.

Cody removed the flashlight and the compass from their respective pouches and did a quick check of the illuminated compass dial to establish which way was east. He did a quick sweep of the terrain with his flashlight beam and slung the bulky pack over his shoulder and began making his way through the darkness. There were some trees in the pasture he had selected for his drop target. They were large trees, but not numerous. There was little underbrush, and he made relatively easy progress to the fence line and found the road. At this moment, he was unsure if his property was close to his current position, nor did he know which direction it lay. He needed to find a culvert or similar landmark where he could stash the parachute package for future recovery. He threw the parachute over the fence and created an opening for himself to slide through two of the middle wire strands. and carefully walked down the incline of the bar ditch that fronted the road, carrying the parachute package.

He checked for traffic on the road in both directions and saw no lights. Because of the darkness, it was impossible to recognize anything to give him reference as to which direction to travel to arrive at his property. He chose a direction to the left and almost immediately found a culvert leading to a gated entrance with pipes into the pasture he had landed in. He stashed the parachute inside the culvert pipe and scrambled up the bar ditch bank to the road. He double checked both directions for traffic and began an Airborne shuffle jog down the road to look for his property. Given the overgrowth and darkness and uncertainty of his position, he had no idea in which direction it would lie. He just needed to be observant and keep looking for clues and familiar signs. He decided he would go approximately a half mile in this direction and then double back and go a half mile in the other direction from his original starting point. One positive sign, he thought, was that he had not observed a burning fire on his drop down to earth. He appeared to be on site early rather than too late. Cody started moving forward in the traditional Army Airborne shuffle, which was designed to cover ground at approximately nine minutes per mile over long distances for troops loaded with gear.

After a few minutes of shuffling, he heard an approaching vehicle on the road behind him and elected to hide himself in the bar ditch on the side of the road that the car was traveling. He crouched down in the ditch until the vehicle passed him and then scrambled out to watch where it went. It appeared to be a truck, and the brake lights illuminated several hundred feet after it passed Cody. The truck slowed and turned right onto a driveway culvert over the bar ditch. *This could be them taking Wiley to the house,* he thought.

He returned to the road and increased his pace, running through the darkness until he saw the driveway and instantly recognized it as the entrance to his and Wiley's property. No evidence of the house being burned nor smell of smoke was noticeable, and Cody crouched at the entrance to check out the activity on the property. The truck was idling with the lights illuminated in front of the old house, and he could make out some voices in the distance. Cody quietly made his way crouching down and ducking behind trees and shrubs as he approached the commotion surrounding the running truck.

He suddenly froze as he recognized Wiley draped over one of the men's shoulders in a fireman's carry. The man slung Wiley off his shoulder onto the front porch like a rag doll and bent over in exhaustion. "This son of a bitch is heavy. Help me get him in the house."

Cody immediately unholstered his pistol from the vest pouch and racked the slide to load a round. He re-holstered the weapon and began to slowly make his way closer to the house while keeping himself hidden from view. He watched as two men dragged Wiley into the home by the shoulders through the front door with his feet dragging behind. Another man followed with a red gasoline can and a small duffle bag from the back of their truck. Yet another man was lingering behind to watch out for witnesses. Wiley appeared to be unconscious and made no movements or indication that he was cognizant of his situation or surroundings while Cody observed him.

Cody stopped for a moment to remove his phone from his vest and turned it off to silence any potential notifications or calls. All three of the men Cody had seen had printed during their movements, and Cody knew they were all armed with holstered sidearms. There was no way to know if the fourth was carrying or not. He did not know yet what his course of action would be, but he did not want to inadvertently reveal his presence.

Cody quickly ran through the options. He could surprise the lookout by engaging him, disabling the truck, and then forcing the three men to flee the burning house into his gunfire. That seemed to have even odds for him to survive and even potentially prevail in the shootout, but it did not give him high odds to rescue Wiley. He could attack now before the house was set ablaze, and he might alter the murder of his nephew from death by fire to death by bullet. Again, not the result he needed, and not that high of odds anyway. He was not convinced that a shootout with three or potentially four armed adversaries would be the highest probability outcome course of action. At the current moment, if the men left hurriedly after igniting the fire, he felt he had a better chance of entering the house and removing Wiley than surviving a gun battle that might take a while to resolve and imperil Wiley even more. If these guys were smart, they would leave Wiley alive but unconscious, to make sure that evidence of smoke inhalation was in his lungs so that a coroner could potentially confirm death due to the fire and not their actions. If they weren't, Wiley was already dead, and burning him was just a cover. Either way, Cody reasoned that the best odds to make a difference was to wait for them to leave. If they didn't leave right away, then Cody would have no recourse than to barrel in with a full-frontal attack to attempt to retrieve Wiley from the house before he burned up.

There were only messy options. Cody thought through the series of events that brought him to this place. He was calling on all his willpower to remain calm and not charge in like a madman intent on killing these brutal thugs who had Wiley. He needed to not only rescue Wiley, but to do it in a way that didn't put him in legal jeopardy if he survived. He was betting his life on his read of the situation and Wiley's life too. If he pulled this off, he had a plan for dealing with all these hillbilly punks that he was pretty sure they would not survive. He had to take care of the first part of the business to get to that, though. He needed Wiley out of their control and out of this tinderbox.

Just then, the three men exited the home and hooted like drunk cowboys as they ran to the truck. Cody saw the huge flames consuming the interior of the home and heard the snapping and popping of the fire as it swarmed the old wooden structure in an intensely hot inferno. All four of the men jumped into the cab and briskly drove up the driveway of the home toward the street. At the street they stopped briefly to look back and then tore out down the driveway toward the road, spinning tires and launching gravel and dust from the rear wheels.

Cody ran toward the house and into the thick smoke belching out the open front door of the home. He got to the front door and attempted to look in but could not make out the interior. The accelerant they poured inside the house was rapidly converting the old frame shack into a raging inferno. The dried-out wood literally exploded into flames when the hot fire spread. Cody knew he had very little time and could feel the floor system sag as he stepped into the house. The roof rafters were groaning, and he could see that the flame was engulfing over half of the ridge beam at the peak of the roof. He crouched down and pulled his shirt up over his mouth in an attempt to restrict the smoke he was inhaling. He squatted and peered across the room and did not see any sign of Wiley. Coughing violently as he stood up, he ran across the room to the doorway into the kitchen area. The flames were creating intense heat as they engulfed the kitchen area. A loud groan from the roof emanated as a portion of the roof decking slid down the back wall, causing a partial cave-in of the back rafters. The flareup of the flames created illumination that allowed Cody to see Wiley attempting to rise to his hands and knees in the kitchen area. He was coughing violently and trying to crawl.

Cody ducked down and quickly crossed over to Wiley and lifted him partially to his feet by raising his arms. Wiley's torso was high enough for Cody to put him in a fireman's carry over his shoulder. Cody bent his legs to a full squat to load him on his shoulder. Straining mightily, Cody elevated back to a crouch and began a rapid walk back out the doorway into the front door. Both he and Wiley were coughing and wheezing from the dense smoke and intense heat. Cody cleared the doorway and made a direct beeline toward the entry. The floor was sagging and giving way with each step and finally, after three steps, the two went crashing through into the crawlspace. Wiley fell heavily on top of Cody and knocked the wind out of him. The crawlspace was acting as a furnace with fresh air flowing up into the house through the ventilation openings into the raging flames above. Wind was whistling through the openings to feed the fire above.

Cody rolled to his stomach and quickly surveyed the situation. Attempting to climb back out onto the floor again to escape out the front door was his first instinct, but he knew that another fall like the one they had just experienced could potentially break a leg or arm and prevent him from being able to get out of the way of the fire. Wiley was coughing furiously and was very groggily trying to regain a crawl stance. Cody fished out his flashlight and surveyed the exterior walls of the house beneath the floor to see if any spaces were large enough to provide an exit. A quick study of the side walls revealed multiple small openings that would not give them an exit without substantial demolition of the framing that created them. Cody shone the flashlight toward the front porch and spied a large rectangular opening that would provide passage to the elevated front porch. Cody knew from memory that the only covering around the front porch crawlspace was an ancient lattice decorative grid that would put up only minimal resistance. The opening was about fifteen feet away with only three feet of head room to negotiate their way under the porch.

Cody looked at Wiley, who was still coughing and struggling to remain awake. He slapped his face and pushed his forehead back to get him to look at him while he tried to explain his plan. Wiley briefly looked at Cody and then his eyes rolled back in his head, and he passed out again. Cody cursed and made his way forward on his stomach toward the front porch. As he passed, he pushed Wiley's arms up over his head and then pointed his own feet toward the rectangular opening. When he got to the end of his arm length, he pulled Wiley toward him and achieved approximately eighteen inches of movement. He pushed his feet backward a similar distance and repeated the movement. He strained, dragging Wiley's body across the dirt. Two more repetitions of the movement and Cody felt his right foot strike the wall of the house. His left foot went through the opening, however. He adjusted slightly and got both feet through the opening and was about to pull Wiley again when the roof of the house began to collapse onto the floor. Cody could see the burning flames and embers of the collapsing structure as he looked backward over Wiley. Embers flew in all directions and burnt his face. He quickly made two more pulls on Wiley's arms and was able to guide him partially under the porch as more and more of the structure collapsed behind them. Cody could feel an increase in cooler, fresh air as they emerged out of the frame of the home and out under the porch. He planted his feet on the wall on a side of the opening and grabbed Wiley by the belt and slightly lifted his head with the other hand and was able to advance him several feet.

Cody swung his body in a semicircle and bashed the thin lattice with his boots and rapidly knocked out enough to create a large opening through which they could both escape. He lay down again at arm's length to Wiley's position and pulled him three times in rapid succession. He could tell that he had Wiley's body largely out from under the house, and he was breathing heavily from the exertion when he heard the roof completely collapse into the house. Flames were scorching their position from above. With a frenzied series of pulls and backward scrambles, he was able to back fully out of the opening until he had Wiley's hands within comfortable reach of the outside. He pulled his knees up and clenched Wiley's hands with both of his and stood up and pulled backward with a mighty pull that fully extracted Wiley from under the porch. To escape the blistering heat of the fierce blaze, Cody continued pulling Wiley in that fashion for another twenty feet to a safer location.

Cody was in the process of standing Wiley up on his feet and putting him in another fireman's carry when the floor joists fully collapsed in the house and an entire sidewall fell into the crawl-space. An immense blast of hot air and embers showered them both as Cody shouldered Wiley and lurched into a fast walk away from the blaze. After he got Wiley to the thicket of underbrush that he had previously used as cover, he leaned him gently up against a large tree and began looking at him for injuries. Wiley was obviously highly drugged and was still coughing forcefully. He slowly opened his eyes and Cody thought he might have seen a spark of recognition that he was out of danger for the moment and perhaps even recognizing him, but he couldn't be sure. He gently backhanded Wiley's cheek several times in an attempt to keep him awake, but Wiley slipped back into dreamland.

After checking to make sure that his breathing seemed stable, Cody pulled his cell phone out and turned it on. As the phone powered up and went through its digital handshake with the new cell system it found itself in, Cody began hacking up the smoke, dirt, and exhaust residue in his lungs with several ragged coughing spasms. He spit up black smoke residue and tried to make his voice sound as normal as he could as he waited for an answer to the call he placed to Wiley's cell phone.

"Hello?" Tiberius's response sounded like a question.

"Tiberius. Cody here. I got him out of the house. They set the house on fire just like you said they were going to, and I barely got him out in time. The whole house is up in blazes and is totally burnt down. Wiley is heavily drugged, but I think he is going to be okay. He is coughing a lot, but I can't diagnose anything until he wakes up more."

"Praise Jesus, Cody! How did you get here from Florida so quickly?"

"Can't explain right now, Tiberius, but we will have a beer and I will tell you the whole story, I promise. Thanks so much for calling me. Until then, you can just know that you aren't the only angel with wings."

"You are an angel too? I never met another angel."

"Listen to me. You know Wiley's girlfriend Lucy?" Cody broke into a hacking spasm and removed the phone from his face. "Sorry about that, Tiberius. You still there?"

"Yes. And yes, I know Lucy. I didn't call her, though, since you didn't tell me to."

"Okay, good. So, I need you to call her now and explain who I am and briefly tell her what happened. Tell her that I am here with Wiley, and he needs medical help. I can't call for an ambulance and I don't have a car. I know she knows where the house is. I need her to come get us."

"I can come and get you in Wiley's truck, Cody. It's right here and I can get the spare keys in his house. I know where they are. Ricky is right here with me, and he can drive us. I can tell him where to go. That will be faster." Tiberius wanted more than anything to be involved in the rescue of his friend.

"I know you can, and I know you would. I need you to leave Wiley's truck exactly the way it is right now. Don't move it and don't touch it in any way. Don't go over to Wiley's house and don't touch anything over there. You got it? I will explain why later. Just text me Lucy's number and then call her and explain who I am and briefly what happened. Then tell her that I am going to call her." Cody began hacking again from the conversation and spat furiously at the ground. His lungs ached when he breathed. He put the phone back to his mouth and asked, "You got that?"

"Got it, Cody. Text you Lucy's number and then call her to tell her you are going to be calling her. Don't touch anything at Wiley's house."

"Good. Thanks again, Tiberius. Looking forward to that beer." They hung up and Cody was pressing the dial on his phone to call Lisa when he felt the vibration of a text message. He smiled. That Tiberius was a reliable dude, he thought. Might have to buy him a whole case of his favorite beer when this was over. He was a pretty thirsty angel himself right now. He smiled in the darkness.

Cody opened the contact forwarded by Tiberius with Lucy's phone number. Enough time had lapsed that he could call her. He bent over to check on Wiley. His breathing seemed better now, and he wasn't coughing as heavily as he had been. Cody punched the button to dial Lucy and stood. *This is likely to be a very strange phone call for her,* he thought.

"Is this Uncle Cody?" she answered. "Wiley already told me all about you. Tiberius told me you were an angel. He was talking crazy talk. Do you need help? Where is Wiley?" She sounded frightened.

"Wiley is with me, and we are in front of his house in the country. You know the one I am talking about, right? He told me you had been there a few times with him."

"Yeah. I know where it is. Is he okay?"

"Randal and his guys drugged him and then set the house on fire. I got there just in time to get him out of the house. He inhaled a lot of smoke. He is heavily drugged right now and not responsive to me. He is coughing quite a bit still, but I think he is stable and will probably be all right with some rest." Cody coughed slightly as he finished.

"Sounds like you inhaled some smoke too."

"Yes, I did." Cody cleared his throat. "Can you come and pick us up? I don't have a car here and he isn't walking. We need a ride."

There was a long pause before she responded. "I haven't ever met you. Other than what Wiley told me about you, I don't really know anything about you."

"I understand your fear. Would your dad come out here with you? Maybe that would make you feel better. I understand he is a doctor?"

"He is and he would come out if I asked him. Is it safe out there? What about Randal and those guys?"

"They aren't here. I want them to think that Wiley died in that fire, so they don't keep looking for him. I need about a week or so before they find out that they didn't kill Wiley."

"Let me call you back. I want to help Wiley, but I think my dad needs to be there to look at him. He probably needs to go to the hospital."

"He does need to go to the hospital. I am asking you to take him to Ada tonight and check him in to the Chickasaw hospital there. You don't have to take me anywhere. Just come and get Wiley, leave me here, and I will walk back into town. I know you don't know me, and all I want is for Wiley to get to the hospital." Cody could tell that she was concerned about whether she could trust him or not.

Another long pause. Then she brusquely responded, "Call you back in a minute."

The call was disconnected, and Cody looked at his battery level. He did not have a lot of charge left in his phone. With all the coordination remaining, he needed to use his phone time wisely. He leaned in again to check on Wiley and found him fast asleep, snoring loudly and coughing slightly. He sounded better than he had after they initially got outside the burning home. Cody was concerned that neighbors might have smelled the smoke and called the fire department. He didn't want to be involved with any investigation of the fire and didn't want anybody to know that Wiley had been pulled from the flames.

His phone rang and he answered it on the first ring. "This is Cody."

"We are coming out there. Should take about twenty minutes. One question before we leave, though."

"Yeah. Ask away."

"If you don't have a ride, how did you get there in the first place? Wiley said you live in Florida, and you just went back there from Oklahoma. How would you have made it from Florida to Oklahoma so fast?"

"A friend flew me here in a plane from Florida." He avoided mentioning the night parachute jump.

"A private plane?" She sounded suspicious. "And then how did you get to Wiley's house?"

"I hitched a ride and walked." There was not time to fully explain. Cody needed to get Wiley out of there before neighbors or the fire department showed up or Randal came over to check on his handiwork.

"Hmmm. Sounds kind of vague. Just so you know, my dad is bringing his gun."

"I understand. This is a very strange night. I just need to get Wiley out of here and get him to the hospital. I don't care about anything other than that. If you promise to get him to Ada, I will be forever indebted to you. Thank you for coming for him."

"Dad agrees that Ada is the best place for him, by the way. We will take him there. He wants you to leave Wiley out where we can see him, and we will pick him up and take him. You need to stay away while we do it."

"That is fine. I understand. See you soon."

The soft snoring coming from Wiley reassured Cody that he was going to be fine. He quickly hammered out a brief text to Lisa alerting her that Lucy had agreed to come and get Wiley to take him to the hospital. He also alerted her to his low phone battery situation. He suggested that they meet at Ole Red in the event his battery didn't make it until she arrived. He had an hour's walk back into town, but after everything he had survived already that night, that seemed like no big deal. A shot of Jack Daniel's followed with an ice-cold beer sounded perfect. He reached into his vest compartment and pulled out some of the jerky that Elliott had given him earlier. He chewed on the end of a stick of the jerky while he watched the smoldering fire begin to die down. *A night of nights,* he thought.

# CHAPTER XXX

The convenience store parking lot behind the building was littered with old cartons, paper bags, cans, and bottles. Cody carried his tactical vest draped over his shoulder as he made his way around to the back of the store in search of a hose bibb to wash off the face paint he had applied prior to making his jump. He needed a place to stash the vest for a while until Lisa came to get him. He could not enter a public establishment looking like a face-painted commando and openly carrying a loaded pistol and two spare magazines. Cody found a hose bibb close to the back door and helped himself to a healthy stream of water for a quick face wash and refreshing head rinse. The hour-long walk to town had provided an opportunity for the smoke smell to diminish on his clothing, but he still smelled like a campfire. *At least it helps mask the sweat odor.* He laughed to himself.

The handoff of Wiley to Lucy and her father had gone well. They had shown up as promised shortly after their last conversation. Cody had moved Wiley out to a conspicuous place in the open where their car headlights would shine on him as they drove up to the house. Cody had remained visible, but at a distance to prevent any misunderstanding on their part. They had immediately attended to Wiley and began trying to awaken him. He seemed to partially respond to Lucy, and they were able to walk him to their car with his arms draped around their shoulders as they walked on both sides assisting. Cody had been able to exchange a few words from a distance with Lucy after her father and Wiley got situated in the back seat of her vehicle. He had asked her not to tell anybody about taking Wiley to the hospital, for his own safety and security. He told her that he would visit Wiley in the hospital as soon as possible and he would appreciate it if she would let him know what room number he was in and the phone number where he could be reached. She agreed to not discuss it with anybody and understood the need to keep it quiet and departed without fanfare. She seemed suspicious about him, but also appreciative that he had saved Wiley. Cody was grateful that they were helping; Wiley was lucky to have so many people who cared about him.

After completing the washdown of his face and removing the last of the face paint residue, Cody helped himself to a nice long drink of the water and closed the hose bibb. He hung the vest on the backside of the dumpster enclosure in a location that would not be seen by anybody emptying trash from the store unless they walked behind the enclosure, which seemed unlikely. Hiding the vest reminded him of the parachute stashed out by the culvert close to his property, and he made a mental note to have Lisa drive him by that location to recover the parachute along with the vest after they reconnected. The rinse-off and long drink of water were refreshing, and he walked with a lighter step the remaining few blocks to the bar where he was intending to meet Lisa.

He made his way to a seat at the bar and sat down. He suddenly felt tired and smiled as he thought about starting the day on his motorcycle, eating pancakes at De Leon Springs in Florida, the ride alongside the river in Daytona, the afternoon with Lisa, the phone call from Tiberius, the plane ride to Oklahoma, the night jump, the rescue of Wiley from the fire, and then the walk here. It was an unbelievable eighteen hours, even by his standards. As he contemplated the day, his shot and beer showed up. Luckily, there was nobody in the bar who seemed familiar, so he had no worry about explaining why he was back. He tossed back the shot and followed it with a full-sized gulp of the ice-cold beer, and suddenly, he felt tired and relaxed at the same time. His phone had died during a conversation with Tiberius to update him on Wiley's status, so he had no communication. It was a perfect moment to absorb this snapshot of his life and celebrate being alive. It had been a while since he went out the door of a plane; he hadn't been sure exactly how he would respond to that challenge. It had been a thrill, to be sure. In the end, the only thing on his mind had been saving Wiley. Nothing could have stopped him from doing everything he could do to make that happen.

It seemed strange, wanting to put his life at risk for someone he had not known three months ago. Life flies by and some people come and go, but others remain and grow in priority. Cody felt proud of Wiley and was protective of him. The guy had something—something hard to explain—something that made you want to be part of the important side of life with him being in it. He felt like Wiley's guardian. Not one to steer events, just to shield and protect from the trauma and harm that life brings. He felt raw anger at Randal and his crew. Anger that came on slow and burned to rage. He needed to dial back his blowtorch temper and think of how he could make this nail his hammer. There was a way to use what he knew against Randal and the sheriff. The stakes were high; he needed to do something rapidly before they found Wiley again, or found Shane and Doris. Fatigue was setting in as Cody was struggling to concentrate. Each time he tried to focus, his temper flared up and turned to violent retribution that he would personally deliver. He knew he needed better. He needed to put these thoughts back on the shelf of his mind and let his subconscious work on the response. It would come, he was sure. Several potential plans were percolating already.

After draining his second shot and following that with a swallow of his beer, he looked up to see Lisa walk in, still dressed in her flight suit. She immediately spotted him and made a beeline to his stool. He stood up to greet her and she gave him a big bear hug and made a heavy sigh. He smiled and kissed the top of her head. The bartender immediately came over to take her order and she shook her head.

"Thanks, honey. I have to take this man home. He is leaving with me now." She smiled sweetly at him and pressed her face against his chest.

Cody made a writing motion with his hand and paid the bartender. He paid in cash for the bill and left a hefty tip. He was glad to be there and happy that Lisa had made it. She had parked immediately in front of the door to the bar, and they both slipped into her car.

"My first ride in the 'Vette!" he said as he slid into the seat.

"My new headlights are working great, thanks to you and Wiley. And Tiberius." She laughed a throaty chuckle with a small snort about Tiberius saving the day on the headlight repair.

"I can't be good at everything," Cody responded with a laugh.

"Don't you worry about it, babe. Any man ready to throw himself out of an airplane at night to save a member of his family gets a pass on the car repair test. No issues." She smiled and looked at him smiling and then broke down in tears. "I am sorry. I don't mean to cry; I was just so scared. I didn't think we had enough time to plan that drop and I was worried I might have made a mistake. Normally on something like that we have several people review it and stack hands on the plan before we take off. I just didn't think I had done enough preparation. It is not how I like to work. You just surprised me, that is all."

"You did great. I landed close to the house, and all went well. It could not have gone any better; you were right on the money with everything you did. On that subject, though, I need to go pick up that parachute tonight. I have my vest stashed around the corner and need to grab that before it disappears also. Can you take me?"

"Show me the way." She sniffled, looked at herself in the mirror, checked her makeup, straightened herself up, and then reversed the car into the street.

Cody instructed her to pull the car behind the building, and he jumped out to recover the vest and handgun hanging off the backside of the dumpster enclosure. All was well with his gear, and he laid the vest in the back area of the car. "Do you think we will be able to get the parachute in the back of this thing?" he asked.

"I wouldn't bet on it with my luggage in the back there already. I think I need to send Elliott out here in a truck to pick it up. Do you think it is secure for a day or two? Let's just head over to Wiley's house and crash. I am so tired. Between the flight and the drive over and worrying about you, I am beat."

"Okay, well, first thing, the parachute is in a culvert that acts as a drainage ditch for the street. If it rains, it will get washed out of the culvert and will probably be discovered. If we don't get it tonight, we need to make sure we get it soon. Secondly, we can't stay at Wiley's house. I want them to think that Wiley died in the fire. His truck doesn't move, nobody enters his house, and nobody talks about him getting rescued. I suggest we go back to our little motel in Duncan and crash there. I am beat, too, but I can drive if you want to rest."

"Okay. I am going to let you drive, then. Let's get to Duncan and take a shower. I need to clean up and get in bed. Luckily, I have my bag with my cosmetics and bath items in it. You don't have anything. What are we going to do for you?"

"Don't worry about that now. I will work it all out tomorrow. Let's just swap places and get going. It's late and I need a shower and some rest myself."

The two swapped places and Cody began the drive to the motel they had stayed at previously in Duncan. Lisa grabbed his right arm with both hands, wrapped her arms around it, and lay against the back of the seat sitting sideways. She was asleep before they hit the city limits of Tishomingo. Cody unplugged her phone from the car charger and plugged his in. He wanted to see if there was any update on Wiley.

The highway to Duncan was pitch black with almost no streetlights at any point on the drive. Cody drove conservatively and ran a couple of different strategies through his mind on how to deal with Randal and the sheriff. After a few more miles, he checked his phone. The phone illuminated and began its handshake with the cell service. After another minute, Cody looked at the home screen and saw there was a message.

"Unk. Wiley here." Wiley then went into a brief coughing fit. "I am calling from Lucy's phone. Thanks for coming to get me, Unk. Don't know how you did it but call me tomorrow. In the hospital in Ada. Lucy is going to text you the room and phone numbers here."

Cody smiled to himself and hung up the phone. He shuddered, thinking of how he would feel if Wiley had not made it. He looked over at Lisa and she was fast asleep and still holding onto his arm with both of hers. So far, everything was returned to normal. Tomorrow, he needed to take action and keep it that way.

# CHAPTER XXXI

**C**ody looked carefully at the beat-up old truck on the dealer's lot. There was not a fender or panel that did not have a dent. The tailgate looked like the previous owner had forgotten to lower it a few times when he was unhitching from a gooseneck trailer. Apparently, he had done a shade tree repair job, and the tailgate did still function, but it looked like Fido's ass. The bed of the truck had apparently never had a liner in it, and there was not a square inch of paint left on the metal comprising the bottom of the bed. Nonetheless, the big diesel engine started willingly, and the transmission and suspension seemed to work okay. It drove surprisingly straight, did not wander on the road, and the motor pulled strong. The dual axle tires on back were brand-new, and the front tires still had some life to them. The truck had a gooseneck ball in the bed and a Class III hitch on the back, with a drop ball insert in the receiver since the hitch was elevated. Looking at the vehicle along the sides, Cody could not find any evidence that it had ever been in a major collision. The frame appeared straight, and the truck did not crab on the road.

The inside of the truck smelled like stale cigarettes, and the seats had some bad tears in the upholstery. The truck had 250,000 miles on it, and it showed. Cody had walked from the motel in Duncan to the used car lot after Lisa left for the base that morning. Cody had found a washer and dryer at the motel and had managed to retrieve the clothes from the machines early that morning, using a bath towel to wrap himself while the only clothes he had with him were washed and dried.

Cody opened the glove box and found a half roll of Skoal chewing tobacco tins. He pulled those out and found a Chris LeDoux CD lying on the bottom of the glovebox, which he removed also. He exited the cab and was giving the old fighter a last once-over when the salesman returned to check in on him. Cody handed him the tobacco tins and the CD.

"What do you think of the old girl?" the salesman asked.

"Well, she is no beauty queen, for sure," Cody demurred.

"Well now, we don't want anybody getting confused. It is a used truck." The salesman squinted at Cody. This was serious business for him, and he wasn't going to get pushed around by some out-of-towner who came walking up to his dealership. He was doubtful that this tall, lean dude could throw the bones to buy this vehicle, anyway. On the test drive he hadn't said a single word.

"Ten thousand dollars you said?" Cody returned the squint.

"Ten thousand for this truck is a deal. You just been shot in the ass with a barrel full of luck, mister. I had this truck sold and the guy cancelled on me yesterday. Good trucks like this don't last long around here. I was thinking about raising the price on it."

"It's strange that you would say that, Herman. I just noticed that the Skoal in that glove box had a sell-by date from a year and a half ago. I guess people around here don't go looking in glove boxes very often."

The man immediately confirmed what Cody told him about the tobacco tin by looking at it. He offered no response. He immediately began launching into a rundown of the features again, however.

"Hold on, Herman. I want the truck; you don't have to say anything else. I will give you $9,000. I have to drive it off the lot today though. Don't have any transportation at the moment."

"Well, sounds like you are in a bit of a hard spot. What did you say your name was?"

"Cody. Cody Houston."

"How are you going to pay for it, Cody?"

"Credit card, debit card, or I can have a wire sent. What would you like?"

"If you want it, you are going to have to do a little better than $9,000. Like I said, I was actually thinking about raising the price on this fine machine."

"I tell you what, Herman, I will pay you $9,500 for that tired old fighter. Take it or leave it. There is another place down the street I will go check out if you aren't interested. Done talking."

"Well now, you do get right down to business, don't you? No need to get huffy."

"Is that a yes or a no?"

"Against my better judgment, I will sell it for $9,500. Let's go inside and get the paperwork and payment worked out. I don't want to send you walking all over town. I get sentimental that way."

Forty-five minutes later, Cody was cruising down the road toward Tishomingo. He planned to end up at the hospital where Wiley was in Ada. He called Tiberius to see if he wanted to come and see Wiley with him and to also ask if Ricky might want to come. Cody did not want to be seen anywhere near Wiley's home, however, so he made arrangements for Tiberius and Ricky to meet him at the store where he had temporarily staged his vest the night before. He also needed to stop and pick up the parachute he had left behind, and he knew that Wiley's father's Appaloosa horses needed tending also. He had no idea how to do that task, but figured he could handle it if Wiley would give him instructions when he got there.

Wiley answered Lucy's phone on the first ring. "Hey, Unk. Break me out of here, please." He started coughing slightly and his voice still sounded hoarse. "The food is terrible, and everybody keeps telling me what to do."

"I am on my way down there, nephew. Driving my new dually. Anything I can bring for you? Some magazines or something? How long are they planning on keeping you? Is Lucy with you?"

"They won't tell me. They are saying I need to stay another few days or maybe a week, for sure. They aren't doing anything for me here. I could be sitting at home. They are worried about my lungs scarring from the smoke and heat. Lucy is in the bathroom freshening up. She stayed here with me last night."

"Try and be patient and listen to your doctor. We had a real bad night last night and we are both lucky to be alive. In the meantime, I was going to stop by and take care of your dad's horses while I am passing through Tishomingo. What do I need to do?"

"Oh, thanks for doing that, Unk. That is really nice of you." Wiley went into a detailed explanation about where to get the water to refill the tank, where to get the grain, how much to feed each horse, and how much hay to put out and how to do that so the horses did not trample it before they ate it. He finished by saying, "Why don't you stop and get some apples for them? That would be a treat and make you popular."

"Ten-four."

"So, tell me about this truck you bought. Diesel dually, eh? Thirty-five hundred, I assume?"

"She is a beauty, with 250,000 miles, but she still runs strong. I figure I will leave it out on the land, so I have something here when I fly out. You can use it too, for towing and other chores. Believe me, you won't be able to hurt it any. Keep you from banging up your truck. Just got it so I am not hitching a ride around here when I come out."

"So, on that subject, how did you get out here so fast, anyway?"

"Parachuted in."

"You aren't serious. Really, Unk. Don't bullshit me. I am hurting here."

"Lisa was flying back last night to Altus, and I dropped out at 3,000 feet right over the neighbor's pasture. I got there when those guys were dragging you into the house and setting it on fire. Barely got you out. We wound up slinking out through the crawlspace just before the roof caved in. We fell through the floor into the crawlspace when the floor gave way and then I dragged you out under the front porch."

"You got to be kidding me. A nighttime jump? What are we going to do to those guys, Unk? I got to get them back for this. Burn down our house and try and kill me. I can't let them get away with that."

"I was going to wait until I got there, but since we are talking about it now, I will tell you what we are going to do. First, I want those guys to think you died in the fire. That is what they think right now. They won't come looking for you again if they think you are dead. So you can't go home, you can't be seen in town, and they can't know you are in Ada at the hospital. We have to keep that quiet. When you get out of the hospital, you need to shack up over at Lucy's house and don't go home. You can't move your truck; you can't tell anybody at work you are okay. Just let them think you are missing."

"Unk, I can't do that. I got to tell them at work what is happening. I can't let them think I am dead."

"You are not going to tell anybody you aren't dead. You are just not going to tell anybody anything. When it comes time, you need to tell them at work that you were laid up in the hospital and unable to call in because the smoke inhalation made it difficult to talk. In the meantime, you are not going to be around to say anything to anybody. I have a plan for the rest of it. I am working on it. Just do what I tell you and it will all work out."

"What about my dad? Can I tell him?"

"Not yet. Trust me on this, nephew. This ends the right way. Just let me handle things. It's better you don't know. I don't want you to know. Give me a week, at least."

"I need to go kick some redneck hillbilly ass, Unk. I can't let them do this to me."

"Listen to me, Wiley. Revenge is way overrated. Believe in karma. Karma will bring them a righteous end. This is something I know a lot about. Give it a week and if this isn't resolved, then we can talk about it again. They won't be getting away with anything. In the meantime, let your uncle handle what needs to happen."

"Lucy just walked back in. Say hi to her." Wiley put his phone on speaker.

"Hey, Lucy. Cody here again."

"Hi, Uncle Cody. Sorry about last night. I just didn't know for sure what I should do when you called. You kind of surprised us. Sorry my dad brought his gun."

"I don't have any problem with any of that. Just appreciate you taking Wiley to Ada. Thanks for staying with him last night too."

Wiley piped up. "She is leaving here around eleven, Unk. You think you will be here before she leaves? I want you to meet her. You know, official." Wiley finished the statement with a small coughing fit.

Cody smiled. *Wiley must really like this girl.* "I am picking up Ricky and Tiberius in Tishomingo, and they are going to help me take care of your dad's horses. We will come after that, but I don't think we will get there before eleven. Sorry. Look forward to meeting you soon though, Lucy."

Lucy replied, "Well, I am going to head home and shower

and take care of a few things at work and then I will be back here again tonight. I just want Wiley to stay a few more days so we can monitor his lungs and his oxygen level. His coughing is way down from where it was, but you can still hear it in his voice. He needs to rest."

"I completely agree, Lucy. He needs a lot of rest. Maybe even a week or so, wouldn't you say?"

"Absolutely. A week would be ideal. That is what the doctor here said also."

"You listen to her, nephew. I will see you this afternoon when I bring Tiberius and Ricky." Cody hung up the phone and sighed heavily. He had a plan and was ready to work it.

# CHAPTER XXXII

**"T**his is Lucas." The man seldom answered calls from un-recognized numbers, but this one originated from an area code where he had some activity that he was concerned about.

"Lucas, you don't know me, but I work with Randal in Oklahoma. We do work for you. You know what I mean. I am calling to give you a heads-up about a couple of things you prob'ly want to know about." Cody did his best to talk in the accent of the area. It helped that he grew up in Texas and could easily swing back into that way of speaking.

"I am listening," Lucas responded after a pause.

"Randal is drinking way too much and taking drugs every night. Dude is messed up most of the time and not thinking right. He has decided he can't pull off those three jobs you gave us, and he is planning on blackmailing you. He has been talking about you guys in Kansas City and mentioning your name in particular to a number of people. He is getting stupid. He knows you are going to kick us off your team, and he wants to get something from you before you do. I quit on him last night. Some of the other guys are probably going to quit too. You need to do something or it's going to get stupid fast, and we are all going to get in trouble."

"And what did you say your name was?"

"Didn't say. Not going to. You clean this up, though, and we let things settle down again. I will reach out to you about picking up where things left off. I am the brains of Randal's operation anyway. Nothing happens unless I think of it first. Randal is a certified idiot in case you hadn't figured it out by now."

"And how did you get my number?"

"That stupid bastard passes out every night. I got it out of his phone. He talks about you all the time, and you are in his phone directory. Not hard to find you. By the way, that drunk sheriff down here is in on the blackmail plan. He knows about you too."

There was a long pause without a response. Cody knew that Lucas was being careful in case the call was being recorded.

"Well, frankly, I don't know why you are telling me all this. You must have a very active imagination, son. I don't have anything involving anybody that they could blackmail me with. Please don't call me again and lose this number." He hung up the call without saying goodbye.

Cody smiled. Lucas had responded in the way that he had privately predicted. He knew that Lucas was immediately shifting into damage control and probably already had a contingency plan for this type of event; ending the call that way meant he was writing everything off with Randal and his crew.

There would be no way to be certain about what his response would be until it actually happened, unfortunately. Cody knew his challenge now would be to keep everybody in hiding and off the radar until Lucas had time to respond. He calculated that if something didn't happen to Randal in the next week, however, then he probably did not take the bait. He surmised that Lucas would most likely execute some kind of response in the next several days if he was planning on taking action. He doubted that he would just ignore the phone call, in any case. Worst case, it would still cause some friction between Randal and Lucas and get him kicked off Lucas's team of henchmen. Best case, Lucas would take Randal and his gang out entirely. If he dealt with the sheriff in addition, so much the better.

Cody carefully turned off the phone that he originated the call to Lucas on. It was a burner phone that he purchased at Walmart for cash. It was only potentially traceable by government investigative entities, but it wasn't likely that Lucas had the connections to make that happen. He placed the phone and the charger that came with it in the glove box of his "new" old beater truck and closed it up. In the event some follow-up was needed with Lucas, he wanted to keep the phone around for a bit.

He started the vehicle up and turned on the air-conditioning to cool down the cab and pulled out his normal cell phone. He needed to plan out the balance of his day, and it might involve some driving. He went to his stored number screen and pushed the entry to originate a call to Lisa. When she answered, he immediately started in on her.

"I have this problem that I need to talk about." He smiled while he was speaking to her, which came across in his voice.

"What is it? Maybe I can help," Lisa replied playfully.

"I want to take my girlfriend out to lunch."

"That is your only problem?"

"My girlfriend is a busy lady and very important. I didn't get to see her last night and I think she misses me."

"Well, I am sure she can make time if she is interested, that is. If she isn't interested, she will probably go on and on about how busy and complicated her schedule is."

"Yeah. Well, the other thing is that I have this parachute in the back of my truck and I need to do something with it. I cannot just go driving into the Air Force base looking for my girlfriend with government property in my truck. Sounds like a good way to get people in trouble." Cody smiled as he said it, remembering the night of the jump.

"Since you are calling me fairly early in the morning, and I haven't made plans for lunch yet, and since Elliott is standing right next to me with the keys to an Air Force truck in his hands,

I think I have a solution to your problems, sir."

"Ahhhh. I knew there was a reason I called," Cody responded.

"Elliott is going to meet you in the Palomino Club parking lot just outside the base gate and take that parachute off your hands. I suggest that you meet him around the back of the building so nobody sees you guys unloading a bulky canopy and harness out of your vehicle into his. As for the other part of the problem, like I told you this morning, I have duty today. I can't leave the base, so I am going to take you to the officers' club for lunch. I will alert the gate guard that you are coming, and they will call me when you are at the gate. I will come and get you and show you around a bit first. How does that sound?"

"You are a problem solver."

"No going in the Palomino Club, however. Neither of you."

"You think Elliott might try and look at those poor girls' pale parts, Boss Lady? I can't believe he would try that old trick. Put money in their panties and try and peek? Those girls just want to get through college."

She ignored his comment about the Palomino Club. "I am going to parade you around the O club like a show pony, and everyone will soon be talking about you, Mr. Houston. Are you prepared for it?"

"Do I need to buy a new shirt before I come? You know how I am dressed. Hardly show pony quality. Why don't you just tell them I am your maintenance man or something."

"Since I live in base housing and don't own a house, exactly what is it that you would be maintaining for me?"

"I never have felt that everybody needs to know everything. Your call, Captain. Just don't want to let down the side."

"You are the most handsome, sexiest man I have ever known. You would look good in a trash bag. I am proud to be with you no matter what you are wearing. I like a guy that doesn't try too hard."

"Well, between my Sanford and Son truck and my jump boots and tactical pants, I can't wait to hear what they would say about me. I think I will stop and buy some jeans and a shirt along the way, assuming I can find a place here in Duncan that has such things, that is. I don't get taken to the fancy officers' club very often."

"It ain't that fancy, believe me. Mostly just a bunch of old pilots playing cards and telling the same bullshit stories that they have been telling each other for the past year. I would offer to come off base to meet you if I could, believe me. I have always hated duty nights, but that is how the military works, as you know."

"I never had too much duty since I served on the teams. Only time we ever had duty or stood a watch was because we were on an Op."

"Okay, Frogman. You have just always been special, haven't you?" She tweaked him.

"Listen, Boss Lady, you know if you call me Frogman, that makes you a Frog Hog."

"Okay, please don't get all military man on me! That is exactly what I am trying to get away from. Don't ruin a good thing for me, for God's sake."

They both had a good laugh and hung up the call.

The drive to Altus went smoothly. Cody found a western wear shop on the way out of town and found a pair of jeans and a nice shirt. He decided to stick with his web belt and jump boots, though, and his outfit still felt partly in uniform and partly out. It would have to do for now.

He met up with Elliott in the Palomino Club parking lot, and they shared a good exchange about the jump. Elliott thanked Cody for being conscientious about bringing the parachute back so soon, and they transferred it over to the Air Force vehicle he was driving. After the needling back-and-forth between them ceased, Elliott looked at Cody with a serious face.

"You know, Boss Lady gave her official notice about leaving the Air Force. They were recruiting her hard and everybody was sure she was going to change her mind and stay in, but she surprised everybody by getting out. They almost guaranteed her a promotion to major in the next cycle and a big bonus to stay in. She told them thanks but no thanks. She must have a bad case of you to do that. I have never seen her more relaxed or happier, though. I hope you take good care of her."

"I knew she was leaning in that direction, but she hadn't told me that she officially gave them notice." Cody tried to act as though he had not been actively talking to her about the subject every night.

"Yeah, they promoted Jacob to left seat, and I am going to be staying on with him in his crew. We are waiting on them to find a co-pilot for the crew now. I guess we will be grounded for a while until they get us somebody new. They took Boss Lady off flight status since she is leaving. They are probably going to release her early. Colonel is all pissed off at her and being shitty about it. That is why she is pulling duty now. He is a dick."

"Well then, I might not be seeing you again. Thanks again for the good help on the jump, Elliott. I appreciated it. Just happy it didn't end up with a bad case of dirt poisoning for me." Cody reached out with his fist and smiled at the young man. He liked him and appreciated that he was so loyal to Lisa.

"Take care, Frog." He bumped fists with Cody and opened the door to the truck cab. "Hope I see you again. Maybe at the wedding, eh?" He smiled at Cody as he climbed into his truck and started the motor.

Cody waved and smiled back without responding to the tweak. He called Lisa and waited for her to answer.

"You at the gate yet?" she asked.

"On my way. Still at the Palomino Club. Elliott just left."

"Okay, I am just about there. I will probably beat you."

As Cody hung up, a thought crossed his mind that hadn't occurred to him before. Since Lisa was tied up on base for the night,
and he was so close to Texas, he wondered if the Musselwhites
might be at home. This seemed like a good chance to pop in for
a quick visit if Ernie was there. It would get him out of town
and keep him from being seen in Tishomingo, and it also would
provide a watertight alibi for him if something did go down with
Randal. An alibi could be important and would serve to keep him
from being blamed for any attack on Randal's compound and
becoming a person of interest in the ensuing investigation. After
she got off duty, Lisa might be able to come down herself to stay
for a few days and meet the Musselwhites also. He would bring
it up at lunch.

# CHAPTER XXXIII

The four men in the back of the box truck did not know each other. They had been summoned together from different locations for this special one-time operation and instructed not to exchange information. The appointed leader referred to himself as Viper and gave each other member of the team a call sign; that was the only way they could refer to each other. Rattler, Cobra, and Boa rode in the back of the truck with their leader and silently awaited delivery to the attack site. Each had a Ruger PC-9 nine-millimeter carbine, modified to accept large Glock magazines, and bulletproof vests with two extra thirty-three-round magazines. Each vest had a nine-millimeter Glock handgun for backup that could share the same magazines as the carbines. Each carbine was outfitted with a suppressor, and all four of the men were out-fitted with radio transmitter earpieces and boom microphones for communication. The ammunition was 147-grain, subsonic hollow point for minimal noise when shot out of the suppressed carbines. All the gear had been checked, ammunition distributed, plates inserted in vests, and the men given a brief rundown of the site at a remote location. They would not be overmatched with firepower in this exchange. Viper had seen to that.

The driver was to drop them off on the road, and they were to infiltrate with three men approaching the backyard area, where Randal's men normally assembled, and attack from a flank, forming a field of fire in only one direction to avoid any injuries from friendly fire. It was anticipated that a substantial number of the intended victims would be drinking and drugging outside as usual. The fourth member of their team would overwatch the front door and take down any escapers and snipers from the house. Once those outside were killed, Viper would lead a sweep of the house to ensure that all intended victims were taken out. The goal was a swift kill and rapid departure with no survivors or witnesses and no unnecessary evidence left behind.

All corpses were to be left as-is on site, and the team members were to immediately return to the truck that would circle back to the site on call. This was a pure kill, and there was not going to be any attempt to clean up the crime scene. Lucas had brought some bags of cocaine, however, that he intended to spill on site to provide a false lead to disguise the motive. If he could set up a false narrative on motive, he would wrongfoot the detectives investigating and complicate the investigation. Once the job was completed, Lucas intended to circle back with the sheriff and confront him with his options. He was confident that he could make the sheriff close his eyes and conduct an unfruitful investigation. He had plenty of ammunition against the sheriff based on what Randal had told him, and he had plenty to bribe him with to make him fumble the investigation.

If that failed, then the sheriff would be taken out too. Lucas was prepared to tell him that. Lucas had decided to personally lead the attack. First, he could not afford a mistake on this mission. Second, he had been aching for some action and this would provide a fast-hitting, low-risk op with plenty of violence. Lastly, he just detested Randal and looked forward to watching him die. The guy was a miserable, lowlife, tyrant of a man who deserved to die a hard death. Lucas gave himself the call sign Viper because they were nocturnal snakes, and they ambushed their prey. Both traits lined up perfectly with the intended operation.

He had initially considered coming alone and performing this operation by himself like the good old days. Based on what he knew about these rednecks, he expected them to be drunk, stoned, and completely unsuspecting of an attack. They had the people in the area completely cowed and they had the police in their pocket. He anticipated that there would be either four or five in the compound, including Randal. After reflecting on the possible outcomes, he had decided to bring a heavy crew. Not being certain about how many targets there would be and where everybody would be located when the attack started, he decided that more hands were needed to ensure a successful result with no injuries to any attacker and, most importantly, nobody escaping. If all three attackers emerged firing on the crowd in the back-yard, their gang would be taken out quickly before any counter response could be mustered. With a fourth person on overwatch on the other side of the house, nobody would be able to escape. Even though he only had what he knew about the layout and fea-tures of Randal's compound from his solo visit to the site, he was confident about the plan.

He surveyed his three attackers. They were each the best of the crews that he used on other assignments. They were all on loan specifically for this op. Immediately when it wrapped, they would be returned with a good bonus and a promise not to ever speak to anybody about what happened. So far, he liked what he saw and liked how the op was starting out. He did not need the heat of any failed attempt here or any casualties among his crew. He needed everybody working with precision and out again with no wounded and no casualties. Other than a field medical kit, he had no backup plan for medical attention. He had told them as much in the briefing. They all accepted that and were following his rules and remaining quiet with no personal information shar-ing. They did not know who Lucas was, they were all cowboys down for heavy action according to their bosses, and they were all expert marksmen. They seemed ready to work as a team and split immediately with no information on who they were attacking, what the reason was, and who they were working with or for. He thought he had it perfectly set up. No risk of a leak and, hopefully, if nobody got hurt or killed in the raid on his side, they would be out of the area and gone before they could get caught.

The truck came to a slow halt and Lucas heard the cab door open. Within seconds, the overhead door was being opened and a gust of fresh air hit all four of the men. They all jumped down and followed Lucas to the fence line and through the barbed-wire strands that he held separated by his foot and hands. They gathered in a semicircle around Lucas as they put gloves on and finished their last-minute re-check of all gear. In a low voice, he had them all actuate their microphones and go through the comm check. With a circular wave, they all slinked their way through the underbrush and thickets toward the house in the distance. The lights of the backyard were illuminated, and loud voices and music could be heard from their location. As they made their way, the truck left on a forward track to find a remote, unobserved location to turn around and prepare for the pickup per the instructions that Lucas had given the driver.

Lucas's crew made the approach in silence with no needless chatter. As they approached the house, Lucas made a turn and gave a hand signal for the overwatch to separate and find his station. The other two approached the backyard with him, and they slinked up to the edge of the light. They had the tactical advantage since the illumination of the backyard diminished the night vision of their adversary. Randal's crew were heavily involved in an axe-throwing competition. Judging by the smell of the smoke in the air, they were smoking a substantial amount of weed and drinking heavily, based on the number of beer cans strewn about. There were four bearded men laughing and gambling on the outcome of the axe toss. Recognizing Randal's imposing stature,

Lucas made note of his location and determined that he would personally attack him first.

Lucas waited for his two companions to separate and find their lanes for the assault. Using his microphone for the first time, he confirmed in a low voice that all parties were on station and prepared for the assault. All safeties were off, all weapons were ready, and everybody was ready to move. Everybody was to wait until he initiated the assault. He silently waited, observing and waiting for a moment when Randal would be highly exposed to his attack lane, and then started a simple one-two-three count-down. At the end of the countdown, he rapidly advanced toward the group with his weapon at the ready. When they got within fifteen yards of the table where they were all standing, he opened fire and immediately took Randal out with several body shots. His cohorts took out a man each and then Lucas took out the fourth man with a head shot into his forehead that blew out the back of his skull. Lucas went over and put a round into the skull of the other three men to confirm their kill and then went on comm to ask if the overwatch had seen any motion.

"Four down in back, no casualties here, Overwatch. Any activity your side?"

"Nothing here, Viper. All quiet."

"Ten-four. Stay on station. Rattler, you come with Viper to clear the house. Cobra remains on overwatch in front, and Boa has overwatch on back. Nobody escapes. Nobody."

The two men entered the house and quickly swept the downstairs. Lucas observed a monitor screen in the entry area from the garage that displayed the security cameras' recording. They climbed the stairs to the second floor and found no resistance. They entered each room and found two young ladies clinging to each other in abject fear in the last bedroom. Once the two entered the room, the women began begging for their lives to be spared. Without hesitation, Lucas shot both of the women instantly. After completing the search under the bed and in all the closets for any other possible survivors, he took out the two bags of cocaine in his backpack and slit one open and slung it over the room. He laid the unopened bag in a semi-hidden location in the bedroom to appear as if it had been overlooked in a hasty escape by the attackers.

Lucas keyed his mic. "Any motion on either side?"

"Negative on the front, Viper."

"None on the back."

"All clear inside. Coming out the back door. Prepare for return to the vehicle. Confirm driver in position."

On the way out, Lucas opened his knife and cut the wires leading to the recorder for the outdoor security cameras and stuffed the recorder into his backpack.

"On station, Viper. All clear here."

"Pull up and pick us up at the end of the driveway."

"Ten-four."

The team beat a hasty retreat down the driveway. The driver was out and had the overhead door open. All four of the attackers rapidly jumped up into the back and the driver closed the door. He returned to the cab and drove off into the night. The music continued playing loudly and the light was shining as if the party continued. The box truck made a calculated, nonchalant escape down the gravel road. Lucas nodded at each member of the team. He was relieved. It had gone exactly as he hoped it would, and each of the team members had performed their role perfectly. *A little extra bonus,* he thought.

# CHAPTER XXXIV

**C**ody drove the Cadillac Escalade to the car wash and waited in line for the attendant to take it from him. Immediately upon edging to the front of the line, two employees began vacuuming the interior and prepping the vehicle for entry into the tunnel wash. Cody stepped inside and took a seat next to a table with a stack of magazines and busied himself with a perusal of fashion, movie stars, sports celebrities, and how to lose weight without dieting, while he waited for the car to be washed and then wiped down. When he got the signal that the big SUV was ready, he stuffed a five-dollar bill in the tip box and headed to his destination at the executive airport. Loretta Musselwhite had asked him to pick up her husband Ernie so she could continue with her preparations of dinner in anticipation of his return from Washington, D.C. Ernie liked a clean car and she lamented that she hadn't kept it as clean as he liked it that week. She asked that Cody stop and get it cleaned on his way. He had spent a couple of days doting on her and taking care of countless small chores that she needed done because she didn't want to bother Ernie when he came home. Cody was happy to help; he enjoyed making her happy and she enjoyed taking care of him with nice meals, frequent drinks, and snacks.

Lisa was on her way down as well. She had not been able to depart until after four o'clock, but she was on the road and planned to be there later tonight. Cody could not wait to introduce her to the Musselwhites. Cody was early to pick up his passenger at the private Fixed Base Operation at the local airport in

Lubbock. Ernie always arranged for a private charter from Dallas to pick him up and fly him the last leg of the flight from Dallas to Lubbock to get him home to Loretta faster. His normal schedule had him leaving D.C. in the early afternoon on a direct flight to Dallas and getting home by the dinner hour on the short charter flight. It gave him a nice sense of normalcy being with his wife on a Friday evening, and they had the benefit of the entire evening together just as if he worked locally. In his opinion, it was well worth the expense.

Cody pulled up to the FBO and settled into the pilot's lounge after telling the front desk attendant who he was waiting to pick up. There was a wall-mounted television playing the local news, and several people were watching to pick up the upcoming weather forecast. Ernie had given Cody the tail numbers and type and coloration of the plane he was coming in to help identify when he was landing. He asked Cody to pull his SUV up to the plane to expedite the transfer of his luggage and getaway. He was ready to get home and relax from a long week in D.C. Cody could tell that he was tired of the noise and drama of the capital, and that he appreciated coming home to his wife and home for downtime and peace.

As Cody was making a lap around the conference room looking at the pictures of planes and local pilots, his phone rang with a call from Wiley.

"How you doing, nephew?"

"You back in Florida, Unk?"

"No, I am down in Texas catching up with Loretta and Ernie. You know I wouldn't leave the area without saying goodbye to my favorite nephew. You know that much about me." Cody smiled at the thought that Wiley was looking for him.

"Didn't think you would, but then I hadn't seen or heard from you in three days, so I was starting to wonder. That, and you didn't exactly let anybody know you were coming either. Not that I object to getting saved from a fire or anything."

"I just wanted to get out of town to lie low like I am telling you to do. How you feeling?"

"I am good. Bored to death in this hospital. Read every magazine you gave me three times now. Ricky and Tiberius have been coming to see me every day, though. Did you know that Tiberius sings opera? That dude has been coming in here, steps up on a little platform he brings with him, and he sings opera songs for me. All the other patients have heard him singing and have been requesting him to sing for them too. He has become quite the celebrity around here. That guy amazes me sometimes."

"Well now, I have to say, I wouldn't have thought of Tiberius as being an opera singer. Is he good?"

"Hell yes. Guy sounds like Pavarotti. He only knows three songs though. He sings that 'Nessun Dorma' a lot. From an opera called *Turandot*. You know it? He has been teaching me about opera."

"Tramontante, stelle. Vincero! Vincero!"

"Are you kidding me? You know the song?"

Cody chuckled. "I am not just an old dude that doesn't eat enough vegetables, nephew. I know a few things."

"You never stop amazing me, Unk. That is awesome. You and Tiberius have something to talk about. Just wondering if you know a little about something else?"

"Talk to me."

"There was a very serious crime committed next to our property last night. Six people murdered at Randal's house. All dead."

"Hmmm. Happened last night, did it? How did you hear about it?"

"Everybody in town is talking about it. Lucy heard about it and told me."

"I guess that means that you don't need to stay in the hospital any longer, then. And your dad and Doris can come back too. No need to hide out any longer, is there?"

"Lucy is coming to get me. They are letting me out tonight. I am so sick of this hospital. I can't wait to see what happens when I show up for work. You didn't say anything about what happened. What do you know about the murders at Randal's?"

"I just know that karma exists, nephew. You should always believe in karma. As for me, I have been in Texas for the last few days helping Loretta out with some chores around the house and waiting on Ernie to come back. I didn't know anything about it until you just mentioned it to me. Speaking of Ernie, here is his plane landing now. I need to jump and head out and pick him up. I will be back on Sunday. Catch up with you at your place then?"

"If you say so. Guess I will call my pop and tell him the good news. Say hello for me to Ernie."

"Ten-four. See you Sunday."

Cody breezed up to the front desk and asked the attendant, "Is that the plane that Congressman Musselwhite is coming in on?"

The man peered out the window and nodded his head in confirmation. "Yeah, that is it. You driving out to pick him up? Loretta usually drives out to get him."

Cody gave him a thumbs-up, exited the building to the vehicle, and drove up to the entrance of the airfield waiting for the plane to park. After it came to a rest, he rolled up alongside the door and popped the liftgate on the back of the truck. Ernie politely shook hands with the pilot and thanked him for the good flight, and they agreed on what time to meet for his return flight to Dallas. During that conversation, Cody approached and began loading bags into the vehicle and opened the passenger door for him. After a quick embrace and a few pleasantries, they were on their way back to his house.

"Before you go on more about work, Ernie, I want to ask you something, and I would like to do it before we get back to your house so we can have a private conversation about it. You mind?"

"No, son. By all means, go ahead."

"I talked to you about this sheriff in Tishomingo, remember? There is a lot happening with this situation, including life insurance fraud and a national murder for hire scheme as well as the corrupt sheriff."

"Okay. What can I do to help out? Sounds like you want to do something about it."

"I talked to a lady in your office who gave me some contact information on the FBI office in Oklahoma City, the Oklahoma State Bureau of Investigations, and the governor's office. I appreciated her follow-up and suggestions. I think I need something more specific, though."

Cody paused for a moment for emphasis and waited for a response from Ernie. He looked over at Ernie and saw that he was intently staring at Cody. He accelerated onto the highway toward Ernie's house.

"Waiting for the punchline, son. Ready to help." He smiled broadly.

"I want the FBI agents to call the sheriff and ask to use a conference room or interrogation room in his office for an interview with Wiley's dad, Shane, and his girlfriend, Doris, in Tishomingo. Doris was held hostage by a group of guys in Tishomingo that acted as contract killers for a financial company based in Kansas City that purchases assignments of life insurance contract benefits from people for upfront cash and then has the insureds murdered to collect the proceeds soon after. Obviously, killing off the insureds makes buying the insurance contracts a pretty lucrative business. They do this on a national scale and use groups like this one in Tishomingo to murder the insureds. That group in Tishomingo was trying to use Doris in their scheme to kill a guy in California. The scheme they had in mind for the target needed a female accomplice, and they wanted Doris to be the accomplice. She escaped from them, they were hunting for her, and Wiley, Shane, and I found her and rescued her, and we got her to safety."

"Never boring being you, is it, Cody?" Ernie smiled. "Still listening."

"Doris wants to tell her story to someone and move on in life. She thinks what they have been doing is wrong and wants to share the information that she has on the criminal activities going on with someone who will do something about it. She would normally just take it to the sheriff who has jurisdiction there, but she is not willing to because she believes that he is on the payroll of and involved in some of the activities with this gang."

"Okay, I can understand that," Ernie responded.

"Wiley and I had a confrontation with the leader of this gang, named Randal. Randal tried to restrain Wiley and me and keep us from leaving our property the night that we found Doris and got her away from him. The confrontation went badly between him and me, he got hurt, and we took a weapon away from him. The sheriff came to visit Wiley and me at his house to ask about it and get the weapon back the next day. We told him what happened, and he didn't pursue anything further with us."

"Randal got hurt, did he? Messing around with you and Wiley? He obviously isn't the sharpest tool in the shed." Ernie snorted. "Then what?"

"After I went back to Florida, Randal had his guys kidnap Wiley. They drugged him and put him in the old farmhouse on our property and set it on fire. I got back there just in time to drag him out. He is getting out of the hospital tonight and going home. I am not sure what the motivation was with Wiley, either revenge for the attack or somehow trying to get back at Wiley and Shane for not letting him have Doris back. Maybe he thought that Shane would fold and turn her back over to him or something."

"What the hell? Those guys kidnapped Wiley? And then tried to kill him? In a fire of all things? Are you kidding me?" Ernie's veins were bulging on his neck. He was furious.

"There is more, Ernie. Randal and all of his guys were murdered last night, according to what Wiley told me a few minutes ago."

Ernie cocked his head slightly. "You were here last night, right? You didn't have anything to do with him being killed, did you?" He looked suspiciously at Cody.

"No, I was here in your spare bedroom, Ernie. It wasn't me."

"Good. You know, if you get the FBI involved, they are going to investigate the hell out of everything, and those guys are good. If you were involved in any way, they are going to find out about it. I don't want to do anything that might hurt you, son."

"No issues. I am not involved."

"Good. So, I call the FBI, ask them to meet with Doris in the sheriff's office. Then what?"

"So, last thing. The sheriff thinks Wiley died in the fire at his house. He has been in the hospital in Ada and has not been at his house and has not been going to work either. I think it is likely that everybody thinks Wiley died in that fire. I want the sheriff to see Wiley walk into his office with Doris. I want to watch him shit himself in front of the FBI. I want to put some heat on him. That is why the meeting needs to happen at the sheriff's office."

"I get it. I don't think that is unusual for these different police agencies to help each other out. I doubt if the FBI gets to Tishomingo very often, though. I can call someone in Oklahoma City and recommend it. I bet that sheriff will crap his pants when he sees Wiley and you walk in with Doris. I can tell you that he does not want any part of the FBI investigating things if he was involved with these guys. Plus, he is going to have to answer questions about Wiley getting kidnapped and those guys getting murdered. No turning back, though, if they get on the case. You sure you aren't involved, and are you sure you want the FBI involved?"

"I do. I think it is the only way that town is going to get totally cleaned up. Someone needs to shut these guys down in Kansas City too."

"I agree. I will call first thing Monday and try to get an agent down there on Tuesday. I haven't ever asked the FBI to do anything for me, so I don't know what kind of response I will get, but I will do my best."

"Thanks, Ernie. I know you will. Wiley says to say hi to you, by the way. And Loretta did tell you that my girlfriend Lisa is coming down tonight, right?"

"This is the Air Force pilot? What time will she be there?"

"The drive from Altus is a little over three hours and she left at four. Dinner is going to be a little late tonight, I'm afraid. Loretta wants to wait until she gets there."

"Well, of course we are going to wait for her to get here. Cody, you are a piece of work, son. I am just flabbergasted by everything you told me. We are going to make sure the guys in Kansas City get shut down. I wonder if anybody in my district has been affected by those guys. I need a drink."

Cody wheeled the big SUV up the driveway and parked next to his truck. Ernie saw it and started laughing. "Is that your vehicle, son? That is the one Loretta was telling me about. Where the hell did you get that old beater?"

"Got that fine piece of machinery at a used car lot in Duncan, Ernie. I am planning on leaving it in Oklahoma at our property, so I have something to drive when I fly out here. Maybe I will take you for a ride in it this weekend before I leave. If you are nice to me, that is." The two men laughed and chatted away about old trucks as they gathered up Ernie's luggage and went inside.

# CHAPTER XXXV

**"H**opefully, you got my message yesterday." The office receptionist looked at the sheriff with disdain. "Kind of early for *Fresca*, isn't it, Clay?"

"What are you talking about? What message?" His head hurt and he felt like ass. He just wanted to be left in peace until he felt better. He took the bottle of Wild Turkey off his desk and replaced it in the bottom drawer with the other bottles.

"I left you a message around noon. An FBI agent from Oklahoma City called, wanting to use our conference room for a couple of hours today, at eleven. They are meeting some people here regarding a potential investigation. I called them back when I hadn't heard from you and told them it would be okay." She knew he had not bothered to listen to her message. She had gone ahead and made the reservation for them anyway since she didn't have any reason not to. Seemed to her that cooperation with the FBI is something a sheriff *should* do.

"Who authorized you to do that?" He squinted at her and suddenly felt a surge of anxiety. All of the weird things going on in this place were putting him on edge. He had no idea how to handle the vicious murder of six people. He had sent deputies out to take photos and study the crime scene, but none of them had the experience to handle a mass murder scene like that. They had photographed and marked up the crime scene the best they knew how and sent the bodies to the medical examiner for autopsies, but nobody had started much of an investigation yet. He did not really want it investigated, in fact. He wanted to go through the motions and just let it die down. His top theories were that Wiley Harris's Florida uncle had done the hit as revenge for killing his nephew. Or, alternatively, the outfit that hired Randal and his idiot thieves had gotten fed up with him and wanted him dead. Or, lastly, any one of numerous people Randal had pissed off in the last ten years decided to do him in. Now the FBI was camping out and taking over his office, interviewing people while he stood around like a stooge helping them launch an investigation that might implicate him. It didn't get much dumber than that.

"I talked to Doug about it. He said he didn't see anything wrong with it," she replied curtly.

"Did they say who they were talking to?" he asked exasperatedly.

"They didn't say, Clay. Does it matter? It's the FBI. I imagine they talk to who they want to talk to. This is the Sheriff's Department, right? We are in the business of enforcing the law, right? If you don't get back to people when they leave you messages, then don't get PO'd when they do things without running it past you first."

"Something like this happens again, you make sure you talk to me about it first before you do anything." He was upset. His staff was getting very disrespectful toward him.

"Roger that." She spun on a heel and walked away. "They should be here in ten minutes."

He cursed under his breath and was walking to the bathroom to pour his coffee cup full of Wild Turkey down the toilet when a group of people walked into the office. He stopped immediately in his tracks when he saw Wiley Harris, Shane Harris, Wiley's uncle from Florida, and the woman who had been living with Randal at his house before she escaped. Wiley locked eyes with him and walked directly back to where the sheriff was standing. Edwards was bewildered and had no idea how to react.

"Wiley," he acknowledged when Wiley stopped in front of

him, staring at him. "Can I help you?"

"You look like you saw a ghost, Sheriff. You don't look well."

"Don't concern yourself about me, boy. What brings you here?" Edwards mustered his best steely-eyed stare-down.

"Got a meeting with the FBI in a few minutes. Guess we will just go ahead and sit down in the conference room and wait on them. You got some coffee we can help ourselves to?" Wiley kept it nonchalant. It seemed more deadly to maintain his cool in this chess match. He was going to harpoon this man shortly. No need to rush.

"Well, I don't guess you mind if I sit in on the meeting, do you? Since you didn't do me the professional courtesy of coming to me first." His face got red, and the words came spitting out of his mouth like a serpent's hiss.

"Sheriff, I can't think of anything I would like better than for you to sit in with us. You are half of what we are going to be talking about in our meeting. When I get done with your drunk ass today, you will be halfway back to that shitty mobile home park you climbed out of ten years ago when you got elected."

Cody saw the encounter between the two getting heated and moved forward to intervene. The sheriff looked at him and said, "You better get your nephew under control, Houston, before he gets you both in trouble."

"We came here to make trouble for some, Sheriff. Yeah, trouble for some and justice for others. Trouble for some and justice for others, I say." He grabbed Wiley by the arm and gently made a motion toward the conference room, where Shane and Doris were already situated.

Two men and a woman, all in suits, walked through the front door. They were all serious-looking people.

"You are the lady I talked to yesterday?" The woman nodded her head affirmatively. "I am Special Agent Pybus, and these are my two associates." He thanked her for scheduling them into the room and then asked, "Is Cody Houston here yet? That is who we are meeting with."

The sheriff snorted his disgust and continued into the men's room to empty his cup. Cody raised his hand. "We are here, Special Agent Pybus. We are meeting in there in the conference room." He pointed to where Shane and Doris were seated. "I was just getting some coffee for myself and Officer Wiley Harris, here. Can I get some for any of you?"

"I would have some, black, please. These two don't drink coffee. Thanks."

The three went in and Wiley followed. Cody made a production of pouring the three cups of coffee and entered the room as Wiley was giving a background summary on each of the people that they were to be speaking with. Just as Cody was handing off the coffee to Wiley and Agent Pybus, the sheriff burst into the room.

"Just in case anybody cares, my name is Sheriff Edwards. This is my office. I am responsible for keeping law and order in this county. I think it's downright unprofessional for you people to barge in here and have meetings here in my office without the courtesy of an advance meeting with me to brief me first." Edwards directly glared at Doris as if to tell her not to say anything that implicated him.

Agent Pybus stared down the sheriff with complete professional cool. "Thank you, Sheriff. Allow me to introduce my associates. This is Thomas Callahan from our Kansas City office and Renee Willow from our financial crimes division in Dallas. These two have been part of an ongoing investigation into a crime ring involved in insurance fraud based in Kansas City for several months. They flew in today on short notice based on a reputable report from a credible source that they could have information helpful to our investigation. The crimes under investigation are federal offenses that would not involve participation from your office. That credible source I referenced is a United States congressman who has shared useful information that we hope to corroborate and expand upon today. Your presence is not required nor requested. We will be happy to debrief with you before we depart if you like. However, I think it would be better for our purposes if you did not attempt to include yourself in this discussion. I appreciate your understanding."

The birthing of terror is difficult to watch. When a moment of fear and sudden realization of danger consumes the consciousness of a living being, it can cause involuntary response. In some cases, shock and the inability to respond or move reveal the terror. In other cases, automatic bowel movement is unleashed. In other situations, the sudden shock of the realization causes a frozen expression of psychic trauma in the face that is undisguisable. Edwards looked as if he had suffered a concussion and simultaneously messed his pants. He haltingly backed out of the doorway without speaking another word and slowly shuffled away.

Agent Pybus scanned the room and then looked at his two associates. Callahan wrote a quick note on a page of his notepad and shared it with Pybus and Willow. They all made a nod and continued on. Pybus looked at Wiley. "Officer Harris, thanks for sharing your background and that of the others. We have already done a little research and are fairly familiar with each of you. Who wants to start off?"

Doris sat up in her chair and leaned forward with her hand partially raised. "I would, sir." She pulled out a folder with a typed memo that she slid across the table to Pybus. "Sorry, I only made two copies of this. This is a complete written statement I have signed stating everything I know and all the information including phone numbers and names that I have to support it."

Pybus quickly perused the memo and slid copies to both Callahan and Willow. He watched silently as they both read the memo. Willow looked up at Pybus and nodded her head. Pybus leaned back in his chair, and a casual, friendly, back-and-forth discussion of what Doris knew began that went on for over an hour. Occasional supporting comments and interjections from Wiley and Shane occurred, but Cody did not offer any information himself.

Cody and Wiley had agreed that no mention of Cody parachuting into town to drag him out of the burning house would be made to either Wiley's work or to the FBI. They agreed that to the extent it was necessary to discuss it, Wiley would just explain that he escaped the fire through the crawlspace. After the lengthy exchange of information between Doris, Shane, Wiley, and the three agents was completed, there was a long pause as the agents reviewed and compared their notes and huddled quietly between themselves.

The three agents appeared to be in agreement, and all nodded their heads. Pybus looked at Cody. "Mr. Houston, this meeting was arranged on your behalf. You haven't really spoken. Do you have anything to add?"

"I think you have the most credible people here speaking what they know about things. Anything I would add would just be a secondhand version of something they told me or something that happened directly to them."

"Interesting. I was told I could believe anything you said, even if it sounded unbelievable. Disappointing. I was hoping for something big from you."

Everybody in the room enjoyed the gentle nudge and laughter broke out.

Cody replied, "Well, I could probably come up with something if it's important to you, but I think you have quite a bit here if you go to work on it." Cody knew that Ernie must have spoken to Pybus directly and given him a big promo.

Pybus nodded and continued looking directly at Cody. "We have information that this guy Randal you were speaking of earlier and his group were murdered the other night in a brutal shooting attack at the house they all lived in. Six people killed by gunfire, from what we heard. Do any of you know anything about that?" The question was addressed to the group, but Pybus maintained his steely stare directly at Cody.

Cody immediately picked up on why the agent stared at him when he asked that question. "Well, Special Agent Pybus, if it is helpful to you, let me cover half of what you are asking. I do not know any better than you who was involved in that attack, but I can share some information that you might find helpful in assessing exactly who could *not* be involved in the attack. You can feel free to confirm that on the night that the attack you spoke of occurred, Officer Harris here was in the hospital recovering from the smoke inhalation he suffered in the attempted murder against him. Shane here was in a remote cabin on Lake Texoma with Doris and her two children, hiding from the people who were killed, and they have witnesses to that effect. And lastly, I was in Lubbock, Texas, at the home of the party who called you to request the appointment today. They would be happy to corroborate, I am sure."

"That is helpful. I hope you don't take offense if we check with those witnesses."

"It would not offend us a bit. I think it would be good to get that concern off the table as early as possible," Cody replied.

"Good then," he responded. "Let's debrief with the sheriff." Pybus turned and looked at his two cohorts.

Callahan stood up and spoke. "I will go get him." He purposefully walked out into the lobby.

Doris, Wiley, Shane, and Cody all stood up and were shaking hands and thanking the agents as they prepared to leave. Callahan returned and interrupted. "The receptionist is saying that the sheriff left the office and asked not to be disturbed."

Pybus looked at Callahan briefly and considered the information he had just shared. Expressionless, he turned, picked up his notepad, and announced, "I guess we are done here, then. Thanks everybody, for sharing the information with us. We have your contact information and will get back to you if we need anything further." He smiled pleasantly and followed his team out into the lobby.

Cody looked over at Wiley, who returned his glance with a slight smile. The harpoon had been launched and was a direct hit to the heart.

# CHAPTER XXXVI

**D**illon slammed the bags of ice on the dock beside the boat to break the ice into the original small cubes in which it had been formed. Cody laid the packages of pre-rigged ballyhoo bait on top of the ice to keep them fresh for the fishing they intended to do later. Dillon snatched one of the bags up to study it.

"Good. You were able to find the double hooked 'hoos. Those have been hard to find lately in the large size. Bait has been kind of small lately. I was afraid I might have to start rigging my own baits. We haven't done that in quite a few years, have we?"

Cody flashed a relaxed smile and replied, "No sir, we haven't. I know we could still do it if we needed to, though. Plenty of practice back in the old days. Some things you never forget."

The morning sun had not yet emerged over the horizon, and the two men were working with the boat's T-top light illuminated, and the twin outboard motors were idling patiently while the men put the finishing touches on the preparations. Dillon moved over to the helm station and began programming some GPS coordinates into the unit from a scrap of paper he had carried onto the boat in his pocket.

Ernie Musselwhite, Wiley, and Nate Hill emerged out of the men's room at the boat ramp. Nate Hill was carrying a box that contained the remains of his father, Gordy Hill. Gordy was a Vietnam war helicopter pilot veteran who had become an astrophysicist and director of the Institute of Meteoritics in Albuquerque, New Mexico. His son, Nate Hill, had been abducted in Mexico by some off-the-grid drug lord who was trying to steal a unique meteor that Nate had found. Cody and Gordy had worked together to get Nate back, and the two had made a strong friendship in the process. Gordy had been stricken by leukemia during the time that they were working to free Nate, and knew he didn't have much time to live. His dying wish had been to be reunited with his estranged son and spend some more time with him before he died. Nate had dropped out of his PhD program in astrophysics, which had caused the rift between the two, but had promised his father that he would return to school and complete the doctorate program he was so close to finishing.

In the course of their interaction during the planning of the daring raid to free Nate from his captors, Cody had brought up the celebration of life that a few people he had known had planned for their deaths. It involved their loved ones taking their ashes to the Gulf Stream current in the ocean off the east coast of Florida and spreading the ashes into the stream to go on a perpetual journey around the earth in the three nautical mile per hour constant flow of the Gulf Stream that flowed around the globe as part of the thermal engine of the planet earth. As a scientist and physicist, Gordy was fascinated by this idea, and he had asked Cody to perform this act for him upon his death. Cody had solemnly agreed, and the plan had been discussed in detail with Nate.

When his father died, Nate had contacted Cody and the final plans had been made. Nate was in the final semester of his schooling and had planned it around the end of mid-semester exams. Cody had returned from Oklahoma less than a week prior to the scheduled event, which worked out perfectly. Dillon had the boat ready, and he and Wiley had spent a portion of the previous night rigging tackle and baits and putting some new line on a couple of the Penn rod and reels that Dillon had been using for decades for similar fishing trips. They carefully inserted the rod butts into the T-Top rod holders and secured the outrigger poles and lines pointed in the rear position. The ice, drinks, and bait were all loaded, and the gear was stowed.

The three men stepped onto the boat as a Jimmy Buffet song began playing on the boat stereo. The five men launched from the dock, headed due east thirty-five miles to the Gulf Stream from Port Canaveral basin. The dawn was breaking over the horizon, and the upper edge of the sun was slightly visible in the moist morning air. As they departed the channel, the water became rough, and the waves were slamming the hull as they accelerated onto plane.

Dillon looked at Wiley, Nate, and Ernie and explained, "The waves will calm down a little as we get into deeper water. We have a stretch here where there is a lot of crossing of wave action, and it makes for very choppy water. Once we get past the shoaling that causes all these white caps out here, we will get into calmer water. The current offshore conditions are two- to three-foot waves with a nine-second interval. That is very doable and should make for a nice day."

Ernie nodded and broke out several fat cigars and offered them to the other passengers on the boat. He was well accustomed to going offshore on similar fishing trips and had no concerns about motion sickness, but Nate and Wiley were still concerned that they might not do well in the rough water. Dillon eagerly accepted his offer and Ernie expertly clipped and lit two cigars and passed one to him. Dillon took it and asked Cody if he would take over the boat. Dillon moved around to the front of the boat and began conversing with the other three passengers. Cody could easily overhear the conversation and was tracking the interaction. He felt good being with the important people of his life, enjoying something that was so special to him. He loved the ocean and loved going offshore to fish. A guy never knew what was going to happen on a trip like this. It ranged from absolutely nothing more than a long boat ride to sheer pandemonium caused by mad hookups with any number of different species of fish. This was the time of a trip like this when the anticipation and hope were high, and the adrenaline pumped hard in his body.

Dillon looked at Wiley and asked, "So how do you like riding Nate's dad's bike?" They all four laughed at the crass comment, which seemed awkwardly funny when made by a serial goofball like Dillon. He was so good-natured; it was hard to get upset with him.

Wiley looked at Nate. "It's a great bike, man, and I am going to take good care of it. I named it Gordy after your dad, and I am going to have an Army Aviator badge with his call sign 'Merlin' painted on the rear fender in honor of your dad. I do not know if Cody told you that I was planning on doing that or not. Your dad was a real hero, and I am proud to have his bike."

Nate looked slightly choked up at the mentioning of his father in that fashion and paused before he responded. "That is really awesome, Wiley. Thanks for doing that and I hope you enjoy the bike. My dad loved it but couldn't ride much before he died. I know he would be happy that it is in the hands of a former Army Airborne Ranger. It would make him proud; I know." The two exchanged a fist bump and a bro hug. Ernie took a long pull on his cigar and smiled as he looked at Cody and nodded.

Dillon smiled at the exchange and said, "Now, Wiley, catch me up on yourself. What has been happening with you since we talked last. You were dating some hot nurse you were all wrapped up around the axles about, you were working a lot on your new place, talking about buying an Appaloosa mare so you could breed her with your dad's herd, and you were telling me that your dad had gotten engaged. Anything else new?"

Wiley looked at Cody first and responded, "Well, to tell you the truth, Uncle Dillon, I have some big news that I have been waiting to tell you about. I have been talking to Uncle Cody quite a bit about it and got his blessing. The sheriff in my community has resigned recently and left town. I am thinking about running for sheriff. I haven't quit my job and they tell me I don't have to unless I win, so now that I have that go ahead from them and won't put my job at risk to run for the office, I am going to throw my hat in the ring. There are a couple of the deputies in the sheriff's office that look like they are going to run also, but I think I have just as good a shot as they do. That is my big news."

Cody beamed like a proud father when Wiley broke this news to everybody. Ernie, Dillon, and Nate all clapped and slapped him on the back and congratulated him. Wiley sheepishly looked at Cody, and Cody gave him the thumbs-up. Wiley smiled back at him and fist bumped everybody else.

Ernie spoke up. "Let me know when you get your campaign account opened up, Wiley, and I will send a little something to help out your fund-raising. You know all these other guys will help out too." He looked around and made sure everybody else was nodding in agreement. "You said your dad is getting remarried? Who is the lucky lady?"

"Yeah, Dad is marrying Doris. She is the lady that Cody found in the woods after she escaped from those idiots we had all that trouble with. She is planning on moving in after the wedding in a few months with her two kids. That guy Ricky Hunter has started working for my dad and has moved into the bunk house, so my dad finally has a little paid help around his place. Turns out that Ricky is really good with the horses. We found that out when Dad was staying on Lake Texoma, and I was laid up in the hospital. Ricky did a really good job of taking care of the horses when nobody else could do it, and really seems to love being with them. All he does all day is dote on them, cleaning up after them, and brushing them and feeding them apples all the time. Those horses just follow him around wherever he goes now. It's funny to watch. He is like the Pied Piper with nine mares following him around everywhere he walks. Tiberius comes over to see Ricky quite a bit too. Dad hired him to take care of the yard, so he comes over at least once a week to do that work, and then he comes over some just to see Ricky and hang out with the horses too. Those two are good friends now."

They all broke into grins and exchanged another round of fist bumps. The waves had calmed down as Dillon had promised, and Cody kicked up the RPMs on the two outboards to increase their speed. The old boat handled the waves nicely and provided a nice, dry ride even in rough conditions. Cody motioned Wiley for a beer as the boat sped on toward their destination, and a round of beers was produced for everybody. The sun was clearly breaking over the horizon now and providing good light for the voyage. Cody carefully monitored the GPS to keep them on track for the most direct line to the Gulf Stream and checked the water temperature frequently. The Gulf Stream runs a full three degrees warmer than the interior water of the ocean, and that increase in temperature provided the best indication of when the boat had reached the Gulf Stream current.

Wiley continued, "I got some feedback from Agent Pybus at the FBI. He said the information they gained from our interview has added a lot of energy to their investigation and they are closing in on indictments. He said they got warrants for arrests, but the organization has disbanded. They have identified the principals, however, and are in pursuit. He told me he would keep me advised of progress." Murmurs and high-fives were exchanged, and Ernie gave Wiley a hearty backslap. He looked at Cody and Wiley quizzically.

"In the process of all this, these two bachelors both wound up finding new girlfriends. I haven't heard an update on that front from either of you. Everything good there?" Ernie stared directly at Wiley when he asked.

"All good here, sir. She calls me three times a day. I almost had to bring her out here with me, she is so worried about me all the time. I got a reprieve when we got the update from the FBI. I am looking forward to getting home and seeing her, though."

Ernie nodded his head approvingly and then turned his attention to Cody.

Cody understood what the stare meant. He smiled coyly and responded, "All is fine, Ernie. Lisa is interviewing with a couple of different airlines and trying to get on with a company that can base her out of Orlando. She is going to come out and spend some time with me at my place once she gets out. I am looking forward to having her stay a while. We will see where it goes, but it looks good now."

Ernie smiled and offered an enthusiastic fist bump. "Good boy," he said.

Ernie and Dillon sat down next to each other on one side of the boat and engaged in animated conversation. The two spoke frequently on the phone and really seemed to enjoy talking to each other. Cody enjoyed watching them interact. He was glad that Ernie had agreed to make the trip down for this voyage. He had only met Nate and Gordy once when they came to his house, but he felt connected to them and was eager to participate in the ceremony for Gordy when Cody asked. It didn't hurt that he would be able to spend some time shooting the breeze with Dillon during the outing, Cody suspected.

Nate was well on his way to completing his education at Stanford and had confirmed that he was going to stay on and teach at Stanford when he finished. They had offered him a tenure-tracked professorship, and Nate seemed really happy to land at such a prestigious school. Nate had asked Cody if he would come to his graduation ceremony in December, and Cody had been happy to agree. Nate and Wiley were engaged in a good conversation about something they both found amusing. They were laughing and hand slapping on a fairly frequent basis and seemed to be getting along famously.

Cody kept the boat moving along smartly with good seamanship, riding the waves on a due east heading into the rising sun. He nursed his beer and kept his knees bent as the boat plowed and surfed through the oncoming waves. He made good time toward the destination and clearly entered into the Gulf Stream one hour and twenty minutes into the boat ride. He slowed the boat, idled the engines, and looked at Nate.

"We are on the spot that we talked about, Nate. How does it look to you?"

Nate clutched the box on his lap and bowed his head as if he was suddenly having second thoughts about giving the ocean his only physical connection to his deceased father. Cody cut the engine, turned off the stereo, and gave the lad a moment. Tears were flowing down his cheeks, and he rose to his feet and wiped his face while he held the ashes.

"Dad told me that you would say a few words about him before we released his ashes. Would you mind doing that, after I say what I have to say, Cody?"

Cody nodded. "No problem, Nate. Got it covered." He reached into the dry box in the T-top of the boat and retrieved a flask and five small cups. He set the cups down on the console of the helm station and poured a shot of Jack Daniel's into each of the cups. Dillon handed out a cup to each man and took one for himself.

Nate set down the ashes and took the cup from Dillon. Cody remained standing behind the helm, and the other men stood up in respect for the moment.

"My dad was a good man. I went a long time in life not really understanding him, though. That misunderstanding on my part led to troubles between us at times. As he left me in his final struggles to stay alive, I found out some things about my dad that I never really appreciated until the very end. When I was locked up in Mexico, and I was not sure I was ever going to see him again, I became afraid that I would never be able to reconcile with him before I got killed. I didn't want our last words to be the arguments that we had that made us stop communicating. I was really scared because I knew how devasting that would be for my dad. I started remembering all the good times we had together and wanted so badly to come back home and be with him, just like it had been for us most of our lives together. I became really depressed, but I never gave up hope because I knew my dad would never quit on me. My dad was a small man, but he was fierce, and he was loyal. I knew he would work out something, I just didn't know what it was. In the end, he sent Cody to do what he couldn't physically do any longer. I got reunited with my dad for the last months of his life, and we enjoyed our time together. I had time to really listen to my dad. I mean really listen. In that time, I learned more than I ever have. Wisdom, encouragement, reassurance. My dad had been saying those things to me my whole life. I just hadn't been listening. In the end, my dad knew I was listening, and that made him happy. He knew he was dying, but he was really happy in those final months. That was a gift that I can never replace. I hope my dad is watching us today. If he is, I know he is smiling and happy that such a good group of guys is making a fuss about him. He never asked for anything for himself."

Nate nodded at the others and looked at Cody. Cody held up his cup in a toast and the others followed his lead. The ocean seemed to calm suddenly, and the boat stopped its incessant rocking in the waves for just a moment as Cody spoke.

"Today, we bring a good man to the sea for his final journey as he requested. Gordy 'Merlin' Hill was a father, a scientist, a pilot, and a warrior. He loved his son, he lived with no regrets, and he did not suffer fools. I was proud to be his friend and I am glad he was on my side."

With that toast concluded, the men all followed Cody's lead and threw back the shots. Nate carried the box of ashes to the side of the boat and solemnly poured them into the ocean. When he finished, he returned to his former spot on the boat and became overwhelmed and was trying with all of his might to restrain the emotion. All four of the other men encircled him and locked arms as if protecting him inside their circle. They stood there silently in respect until the wave of emotion and loss subsided in Nate. When he nodded his head and indicated that he was better, the men each looked up and wiped moisture from their own eyes. There was not a dry eye among them and not a bit of shame in admitting to it when the men released each other. They all silently moved back to a comfortable spot on the boat and Cody restarted the motors.

There was a nearby location that marked the start of a lengthy ledge on the bottom of the seabed. Dillon had marked that as the spot where they should begin trolling. As Cody plowed over the surface at trolling speed in the direction of that waypoint, Dillon swung out the outriggers and laid out the ballyhoo baits for rigging. In his efficient way, he had all four lines out in perfect formation in the water fishing as Cody trolled to the starting point at roughly six miles per hour.

Dillon retrieved another beer for Cody at the helm station and offered another to the other passengers. The boat was comfortably silent as everybody reviewed in their minds the act they had just completed and the respect they felt. Thirty minutes later,

Dillon threw a bag of cut fruit to Cody and was eyeballing the sub sandwiches in the cooler when one of the forward rods bent over almost in half with the line leading almost straight downward. The drag on the reel was screaming in complaint as line fed out. Dillon immediately knew they had a trophy fish hooked and began reeling the other lines in and barking orders at the others.

"Nate, jump on that rod and hold on, man! Don't reel against the drag. Let the fish play itself out a little. Ernie, get that other line in next to me here. Wiley, get that other outrigger line in. Cody, slow the boat down to about three miles an hour so we don't strip off all of our line. We got something big on that bait."

After sounding, the fish made several runs in different directions. Nate was holding on valiantly. He was not an experienced fisherman, but Dillon was eagerly coaching him and had him holding his own against the hard-fighting fish. Suddenly, the seven-foot-long billfish crashed the surface close to the boat and Dillon's jaw dropped as he looked at Cody. The fish had been shaking his head and savagely thrashing his long bill in an effort to free himself from the hook and line as he jumped out of the water.

"Did you see that, man? That is a white marlin! We got a white marlin on the line here, Cody! That is a rare fish, man. Keep that rod tip pointed upward, Nate! Make sure you keep that line tight and don't let him shake that hook. We got him hooked good. I saw it when he broke the surface, but after a while the hole gets bigger during the fight and the fish can throw the hook. Keep the line tight and your rod tip up!"

Cody smiled to himself. Dillon was an expert fisherman, and he was coaching his ass off trying to keep this fish on. It would be a bragging right for him to be able to tell his friends at work that they had boated a rare white marlin. It was a real highlight for any fisherman to accomplish that. After another twenty-five minutes of mortal combat with the mighty fish fighting for its life, an exhausted Nate was finally able to pull the spent fish to the boat with its lengthy beak sticking in the air and one of its goggle eyes staring at the men staring down at it. The fish was completely depleted and unable to fight any more. It remained strangely quiet as Dillon bent down with a gloved hand, grabbed its spear, and easily removed the hook from the side of the fish's mouth. He silently nodded and Cody slipped the boat into gear and slowly moved forward to allow the water to flow over its gills in order to revive the fish before they released it. Dillon released the fish when he felt it stir, and it slowly swam back down into the deep blue. He suddenly stood up and looked in disbelief at the other men.

"None of us took a picture of it! I got so amped up about catching that fish that I forgot to have anybody take a picture of it. Damnit! Nobody is going to believe me now. None of those eggheads at work will believe me when I tell them this if I don't have a picture!"

Suddenly they all erupted into cheers and laughter and started high fiving each other. None of them cared if they had a picture or not. They had lived it. No picture could ever top that. Beers were opened, backs were slapped. The men relived the fight over and over. Each felt they had some part in the catch and release of the magnificent fish. Once everybody had a fresh beer in their hand, Dillon stood up on the front of the boat over the anchor locker and raised his beer in the air.

"Here is to Gordy! Thanks for hooking us up, Gordy!"

All of the men laughed and held their beers up in salutation. It was a glorious day.

CPSIA information can be obtained
at www.ICGtesting.com
Printed in the USA
BVHW070745290921
617681BV00002B/129